Praise for

No Alcohol Beyond This Point

"*Pour yourself something tasty, don't let the title fool you. Live vicariously through Joan and Mar as they take on the open road and countless adventures in JB Teller's debut novel, No Alcohol Beyond This Point, that will have you laughing, crying, and singing along as they prove sometimes sisterhood, friendship, and maybe a cupcake or two are all you need.*"

Teresa Ross

"*A laugh out loud joyride from beginning to end. Cheers to the journey, and cheers to No Alcohol Beyond This Point!*"

Dustine Lee

"*From start to finish, No Alcohol Beyond This Point had me laughing out loud. I got so wrapped up in the journey that I lost track of time while reading! I can't wait to see what Mar and Joan get into next!*"

Dana Rohde

First Edition.

Robert Edwin Eklund, Line Editor, Content Editor.

Dustine Lee, Line Editor, Content Editor.

Mary Ann Smith, Cover designer

Author's Website JBTeller.com

ISBN-978-1-7354082-0-0 Paperback

ISBN-978-1-7354-08217 eBook

ISBN-978-1-7354082-2-4 Hardback

Library of Congress Control Number 2020918457

For Joann

NO ALCOHOL BEYOND THIS POINT

By

J.B. Teller

Lying on the Cold Hard Ground

Oh, Crap! Seriously? This is not how I expected to die. Lying here on my sister's living room floor, my head throbbing. I can hear my family all around me; their voices like some kind of psychedelic dream.

"I'm sorry! I'm sorry! Get up Mar! You are so stupid!" my sister, Joan, is yelling and jumping up and down from one foot to the other.

She's frantically tapping the screen of her phone to no avail. Jeez, at this rate I will die, I mean if I haven't already. Wait a minute, am I dead? I can't be. Who is she calling? Last I checked, 9-1-1 only had three numbers.

I try to yell, but nothing comes out. "Joan, Joan! Down here…on the floor… it's your sister. Help!" If that giant purple rabbit would just move aside and stop blocking my view, Joan might be able to hear me! Joan's jumping is making an indention on the surrounding rug. My eyes glaze over. My tongue feels thick and fuzzy. I catch a glimpse of mom sprinting off into the distance towards the kitchen.

Mom quickly returns, "I've got it! Move! Oh, Mija!"

She drops to her knees as she pulls my shirt up and rubs my body with a cold egg from the refrigerator. She begins on my chest and goes down each arm as she starts to chant over and over, "Mal de ojo. Mal de ojo."

Great, she thinks I've been cursed! I'm lying here dying and my mom is trying to reverse a curse. Go figure! "Ojo," is an old wives' tale. Basically, what it boils down to is if someone admires you and doesn't touch you, you get something called "Ojo." I don't believe that nonsense. Honestly, I don't know how anyone could.

Nevertheless, I've seriously lost count how many times my grandma rubbed me with an egg, covered me in Vicks vapor rub, or blew smoke in my ear with a newspaper funnel. We used to affectionately call her "The Bruja!" which means "witch" in Spanish.

I hear sirens in the distance, but it doesn't feel like they're in my world. I'm floating somewhere above, but then not. I see the whole scene playing out. It's like I'm on the outside looking in. Wait a minute, that really means I am dead otherwise how would I be able to see all of this? Crap, I don't want to be dead. Is this heaven? This can't be heaven. Where's God, the pearly gates, or the bright tunnel of light? Heck, where's my dog Duke? If I am dying, I want the whole experience; the light, the gates, the dead relatives...I don't understand what's happening. This rug is nice.

I hear mom mumbling something to dad. I can't quite make out her words. She sounds like the teacher from Charlie Brown, "Mwah, mwah, mwah, mwah, mwah..."

I'm not sure if my vision is starting to blur, or if I'm actually seeing at all. Maybe I'm just mentally making pictures in my head. Maybe this is what happens when you're dead. Maybe this is why ghosts are always pissed off in the afterlife; they can't be seen or heard. I just don't understand what's happening.

I'm going over it and over it in my head. I went on a date, got a call from Joan, drove to Joan's... talked to Joan, drank some wine... now I'm here on the floor with buttercream frosting in my hair. I strain to lift my head to taste it, but my head feels like it's glued to the rug. I may just take a nap. Yes, a nap...that's what I need. I close my eyes. I am exhausted. Maybe too many hours at the bakery? Maybe too many hours of Dirty Scrabble with Marie?

Joan bends down, dropping her cellphone; it hits me on the forehead. Out of the blue, she does something totally unexpected: she shoves two fingers down my throat. I barf on what was once her very pretty, white rug. Who buys a white rug? Joan does, that's who.

I open my eyes slightly. Pretty...rug...red wine and green cupcakes are intertwined in my long, brunette hair. I look like a great night gone to hell in a handbasket. Girls Gone Bile! Uncensored material included. The front of the DVD would have a barf bag attached. It could be ripped off in case of an emergency.

Joan drags my limp body onto her lap like a rag doll filled with wet sand. "You're so stupid! God, I'm so stupid," she whispers in my ear as she rocks me back and forth, holding me to her chest.

Why is she so stupid? I'm the one down here dead with cupcakes in my hair. The doorbell rings. A couple of guys in uniform roll in a stretcher, followed by four other men...firemen. Great, who invited the strippers? Did I miss the party? Maybe I have alcohol poisoning? Maybe I drank too much? Crap, was there a fire?

A man kneels beside me and wraps a blood pressure cuff around my arm. The cuff blows up then deflates. "Her blood pressure is normal. Can anyone tell me what happened?"

I catch a glimpse of my family standing around me, everyone seems as confused as I am. Everyone but Joan that is.

Before I know it, I'm in the back of an ambulance. One of the strippers is giving report and thinks I can't hear him, "About 5'3"...one-hundred and fifteen pounds. No medical history. Her family said that they had no idea what happened, but her vitals are good...and, if I'm being honest, she is beautiful."

What? Is that standard operating procedure?

Before I tell you how I ended up in the back of an ambulance with a stripper, I should probably go back a bit.

It's Only the Beginning

As kids, our summers were spent outside eating Bologna-Dorito sandwiches and drinking bright red Kool-Aid; staining our fingertips orange with fake cheese powder and our upper lips red. Our childhoods were dominated by tree climbing and playing war in the woods.

Joan's favorite hobby was fishing and riding her dirt bike. One time, Joan drove her dirt bike right into our fence and nearly decapitated herself. Luckily, the fence broke and her head stayed attached. Out of nowhere, mom flew across the field to make sure she was okay...and then hit Joan with her chancla for worrying her. The Chancla is mom's worn-out flip-flop she uses to show her love *and* disapproval. When she would hit us, we'd laugh. It's not painful, it's just funny.

My favorite thing in the whole world was my prized possession: go-cart. I named him Sparky. He consisted of a simple, flat metal frame, four wheels, and an exposed motor. Sparky had vivid red paint with yellow and orange stickers running down the floorboards. It was a patched-together sporty contraption, and I loved it.

If there was ever a problem with it, it was my responsibility to figure it out. It rarely started and the chain always fell off. After many trials and tribulations, I realized that the connection was loose between the spark plug and motor. I discovered I could stick a flathead screwdriver in between the spark plug and motor to make a connection. This is how Sparky got his name.

I'm sure my dad was trying to teach me a life lesson somehow... maybe it was, How to Get Electrocuted and Not Die

201? That's the class right after mom's How to Outrun "*The Chancla*" 101.

God only knows how we managed to survive.

On most days, Joan and I had no problem keeping ourselves busy. We were always doing something. Our dad had a small work shed next to the house that we confiscated by dragging it to the far side of the yard with the tractor. We turned the shed into a museum of sorts, by adding some old shelves to the walls and posting a sign on the door. We spent time collecting dead animals and insects that we would display in jars.

Our biggest attraction, however, was the rattlesnake that we skinned. It was slithering too close to the house and was the only animal we ever killed. Dad had taught us how to kill snakes at an early age; almost a necessity in Texas. We dissected the rattlesnake and put each part in separate, glass mason jars.

We were so proud of our exhibit. Normally, we charged fifty cents for the neighborhood kids to see our curiosities, but the rattlesnake was a special showing. We charged a dollar! Joan and I were early entrepreneurs and thick as thieves. I guess that's why I felt so betrayed when our happy Ya-Ya sisterhood abruptly ended.

Joan was thirteen when the boys came knocking and all of a sudden, I was out. Her jeans and the museum were traded for a bikini and the local swimming pool. It became the *it* place to be. The pool was only a couple of miles from our house, most days we would walk there by climbing down the bluffs and following the outline of the bay.

We would scrape just enough money to get into the pool and buy snacks from the vending machine. And by "scrape" I mean leave IOU's in dad's wallet promising to pay him back in the future. We would stay all day eating candy and sipping Coke, swimming, and sunbathing in the hot Texas sun.

Everybody knew everybody and it was seriously a village raising you. It also helped that The Bruja lived directly across the street. For all we knew, she could use her witchcraft to see us from her kitchen table, which made us walk somewhat of a straighter line.

Things always seemed to come easy for Joan, or maybe that's how I perceived it. It's one of the reasons I always wanted to be like her or, at the very least, be around her. I thought that we would meet boys like we did everything; together. She never realized I was running interference in the background by running off any unworthy potential suitor. I would spend all day observing them at the pool. If they were looking at other girls and trying to date Joan also, I would run them off by kicking them square in the nuts.

Kicking boys in the nuts was my newfound weapon and I wanted to try it on every one of them. As kids, Joan and I were both tomboys. Joan sprouted up, quickly. Unfortunately, it took longer for me to develop. It was a relief when I finally stopped having to stuff my bra. It seemed to happen overnight. One day I was willing my chest to grow, the next, there they were, like magic. Shortly after my chest developed, I discovered Cosmo Girl. I read article after article; it was like I was studying for the most important test of my life. In my preteen mind, I was.

We are both a good mix of German, English, Hispanic, and Apache. Our family is a true American melting pot. At 5'8" Joan is ginormous compared to my tiny 5' and change height, and she never lets me forget it. She is slender with a raw beauty that caught the boys' eye from an early age. She looks more like our dad with blond hair, striking indigo eyes, and light skin. I call her translucent, and she calls me an ass. I have my mom's tanned olive skin and dark hair. As a kid, Joan use to tell me my parents found me in the trash. I turned it around on her. At one point I convinced her she was adopted since she is two inches taller than dad and looks nothing like mom.

Although Joan is almost three years older than me, sometimes, it seems more like ten. She is more focused on what she wants out of life. I, however, plan a little less when it comes to the big picture. I tend to go with the flow of the river, lazily floating on my innertube down the Frio. Joan, on the other hand, methodically hops from one stone to the other picking out her path perfectly. However, we've always shared the same sense of humor (we both still inappropriately laugh when someone hurts themselves).

Joan and I grew up in a very small, Texas gulf town. Our town was so small, in fact, it was combined with our neighboring town to make up one high school. The combined high school was named G-P, which stands for Gregory-Portland High. The town's main street had a Whataburger, K-mart, and, of course, my dad's gas station. Main Street was named after our high school mascot; the Wildcat. It was the kind of small town where coaches were kings and the whole town closed for high school football's Friday night lights.

After the game, all the high school kids would make a beeline to the Whataburger, a Texas religion, to socialize and celebrate the inevitable win. On Saturdays, Joan and I would cruise up and down Wildcat Drive in dad's white and yellow Chevy truck flirting with the boys. Joan would drive and I'd play it cool with my feet on the dash. Our house was just outside of the city limits and, for us, it was magic.

It's crazy how time changes as you grow up. When we were kids our days seemed to drag, but now, as I look back, it seems like it all happened in a blink of an eye. Our magical, lazy summer days quickly turned into high school and hours of homework. Before I knew it, Joan was graduating.

College Life

Joan traded boys for books and left me behind. She got accepted to the University of Texas. With her at college, things were different. Her absence left a quietness in the house. I could only hope that she was missing me like I was missing her. Three years later I followed, choosing the same school mainly because Joan was there. Plus, let's face it, who wouldn't want to see Matthew McConaughey at a UT game with an armadillo on his knee?

Joan and I shared a house just off campus with my childhood best friend, Marie. She is like a second sister, too much like us to really be counted as just a friend. When we moved in, the house had been freshly remodeled with hardwood floors and a bathroom for each bedroom, it was the ideal size for three college girls. The exterior was gray with white trim, and it had a big backyard—fantastic for the epic BBQ parties we held every month. Dad bought the house as an investment for us girls. We got along well sharing chores, dating advice, and groceries. Things ran like clockwork.

Joan and I each had a car. Marie didn't, but it didn't matter. She shared mine. Joan drove a black Lexus and I asked for a 1969 Mini Cooper I named, of course, Cooper. Cooper is a red convertible. He is marvelous! In a way, he reminds me of Sparky, my old red go-cart.

Marie and I had some of the best times in college. We quickly were enlightened to the importance of experiencing college life. We took the whole "you only live once" phrase to heart. In fact, with our blood-alcohol ratio we were sometimes closer to death than we knew. We "experienced" way too much Vodka. Vodka, by the way, is completely tasteless. Someone should put in some kind of additive like they do for gas in houses. You know, so you can smell the gas and get out before you kill yourself. Same idea. File the tastelessness away in your guidebook to college life. It's a hard lesson we learned after eating way too many Jell-O shots while setting up for a BBQ. We must have eaten ten each. It was so hot that day; another intoxication accelerant. I don't remember the party at all. We ended up sitting in Marie's shower completely clothed, singing old NSYNC songs. When Joan finally found us, she turned the cold water on us. We felt nothing.

Joan was much more of a homebody. She chose to paint instead of going with us to the local piano bar or weekend party, which made it more surprising when she told us she met a boy named Frank. We pulled up a chair and made popcorn. Figuratively. I was pretty sure she was hallucinating but it turns out she wasn't. She met him walking home past the Law building. As cliché as it was, she dropped her books, Frank picked them up and asked her out. Joan had never been much of a dater, even though she had been asked out plenty. When she started seeing Frank regularly a couple of weeks later, it just kinda stuck.

Frank was, and still is, a clean-cut type of guy; the kind you always find with his head in a book. He's lean and a bit on the nerdy side. He's from New York and has one of those thick New York accents. Listening to him reminds me of The Fonz from the reruns of *Happy Days*. Frank has thick, jet-black hair and deep-set brown eyes. Envision John Travolta from *Grease*. He's four years older than Joan and was getting his Law degree while Joan was working on her undergrad in Art.

Joan creates these beautiful paintings depicting our childhood. Her senior year was her landmark year. That's when she began to sell her art in local galleries, it's also when she became more serious about Frank.

Joan and Frank married just after she graduated. They left Texas and moved to California to pursue Joan's dream of making art in wine country. When Joan moved, it once again left a hole only she could fill. I felt lost without her.

Mom and dad bought Joan a house in Yountville, California. Yountville is a small town in the Napa Valley smack dab in the middle of wine country. The house was a graduation gift. My dad thought houses were a good investment, more so for the land than the house.

He always said, in his rough but kind voice, "Buy land, they're not making anymore." In retrospect, I'm pretty sure Mark Twain said it first, but my dad took it to heart.

That's how Frank ended up in San Francisco working at a law firm downtown near the Transcontinental building.

I Left My Heart in San Francisco

In hindsight, I wish I had kicked Frank square in the nuts. You know, for old times' sake. But I'm getting a tiny bit ahead of myself.

I graduated with a Business degree but spent a year dinking around Austin after college with Marie. Most of my time was spent listening to music, drinking coffee, and discovering my true passion for absolutely everything and nothing before deciding to move west. It turns out my skills are more creative than businesslike but, if you ask me, they're one and the same. If you are creative, then you can sell what you create.

My creativeness manifests itself in many ways. Joan is strictly a painter; I, on the other hand, bake, doodle, and paint. One point for Joan / three points for me. Even though I'm better than Joan (enter sarcastic laugh here), she lets me hang a few pieces in her art gallery. My main source of income, however, is a small cupcake shop I co-own with Marie.

As you know, I've known Marie practically my whole life. As kids, she lived about half a mile down the road from us, just inside city limits. I'd drive Sparky to the edge of the city limits and pick her up. Along with Joan, we called ourselves...wait for it...the Texas Tater Tots. We changed the name later when we were in college.

Marie has dark hair, a skinny frame, and a fiery personality when excited. The funniest of the group, she spent most weekends at our house. This allowed her more freedom. As a kid, her parents were strict, not allowing Marie to watch rated R movies, or have a cellphone until she was eighteen. That didn't stop us from introducing Marie to *The Hangover, Zombieland,* or all of the Adam Sandler movies.

Joan and I wanted to adopt Marie in the hope nobody would notice, but we didn't have to since her parents liked our parents and let her come over all the time. If you saw me, you saw Marie; especially after Joan went off to college.

Marie's dream has always been to move to San Francisco. She was fascinated with the Golden Gate Bridge and reruns of *Full House.* The whole bakery idea was born while binge-watching *Cupcake Wars* and partaking in a couple of really great bottles of wine. A bottle and a half in, Marie asked me if I would move to San Francisco to open a bakery; I guess you could say the rest is history. We made plans and packed up a U-Haul a month later.

I love anything that allows me to be creative, and the bakery was a perfect idea. The icing on the cupcake was that it wasn't too far from where Joan lives. Our bakery is called "Feeling Whisky." Originally, it was supposed to be a funny name for our shop, but that completely backfired on us. I can't tell you how many times people have mistaken it for a bar. We used it to our advantage. It happened so many times that we started reopening after midnight for the bar crowd. It turned into the thing to do after bar hopping.

We even invented a liquor line of cupcakes–Whiskey Wednesday, Time to Forget Thursday, and Fuzzy Navel Friday (which included fresh peaches). Seductive Saturday is a double chocolate cupcake with a molten center and a fresh strawberry on top. You get the idea. We use the philosophy: "what stands in the way becomes the way," and it actually worked. We were even featured in *The San Francisco Chronicle*, "FEELING WHISKY CUPCAKE GIRLS TAKE BAY BY STORM."

Our cupcake shop is only a couple of blocks from the wharf. On weekends we get a lot of pedal car traffic, and business has really been good. Thanks to Marie and her wizarding ways with social media.

Dad bought the building our shop is in, of course. He said it was my graduation present even though he gave me a stack of cash when I tossed my cap the year before. Dad flew in and helped us pick the perfect spot for the bakery. At one point, the building had been a four-plex. After dad's renovations, Marie and I now share a ginormous 1,800 square foot upstairs apartment. It's a mansion compared to most apartments in San Francisco. That is, unless you are a billionaire; which, by the way, you almost have to be. If it wasn't for my graduation gift, we wouldn't be able to afford the shop's rent. In fact, we probably wouldn't be able to afford rent in San Francisco at all. The downstairs is split into an apartment and our small cupcake shop.

Which brings us to Mr. Horowitz and the date of the incident.

Mr. Horowitz

Mr. Horowitz is in the apartment to the left of the shop. He has called the apartment home since the 1970s. Instead of having him move, dad set him up in a local hotel for the three months it took to renovate. Dad later struck up a deal with him; free rent as long as he keeps an eye on me. Dad's heart is as big as Texas.

The building has a cute brick front with large windows. It wasn't originally zoned for business, so the front has two small porches. Dad was going to have them removed when he renovated, but because it was important to Mr. Horowitz, he kept them. Besides, it is the perfect place to sit after ordering cupcakes.

The inside of our shop is a colored combo of pink, white, and turquoise creating the perfect cotton candy dream. Two adult-size wooden swings hang from the ceiling with a small patch of grass underneath each. Nothing makes you feel more like a kid than swinging and eating cupcakes while dragging your feet through the grass. We also had a fireman's pole installed. It runs from our upstairs apartment to the downstairs bakery, giving us the ability to slide right behind the counter if need be. If I run upstairs for a minute and hear the shop's front bell, I can immediately be back behind the counter like teleporting. Genius, I know. Being located in downtown San Francisco has its pros and cons. We have quite a bit of...um, "interesting" people come through. To be fair, we have our fair share of hot guys as well. It's like a conveyor belt in a meat market.

Speaking of "meat market", I have a date today with a man named Chris. We met on the wharf last week while I was out for my morning jog. I was petting the usual suspects in the park when Chris struck up a conversation about how he loved to come and pet the dogs since he didn't have one of his own. Some people need that, and some people don't. I liked that he did, so I agreed to a lunch date later in the week. We are meeting at a super trendy restaurant that recently opened in The Tenderloin District. The word is that it's a pretty fancy place for lunch. I've never been there so, who knows, they may have a great lunch menu.

As I lay in bed with my eyes closed, I mentally select my outfit for today. It has to be put together but not too fussed over. Rolling out of bed, my feet hit the wooden floor with a thud. I throw on a sweatshirt and yoga pants for my morning jog. I give Marie's door a double tap as I walk by. It's cracked open. I yell into it, "I'm going!"

Marie opens her door with her elbow. She's pulling her hair up in a messy knot. "...kay, see ya!"

It's still dark out. The sun hasn't come up as I pull on my running shoes and quietly shut the apartment door and jog down the wooden steps. The air is crisp. It always is here—especially this early. I blow out as I stretch and faintly see my breath. The first time I visited San Francisco, I was dumbfounded by how hot it was in the city but how cold it was on the wharf. It was, seriously, at least twenty degrees colder. Joan and I practically ran through a tour of Alcatraz freezing our assets off.

The city comes alive around me as I jog along the rows of apartments. Little by little, I'm joined by familiar faces. I nod my "hellos" as I start on the route I take day in and day out. My dad always tells me to change it up. He worries about someone knowing my habits, but I think it's a good thing; if people are used to seeing me and I'm not where I am usually, then they are more likely to notice when something is wrong. My route runs to the end of the wharf before I double back. On days I have more time, I extend the route to the yacht harbor. Today is my day off, so I can afford a long, relaxing run. I do my best thinking when I run.

On the way back, I plop myself down onto the grass and watch the waves hit the concrete steps. The fog on the bridge is thick this morning as the dogs play in the park. We don't have a dog of our own and playing with them is one of my favorite things. I get in some cuddle time with the usual suspects before heading back.

My return jog is slower. During this more leisurely paced run I enjoy watching waiters pull out tables and chairs onto the sidewalks. A line of seagulls Charlie Chaplin scuttle their way to the fish market on the corner and the pedicabs line up for business.

On the weekend, the wharf is bustling with tourists and energy. I love that. The air is filled with the smell of the morning's catch. I say "Hi" to Vinnie, cleaning his boat. The smell of Wesley Owen's freshly ground coffee floats through the air. It's my favorite coffee shop. I stop for a cup and a chocolate zucchini muffin.

I have always loved small town living and wasn't sure how I was going to adjust to the big city; honestly though, the world is as big or as small as you make it. I've grown to love the cracks in the pavement and the chill in the air. Within a few minutes, you can karate kick a guy dressed like a bush scaring tourists or enjoy numerous local musicians trying to make a little money. The weekend Farmer's market is always buzzing with local foodies picking over fresh fish or smelling local organic vegetables. Marie and I make it a point to buy all our bread, flowers, and produce there. We feel like a couple of city girls shopping at the market in the old ferry building. It's completely different from the way we grew up, shopping in an old box store.

As I approach our building, Mr. Horowitz is shuffling down the steps carrying his trash to the curb.

I wave to him, "Mr. Horowitz, you know you don't have to take your trash down. Just leave it on the porch, I'll get it." I grab the bag from him and place it in the bin at the curb.

"Anything else you need while I'm here?" I say following him up the steps. I know exactly what he's going to say. It's the same thing every Sunday, but I pretend to be surprised.

"I could use some company." He adjusts the chairs on his front porch. The tea is hot and already sitting on the small table in between our two chairs. Mr. Horowitz pours the tea and sits back to enjoy the sun. I join him, smiling. He's sharp as a whip. We normally talk about art, Jeopardy, or his parents. Occasionally, we talk about books. I bring him one every couple of weeks. He loves historical fiction; Dan Brown can't write fast enough. I enjoy our conversations because, even after all the things he's seen, he always ends with something profoundly positive.

As we sit, a scrawny gray kitten twirls itself around my legs then jumps onto Mr. Horowitz's lap.

"Oh, you got a cat?" I say giving it a rub from head to tail.

"No, I didn't get a cat, she got me. She wandered up here about three days ago. Now… I suppose she lives here." He puts the kitten down and covers his knees with a knit blanket then snaps his fingers and the kitten returns, curling herself into a tiny little gray ball.

Mr. Horowitz is always impeccably dressed. His dress pants always have a crease down the front and most of the time he wears a long-sleeve buttoned up shirt under a cardigan. I saw him only once with his sleeves rolled up and noticed a six-digit number tattooed on his arm. I knew exactly what the number meant. Maybe that's why he always wears long-sleeved shirts. The thought makes me sad; I reach over and grab his hand. His dark brown eyes are kind. His face is wrinkled now, but I can tell he was devastatingly handsome in his time.

I squeeze his hand, "…Need a haircut today?" I look at his hair, which is always combed to the side with a little wave in the front.

"I suppose I'll get one next week, if you have time?" he says petting the sleeping kitten on his lap.

I gesture to the kitten, "What are you going to name her?"

"I've named her Eleanor…after my mother." Mr. Horowitz turns to look up the street as though he can see her walking toward us.

I squeeze his hand tighter. We sit in silence watching the cars drive by. Prius…Prius…another Prius.

I glance at my watch, its half past ten and I reluctantly stand to go. "Alright Love, you know how to reach me if you need anything. By the way, I have a date today. Want me to bring you something from the restaurant?"

Mr. Horowitz waves me off, "I still have the meatloaf you brought me yesterday, but thank you. You spoil me."

I lean in and kiss him on the cheek. "You know I love you."

Mr. Horowitz's wrinkled cheeks flush. "I love you too and, remember, never wrestle with a pig. You just get dirty and the pig enjoys it."

I laugh while pondering his wise words.

I hop up the stairs to my apartment two at a time. While waiting for the shower to heat up, I grab my clothes from the closet. I take a long shower and afterward I wrap myself in my comforter, making a make-shift fort. I'm going to take a nap before I have to get ready for my date.

An hour later, I pull on a pair of dark washed, skinny jeans and a cream-colored sweater; I pair the ensemble with my cognac brown, ankle boots. I twirl around, giving myself a once over in the mirror. Satisfied with my date outfit, I slide down the fireman's pole and land right next to Marie.

"Hiya!" I slap her on the butt. "Got a date, see you after!"

Marie slaps my hand away, "Have fun!"

I hate being late. I'm leaving a few minutes early just in case parking is a problem. With Cooper, it usually isn't, he could fit almost anywhere. Heck, I could park him on the sidewalk, but I don't want to ever make that call again to my dad. Who knew you couldn't park your car next to your apartment stairs…even if it fits?

Mr. Horowitz is still sitting on the porch with Eleanor curled on his lap as I pull out of the driveway. I give him a quick wave.

The restaurant isn't too far from my apartment, but the twenty blocks will take me thirty minutes, give or take. I park Cooper and check my face in the mirror.

Walking into the restaurant, I am delighted to find Chris is already sitting at a cute table in the corner. When I reach him, he stands; I love it when a man stands for a woman... extra points for him. I make a mental note of it. He's attractive and actually seems to have thought about what he's wearing: navy blue slacks and a white button-up shirt rolled to his elbow; nice.

"Hi," I say, brushing my long, brunette hair behind my ear with my hand. "I hope you haven't been waiting long..."

He straightens his shirt then sits. I'm taking him in as he leans over towards me. He must be going to say something pleasant about the afternoon or maybe something nice about my outfit, I lean in closer and smile.

"You look hot!" he says as he pulls his seat closer to mine. My skin crawls, and I force myself not to curl my lip in disgust. Before I can respond, he continues, "Order off the kids' menu, that's what I usually do. It's cheaper."

He's so matter of fact, it catches me off guard. I glance around to see if anyone is looking our way. I'm sure my facial expression is telling a thousand stories right now. I mean, I don't need a date to take me to a fancy, expensive dinner; but if he does, I sure as hell am not ordering off the kids' menu. If expense is the case, he should've just taken me someplace different. Heck, I would have been happy with a picnic in the park. I run my fingers over my brow trying not to make eye contact. I pretend to study the menu, buying time to collect myself.

Chris grabs the menu out of my hands and slides it across the table. "Don't worry, I've picked out the absolute perfect thing for you. Just leave it to me, hottie," he says with a wink.

I swallow my disgust. He must be mistaking my dumbfounded expression for confusion on what to order. As I sit in horror, I mentally argue with myself on what to do. I scoff and mull over if I'm being too pretentious. The waiter scurries up.

Chris straightens in his seat and begins to order like an aristocrat in 17th-century France, "The lady will have the chicken nuggets with the French fries."

I nearly choke on my water. Is this a test? Is Ashton Kutcher going to pop out somewhere? The only thing funnier would be if he added a monocle and a French accent. I try to hide behind my glass of water. I clear my throat, half embarrassed, half not believing the situation. I try to contain my laughter. I choke, and my cheeks blow out like a pufferfish. I'm a complete mess. My eyes begin to water as I take another gulp of water. Still trying to pull myself together, I carefully wipe the tears from my eyes. 'Pull yourself together Smalls'… my inner voice says.

Maybe he has a good reason for ordering off the kid's menu. Even if he, literally, just told me it was because it was cheaper. I am trying to give him the benefit of the doubt. Chris finishes placing his order. The waiter, looking confused, claps his black notebook shut, turns on his heels, and walks off.

It's difficult, but I'm trying my best to make small talk. He's a software engineer in Cupertino and an avid runner, which makes sense since I met him running. He was wearing a pair of those ridiculously short running shorts, but I don't hold it against him. (You do know you can run in longer shorts; it isn't imperative you run in shorts that show your undercarriage.)

"So, what do you like to do for fun?" I ask, mostly out of politeness.

"I run and I work, mostly in that order," he says, smiling back at me.

I sarcastically think to myself, 'This is going well. He sounds like a barrel of monkeys.' I give my head one, hard shake, like my sarcastic thoughts will just vanish into thin air or come bouncing out of my ear.

The gourmet nuggets arrive. I mindlessly start to eat while trying hard to listen and focus. Chris definitely likes to talk about himself. He went to Caltech, uber smart…blah, blah, blah. My mind strays to think about the order I need to make for the bakery. I shift in my seat. We've been here for thirty minutes and he has yet to ask me anything about myself. Honestly, at this point, I'm not sure it matters. This isn't going any further than it already has. I casually look around, trying not to seem rude, but I'm completely over this.

A bead of sweat starts to run down the side of Chris's face. He becomes quiet. Maybe he's nervous. Maybe that's why he is talking so much. There's a lull in his one-sided conversation. He clears his throat and begins to wiggle in his seat. The same wiggle little kids do when they have to potty. I fight the urge to ask him if he, indeed, has to go potty.

Instead, I look over at him, "Is everything okay?"

He's actually turning a little gray and moaning a bit. I don't know if it's because he's nervous or just doesn't care. To my horror, he lifts his leg and farts the loudest fart humanly possible.

I immediately throw the nugget I'm eating straight into the air, startled. My eyes widen and I jump up, going into a karate stance. A snippet of 'Kung Fu Fighting' begins playing in my head. Can't I ever be serious? Taking a step backward, I laugh out loud, "Jiminy Christmas!!! Chris, um, this isn't working," I wave my hand in a circle between us. "I have to go."

Digging cash out of my wallet, I throw it on the table and start making my exit.

Chris shoves his seat back to stand, "I'm sorry, did I do something wrong?"

Apparently, farting during a date is okay with him. I wonder, did he just blackout the last two minutes? The smell is so overwhelming, it's like week-old Chinese takeout. My super sensitive gag reflex kicks in and I begin to gag. Once it starts, there's no stopping it. I sound like a cat trying to hack up a hairball. Pausing, I glance back over my shoulder, "Please don't follow me." I get my wits about me and make a mad dash for the door, gagging as I go. The waiter follows behind me, making it to the restaurant's door before me.

"That was the weirdest thing I have ever witnessed," he laughs at my misfortune.

"I'm glad you got some entertainment out of it," I roll my eyes at him and continue my mad dash to get the heck out of there. The waiter follows me to Cooper parked on the street in front. He seems amused and concerned, but I was one barely controlled gag away from losing my gourmet lunch.

"Please. I'm trying very hard to stop thinking about it." I rest both hands on Cooper taking deep breaths. This whole thing could go south, and I'd barf. I swallow hard.

"What the hell was wrong with that guy? He just wasted his shot," the waiter says with a twinkle in his eye.

I put my hand on his shoulder, steadying myself, and laugh. "You got that right, but you can never wrestle with a pig." Never in the history of someone being right, has anyone ever been so right. I fumble in my jeans pocket for my keys while silently thanking Mr. Horowitz.

The waiter leans in, giving me a wide grin, "I'm Josh. If you ever want to go on a real date," he scribbles his number on a slip of paper and hands it to me, "call me."

I hold out my hand and shake his. "I'm Mar. Give me a bit to recover from whatever this was." I make a big exaggerated circle with my hand gesturing at the restaurant. "Then, maybe…"

He opens Cooper's door, and I hop in.

"Until then," he says, bending his head down to my level to give me one more charming smile before he closes the door.

"Until then…" I repeat his words. Every time I say, 'until then' I fight the urge to yell 'Toot-a-Lou Mother Fuckers!' like I have Tourette's. I honestly don't know what's wrong with me.

Joan is going to flip when she hears about this. We have a running conversation about my love life—or lack thereof. It's not like I'm really looking…at almost twenty-five, I have my whole life to find someone. Don't get me wrong, I do my fair share of dating. I'm just not willing to settle. It doesn't make sense to give my life to someone I'm not "all in" with. I only have one life and it's going to take someone pretty awesome to change my relationship status.

The movie *Notting Hill* set the bar, which, turns out, is too high for most men. Someone would have to do something pretty daring to get my attention. I imagine Hugh Grant and a gaggle of people rushing about in a car trying to find me. I like who I am and what I'm doing right now. I'm a cautiously optimistic, total romantic. You would think I'd stop that nonsense with my built-in BS meter. My BS meter is located directly behind my pesky judgmental frontal lobe, whereas my romantic advisor consumes my whole heart. They both have strongly worded arguments from time to time.

That said, I hold out hope an amazing guy is out there...somewhere. Right now, however, he strictly lives behind the blue door with a flat mate named Spike, next to a secret garden in *Notting Hill*. Not Hugh Grant himself, but the idea of such a romance. Maybe he's just a guy named Joe, with a flat mate named Bob, sitting on a rooftop, eating tomato soup. But he's out there. I just know he is.

Gosh, I can't believe I just had another date with a weirdo! I'm half-laughing, half-wondering if I just have that thing on my forehead that says, 'Weirdos - Please apply.' I can't seem to find the right makeup remover to remove it. It's beyond annoying. Maybe I'm doing something to attract this type of person? Maybe I'm just too nice? Don't get me wrong, I've had some fantastic dates, but right now the strange ones are outweighing the good ones. Just two weeks ago a guy showed up in a chipmunk costume. Turns out that he was just coming from a job, but still—change your clothes! You can't show up in a chipmunk costume and expect to get the girl.

Tonight, I'm headed to Joan's. For the last few of years, my parents make it a priority to visit us girls every couple of months. This works for me since I'm not dating anyone. Unless you count my love affair with wine...and coffee...and chocolate. Rightfully so, because they are all fantastic! My wine affair beats the guy I just went out with. I mean wine is acceptable anywhere. You can bring wine to a party and you can bet he won't make an ass out of himself. You can make an ass out of yourself with wine, but it can't happen the other way around. And generally, everyone is always happy to see wine. Not to mention, he always smells good and makes you feel nice. Unlike wine, you can't bring an inappropriately farting guy to a party. No one likes that.

A major selling point for me is that Joan's place is only an hour and fifteen minutes from the city, depending on traffic. I make it a point to see Joan every other week, often dragging Marie along for the ride. We stop at the Oxbow Market for coffee and everything delicious we can possibly pair with our wine. Napa's indoor Oxbow Market is a foodie's paradise that one can't pass by without stopping to check the cheese selection. Marie and I keep talking about making plans to do an actual wine tour, but we haven't gotten around to it. The shop keeps us fairly busy even though we have eight people on staff.

Besides, we usually spend our wine drinking on the couch, in our pajamas, playing Dirty Scrabble. Dirty Scrabble is our version of Scrabble. We made it up after a couple of drinks and a night of complete boredom. The rules are as follows: All words have to be a dirty word, in any language. If you don't have a word, you drink a shot of wine. I know, wine isn't for shooting, but tequila makes me Hulk out. You can phone a friend, like in *Who Wants to Be A Millionaire*, but only after two a.m. Words can be made up, as long as they are sexually suggestive, like "dicklicious."

The Scrabble board is always sitting on our living room table. Our games go on and on and…on, for weeks. Sometimes, I wait until 2 a.m. to start playing just so I can phone Joan. We put her on FaceTime, so she can join in. She pours herself a glass of wine, sits at her kitchen table, and we travel back to our college days.

Meet the Parents

My parents arrived yesterday from Texas. My mom is a tiny little thing, she's all of 5'1" and ninety pounds. What she lacks in size, she makes up in her feisty personality. As a kid, my mom was a stay-at-home mom. Basically, she kept us from killing ourselves or each other, which was definitely a full-time job. While mom spent all her time keeping us alive, dad was busy building his gas station empire.

What started out as one gas station has turned into 150 all over the state of Texas. On a day-to-day basis, he works at the original one on Wildcat Drive. The stations are the kind of stations where uniformed attendants pump your gas for you. Dad has always done it that way and I don't see him changing anytime soon. He calls it "Customer Service."

Dad goes to "work" almost every day, mainly because of Tex, who has been working there since day one. I get the feeling dad goes just so he and Tex can have something to occupy their days. Going to "work" allows my dad the opportunity to chew his cigars without my mother yelling in his ear about it and hitting him with her shoe. They never do any actual work; they just sit around playing cards and shooting the breeze with the regulars that come in. Occasionally, other old guys come in and they have a Pow-Wow around a card table dad set up in the back. They call themselves, "The Good 'Ol Boys."

Tex is my dad's righthand man and runs the operation when he is out in California visiting us girls. He's been a loyal friend since as long as I can remember. He came back with dad from the Vietnam

War. They had shared a trailer on the outskirts of town and had been painting houses until dad saved enough money to open his first gas station on the main strip in town. Tex was the first person he hired. Scratch that, "hired" is a strong word. Tex just showed up the first morning it open and stayed.

Surviving something like the war together really bonded them. They have an understanding few can fathom. I never really hear them talk a lot, just a sentence here and a sentence there, then the occasional "Yep." I think it's mainly because Tex doesn't talk a whole lot. Dad talks enough for the both of them. He is a real spitfire.

Dad used to pull the best shenanigans at the grocery store. As a teenage girl, I was mortified. Now that I look back, he is pretty epic. He'd walk around adding things to other peoples' baskets and throwing handfuls of uncooked pinto beans over the shelves lining the aisles, making it "rain" on unsuspecting shoppers. Dad's antics made going to the grocery store with him an ordeal. It was a mission to get out of there without being completely embarrassed. I always considered it a success if we left without him knocking down a feminine product display, or asking if they had the plastic Barbie doll shoe in my size. Mom figured it out early and never went with him. I don't know why I continued to go with him, I suppose I secretly thought it was funny. Plus, it gave me the chance to spy on Eric, Joan's boyfriend, who bagged groceries. Those were the best of times, even if we didn't know it.

I snap back from my daydream and look at my watch. Since my date abruptly ended early with the whole "Fart Fandango" episode, I have a couple of free hours. I pull into my driveway and rest my head on my steering wheel. That was horrible.

Mr. Horowitz is still sitting on his porch counting cars. He yells as I get out of the car, "Back so soon? I take it he wasn't 'the one'?"

"Nope, not today," I say giving him a smile. "Did you eat lunch yet?" I ask, standing next to my car.

Mr. Horowitz holds up a plate the kitten had been licking.

"Okay, good! Have a good day!" I blow him a kiss as I walk up the steps to my apartment. This time, only one at a time.

Marie steps out onto the porch and follows me around the side of the building and up the stairs to our apartment. "How was the date? ...Not so great, huh?"

I grab a small duffel bag out of my closet and start casually putting things in it when Joan's face pops up on my phone. It's a picture that we took while visiting Sacramento; she's wearing aviator goggles upside down and giving me a thumbs up. I pick up the phone.

Before I get a word out, Joan's voice comes booming over the other end of the line. "That son of a bitch! The chicken is in the pot. I repeat! The chicken is in the pot!"

The Chicken is in the Pot

I put one hand under my arm to make a chicken wing, throw my head back and yell, "Cock-a-doodle-doo, Motherfucker! COOK IT!" I press the button to hang up. Immediately, I zip my bag shut. Marie knows us well enough to know I need to get to Joan. I slide down the fireman's pole, skipping the stairs altogether. Snatching a box of cupcakes off the counter, I rip through the shop door before Marie has a chance to say anything.

I throw my stuff in the backseat of Cooper, hop in, and open my Amazon music app. "Alexa, play my playlist: *Cock -Doodle-Doo, Motherfucker!*"

I made a playlist just for such an occasion. The first song that comes on is "Goodbye Earl".' It seems fitting since Frank is now a "Son of a Bitch!" I mean, I guess it's Frank? Who else would it be? Joan and I have all kinds of secret code phrases for different circumstances. The codes were born from the need to be able to talk in front of our parents without them knowing what we were saying. It's kind of our version of Pig Latin. Our parents thought we had hit our heads when they first heard us. Dad just blew it off, laughing at our ingenuity. Mom, unfortunately, quickly figured out that we were speaking in code and slapped both of us on the back of our heads with her chancla.

'The chicken is in the pot; cook it!' is the mother of all Code Reds. These eight simple words speak volumes. It means drop everything; I need you here, right now, no matter what. Whoever is in trouble, they say, 'the chicken is in the pot,' and the other yells, 'cook it!' confirming it was heard. Kind of like when you say, 'Roger that.'

I double honk at Mr. Horowitz as I pop Cooper into second gear and speed down the street. I frantically drive through the stop-and-go streets of San Francisco, slowing only enough to see if anyone is coming, then slamming my foot down on the accelerator. By the time I hit the Golden Gate Bridge, I'm in pure panic mode. Luckily, all three lanes are wide open. I shift into fifth gear and press the pedal hard to the floor. Cooper gives a little resistance but begins zipping along at a good pace.

I think I need a cupcake. I tend to eat when I'm stressed, which is not often. I stretch my arm back, straining to reach the cupcake box. Yoga is not paying off for me, at least not in this situation. To be fair, Sun Salutations doesn't include The Downward Cupcake, nor does it make my short T-Rex arms any longer! I hit a bump sending Cooper flying into the air. In Cooper, it feels like a ten on the Richter scale. His four tiny tires bounce high in the air. The cupcakes go flying. A couple hit me in the back of the head, but one gloriously lands close to my hand.

"Score!" I yell like a crazy woman who just won half-off at Starbucks for life.

I make the hour and fifteen-minute drive in forty-five minutes. I park Cooper like Mario Andretti gliding past the finish line; I don't even allow Cooper to come to a complete stop as I hop out and practically run beside him as his tires bump against the curb. Sprinting around the back of the house to the kitchen, I intentionally avoid the drawn-out hellos from my parents. I catch a glimpse of Joan through the kitchen window. She has one arm across her chest and the other holding a glass of wine. She is casually sipping wine staring blankly across the kitchen sink. I creak open the door and slip in.

I grab Joan by the elbows, with a worried whisper I ask her, "What happened?"

Joan lets out a breath and blurts, "Its Frank…he's been cheating on me!" She starts crying putting her free hand on her forehead, as if she's trying to hold her head together. "Oh! I feel like I just got kicked in the stomach. I think I'm going to barf again," she turns to the kitchen sink and leans in. It's a waste of good wine, but, hell, if I was being cheated on, I would throw up, too.

"Oh, crap!" I gasp as I snatch a glass of wine from the tray, settling in. "We need to come up with a plan." I plant myself directly hip to hip with Joan and try my best to reassure her. "We've got this, Joan, whatever you want to do about it."

Joan shakes her head, "I just feel so stupid for not realizing it. I mean he was still sleeping with me…Oh, God! We were still sleeping together!"

The realization hits Joan like a ton of bricks. She leans in and dry heaves into the sink. I feel the blood rush to my ears and turn red-hot. My ears are my give away. Every time I'm mad, my ears turn bright red. My cheeks do the same thing when I'm attracted to someone. That's the funny thing about blushing, it always calls you out. Every. Single. Time. Fury courses through my veins. I'm going to put Frank's head on a spike.

"Where is that bastard?" I shout forgetting we are trying to keep quiet.

Joan points her finger up, indicating that Frank is still upstairs.

My mouth drops open, "He must have some balls!"

I've never seen Joan so broken; I feel like I'm stuck in place. I have to be strong for her. I gulp my wine to gain some strength as Joan tells me Frank has been cheating with a girl from work. "It's been going on for the last year…the whole year!"

I finish the first glass and trade it out for a full glass from the tray. "Do not the girl you know?" my words come out in a jumbled mess.

Joan's face screws up in confusion. That didn't come out like I planned. "Do you know the girl?" I slow my voice down and choose my words more carefully.

"Are you okay?" Joan asks, looking a bit confused.

My tongue starts to feel thick and fuzzy. My lips begin to tingle, so much so I think I can actually hear them make a buzzing sound. I can hear my words like someone else is saying them. It's like I'm outside of my own head.

"Joan, Joan, look at my feet! I'm floating!" I say, shocked. I wiggle my toes.

Joan looks at me puzzled.

"Bunny rabbits...cupcakes...Chris...fart fandango...blurry," I mumble.

Mom swings the kitchen door open and walks in. "Oh, Mar! I didn't know you were here." Mom's voice drags out. She reaches up and pinches my cheek, "Ey mija, mi corazón. Give me a big hug and come see your dad."

Mom pulls me by my arm towards the living room. "Get on to him, he still hasn't given up those damn cigars," Mom says, pushing me through the swinging kitchen door. "You tell him something. Maybe he will listen to you."

As the door starts to close behind me, I shoot a wide-eyed glance over my shoulder to Joan and shrug.

Mom looks at me, finally getting a good look at my hair. "Why do you have cupcakes in your hair Marguerite?" Mom sounds disgusted and tries to untangle one.

I feel like one of those floats in the Macy's Day Parade; I'm weightless, bloated, and bobbing around. I begin to do high knees to see how high I can float off the ground. Mom gives me a strange look. I reach my finger up and touch the tip of her nose, "Boop," I say. I start to imitate her, "Ey, Mija.... Mi corazón..." I make kissy lips all over her cheek.

"For heaven's sake Marguerite, are you drunk?" Mom says as she marshals me closer towards dad so that I'm standing right in front of him like, 'Look at Mar, she's drunk...again.' Jeez, you have one drink at a family reunion...and it turns into this: mistrust and a judgmental eye from a five-foot, one-inch Hispanic mother. I cup my fist to my mouth like I'm blowing a horn to introduce the arrival of royalty.

"Buh ba bah bah! Hi, dad!" I say with over exaggerated jazz hands. Dad looks up, surprised and confused by my hair. He puts his unlit cigar in the ashtray and stands.

"Hello, Punky! Did you just get here?" dad gives me a bear hug, lifting me off the floor.

My lips are tingling and going numb at the same time. How is that possible? I'm beginning to see double. The light around dad's head is a hazy glow, making him look like he has a halo.

"I've been good, dad. But I'm awfully fizzy. I mean dizzy."

Dad gently lowers me down to my feet.

I rest my head on his shoulder and mutter, "Cupcakes... sunshine...oil change..."

My body feels like a piece of paper floating down slowly, but I hit the floor like a ton of bricks. The only thing that cushions my head is the remaining cupcakes tangled in my hair. What's happening to me? My arms feel so heavy. My mouth won't work. This is not how I expected to die, I think to myself. Or maybe I say it out loud. At this point, I'm not sure.

I feel like I'm underwater. Lying on the floor I can hear my family, their voices like distant echoes all around me. Mom yells for Joan. Joan comes running in like a herd of elephants.

"What? Oh, no! I'm sorry! I'm sorry! Get up stupid!" My sister yells as she jumps around.

Mom runs to the kitchen and grabs an egg. "Oh, Mija!" she drops to her knees and pulls up my shirt. Mom rubs my body with the egg. She chants over and over, "Mal de ojo." She whips her head around to look at my dad, "This is your fault, Henry! If you weren't so good looking, we wouldn't be in this situation!"

Is she flirting right now? I can never tell with my mom. The only emotion distinguishable is anger. It doesn't help she switches back and forth from English to Spanish faster than J. Lo changes clothes at a concert.

Dad shakes his head, "Olivia, this isn't something an egg is going to fix." He wipes the hair from my face. He looks at my sister, "Why does Marguerite have cupcakes in her hair?"

As if this matters right now.

"For heaven's sakes, stop hopping around and call 9-1-1, Joan!" Mom barks like a Chihuahua on crack.

I feel my heart thump in my chest each and every time. It's like a really loud clock you are watching near the end of class. 'TICK. TICK. TICK.' Look on the bright side; at least my heart is still beating. It feels like an eternity before I hear sirens in the distance. Am I dying? What the heck is happening? This rug is nice…I feel it under my fingertips. Joan is walking circles around me.

I strain to open my eyes, but only one manages to somewhat pop open.

Joan sees me. She clumsily bends down, dropping the phone on my forehead. Out of nowhere she shoves two fingers down my throat. Confused, I bite down hard, and then barf everywhere! I hate throwing up, even when I'm sick. I'd do anything not to throw up, even if I know it will make me feel better. Joan knows this. Why would she do this to me?

I press my hand down feeling the rug again.

"Hello people I'm in here!" I shout but nothing comes out of my mouth except hot air and the smell of barf.

No one can hear me. I must look so awesome, lying here with pieces of cupcake in my hair. Even dead, my inner sarcasm spills out. I look like the remains of a wild party. My other eye finally pops open. I'm staring into the air. My eyes gloss over.

Joan vigorously rubs my face "I swear to God…are you dead? Blink! If you die, I swear, I'll be so mad at you!"

Frank slithers out the door trying to avoid the confrontation that is inevitable when dad finds out what he's done. Wait a minute; did he do this to me?

Dad rubs my hand, trying to get me to look at him. "Pumpkin, say something…anything."

I can't shift my eyes to look at him. Everything is so heavy. Joan holds me, and everything goes completely black; even my thoughts…no light, no sound. Just blackness.

Bra on Credit

Where am I? How long have I been out? I open one eye. I'm groggy and disoriented. My other eye seems glued shut. I feel like I'm in between a dream and being awake. It's like when you dream in the morning, you know you are dreaming, but you can also make decisions. My other eye slowly opens and I try looking around the room.

It's really hard to focus.

My mind begins to register...white sheets...a metal pole...a rhythmic beeping noise, and my sister holding my hand. I can hear mom just outside the door. She is on the phone with someone speaking Spanish a million miles a minute. Dad's heavy footsteps are pacing the hall next to her. I squint; the fluorescent lights are way too bright.

Joan realizes I'm waking up and squeezes my hand three times. I immediately know what she is saying. It's our silent way to say, I love you. It all started when I was eight. I got my tonsils taken out, Joan stayed in my hospital bed until I woke up. I wanted to tell her that I loved her so bad. I was so scared and so thankful she was there, I squeezed her hand three times. "I want water...I want food...have to pee...I want chocolate," Joan was trying so hard. When she finally figured it out, I gave her a huge thumbs up. We've used it ever since.

I reach my hands below the sheets, exploring my body. Why do I feel naked? It's because I am naked! Well, not completely. I'm wearing a hospital gown with the saddest looking flowers on it and no panties. Dang, those were my favorite silk panties. What could have possibly happened that I would be missing my panties? I don't even want to think about it. I want to just lay here and not think about anything. Wait a minute, why am I in the hospital? Was I in an accident? Slowly things start to come back to me. Joan called me. She was crying. There were strippers. I blacked out.

Joan leans in closer and cautiously, but frantically whispers, "I meant to poison Frank. You must have grabbed the glass meant for him. I was just so distraught that I didn't notice you picked up his wine glass. I was just going to give him enough of my sleeping pills to incapacitate him. Maybe come up with a plan to humiliate him; maybe strip him and leave him in the foyer of his office building." Joan trails off slapping her palm against her forehead, "Oh, gosh, I'm so dumb!"

That's right, Frank is cheating on Joan! Without turning my head, I look at Joan sideways, a smile slowly stretches across my face. I put my hand over my heart and silently laugh. My abs hurt too bad to laugh any louder.

"Classic," I manage to whisper. I slowly lift my arm just enough to give her a fist bump. I mumble, "Stupid."

Joan laughs, "Stupid-er."

"Why do I feel like I got run over by a truck?" I say as my eyes begin to dart all over the room.

Joan looks down at her feet, "They had to pump your stomach. I told them you already threw up, but they wanted to make sure you didn't have anything left in your system."

We sit in silence for a good ten minutes. Thank goodness it was me and not Frank, otherwise Joan would be in jail. I break the silence softly, "We have to be better than that...If we are going to poison someone, we need to be sneakier...and not poison each other."

"I know. I was just hurt," Joan says in a broken voice.

I hate to see Joan like this. I try to get her to laugh. "Just think of the things we could do to him..." I say in a sly voice.

He has it coming to him. At any point, he could have told Joan it wasn't working. He could have stopped sleeping with her! He could have said, 'I'm a douche bag and a walking STD, sorry.'

The doctors are talking to dad in the hall. I only catch snippets, but I get the gist of it. They are telling dad I'm going to be here for a few days for observation. Apparently, they are concerned I overdosed.

"Does she have a history of depression?" I hear one ask.

OH MY GOSH! I'm going to kill Joan. I knit my eyebrows together and scowl at her. Jeez, is this going to be on my medical record forever? I did overdose if you want to call it that, but I only overdosed because of Joan. There's no good way to explain it though…not in a way that wouldn't get Joan into major trouble.

Joan presses her face into the hospital bed.

I put my hand in her hair and tug it. "You owe me big time," I hiss.

By the third day in the hospital, I discovered there's not much to do. There is only so much television you can watch before you start losing brain cells.

"Wanna take a walk around the ward?" Joan asks, shoving the last spoonful of Jell-O into her mouth.

Jell-O is about the only edible thing this place serves. My throat is still a bit sore, so Jell-O hits the spot; the red kind, not the green. Whoever invented green Jell-O needs to be fired immediately.

I start to scoot to the edge of the bed.

"Where do you think you're going young lady?" the nurse says as she walks into the room.

"Oh, we're just going to walk around the hospital since it's after visiting hours," I say happily.

The nurse opens the door. "You can go, but you aren't walking anywhere unescorted."

I swear, Joan is so dead! "Fair enough, will my sister be an acceptable chaperone? We want to talk." I poke out my lower lip.

The nurse nods to Joan.

I follow Joan out of the room, marching close behind her.

"So, where too?" she says leaning over to look at me as I walk to her side.

I randomly pick a floor, "Let's go to the fifth floor and find a vending machine. Do you have any money?"

Joan pushes the button for the elevator. "Next stop, the fifth floor. Of course, I have money," Joan says pulling a credit card out of her bra.

"Why, the hell, do you have a credit card in your bra?" I lean forward pretending to look for anything else stuffed down there.

"For emergency vending machine purposes, why else?" Joan says pulling her shirt up to her chin.

"What else do you have in there? This whole time I thought you were a natural C cup; it turns out you've been stuffing," I say with a laugh.

We stroll down a long hall looking for the vending machine, when I giggle, "Remember that three-legged dog we had?"

"Oh, yeah! We found it at the feed store," Joan said laughing.

It was good to hear her laugh for a second. Dad didn't even know we had a dog in the truck until halfway home. Mom, of course, knew we had the dog the whole time. She pretended she didn't see us sneak it into the backseat until Dad looked at her, and she burst out laughing. This is what Joan needs to be doing; not thinking of that worthless bottom feeder of a husband, Frank. I need to get Joan laughing again.

I gently grab Joan's hand, "I know you think that Frank cheating is the end of the world, but it's not. It's just the end of your time with him."

Joan squeezes my hand, "I just wish Frank had been man enough to handle it correctly."

"Yeah, me too... but he didn't. He'll get what's coming to him, the Universe has its way of righting things…Hey, I have an idea, what would you say about going on a road trip?" I examine Joan's face for a reaction. "Well…?"

I stop Joan and turn her towards me. Joan shrugs her shoulders, "It wouldn't be the worst idea."

"I mean it's not as exciting as trying to poison Frank, but…" I add, poking Joan in the ribs. "You know you want to be trapped in a miniature car with me across the country."

"Across the country?" Joan leans back, thinking, "Hell, why not? I've got time. I don't want to go back to the house anyways."

"Then it's settled, we are going on a road trip!" I throw my hands in the air.

Joan and I stroll up to the vending machine. Joan swipes her card and I press C4. A package of chocolate donuts drops to the plastic door.

Joan stares at all the choices and then presses C4, choosing chocolate donuts, too.

"I don't know why you even look. You always get the chocolate donuts or a honey bun," I smile at Joan. I could have totally picked for her and got it right. I turn around and yell, "I'll race you back to the room!"

As we get back to the room, the nurse is unplugging and rolling my IV pole to the door. She puts the rail down on my freshly changed bed. I crawl in and lay on my side, unwrapping my snack.

Joan crawls in next to me and pulls the rail up to keep from falling out backwards.

I tug the scratchy hospital sheets up around my neck. Joan cuddles in behind me. I'm the little spoon. I eat my donuts and fall fast asleep.

I wake up in the dead of night and lay in bed thinking about life. The only sound is the sing-song noise of beeping monitors somewhere in the distance. What if we take this road trip? Did she really mean it when she agreed to go? Joan has been my rock, now it's time for me to be hers. I roll over to my side to face Joan.

I tap Joan's shoulder. "Hey, stupid…Joan, wake up. Hey, I was serious about taking a road trip."

Joan wipes her eyes and looks at me, "Okay, but where would we go?" She reaches down and pulls the covers over us, making a make-shift fort.

I push the button on my phone for light. "Anywhere but here. Everywhere. Let's just go. Marie can take care of the shop for a bit," I say in my most convincing voice. I make a mental note to call Marie later to run it by her.

"Well, I guess I can go…I have enough inventory in the gallery. The staff can hold it down for a while," Joan whispers.

I can see a tiny glimmer of doubt in her eyes.

"You're going! You almost killed me; you owe me!" I say in a stern voice. She does owe it to me.

"Okay, okay…I'll go on your stupid little road trip. Just stop breathing on me," she smiles as I put my head on her shoulder and fall back to sleep.

Out for Good Behavior

The next morning, I wake with Joan still sleeping next to me in the hospital bed. I'm itching to get out of here. I've been here four, long days, but it seems more like two weeks. I'm ready to blow this taco stand, if you know what I mean. I feel too good to be here any longer.

The doctor peeks into the room then walks in.

He flips open my chart and begins reading over the notes. "Ms. Becker, You are being released today."

"Am I being released early for 'good behavior'?" I ask in a snarky tone.

The doctor gives me an amused look, "The nurse will bring your paperwork. You're out of here today…for 'good behavior'." He salutes me with his clipboard as he turns to walk out of the room.

I nudge Joan, "Hey, I get to go home today."

Joan wraps her arms around me and pulls me in tighter. I know she feels horrible about what happened.

Mom knocks on the door as she and dad walk into the room. "Are you up? I knew I would find you girls sleeping," she says this like we are goofing off somehow.

It's only 7 a.m. Besides, what else are we supposed to be doing? Joan slides out of bed and sits in the metal chair beside me.

Dad leans over and kisses me on the head. "Are you feeling better, Punky? I was really worried about you."

"I'm better. I get to leave today," I grin.

Mom starts running a brush through my hair. "Do you want

some coffee, mija. I'll get you some, I'll be right back."

As mom shuts the door behind her, dad turns back to me. "Okay, I can tell you girls are up to something, what is it?" he asks with his famous, crooked smile.

I love dad's smile; it lets me know everything is going to be alright; that all is right in the world. There's a warmness in it that I can't find anywhere else. I give him my cheekiest grin. Out of the corner of my eye I can tell something is going on with Joan. She has that look in her eye, the same look she had when she told dad she smashed into the back of a parked car at the football game.

Joan begins to speed up the tapping of her foot. Almost as if she can't possibly hold it in anymore, she blurts, "Dad, Frank cheated on me. I found out and tried to poison him. But Stupid here," she points at me, "drank the tainted glass of wine instead." She makes a silly face at me, "We really need to look into your drinking problem."

My mouth drops open. I begin pulling at my covers, pretending like they are stuck under me.

Genuinely concerned, Joan hops off the chair and begins to help me pull the sheet from under me. As soon as she realizes what is happening, she throws her head back and laughs, accidentally snorting like a pig.

"Dad, Mar is shooting the finger at me," Joan whines.

She falls for it every time. It's a joke we have played on each other since high school. I would pretend to have something in my pocket for her. I would gesture for her to come closer because it was a secret, then I would whip my middle finger out of my pocket and flip her off.

I hear mom's voice in the hall talking to a nurse.

She pushes the door open with her shoulder, "You girls knock it off." She snaps at us like laughing is a bad thing. "This is serious! You girls never take anything seriously!"

I guess this is her way of dealing with how worried she is.

"Mom calm down. I'm fine," I say, reaching for her forearm. I lie, "We were just laughing at that three-legged dog from the lumberyard that one time..."

Mom cracks a smile, "We did pull a fast one over on your dad, didn't we?"

She sits at the end of my bed and leans over my legs. "Mar, I was so worried about you."

Dad pipes up, "You never pulled a fast one on me. I knew all along the girls had that dog in the backseat."

Mom rolls her eyes, "You did not, Henry Becker. Don't lie!"

We laughed and reminisced well into the late afternoon when the nurse and doctor finally reappear to make their rounds. "Well, Ms. Becker, we are ready to discharge you, I just have to go over some items. We kept you here for observation because when you were brought in you had some Ambien in your system which was mixed with alcohol and created a very dangerous combination. I don't see that you have a prescription for Ambien, was this a new medication?" the doc says slowly, searching for me to add more of an explanation.

Whatever happened to patient confidentiality?

Mom stands on her tiptoes and glares at me over the doctor's shoulder. I'll just add this to the guilt she gives me about the family reunion.

I nod my head and lie, "I hadn't been sleeping very well. I took a couple of my sister's sleeping pills to catch up on some rest. I guess between that and the wine, it took me down. I've never taken sleeping pills before. I didn't know I couldn't mix wine and pills." I'd rather sound stupid than get Joan in trouble.

I casually glance at Joan and my dad gives me a wink. Mom narrows her eyes at me. She knows we aren't being completely honest.

The doctor begins to drone on in a monotone voice, "Taking prescription pills that aren't yours is never a good idea. Neither is

43

combining any medication with alcohol…"

My mind begins to wander off.

The doctor presses his lips together in a straight line and raises an eyebrow, scolding me like a three-year-old. "Got it?"

"I got it," I nod my head reassuringly as he walks out the door closing it behind him.

"Dad, could you go pick up Cooper back at Joan's? I have to go back to the city tonight." I lie yet again but I don't want to tell him our plan in front of mom.

"Sure thing, Punky. I'll go now." Dad kisses me on the forehead, "We'll be right back."

I secretly hope he runs into Frank, that bastard. Dad is in his seventies, but you wouldn't know it. He has always been in excellent shape. Except, of course, for the cigars.

I slide myself out of bed and turn on the shower. After my shower, I pull on my clothes that mom brought me in her purse. I curl back in the hospital bed.

Joan is sitting on the chair next to me when a nurse pushes in a wheelchair.

"You've got to be kidding me? I have to be wheeled out?" I question.

I swear, Joan is seriously going to pay for this.

"Yes, dear, you don't want to fall on the way out. You've had quite the episode. It's hospital policy, we have to wheel you to the curb," the nurse says, locking the brakes on the wheelchair.

I guess the hospital doesn't want to be responsible if you injure yourself walking out, but to hell with you after that. This is beyond humiliating. But I guess no more humiliating than having cupcakes washed out of your hair. Not to mention, I still don't know what happened to my favorite pair of panties. I think I'm more upset about having to be wheeled out of the hospital versus the whole "accidentally poisoning me" thing.

I make a mental note of all the things Joan owes me for. I look at her to make sure she's watching me as I reach my hand up and make an invisible check mark in the air.

She laughs, "You don't get a point, Stupid!"

I raise both my eyebrows, "I certainly do! If not for this, then what? I almost died...Stupid-er!"

Joan shrugs her shoulders in agreement, "Let's go. I don't know why you're still talking."

Just as we make it to the sidewalk, dad pulls up in Cooper. What great timing. He honks the horn and waves. Dad hops out of the car, grabs the wheelchair, and pushes me to the driver's side. How this seems safe is beyond me. I shouldn't just be wheeled straight to my car. Talk about irresponsible; I would usually have something snarky to say about this, but nothing comes to mind.

"Mar, just so you know, I gave it a tune up and changed the oil yesterday. When was the last time you changed your oil?" Dad points his chin towards the ground and looks up at me; he knows it's been too long.

I poke my bottom lip out and give a sheepish shrug, "Maybe, never...probably never. I guess not since you did it the last time you did it."

"What am I going to do with you, Marguerite? You'll burn your motor up. I've told you to change it with synthetic oil every 8,000 miles." Dad points to Cooper's hood.

"Sorry, dad. I'll try to remember," I say.

In unison Joan and I plead, "Dad." We scoot together and look at dad with puppy dog eyes. Something we've done since we were kids. He knows something is coming. It always does when we huddle together like this. I can tell he is bracing himself.

"What? What are you girls up to, or do I even want to know?" dad says, crossing his arms over his broad chest.

"Joan and I have been talking. We are headed off on an adventure. We are going to drive from California to New York and back again. Don't worry about us," I say with enthusiasm.

Dad gives me a cautious look. I slowly scoot up to him, tiptoeing to give him a hug around the neck.

"An adventure, huh… Where exactly are you girls headed?" dad asks curiously.

"Wherever the road takes us, and everywhere in between." Joan quickly chimes in.

"We will take Cooper, now that he's in tip-top shape," I add giving dad a wink. "And we are leaving today. Right now."

"In light of what's happening at the present moment, I think it's a great idea. You two girls have always had each other's backs. Just make sure to call your mother and I from time to time," dad says.

Joan hugs dad tight, "You're the best, dad! Please give mom the edited version of what happened to Mar. I just don't think she can handle it."

Dad huffs, "Your mom can handle more than you think. She raised you two girls, didn't she?"

He pretends to tip his hat like he just counted that as a point for himself. Dad reaches in his wallet. "Go have fun girls, life is short." He hands me his credit card with a wink, "Give 'em hell!"

I try handing the credit card back.

"Dad, we are more than capable of paying for our own trip, you know? I'm almost thirty," Joan says, schooling Dad.

Dad smiles his crooked smile at us again, "Awe, but it's a lot more fun spending my money. Just let me do this for you girls."

"Hang on!" I reach into the glove box for a pen and piece of paper. I quickly write on it and hand it back to him.

Dad unfolds the paper and reads it out loud. "IOU! Love, Mar and Joan."

He folds it up and places it in his wallet, like when we were kids.

Joan and I wrap our arms around dad at the same time, "You're the best!"

Dad whispers, "No, you are. Go on girls, mom will be along

shortly to pick me up."

I give Dad one last kiss on the cheek. We hop in Cooper and slowly start to drive away. I adjust my mirror and catch a glimpse of him in it. He is wiping his eyes, and my heart drops. Saying 'bye' to Dad is never easy.

Joan snaps me out of it, "What's the plan, Stan?"

I raise my eyebrows and say, "New York or bust?" That sounded more like a question than I wanted it to.

"New York or bust!" I say with a little more authority.

"New York or bust," Joan says, repeating what I just said in agreement.

I grab my phone and plug it into the aux cord and type in Paul Simon. I skip to my favorite part, the chorus.

Joan snatches the phone from my hand, "Don't mess with your phone while you're driving. I'm in charge of the music."

Our plan is far from solid, but as they say: 'A good plan now is better than a great plan next week.' My thought has always been, if you have a car and gas, just drive. Everything else will work itself out. Joan only has the clothes on her back. Luckily, I have the duffel bag containing my laptop, running shoes, and a few essentials.

Two Drunks on a Trike

We make it as far as Napa when Joan gets that look in her eye. I know it too well. "Hey Stupid, Let's do a wine tour. I mean, unless you've given up drinking."

I look at Joan like she just grew a second head, giving myself ample time to consider if I'm going to have some kind of residual aversion to drinking. "Nope I'm good. It's going to take more than a little poisoning to stop me from drinking. College is evidence of that." I jut out my chin and give Joan a mischievous grin.

I've never been on a wine tour. Unless you count perusing the aisles at The Liquor Lot as a wine tour.

"Hey, let's ride bikes though, and make a day of it," Joan says.

"That's a brilliant idea! I mean, how much trouble can you get into drinking and riding a bike?" I shake my head, agreeing with myself.

I pull into a coffee shop parking lot and begin to work my way through the list of bike rental shops. I call a few shops with no luck. Bikes must be one hot commodity. Who knew?

"How many darn people are riding bikes around and drinking?" I ask Joan. "Is there some kind of Tour De France going on this weekend?"

"Tour De Drunk," Joan giggles.

I shake my head at her. Sometimes she can be so corny. But I love it. "I'm going to try one more place. If they don't have a bike, I say we press on."

The phone begins to ring, then a click. The girl at the other end of the line squawks loudly, she's the female equivalent of Gilbert Gottfried. "Hello…Hello. Tandy Dandy Bike rental."

"Ummm…Hi, I was wondering if you had any bikes for rent…for today?" I look at Joan and stick out my tongue.

The girl on the phone squawks again and I wince. "Yes, we rent bikes, but all we have left is one adult cruising tricycle."

"We'll take it!" Joan yells in the background. My eyes widen. I shoot Joan a look. She throws her hands in the air, giving me the "I didn't think that through" look. I suppose she was so excited she didn't realize one of us would not actually have a bike. "Thank you, we will be there in a few minutes." I say pausing before hanging up, hoping Joan would add something.

"What are we going to do with one tricycle Stupid-er?" I say to Joan.

"One of us could drive, and the other can ride in the back basket?" Joan says with a smile stretching across her face like she just came up with the most brilliant idea.

"I don't think that's safe, Joan," I say, blowing out my breath and squinting at her.

"I'm just brainstorming here!" Joan snaps.

I roll my eyes at her; she does have a point. It gives us both the opportunity to enjoy the ride and the other to sweat out the wine from the previous vineyard. We arrive at the bright yellow bike shop, and park Cooper right in front.

"Hello, we are here for the adult tricycle," I say politely, pulling my dad's credit card out of my wallet.

The girl behind the counter gives us the strangest look. It's obviously because she's never heard of such a brilliant idea, or maybe she's never seen two adult women on one tricycle. Either way, I'm going to think we're the first.

"You know you can still get a ticket for drinking on a bike?" the girl says like it's going to change our brilliant idea. She just doesn't share our vision. Plus, it beats drinking and driving a car. On a bike, we can only hurt ourselves, at least in theory.

"Ah, thank you, Debbie," I say sarcastically.

She furrows her brow, looking confused, "My name is Becky."

I turn towards Joan and block the side of my face with my hand and mouth "Debbie Downer."

Joan claps her hand over her mouth, trying to control her laughter. Her face is turning bright red, and her hulk vein is bulging across her forehead. She turns and pretends to look at the bike accessories. I grab two helmets, shove one at Joan, and begin strapping mine on when I feel a sharp sting. The back of my head still hurts from bouncing it off the floor.

Joan pulls out the wine tour map and hops into the back basket. I steady the trike and glance back at her. As we ride off, she gives Becky a two-fingered salute.

I don't know how I got the job of pedaling first. I did just get out of the hospital for what I would call, "malicious minor poisoning."

The Mondavi Winery is first on our list. It's a bit of a jaunt, but we decide to just enjoy the adventure. Joan settles in and makes a playlist for our ride. She labels it, "Two Drunks and A Trike."

Joan is behind me spitting out names of songs. "How about anything by Elton John, or The Beatles or how about anything by Benny Blanco?" Joan asks, shuffling through her phone.

"'Eastside' by Benny Blanco!" I yell into the wind.

It's a dreadful hundred degrees and the dirt is more or less just dust. The road to the wineries is a narrow, two-lane road with not much margin for error. Sidewalks are nonexistent. There's a single bike lane on each side of the road, but neither wide enough for a tricycle. It makes me wonder why they rent tricycles if there really isn't a place to ride them.

The only choice I have, is to drive really carefully on the side of the road where the single bike lane is. I start off slow, holding the trike steady, while riding the edge. This is the worst idea ever. Cars zoom past us. A little too close for my comfort, but I can't let on too much or Joan will flip out. Literally.

A bead of sweat rolls down the side of my face. "Crap!" I grip the handlebars tighter, trying to keep the trike going straight.

Joan seems oblivious to the passing cars. She's belting out the lyrics to 'Rocket Man.'

I look up and notice a delivery truck coming straight towards us. My legs begin to shake a little as it gets closer and closer. I reach up with one hand and wipe the sweat that is now dripping into my eyes. I watch as the truck's wheel rides the white line. He's too wide. I have to make a decision, quickly!

"Joan!" I yell, jerking the handlebar of the trike.

It's just enough that we veer off and speed down the dusty embankment straight for a row of rose bushes. We bounce and thump down the hill hard and fast. I'm managing to keep the trike upright. Glancing over my shoulder, I see Joan squatting in the basket. She is clutching her phone high above her head in her right hand and holding on to the basket with her left. I laugh! She looks like she's riding a bull.

One of the back wheels pops off and comes bouncing down the hill beside us. The trike tips sideways. I brace myself for the inevitable fall when suddenly the other wheel pops off. Joan bounces into the air and comes crashing down, landing with her butt flat against the bottom of the basket. Joan's butt and the basket are dragging against the ground like a giant cheese grater.

We come to a quick stop. I immediately hop off to get a good look at Joan. She has dirt everywhere. She stands up and steps out of the basket. I walk around her, inspecting the damage.

"Uh, Joan!" I jump up and down, laughing.

The back of her flowered dress is shredded up to her bra strap showing what's left of her panties and bottom. So much for those very expensive silk panties...They are merely a string now, or maybe they were only ever a string.

"My butt stings!" Joan says reaching back to feel what has

happened. She slowly touches each butt cheek and her eyes widen, "Where's my dress?"

I put my hands on my knees and laugh, "Oh! Joan, your butt cheeks are super red and scraped!"

I look a bit better than Joan. I mean I didn't just get my butt grated like a giant piece of cheese so, that's a plus. We both have a good laugh as we plop ourselves down in the dirt.

In the distance I hear a shout, "Hey!" Over the hill, comes a guy rushing down towards us. "Are you two okay?"

Joan and I pretend like we are sunning ourselves on a beach in Cannes. Like it's perfectly normal to be at the bottom of a hill with a broken tricycle lying mutilated in the dirt.

Dryly, in a southern accent, I say, "Oh, yes honey...Why do you ask?" I pretend to put sunscreen on my arms.

Joan adjusts her imaginary sunglasses, then crosses her legs and pretends to sip a drink. She taps her pretend glass, "Just in time sugar, I am due for a refill. Could you please bring me another mint julep?"

I can see confusion cross his face as he reaches up and scratches his head. A smile stretches across his face. "Hi, I'm Will."

By all standards, 'Hi, I'm Will' is very handsome. He's about six-foot tall with dark brown hair and deep green eyes. He looks like he is in his early thirties. His chiseled chest is obvious through his gray t-shirt. He looks like a rugged Adonis. I reach up to shake his hand; he pulls me to my feet.

"Thanks," I say as I shake myself off. "I'm Mar. This is my sister, Joan."

"Are you guys really okay?" he asks realizing we were playing with him.

I'm sure he thinks we are drunk. Little does he know we don't have to be drunk; this is our normal. He reaches down to shake Joan's hand and begins to pull her up onto her feet. Joan, not wanting to stand, realizes that he is trying to pull her up. She starts to dig her heels into the dirt and lean backwards. Will gives her an extra tug. Joan throws her weight backwards to keep her raw bottom from being discovered. Puzzled, Will grabs her with his other hand and finally pulls her to her feet.

"Um..." Will immediately realizes Joan is missing most of her dress, and instantly regrets pulling her up.

His cheeks turn bright red and his eyes begin to dart everywhere...everywhere but Joan that is.

Smiling, I step in front of Joan, interrupting the awkwardness. "We stopped to do a wine tour on a whim and had this, obvious, brilliant idea," I point towards the dismantled trike lying in the dirt.

Will rubs the back of his neck, I suppose, considering the options. "Can I help you get the trike back somewhere?"

I make another quick observation of the trike. There's no way we are getting it back without help. The wheels are lying broken in the dirt and Joan is injured and half-dressed.

"Let me give you a ride, I insist," Will says, still not making eye contact with Joan. He starts laughing, "You two are funny. For a second I thought I was a cabana waiter at a beach."

I look at Joan and snicker, "He doesn't know the half of it."

Will half-turns towards me. I can tell he is rethinking giving us a ride, so I give him a slug on the shoulder and laugh. "We aren't going to kill you. Do we look like murderers to you? I mean with our broken trike and all...and her missing dress?"

Will slings the trike onto his back and carries it up the hill. I pick up both tires and follow Joan closely in an effort to hide her exposed butt. Although, I'm not sure who I'm hiding it from, there's no one in the field, except a few crows.

When we get into his truck, I quickly type out a text to Marie. I do this when I'm in a car with someone new; too many nights of watching crime shows.

Getting a ride back to a bike shop in Napa. Guy, 30's, brown hair, and green eyes. His name is Will. We are in a silver Chevy truck.

Marie sends a text back. *Gotcha!*

We hop in Will's truck and start to make the short drive back to the bike shop.

"Is it the yellow bike shop a mile or so back?" Will asks, hunching over his steering wheel and glancing sideways at us.

"Yes, the bright yellow one," I say.

Will pulls his truck up to the front of the building. Before we step out of the truck, he grabs a jacket from the backseat and hands it to Joan who puts it on.

I spot Becky inside the shop following us with her eyes, slack jawed. She gives us a glare as Will grabs the trike out of the back of his truck.

Joan rushes around me, beating me to the counter. She blurts, "The wheels popped off, then we ran off the road and down a hill! A hill!"

I walk up beside Joan and gently move her over.

She laughs as she twirls around to stand behind me.

"We ran off the road, down the hill, and then the wheels popped off," I say. Looking at Joan, I shake my head and giggle. Under my breath I whisper, "Stupid."

She kicks the back of my heel with her foot, "Stupid-er."

Dad is going to get a kick out of this story and the six- hundred-dollar charge on his credit card. I can see him now, laughing as he adds the receipt to the memory box he has kept since we were kids. Lord only knows what's in that thing.

"Thanks for all your help, Will," I say, extending my hand.

He shakes it and looks past me directly at Joan, "You're welcome." His voice comes out clear and warm.

I elbow Joan. Will pauses slightly, the same pause someone does when they want to say something but don't. He casually glances at Joan's left hand…her wedding ring is still on her finger. Damn it! I should have reminded her take it off. I can almost feel the air drain out of his lungs. He turns to grab the door handle of his truck.

Seizing the opportunity, I turn to Will, trying to control the eagerness in my voice, "Hey, Will! How about joining us for dinner tonight as thanks for rescuing us?"

Am I the only one that can feel the attraction between these two? It feels like some kind of human magnet. You better believe I'm not going to let Joan pass this up that easy. When one door closes, another one opens.

"Meet ya at Bowen's Chophouse at 6:30?" I hold my breath, waiting for his answer.

"Sure, that would be nice," Will replies warmly.

I turn and give Joan the Groucho Marx eyebrow raise. "It's a date!" I say, turning back to Will.

Will nods his head and smiles, "I look forward to it."

I smile back, "We look forward to it!"

Patch Yourself Up, Buttercup!

"Now what?" I raise an eyebrow at Joan.

"I'll call around and find a hotel." Joan begins Googling on her phone, "Let's see...found one, head north while I call to make sure they have a room."

I give Joan a puzzled look, "Which way is north? Left, right or straight?"

"You really need to get your directions down. If you can't, then maybe you should get a newer car that tells you which way north is," Joan says still looking down at her phone.

"Hey!" I say, patting Cooper on the dash. "She didn't mean it Coop."

Joan glances up from her phone, "Take a left, Stupid."

We arrive at a cute, little, vine-covered hotel with a cobblestone drive. On each side of the main hotel are four, small, white cottages. "Good choice," I say to Joan, pleased.

Joan hops out to check us in. I look in the trunk and slam it shut. Our options are scarce, that's what we get for leaving on the fly. Joan and I will need to go shopping. Which is one of my least favorite things in the world. Nevertheless, we did need something to wear, especially Joan! Wait a minute, why is Joan the one checking us in? She's the one missing half her clothes. Well, I can't change that now. I lean against the back of Cooper to wait.

Joan walks back towards me, holding the key in her hand.

I point at her and laugh. She has completely forgotten about the back half of her dress. Will's jacket is quite long, though, and comes down to her mid-thigh. She looks odd with a jacket in a hundred-degree weather.

I turn my wrist over to check the time. The face of my watch is cracked. I must have broken it somehow in the fall. "We have about four hours before we meet Will for dinner."

"Okay, I need a shower, clothes, and bandages before we go anywhere," Joan says pointing to her butt.

I give Joan a smug grin, "Okay, I'll be the nice sister and go out for supplies while you take a shower, I'll get some peroxide, too." I throw my duffel bag on a bed, claiming it. "Check ya later, wish me luck," I say, shutting the cottage door behind me.

The store is two miles up the road. I drive past it and have to make a U-turn to find it. It almost looks like a resort instead of a grocery store. As I walk in, I begin to make a mental list, gauze, peroxide, Neosporin...Got it...Check. Clothes...I don't think I can find clothes here. I pass the tourist aisle. Sunscreen, hats, sunglasses, towels—I've hit the mother lode. I can surely find something here. It's as good as it's going to get. I find a blue, boxy shirt that says 'Napa, California' on the front with a generic picture of a vineyard, and a pair of boys' swimming trunks in large. I check out and quickly make it back to the hotel.

Joan is sitting on the bed wrapped in a towel. "What did you get?" Joan asks, peering into the grocery bags.

"It wasn't exactly couture at the grocery store, but I got you some stuff for your bottom. Here is something to wear so we can go shopping for some real clothes," I say feeling pretty proud of my finds.

I spread out the shirt and shorts on the bed.

Joan picks up the shorts and smirks, "Mar, little boy swim shorts?"

I could have done worse. "Be thankful for what you get." I shrug my shoulders at her, "Patch yourself up, buttercup, and let's go. Stop being vain."

"I'm the furthest thing from vain!" she tries to defend herself.

I know she's not vain. I start to hum the Carly Simon song, "You're So Vain", and dance around just to get under her skin.

Joan snatches a pillow off the bed and smacks me in the face with it.

I fall back on the bed and begin scrolling through my phone. "Hurry up," I yell.

Joan strolls out of the bathroom in her new attire. I don't think I've seen anything funnier. I snap a picture with my phone and send it to dad.

"You look like the Jolly Green Giant!" I blurt out through tears of laughter. She looks ridiculous in the little boy shorts I bought. "Now you've ruined my mascara!"

"Well, you shouldn't buy cheap mascara," Joan slings back at me.

I pretend to cast an imaginary fishing rod and start reeling as my middle finger goes up, flipping Joan off.

Joan grabs my cheek, "Aw, you're so cute. First stop: jeans."

I shake my head in agreement. "Yes, first stop is for sure jeans. We can't have you going around town looking like a scrawny, twelve-year-old boy," I say. "You look ridiculous."

"You know, sometimes I really hate you," Joan says, grabbing her purse off the chair.

"That's not true. You love me and you know it. I'm irresistible," I give her a wink.

"I poisoned you, didn't I?" Joan says jokingly.

"Oh, that was low. Inconceivable!" I say with a made-up lisp.

She reaches her hand up and gives herself an imaginary point.

As we walk down the main street, we notice most shops are high-end boutiques. The price tags are way over-priced. Who are they kidding? Used bedazzled Levi's are $250.00! Reluctantly, we go through each shop, one by one, eventually gathering enough of the things we need. I grab a couple of jeans, shorts, and a few shirts. Joan and I wear roughly the same size, except for pants. We could share clothes if we had to.

"You should wear something cute tonight," I say, trying to casually persuade her. "It will make you feel good about yourself. If you have the body, flaunt it," I slyly remark. I have to admit, I have ulterior motives. I know Will likes her; I could tell from the way he looked at her today.

I opt for skintight jeans and a gray shirt coupled with nude, stiletto heels that I paid way too much for. Joan opts for a flowing, mini dress and ankle boots. Mainly because anything rubbing her rear is not the best idea. Plus, Joan has killer legs. We give ourselves a once over as we clasp our hands together and chant, "Unbreakable." It's our sister handshake we made up when we were little.

I stare Joan right in the eyes, "We are just going to have fun tonight. No worries..."

As we pull into the restaurant parking lot, Will's truck is parked in front; prime parking. The restaurant is packed tonight, but I can practically park Cooper anywhere. I parallel park in front of a big eucalyptus tree and bring his top up. I don't want any surprises from the birds.

Walking into the restaurant, I make a quick survey of the room. One of Joan's paintings is hanging in the entryway.

"Hey, look one of your paintings is hanging over there." I point and notice Will's head pop up from across the room.

I get an uneasy feeling. The hair on my arms stand straight up and alarm bells go off in my head. My mind registers someone familiar.

Backwoods Texas Girls

I scan the crowd. It's Frank! Holy hell, Batman! He's just sitting there, looking smug with some girl dressed like a hooker. I can't believe he's here. Out of all the places…I mean it wasn't more than a week ago that Joan found out he had been cheating on her. He's got some nerve! I mentally start making a game plan. I could pretend to feel immediately ill, which wouldn't actually be a lie. I do feel sick to my stomach, all of a sudden.

Joan grabs both of my hands and stares at my face. I know she can tell something is happening even though I'm trying to keep my face blank.

"What? What's wrong Mar?" Joan says as she begins to glance around.

Joan's face drops. I know she sees him. It seems as if hours pass as we stand there but in reality, it hasn't been more than ten seconds. I stand completely still. I'm rattled. I can't imagine how Joan feels. I get some sort of PTSD tunnel vision. It's like the whole restaurant has gone dark, except one, large industrial spotlight on Frank. I want to wrap my hands around his neck.

From the corner of my eye I see Will walking towards us.

"Hello ladies, good to see you upright. I mean tonight." He kisses both of us on our cheeks, then ushers us to the table. The best one in the house it seems, the table sits in front of a giant stone fireplace.

The restaurant is exactly like you would imagine. It's a mixture of heavy wood, stone, and beveled glass. Joan and I have been here a couple of times before. The food is outstanding.

I try to maneuver myself so that I'm facing Frank. Apparently, Joan has the same idea. We look like a couple of awkward teenagers at a middle school dance, or two roosters posturing. She is making it completely impossible for me to sit facing Frank. Will is standing behind us probably feeling just as awkward, as he waits for us to sit. I give up and sit with my back to Frank.

"Hey, 'Hi, I'm Will!' How was the rest of your day, not as interesting as the first part?" I say loudly, like old friends.

I'm hoping if I talk loud enough it will bring Joan's attention back to the table. I lean forward, grab Joan's hand and bump it on the table, in effort to bring her focus back.

"Nothing will be as interesting as that all year," he jokes.

Joan shifts in her seat.

I try in vain to make small talk, but it isn't working. "So, what do you do, Will? What's your passion? Joan is an artist; she paints these amazing paintings of our childhood." I try to fill the space with noise so the inevitable doesn't happen, even though I know it's coming.

Will leans forward, "I love art. One of my favorite pieces is the one hanging over there by the front door."

Joan looks up, "It's one of mine."

Will's eyebrows raise. "I'm impressed. It's beautiful. So, I take it that the two little girls are you and Mar?"

Joan grows silent. A small tear rolls down her cheek.

I become instantly furious. I want to march over to Frank's table and rip him out of his seat. Funny how anger makes you stronger than you actually are. The whole dynamic of the table shifts. Why did we stay here? Why didn't I insist that we go farther so something like this wouldn't happen? I didn't honestly think we would run into Frank. I mean, what are the odds?

Will's eyes drift to Joan's. "What's wrong? Is everything okay?" he asks urgently.

I can see that Will feels the hurt in Joan's eyes. There's

something about him. It feels like he's always been here.

I lean in to whisper and Will leans in, copying me. "You see, Joan's cheating soon-to-be ex-husband is sitting over there with the bimbo he's been cheating with." I point with my thumb. "He is directly behind me. White shirt, blue tie."

Will straightens up and looks over my shoulder and frowns. I can tell he is relieved Joan is no longer attached, but mad she is hurt.

"Joan let's go. Let's just get out of here," Will says in a pleading voice.

"Let's key his car while we are at it," I say, trying hard not to cry. Crying seems to just happen when I am super pissed.

Joan wipes her face, stands, and excuses herself to the bathroom. As she turns around, the girl gives an intentionally loud, high-pitched laugh. The laugh is obviously fake, just like her boobs.

Joan and Frank lock eyes. Frank looks like he's just seen a ghost. He stands and grabs Joan by the arm as she tries to pass.

"Joan," he says, exasperated.

Joan shoots him a sideways glance without turning her head. If looks could kill, Frank would be six feet under.

The girl then stands up right behind Joan and blurts, "If you were a better listener, or lover, Frankie Baby would have never been unhappy. I'm a much better fit for him."

Frankie Baby? Wow, what kind of bimbo says Frankie baby? I guess the same kind that knowingly has an affair with a married man. She's standing there, wearing a tight, hot pink top that's two sizes too small and a small, black skirt. I think I remember this outfit from the movie *Pretty Woman*, but Julia Roberts got paid twenty million to wear it. This bimbo's wearing it for free. Julia Roberts also ended up marrying a rich guy. Too bad for *Pretty Woman* here, most of Frank's wealth is Joan's.

The bimbo presses herself against Joan. This is the wrecking ball that breaks the camel's back. Before I realize it, I'm standing at their table. I close my fingers into a fist and punch the bimbo right in the face. I'm having an out of body experience. I've never been in an actual fight, ever. But my instincts to protect my sister are primal. Tears stream down my face. I hate that about myself. Some think this is a sign of weakness, but I'm not crying because I'm hurt, I'm crying because I'm furious.

Frank rushes to the bimbo's side and covers her bloodied nose with his napkin.

"Cindy, are you okay? Someone call the police! This is assault! Where's the manager?" Frank asks, squealing like a pig.

I can almost imagine his face morphing into a pig's face.

Frank walks around behind me and pulls me hard by my shoulder, "What the hell are you thinking?"

I guess not much because I pivot and 'David Beckham' him right between the goalposts, just like I should have done years ago. He turns red and all the veins in his neck bulge out. Holy hell, I can't believe I just did that. Surprisingly, my crying has stopped. Maybe it's true what people say—having an outlet to reduce your stress really does work.

Will calmly walks up behind us. What a mess he must think we are. He gently puts his hand on Joan's right shoulder and pulls her behind him. He gives Frank a very stern look; he means business.

"Hi," he raises his hand and motions a waiter over. "Your meal is on me," he says evenly.

Will is trying his best to stay calm, "Sorry for the inconvenience your affair has brought you."

Wow! I think he just told Frank all of this was his fault. I'm beginning to really like this guy.

"Everyone here is a witness! These two, backwoods, Texas girls assaulted us at our table!" Frank continues to whine like a sweaty pig.

I never noticed how whiny Frank could be.

"I'm a lawyer, I'll sue!"

All I hear is squeal, squeal, squeal.

"That's not the way I saw it. You clearly assaulted this lady," Will gestures towards Joan.

"I saw her walking towards the bathroom, you stood up and grabbed her by the arm, preventing her from passing while this lady bumped her." Will turns to look at me, "It looks like her sister here was just defending her."

"This is ridiculous! Where is the manager? Who's running this place?" Frank yells and looks around the restaurant.

"I'm the owner," Will says sternly. "Now leave before you make more of an ass of yourself."

I let out a deep breath, one that I didn't know I had been holding. "Thank you 'Hi, I'm Will' for saving us for the second time today," I whisper.

He gives me a warm look and slugs me on the arm, "You know, it wasn't a challenge when I said nothing would be as interesting all year."

A devilish smile spreads across my face.

Joan gives a quiet laugh and whispers, "Challenge accepted."

Take Me to a Castle! I'm a Princess

"Want to get out of here?" Will asks in an upbeat voice, trying to lighten the mood. "I'm going to a birthday party tonight; will you guys join me?"

To be honest, swimming with sharks with a rib-eye attached to my body would be better than staying here. "Let's give it a go!" I say.

I would do anything to get Joan's mind off of Frank. That would include hopping in Will's truck to go to a stranger's birthday party. I text Marie my intentions.

We hop in Will's truck, deciding to leave my car in the parking lot. Will slides in next to me and cranks the engine. Joan is looking out the window and, for a few seconds, it is completely silent.

Will leans forward on the steering wheel and turns to us, "I forgot something inside, I'll be right back." He hops out and puts his index finger in the air as though to tell us that he'd be back in one minute.

I break the silence, "I can't believe that asshole was in there, acting like everything is normal."

Joan and I laugh a quiet laugh and look at each other. Joan's is more of a cry than a laugh, but I ignore it.

"It hurts so bad that if I don't laugh, I will cry," Joan says putting her face in her hands. "It's just the betrayal of the whole thing. You really think you know someone, and it turns out, you don't know them at all. He was sleeping with her while still sleeping with me! He may have given me a STD!"

I throw my arm around her shoulders. I don't know what to

say…we sit in silence for a second. "Joan, you can't control what is happening, you can only control how you respond to it. You are stronger than you think. You may be a little broken now, but you won't always be."

I'd do anything to make things better for her, even if it meant making an ass of myself, or if it meant dropping everything in my life to drive across country with her. I pretend to grab a mic off a mic stand.

"Testing, testing one, two, three." I clear my throat. I begin humming the first part of an old Coldplay song. I have to admit, it's choppy. I can only remember half the words. I'm overexaggerating my hand movements to passionately act out the lyrics. When I get to the part of the song that mentions "reverse," I grab the gearshift to the truck and cleverly pretend to shift it into reverse. To my surprise, I accidently shift into neutral. The truck starts to roll backwards. Joan looks at me and her eyes are as big as saucers. We both let out a yelp! I jump halfway into the driver's seat and slam my foot down on the brake.

Joan snaps, "Jeez! Stupid! Are you trying to kill us?"

I scuff, "I hardly think we were in danger of dying, that's a bit dramatic."

Joan clamps her hands over her mouth, she's laughing so hard she snorts. Mission accomplished. She's not thinking about Frank. I throw myself back and laugh. It was just what we needed. Laughter is indeed the best medicine. But, not at the price of crashing Will's truck.

Will walks out of the restaurant holding two bottles of Chateau Margaux. His face drops and he shakes his head. A look of bewilderment spreads across his face. I can tell, he's trying to figure out why his truck is twenty feet from where he left it. He looks at us in the truck, then back to the spot where he parked it, then back to us. Joan and I sink down into the seat of the truck so we can't see Will and he can't see us. A shiver runs through me. The same shiver you get when someone is about to find you while playing Hide and

Seek. The passenger door opens; Joan and I both look up.

"Jump out of the truck!" Will says.

Joan and I both slide out, not sure if he's mad. I instantly begin apologizing, "I was acting out a song..."

Will hears the regret in my voice and cuts me off, "I'm not mad, I was just confused...I'm starting to get used to that around you two."

A black shiny limo pulls up. Thank goodness. I was getting nervous about being in Will's truck.

"I thought this would be a better idea tonight." Will opens the door, "Your chariot awaits, ladies."

We both look at each other and happily jump in. This totally reminds me of that 'How to kidnap me' meme; the one that has a white van with the words, 'Free Tacos' on the side. I guess this is the way we get kidnapped; just bring a fancy limo and Chateau Margaux. I shake the thought from my head.

"Whose birthday party is it anyways?" Joan asks.

Sitting in silence, I stare out the window at the view. I figure, I better keep a lid on it for a bit.

"A friend of mine owns a winery not too far from here. It's his birthday." Will looks directly into Joan's eyes and gives her a wide smile.

Joan melts a little in his gaze and replies, "Sounds good."

There are vines as far as the eye can see on both sides of a long driveway. As we get closer, the top of a castle emerges.

"It's a castle! Joan! It's a castle!" I shout to Joan in my excitement. This is amazing! A bolt of excitement runs through me. The limo pulls up to a front pathway. I grab Joan by the hand and yank her out of the limo.

Chickens are running around freely. I reach down grabbing a chicken and tuck it under my arm. A small cat is hiding in the first row of vines. I spin around, trying to take it all in. I let out a squeal, "There's a goat! A goat!"

Goats are my favorite animals of all time. Joan and I had a goat when we were kids. It used to jump on the trampoline with us. I set the chicken down. I immediately try to call the goat over to us.

"Here goat, here sweetheart…" Joan calls while making a clicking noise with her tongue. The goat comes trotting over. In my excitement, I jump up and startle it. To my surprise it falls over with a hard thud to the ground, like it fainted.

I look at Joan and shrug my shoulders, "Jeez! I've killed the goat." I bend down and try to stand it up. I stand it back up on its four tiny hoofs but its legs are rigid, it falls over again and rolls onto its back with its tiny feet sticking straight in the air. I squat, staring at it. I don't know what to do. I rub its shoulder until it slowly starts to move.

Great, first Will's truck and now I've killed his friend's goat. An older man walks up to us. I stand, stepping in front of the goat.

The goat steps around me, as the man lifts his hand and waves it off. "Don't worry about him, he does that. He's a bit dramatic. He's what is called a fainting goat."

Will gestures to the older man, "I would like you to meet Howard."

Howard is in his early seventies and very distinguished looking. His hair is a brilliant silver and it matches his goatee. His eyes are almost the same bright green as Will's. Reaching out to shake my hand, I can feel how callused his hands are. He must work in the fields.

"Hello there, welcome to the castle, ladies," Howard manages to say modestly. He has a warm glow about him; a calm about him.

"These are the ladies I was telling you about earlier; the ones that crashed their trike," Will says, letting out a small puff of air while trying not to laugh.

I interject, "I'll have you know we didn't actually crash. It was more like we 'gently rolled' down the embankment. I was able to keep the trike upright. No crashing involved."

Leaning in next to me, Joan says, "Both back wheels fell off."

True, the wheels did fall off. In what order the wheels fell off is still under investigation. As we walk towards the castle, I soak it all in. The front doors are massive wooden doors, rounded at the top. They seem very heavy and are lined with old, iron studs. The floors are cold, gray cobblestone. The ceilings are high. It must be at least thirty feet from floor to ceiling. The entry room has a massive chandelier hanging over a circular marble table; I picture myself swinging from it.

The attention to detail is incredible, it feels like we are in a European castle. The room opens up to a long dining hall. It has a gargantuan custom, wooden table with fifteen chairs on each side and one on each end. It can seat thirty-two people! That's quite the dinner party. A catering staff is busily setting the continent of a table.

A look of awe crosses my face and Howard notices, "I like having people over."

"Did you build this?" I ask in admiration.

Howard smiles at me, little lines form around his eyes. "Yes, I did. But that's a long story and I don't want to bore you."

"Oh! I promise not to be bored," I say, winking at him. It works.

"Well, how can I turn down a request from such a beautiful lady? It began in the eighties when I drove my 1976 Datsun up from San Diego. I was searching for my soul and a place to dig my toes into the dirt when I found Calistoga. It was love at first sight. Immediately, I fell in love with the land's wine-making abilities and the energy of the place. I had a little bit of money and put it all into a failing vineyard," he nods his head, thinking of the memories.

"We started small…I use to work in the fields all day alongside the workers. People with the same dream as me. Our wine got better year by year, grape by grape. Once we made enough money, I knew we would need a better distillery and tasting room. I always loved the castles of Europe, so brick by brick we built what you see now. I started with nothing but a dream. I didn't care what I had to do to make that dream a reality." He puts his hand on Will's shoulder.

"In the beginning, I couldn't even afford a mattress. I had a cot I would roll out at night and hide during the day. I was too embarrassed to let anyone know I was sleeping here. Only some of the workers knew because they would sleep here, too. Most were immigrant workers. Every single worker that worked here then still works here now, in some form or fashion. We are a tight-knit family. At times, I was down to my last penny. But, some way or another, I found the money to keep going."

Howard bends, looking Joan and me straight in the eye, "It is not where you begin, but where you end." He emphasizes each word. With that, something hits home for Joan. I could tell she is taking his words to heart. "Would you enchanting ladies like a tour?" Howard walks us towards the back of the castle.

"That would be amazing!" we say in unison as we follow.

"I imported the stone from France," he says as he runs his hand over it. I believe he remembers each and every one of them. We step into the back courtyard; it looks like something out of a movie set. Lights hang from olive trees, groomed grass grows in between the old flagstone, a few wooden tables are scattered around the patio. Howard wrings his hands and looks around, inspecting the courtyard for tonight's party.

"Thank you for allowing us to crash your party tonight," Joan says.

"Any friends of Will's are friends of mine. Plus, who can resist spending their birthday with two lovely women?"

He turns, with a spring in his step. We follow, with a little spring in our step now, too.

"When is everyone arriving?" Will asks.

"People should start arriving any minute now," Howard says looking around, then glances at his wrist. He wears a simple black Timex. The watch, just like Howard, is timeless. As we make our way back inside, we notice a few people have arrived.

"I must check on dinner," Howard excuses himself, walking towards the kitchen.

Will drags us around introducing us to various people. Most are other vineyard owners, the original staff, and old friends. Everyone is so nice here.

A man catches Will's eye. He turns to us, "Come, you have to meet one of Howard's oldest friends."

We walk up to a man in a dark gray newsboy cap. He looks vaguely familiar. Will claps the man on the shoulder, "Joan and Mar, I'd like you to meet one of Howard's oldest and dearest friends. This is James."

The man leans forward, "Hello. It's nice to meet you. Are you friends of Howard's?"

Will interjects, "They are friends of mine. I met them today in Cannes," he turns and gives us a wink.

I am studying the man like I'm the top agent on a murder case. Then it hits me like a ton of bricks. James Freaking Jack, the famous folk singer—I love his songs! Why in the world is he here? That's a stupid question. How are James and Howard friends? It's just weird to me because I've never actually known anyone to be friends with anyone famous; especially someone like James Jack.

"Where's your dad, Will?" James asks.

I'm confused, who is he talking about?

"He is checking on dinner," Will replies, pointing towards the dining room.

"Aw, I'm going to say a quick hello. It was a pleasure to meet you," James says as he makes his way to the kitchen.

I feel like we stepped into another universe, one where music legends just walk around drinking wine…Wait a minute, maybe Joan poisoned my wine again and I'm hallucinating. I turn on my heels to Will and rattle, "Is Howard your dad? We crashed your dad's birthday party? It was bad enough crashing a friend's party, but your dad? Did I just meet *the* James Jack?"

"Howard is actually my uncle, but he raised me since I was six," Will says with a hint of sadness in his voice.

I wish I had never asked the question; Joan elbows me in the ribs. Man, can I do anything right tonight? We continue making our way around the room meeting everyone. Howard walks out to the center of the main room. Everyone turns to look at him.

"Hello everyone, welcome to tonight's dinner. It is being served in the dining room." Howard glides his arm behind him, pointing towards the dining room. People start making their way in, searching for their place cards. Surprisingly, we find our names. One of the staffers must have quickly made them. That's impressive. I think about stealing James' place card for a memento.

Joan looks at me; she knows what I'm thinking. "Act like you've been somewhere before," she says, placing her napkin on her lap and scooting in her chair. As the staff serves, the smell of steak and mashed potatoes floats through the air. I'm hungrier than I thought. I guess kicking someone in the nuts really works up an appetite.

I always thought that someone had to throw you a birthday party, but from now on I'm going to take one out of Howard's playbook and throw one for myself. Wine is passed around like water.

Joan leans over and says, "Jesus must have been invited, too."

I choke on my wine and almost blow it out my nose. People start looking at me. "I'm okay," I say, patting my chest. "Wrong pipe."

The conversation is good on both sides. I really think Joan is having a good time. I give her a slight nod in confirmation. She nods in agreement.

Will pulls up a chair next to Joan and asks, "Are you enjoying yourself?"

"The food is fantastic! Don't tell me you have Gordon Ramsey back there," Joan says, leaning slightly towards Will.

After dinner, we all walk out to the garden. James picks up a guitar and starts playing. I work hard not to stand there slack-jawed. This is such a surreal moment. Could this possibly be happening? I must be dreaming. No one here seems star struck. It's obvious that these people have done this for years. This is the craziest thing that's ever happened to me. Scratch that, I was just poisoned by my sister by accident. So, this is the second craziest thing that's happened to me.

I look around, trying my best to keep my cool and not go all fangirl. I wonder if anyone else is seeing what I'm seeing…Gosh, if this is a dream and I'm still in the hospital, I'm going to be pissed.

James begins to sing a song I immediately recognize. I put my arms around Joan and rock back and forth. Joan buries her head in my shoulder and snobs (snotty sobbing). I wrap my sweater around her, so no one notices her crying.

Howard grabs a guitar and joins in. Where are all these guitars coming from? Are there just random guitars in the bushes here? Could this possibly get any more amazing?

Just as the song ends, Joan lifts her head off my shoulder and pulls herself together. She dabs her face with the inside of her shirt. I lean in towards Joan and whisper, "Are you okay? Wanna get out of here?"

Will stands, positioning himself between James and Howard. Jeez, if he starts to sing… "I'd like to wish my dad a Happy Birthday. I am the luckiest kid in the whole world to have had someone so amazing to learn from. Not just for teaching me about the wine business, but for teaching me how to be a man. Not just any man, but a good man. I strive every day to make him proud. Most of you guys don't know, but Howard isn't my biological father. He took me in when I was six. He was single. His winery was finally beginning to take off; he was busy. All of a sudden, he had this kid shoved in his life. But there he was, taking care of me. I will forever be grateful. So, raise your glass to the best man I know. Happy birthday, dad! This is for you."

Will points his arm towards the castle doors. Everyone shifts in their seats to turn and look. The doors open. You can almost hear a pin drop. I hold my breath in anticipation. I hear a voice behind us. The lights are too bright, I can't see who is talking. I raise my hand to shield my eyes. NO FREAKING WAY! This has to be an impersonator with a voice track. My eyes grow wide. Joan and I start to clap our hands together in excitement. There's no keeping my cool now.

I'd know this guy anywhere, even though he is wearing a casual, black turtleneck and blue jeans. It's Neil Diamond! My dad used to have his vinyl record when I was a kid. Joan and I would play it over and over and over. We'd prop the cover up against the back sliding glass door and watch the rain. That's when we listened to most of our records; on days we couldn't go outside. The album cover had a wagon on it; like an old time traveler's wagon. We'd stare at it for hours, making up stories about where they were going, or where they'd been. We're the product of having an older dad, growing up. He has gifted us with a wide range of musical knowledge. We learned everything from Hank Williams to Frank Sinatra.

As Neil Diamond walks down the path to the patio, his aura is such that it feels like little tiny puffs of glitter and a spotlight are following him. We are completely awestruck. His voice is crisp. It's not often you find a singer that sounds just like the recording. Joan and I jump out of our seats and pump our fist in the air, as we join along singing about love. I mean, how could we not? I grab Joan's hands as we jump around in a circle and wave our arms in the air. I grab the lady sitting next to me, Joan grabs the man. It's like a ripple effect, as one by one everyone starts to stand and jump around. We fall back into our seats and laugh. What an amazing night! I'll never forget it.

I catch Will's eyes, and mouth, "Thank you."

He shrugs his shoulders and makes his way back to us. Joan jumps up in her excitement and throws her arms around his neck. Will lifts her off her feet and spins her around in a circle. I jump in and put my arms around both of them. This is just what we needed.

"Thank you, Will! Thank you!" I yell.

The electricity can be felt all around us. This is the craziest birthday party I've ever been to. It makes the restaurant incident seem like a million years ago. This has been the worst and best day ever.

"Happy birthday, Howard," Neil says before putting down his microphone. I shake my head in wondered disbelief. What's going to happen next? Is Lady Gaga going to drop down from the sky like in the Super Bowl?

"Hey, how about a tour of the rest of the vineyard?" Will looks at Joan for an answer. All of a sudden, she's lost her ability to talk; I elbow Joan. I guess she was functioning off pure adrenaline and now she's finally realized what just happened.

"Of course, that would be magnificent," I say, answering for Joan.

I hiss at Joan, "What the heck is wrong with you?"

She shrugs her shoulders, "I just got overwhelmed with all the excitement!"

"You weren't 'overwhelmed' a couple of minutes ago, pull yourself together. Act like you've been somewhere before." I shake her by the arms.

She then gives me a quick wink.

Will pulls up in a golf cart. Thank goodness, I was beginning to wonder if we were going to have to act cool while walking through soft dirt in heels.

"Hop in, ladies," Will says.

I hop on the seat in the back facing backwards as Joan grabs the seat next to Will. He begins giving a brief history as we begin our tour. Howard bought this land with the vineyard already here. The original vines were planted in 1890. The land needed a lot of work. Howard immediately began working on bringing the vines back to life. The vineyard itself is just over fifty acres. Keeping it small allows Howard to really focus on small batch wine, which makes the wine exclusive. Howard bought the adjoining land and built the castle to replicate one he saw in Europe as a boy.

There's a small farm in the back and a vegetable garden where Bowen's gets most of our vegetables. There are also four houses for the original crew that helped Howard in the beginning. But that is a separate adjoining piece of land Howard deeded them individually. Howard loves animals. So, all the animals here are pets. He has five goats, two llamas, numerous chickens, and one cat that somehow became ten. They are free to roam the land during the day and sleep in the barn at night. Visitors really gravitate toward seeing animals during tours. The llamas were even used in a wedding here last year."

"Mar and I had a goat growing up," Joan says reaching out to pet one of the llamas on its neck. What a friendly llama. I'm trying to be cautious. I'm sure this is just a front and this thing is going to spit on us. I guess that's a camel I'm thinking of, not a llama, but still. Feeling like a bit of a third wheel, I call to a goat that has been trotting behind the cart. It's the same goat from earlier. I guess it lived after all. I call it and it jumps onto the seat next to me.

Joan turns to me, "Put the goat back, Stupid." I pull the goat tighter and shake my head no like a four-year old, holding her favorite toy. Joan points at me with her index finger and presses her lips together. "Put the goat down!"

In a playful voice, I say, "Nope."

Knowing she could never convince me, Joan turns back to Will, "Thank you for this night Will. You really turned an awful night into something amazing. You invited us when you didn't have to. I appreciate it more than you will ever know."

Joan is gazing at Will. I consider jumping off with my goat and walking back. However, I know Joan wouldn't be happy with me. I sit there pretending like I don't notice Will's heart about to jump out of his chest.

I start a conversation with my newfound friend, "Come here

often, who's your dentist?" The goat's bottom teeth jet out as he bleats at me. "Oh! That's nice, what are your hopes and dreams?"

Joan casually leans back to look at me, "Are you kidding me right now? Stop it!"

We drive up to the front of the castle. The party is in full swing now. I can hear the laughter and it makes my heart happy. Howard worked his whole life for his dream, and the laughter is like a soundtrack to his success. He made it, it wasn't easy, but he made it.

"We should call it a night," I say reluctantly, looking down at my feet then back up at Will. "We had the best time Will. Thank you for including us, it was truly special."

I notice Howard walking towards us, "I was wondering where you guys ran off to."

"Happy birthday, Howard," I lean in and give him a hug.

He turns and kisses my cheek, "Come back anytime, ladies. You're always welcome here."

He then gives Joan a kiss on the cheek.

"Happy Birthday," I say, giving Howard a wave. We hop in the limo and make the drive back to Bowen's. Cooper sits alone in the parking lot. Frank is leaning against the side of my car. Whatever happiness the night brought is gone in an instant. It's like we got drug back into reality kicking and screaming.

"Do you want to keep going?" Will asks.

"No, I have to see him some time," Joan says quietly.

"That sometime doesn't have to be now," I say. The limo's tires make a crackling sound as we roll over the gravel to a stop. Will gets out of the car and instinctively places himself between Joan and Frank.

Frank looks around Will.

"What? Is this douchebag your boyfriend now? Have you been cheating on me?" Frank says in an accusatory voice.

Joan pivots on her heels, and I finally see the Joan we all know and love, "Frank, you are the one cheating on me. You have no right to be here harassing me and questioning me. Why are you even here? Why does it matter what I do? You are the biggest mistake of my life! Thank God I never have to see you again. Ever!"

"I know what you did. I know why Mar was in the hospital," Frank says in a rushed voice knowing he's losing ground with Joan.

"You have no idea what you are talking about Frank. Go home, go to Cindy's, I don't care where you go. Just go away. It doesn't matter anymore. You don't matter anymore," Joan says with more anger in her voice.

Her anger comes out hot. I've never seen her this mad, it makes me jerk my head back in surprise. Will walks around the car and opens Joan's door. Joan slides inside and buckles her belt. Will shuts the door, securing Joan inside. Joan reaches over and locks the door. Frank, standing at Joan's window starts yelling again, but she doesn't flinch and keeps her eyes straight ahead.

Will walks to my side and opens the door, "Get in Mar, I'll take care of this." He hands me a small piece of paper, "Please give this to Joan. Please consider staying another night. This can't be the way this ends."

I nod my head and start the engine, "Thanks again for tonight, Will."

I glance in my rearview mirror and see Will walk over to Frank. This can't be good. But at least Frank can't follow us. Maybe that's Will's plan.

Hi, I'm Will

"Hey," I shake Joan's leg. "Wake up, let's go get breakfast."

Joan raises her wrist to her face and tries to focus on her watch, "It's almost eleven!"

"Okay, then brunch," I shrug, sticking my tongue out at her.

"What are you feeling like?" I notice her bare butt cheeks have two, big, brown scabs on them.

"Your butt is healing nicely," I say as I roll to my side and sit up.

She squeezes her eyes tight and groans, "Oh, I almost forgot about that. Thanks for reminding me. I really don't care where we eat, pick a place."

I lie back in bed, pulling the covers up to my chin. I guess this time is as good as any to tell Joan about Will's number. I look over at Joan, "Will gave us his number. He wants us to stay another night." I pause, trying to gauge Joan's reaction.

"Well, what do *you* think? We really don't have a timeline at the moment." Her words come out faster than normal and I can tell she is trying to keep her voice even.

"Then I guess it's decided," I toss Will's number to her. "Call him…invite him to brunch."

"I'll call him after my shower," she says with a wide grin.

I eye her carefully as she nonchalantly picks up her phone and carries it in the bathroom with her. As she shuts the door, I tiptoe over and press my ear to the bathroom door.

I hear Joan, "Will? This is Joan from last night."

Does she honestly think he forgot? I'm hanging on her every word.

Joan sucks in a deep breath, "Umm…we just woke up and are headed for some brunch. Would you like to join us?"

I press my ear harder to the door, hoping to hear his answer, but I can only hear Joan's side of the conversation. "Oh, okay. Yes! See you at 6:30 tonight. We are staying at The Inkwell, the little white cottages past the railroad tracks. Room 26. See you then, bye."

I bound back to my bed in one huge leap as Joan walks out of the bathroom. "Well? What did he say?"

"He has to work today, but wants to pick us up tonight for dinner," Joan says, unable to hide her excitement this time.

"You like him! I can tell!" I say, pinching her side.

Joan slaps my hand. "Okay, I like him. He's nice, but it's just not the right time. I still need to deal with everything that is going on with Frank. I can't possibly even think about any type of relationship."

"Yeah, I get it. I knew since the bike shop that Will liked you. Then it became more apparent at the castle. Maybe you don't want anything now, but don't count him out—people come into your life for a reason. You have to find out if he's a reason, season, or a lifetime."

Joan screws up her face, "Who are you, Yoda?"

"Powerful you have become, the dark side I sense in you," I say in a Yoda voice.

Joan reaches up and grabs my ponytail, "Shut up, Stupid."

Will He or Won't He?

I hear Will's truck pull in front of our cottage. I peek out the window and watch him walk up. He's ten minutes early, but we are ready.

I swing open the door, "Hello, Will!"

"Hi, Mar. Fancy meeting you here," he jokes.

Joan pops her head over my shoulder, "Hello, 'Hi, I'm Will!'"

Will's face lights up like the Rockefeller Christmas tree. Joan walks in front of me as I grab my bag from the chair.

"Mind if we take my truck?" Will asks, shooting a look at my car. "We need a truck for where we're going, and I'm not sure I can fit in your car," Will says pointing at Cooper.

I look at Joan. I still have reservations about just hopping in Will's truck. I mean the limo was different. We had a limo driver. I stop and think for a minute; I guess they could have been in on a kidnapping together. I put a pin in that thought and will have to think about it more later. I pull out my phone, "Do you mind if I take a selfie really quick?"

I turn and pretend to snap a picture of myself. But I take a picture of Will, standing in front of me instead. I send it to Marie along with a text.

> *Out to dinner. Will, same guy as before. Drives a new Chevy truck. Silver. Uncle owns a castle winery. Howard. Owns Bowen's steakhouse. Sending my location.*

Feeling a little more confident, we both hop in the truck. Joan looks back at me and we silently decide that if something goes down, then we have no choice but to take him out. She gives me a confirming nod.

"So, where are we headed?" Joan asks.

"You'll see," Will says with a cheeky grin.

I know the area fairly well; Joan and I drove out this way last year while shopping in Calistoga. We were also looking for Calistoga's "Old Faithfull," which happens to be a very flaccid but small geyser behind a worn-out wooden fence. Needless to say, it is nothing like the real Old Faithful.

As we pass the last main road in Calistoga, the sun starts to go down. I know there isn't much past the main road and my anxiety starts to kick in. How well do we know 'Hi, I'm Will?' What did he say to Frank last night? What if he is driving us to Frank? My mind immediately begins to go through a list of serial killer traits. Ted Bundy was charming. Maybe this was his ploy the whole time. Charm us so we wouldn't see it coming. I make a mental note—no more CSI for me.

I click my home screen off and dig around in my purse to feel for my pepper spray. I feel the small canister in my hand and flip off the safety. I let out a sigh of relief. Joan looks over at me and shakes her head. She knows me too well. She knows I'm making a mental list of scenarios on how to escape and what I would do in a serial killer situation. There's nothing out here except hills, rocks, and dirt. I begin counting trees, 'one, two, tree, tree, rock, tree'…I look for the nearest sign of civilization. We turn down a well-used dirt road. The last bit of sun is disappearing behind the hills, it's casting the most beautiful glow over the landscape.

There are tiny grapevines as far as the eye can see. A large, willow tree sits in the middle of the tiny plants. We drive to the end of the road. Will positions his truck facing the tree and puts it in park.

"This is my vineyard. We planted the vines three weeks ago. I plan on opening in the next couple of years," Will says proudly. He points to the right, "Over there, will be the winery."

He turns the engine off and slides out. Joan follows him. He pauses, and looks precisely at me, and waits for me to hop out of the truck. Jeez, talk about trust issues. It's not like I actually wrecked his truck. As soon as I'm out of the truck, he presses the parking brake and shuts the door with finality. Will grabs a blanket and wooden crate out of the truck bed. He leads us over to the base of the willow tree; he spreads the blanket out. I relax, my anxiety about being in Will's truck disappears.

It looks like he actually brought some really great food and wine. I'm impressed. He pulls out two bottles of Du Vin Château, Howard's label.

"Wait here, just a second." He runs back to his truck and grabs a round board. He sets it down on the blanket. The round board has four tiny legs that bend out, making a short picnic table. It's a pretty clever design. He spreads a white tablecloth over the top and begins setting out the food.

"First, ladies, is…Chateaubriand," Will says pulling out three hot plates from the crate.

I pull the silver top off my plate. There is the most delectable cut of meat on a spotless white plate, a mound of mashed potatoes, and boiled tomatoes on the side with baked cheese on top. How he got it here without the tomatoes wilting is beyond me. Next, he pulls out three sets of silverware. Actual silverware for a picnic! This guy…

He continues, "To accompany the Chateaubriand is a freshly baked loaf of French bread." He raises his hands, "Dig in." The conversation flows while we eat and we know he's our kind of people.

"This is amazing, Will." I stuff the last bite of meat into my mouth, savoring every bit of it. "Did you make this or is it take out from Bowen's?"

"I went to The Culinary Institute of America after high school…I like to tell people I was in the CIA," he laughs. "When I opened Bowen's, I did all the cooking. Now, I have a new chef that uses most of my recipes."

This guy can cook! He's single, what's wrong with him? There has to be something wrong with him.

"You can cook, and you're hot!" Joan blurts out before she can catch herself.

"Ummm, Yes? Thank you?" He laughs and wraps his hand around the back of his neck.

Poor guy. I feel uncomfortable for him. I try to break the awkwardness, "Hey, I gotta walk this meal off a bit before dessert." I pull out my phone, "Do you mind? I have a playlist for this type of night?"

"What 'this' are you talking about?" Joan asks.

"Just a beautiful night," I giggle. I dust my bottom off with my hand, hurrying to the truck to set up my Bluetooth. Will eyes me suspiciously. I don't think he will ever get over the whole truck rolling backwards thing.

As I breeze back past Joan and Will, Sinatra comes on.

Joan's eyes widen, she knows this playlist.

I casually look over my shoulder as I leave them sitting on the blanket. She runs her thumb across her throat. It's the international sign for I'm going to kill you. I wink and blow her a kiss. As I walk, I gently run my fingers over the vines, touching each tiny plant, talking to them, the universe, and myself.

I whisper, "Please, heal Joan's heart." I look up at the moon, "Man in the Moon, if you are listening, we could use your magic tonight."

I study the giant craters. It almost looks like the moon has a giant smiling face. When Joan and I would fight in the backseat of the car, mom would tell us if we didn't behave, the man in the moon would come and take us; that we would be trapped there…forever. In fact, the craters were actually two people that he took because they were fighting. I was terrified as a kid that I was going to be kidnapped by the moon. I was on my best behavior. That was, until Joan would reach over and kick me…and then I would have to stab her foot with a pen.

Behind me the song switches. The music floats through the air.

I turn back to the headlights in the distance. Will is extending his hand down to Joan sitting on the blanket. She hesitates but gives him her hand. He pulls her up to his chest. He slowly raises her hand and places it on his shoulder. He puts one of his hands around her waist. I squat down trying to hide behind the twelve-inch seedlings. I hope they don't look my way and wonder if I'm relieving myself. I standup quickly but then think better of it and squat down again. It looks like I'm playing a one-person game of Whack-a-mole.

Joan's heartbreak is visible even from this distance. Dust is floating in the air, lit by the headlights causing a fuzzy, glowing aura around them.

Will leans towards Joan and, in the softest voice, he sings with the song. He spins Joan around in a circle.

I stand without thinking. My heart gives a hard thump and makes me take a step back. Whoa, who is this guy? Where was he when Joan was in college? Before she met the loser. Joan bends her head down and takes a step back, breaking the mood.

The next song comes on, it's "Werewolf in London". Joan lets out the loudest laugh (When Joan laughs, you can hear it from space. I can always pick out her laugh). I run from the field, hurdling row after row of tiny grapevines like an Olympic hurdler and land at her side. I hand Joan her make-believe mic and pretend to grab mine. I tap it to see if it's working. We turn pressing our backs together and throw our heads back howling at the moon. Will laughs in amusement and a hint of awe. I act out the part of the wolf, howling on cue, while Joan sings the song. The playlist is actually called *Cry and Laugh It Out*. It's the product of wine, dirty scrabble, and a not-so-great date.

After the song ends, we spend another few minutes staring up at the stars in complete silence. I reach down and put my hand in Joan's and squeeze it three times. Poor Will got pulled into our vortex of craziness, but for some strange reason it feels like he belongs here. Some people just feel like that.

"So, why did you stop in Napa for a wine tour?" Will asks, bringing us back to reality and thoughts of Frank.

"We wanted to get away for a while. We wanted to travel, see the States, soul search," I say, trying to avoid the real reason we decided to take a trip.

Out of nowhere Joan snaps, "It wasn't the best plan. As you know, my husband cheated on me. What you didn't know is that I stupidly tried to poison him to embarrass him in some way, but Mar drank the tainted wine instead. Like I said, it wasn't the best plan."

Joan must have really needed to get that off her chest.

I clear my throat. "We thought doing a trip across the U.S. would be just the soul searching we needed," I say, hopefully making Will see our point of view. And maybe forget that Joan tried to poison Frank.

To my surprise, Will shakes his head, "Any man that would ever cheat on you has to be completely out of his mind. And by the looks of the woman at the restaurant, your ex is delusional."

That's a nice way of putting it. He's right, Frank is a massively delusional moron. An uncomfortable silence settles over us. I can't tell if it's coming from him or us. Crap, have we shared too much? What if he calls the cops?

"Do you think I'm crazy?" Joan asks, looking Will straight in the eye.

"The only crazy person is your ex. Honestly, I don't know what I might have done if I found out my spouse was cheating on me. I'm not one to judge. I'm also not one to cheat." Will pauses and stares at Joan for a second.

"You aren't until you are," I say feeling cynical about the whole subject. I don't like Joan getting hurt. She wasted her twenties on this guy.

"Thanks for everything you've done for us, Will. It's been a crazy couple of weeks, and I really needed this," Joan says sincerely.

Will steps forward and hugs Joan. It's the type of hug that heals a heart. He whispers in her ear, "Joan, I've only known you for a few hours and know how amazing you are. Don't you ever forget that."

Joan flushes, fixing her eyes to the ground. He raises her chin up with his hand, "Keep your head up, it won't rain all the time."

"We should get back to the hotel. We have to get going first thing in the morning," Joan says, looking uncertain.

There's something in her tone that makes me think she doesn't want tonight to end, but we both know it has to.

Will hesitates, "I'll drive you ladies back to the hotel. I really enjoyed meeting you two. I will never forget these last two days."

"Believe me, we won't either. I mean who meets James Jack, Neil Diamond and a fainting goat in the same night?" I shrug my shoulders.

Awkwardness hangs in the air as we ride back to the hotel. It feels like something needs to be said here, but not from me. I need to take myself out of the equation. As we pull up to the cottage, I hop out of the truck first, hoping that it gives Joan and Will the opportunity to talk. I extend my hand to Will. He grabs it pulling me in for a brotherly hug.

"Thanks for interrupting our time at the beach." I slug him on the arm.

He laughs, "Take care, it's been anything but boring. I've never met sisters with such a close bond; your sense of humor is contagious."

I bow and nod my head, "Yep, we're weird and I love her." I hold Will's hand a little longer, and pull him back to me, "Don't hurt her or I will kill you."

"I wouldn't put it past you," he says, giving me an anxious smile.

"I'm kidding...or am I?" I give him *The Focker's* 'I'm watching you' hand signal as I walk backwards into the room, giving them privacy.

Will looks at Joan, "When you are back this way, or any way, call me. We could have dinner, but no pressure."

She shrugs, then raises her head and nods, "Yes, I might like that. I might like that very much."

"I know this isn't a good time for this, but I'd like to stay in touch with you in case there is ever a good time," Will says, grabbing Joan's hand and raising it to his lips.

He gives her a sweet kiss on the top of her hand and holds it there as his eyes look straight up at Joan. Joan tiptoes and kisses Will on the cheek, accidentally brushing the corner of his mouth. I close the curtain a little more, so I don't get caught spying.

Will turns fully to Joan and presses his mouth to hers. Joan goes ridged.

"I'm sorry," Will says pulling away. "I'm sorry I just did that. Gosh, I'm sorry."

"It has truly been an amazing time. It's just not the right time," Joan says quietly giving Will a big hug. She waves over her shoulder, "Goodnight, Will."

Joan enters the room looking frazzled.

"You look like you're in shock. What happened?" I ask, knowing darn well what happened.

"Will kissed me," Joan says, putting her fingers to her lips as though she can still feel his.

"And...that's a bad thing?" I ask, eagerly waiting for the answer.

"Yes...no...I don't know," Joan answers quietly.

She pulls her jeans to her ankles and kicks them into the air. I watch her, waiting for some flicker of something, of anything. I watch her as she brushes her teeth and stares into the distance in a daze. She slides under the covers next to me. We always slept in the same bed as kids. We'd even sleep in the same bed as teenagers. Even when we had our own rooms. I'd sometimes slide into her bed and ask questions or comfort her when a boy had broken her heart.

Joan breaks my train of thought. "Do you believe in fate?"

I turn to her, and grin "Absolutely. Why? Do you think meeting Will is fate?"

Joan shrugs her shoulder and presses her face into her pillow.

"Does he make you tingle in all the right places?" I giggle, wrapping my arm around hers. Joan lets out a small sigh. This isn't the time to make jokes. Instead, I hold her arm until she falls asleep.

The Road

I reach out and pat the bed next to me. Joan isn't in bed. I always sleep the best next to Joan. I raise my hand to block the light from my eyes and look around the room. She's sitting at the small table with a huge bouquet of flowers in front of her.

I draw in a deep breath and throw my arms over my head in a stretch, "I assume the flowers are from 'Hi, I'm Will.'"

Joan sniffs one of the flowers, "Yes! He really knows how to charm a lady."

"Well? What does the card say?"

"Joan, it was a pleasure. Enjoy your adventure…Hi I'm Will."

I laugh out loud, "Are you going to call him?"

I know this is all too soon for Joan, but Will is a pretty awesome guy. There is no reason not to keep in contact with him, at least a bit.

"I think I will," Joan says, leaning over to smell the flowers again.

"Let's get going. We can eat on the road," I say, sifting through our clothes. "I think we are going to need more than my duffel bag and your makeshift luggage. We should buy some suitcases before we leave town. You know I need my stuff organized," I say as I line up my clothes in a neat, little stack.

Joan pops up like a rabbit on too much coffee, "I've been ready for an hour! Why are you fretting about luggage? Let's just throw everything in the trunk, we can get luggage later." Joan pulls her hair into a messy bun.

We jump into Cooper and Joan settles in pulling a miniature atlas from her purse. Oh, for Heaven's sake, we can totally use our phones. Google has a thing called Google Maps that is amazing. But nope, there's Joan with a map chiseled into a stone tablet.

I scroll to my newly made *The Road Trip* playlist. I'm in the process of making it, I should say. With the trip being last minute, I only have a couple of songs on it. Joan leans her seat back and puts her feet on the dash. Willie begins to sing, 'On the Road Again.' A classic road trip song. "Where to, Smalls?" I ask.

"Definitely east, maybe towards Lake Tahoe? Maybe head towards Zephyr Cove?" Joan says like she's asking a question.

"Is that a question?" I give Joan a quizzical look.

"We are headed to Zephyr Cove," Joan says with authority. "I have something to take care of there."

"That's more like it! What sort of something do you have to take care of in Zephyr Cove?" I ask. "And which way is east?"

"While we are there, we could have one of those famous skillet cookies I told you about," Joan says.

"Well, why didn't you say so in the first place?" I say with a wink.

After a few miles we both get quiet and zone out. There's nothing like the open road, good company, and great music to facilitate a little soul searching.

"What ya thinking about?" I ask, reaching over and squeezing Joan's knee.

Joan is resting her chin on her fist, staring out the window. "I'm thinking about everything…Frank, all those wasted years. Will, and what an amazing guy he is…or at least seems to be. He could turn out just like Frank. Frank didn't start off as a cheater, or maybe he always was. I don't know. I just can't bring myself to even think that."

"Frank is a cheater. It doesn't mean that all men are cheaters, despite what I said earlier. Don't let one asshole ruin you forever," I say with a frown. "Think of it this way, you know now, and you don't have to waste one more day giving love to someone who, obviously, doesn't deserve it."

Frustrated, Joan adds, "Easy for you to say, it doesn't seem like you've ever given your heart to anyone."

"That may be true, but I know I want to. And, even if I find one bad apple, I know there are more good apples to choose from. Fiji, Golden, Granny Smith…" I trail off.

"That's not how that goes, Stupid. You have two sayings mixed together. The saying is, 'there are more fish in the sea' and, 'one bad apple spoils the whole bunch.'"

"Exactly, I'm glad you agree," I pinch her side.

I have a knack for getting Joan to laugh. I mean, that's the whole point of this trip, isn't it?

"Look at us, two sisters on an epic adventure! I know exactly what you need!" I pop open the glove box and move some papers around. I shoot Joan a confused look, then slam it shut and dig under my seat. "Ah-ha! I found it!"

I hand Joan her pretend microphone, then I grab my phone and shuffle through some music. Joan pretends to tap the top of the microphone to check if it's on.

"You're so stupid!" Joan says, shaking her head at me.

"You know you love me," I give her a cheeky grin. I sing the first line of Pink's song about her husband. I feel her angst. I feel like she knows what she's talking about.

Joan looks over at me, and gives in.

We both start screaming at the top of our lungs, lyric after lyric. I look over at Joan; her smile is the biggest I've seen in days.

"I needed that," Joan says leaning back in her seat out of breath. "Oh, crap! Turn, turn! It's right there!" she yells, pointing in excitement.

We pull into a gravel lot beside a large, log cabin restaurant. It sits at the edge of the crystal-clear shore of Lake Tahoe and has smaller cabins tucked behind it. The hostess ushers us in and puts us at a table facing the lake. The waitress walks up, scowling. She flips open her notebook. I'm not sure if she's going to give me a ticket or take my order.

"Do you need more time, or do you know what you want?" She begins to scribble something on her pad.

I ignore her lack of customer service. "I hear you have a world-famous skillet cookie. We will take two."

"I don't know about 'World Famous' but we have several skillet cookies on the menu; chocolate chip, peanut butter, and s'mores." She looks up from her pad for an answer.

"Yes, please," I say.

The waitress looks over at Joan for a clarification.

"She means, we will take one of each," Joan says, giving the waitress a smile and shutting her menu.

The waitress looks Joan up and down, "You know that each cookie is about eight inches around? They are meant for sharing."

Joan nods her head, "Yes, thank you."

The waitress smiles, raising her eyebrows, "I would expect you two to be a whole lot bigger than you are if that were the case honey...but, the customer gets what the customer wants." She slaps her notebook shut.

Joan was right; skillet cookies are the best! The cookies come out hot with a scoop of ice cream on top. It turns out the waitress knew what she was talking about, our eyes were bigger than our stomachs. We only manage to eat what amounts to one whole skillet cookie together.

"Let's drive down the road a bit and see what we can see." I place my napkin in the middle of a skillet cookie, forcing myself to stop eating it.

Joan pulls out her phone, "Hey, can we stop at the hardware store? I need to buy a chainsaw."

I furrow my brows at her. "What do we need a chainsaw for?"

"Do you trust me?" Joan asks, sliding the phone into her pocket as we walk to the car.

"Of course, I do." I hop in Cooper. "Just tell me where to go."

Joan puts her Google map directions on and sets her phone on the dash. I'm so proud that she finally made it into the 21st century.

"What are you doing?" I glance over as Joan is writing a note.

She puts the pen to her chin. "I'm writing a list of the things we need from the hardware store."

As we walk into the store, Joan rips the list in half and hands me part.

I scan the list in silence.

1.   A gas can, gas
2.   Matches
3.   Trash bags

I check out and wait for Joan at the front of the store. I look like I'm about to do something very illegal. Just as I'm finishing my thought, Joan walks up holding a bright orange chainsaw. I smile at her and lead the way to the car without a word.

I pop open the trunk. Joan wedges the chainsaw among our other things, like it belongs there. I round Cooper and Joan slides into the passenger seat. I don't say a word. I wait until we get back on the highway before I ask, "What the hell is the chainsaw and gas for?"

"Remember when Frank and I moved to California?" Joan says, prompting my memory.

I nod my head yes, but I'm still confused. "Okay…"

"Well, I was thinking…We carved our names in a post by the beach…" Joan continues.

"And you want to cut it down and burn it?" I ask in a rush.

"Mar, that's a great idea!" Joan says, grabbing at my arm.

"What? I didn't come up with this idea! I just put two and two together!" I turn to Joan and narrow my eyes at her. She sits in the passenger seat looking smug.

"OKAY criminal, where is this so-called post?" I say, giving into the idea.

Joan casually points straight ahead. "Just go back towards the main highway. When you get to it, take a left."

I get back on the highway and drive about six miles. Joan points at a line of posts lining the road, "Hey, make a U-turn and park along the side of the road behind that blue car."

I make a quick U-turn and pull behind a few parked cars. There isn't much of an edge, so trying to get out of the car is like playing a serious game of Frogger. Nevertheless, I managed to get out and slink around to the back of the car. It is obvious this is the place to be, even though it just looks like a bunch of trees. I hope we aren't crashing someone's party. I don't want to make a habit of that.

Joan meets me at the back of Cooper. "Okay, it's one of these posts. We are going to have to find it."

I peer around. There's a fire station directly across the road from us. How are we going to do this without getting caught? I grab two extra layers of clothing from the trunk. Jeez, it's freezing here. "Let's leave the supplies here until we find the post and come up with a game plan," I say as I shut Cooper's trunk.

"I'll go this way if you go that way," Joan points.

I start walking by each post, looking for the engraving. I make it about 100 feet before I find it. "Found it!" I yell to Joan.

Joan hops the wooden fence with ease and meets me at the post. "Yep, that's it!"

"Now what?" I stand there, staring at the post.

"We need to cut it down. We could make a bonfire on the beach." Joan kicks the post.

"How do you expect to do that without getting caught destroying public property?" I run my fingers through my hair. "Let's think about it for a bit."

I stand back, sizing the fence up. I don't know if it would be easier to try climbing over it or squeezing in between the wooden posts. I decide climbing over it would be the lesser of two evils. We make our way through the woods, following the path. It breaks out onto a beach covered in black sand with little specks of gold in it.

"Wow, this is fantastic!" I exclaim, raising my arm, shielding my eyes from the sun.

Lake Tahoe is crystal clear with large pine trees almost all the way to the beach shore. I drag my toes in the wet black sand at the water's edge. It's colder than I would have thought. Big boulders dot the shoreline. The wind is picking up. I throw my extra shirt over my back. From the corner of my eye I see something scurry to the trees, deep into the forest.

"Did you see that? What was that?" I turn, looking behind me.

"What was what?" Joan says looking in my direction.

"I think I just saw a mouse or something," I say gesturing for her to sit down in the sand next to me.

I never would have in a million years thought this place was here. Growing up, back in Texas, there weren't trees all the way up to the beach. We didn't have to walk through a forest to get there. We would drive right on the beach and park. The end.

Joan and I sit in complete silence as we watch the sun glisten off the water. The way the ripples in the water catch the sun's reflection looks like thousands of gold coins dancing on the lake's surface. I catch something out of the corner of my eye again. I gently elbow Joan and point with my chin. There is the smallest chipmunk sitting on his rear end next to me in the sand. What in the world is a chipmunk doing on the beach?

As we sit there in silence, more and more tiny chipmunks start coming out from the woods and scurry all over the beach. I can't blame them; if I had a choice, I would probably pick this place too. I dig my toes into the cold, wet sand next to Joan's. I've never seen such beautiful sand. I scoop some up with my feet and pile it on Joan's feet. I put my arm around her shoulder as we watch the sun go down. We sit, enjoying the silent moments. Talking without talking.

"I think it will be dark enough to cut the post down soon," Joan says, leaning into me.

"You're right. I just don't know how we are going to hide the noise." I stand up and stretch.

Joan stands. "Let's park Cooper in front of the post. You rev his engine as I cut it down."

I shake my head. Sounds like a good enough plan to me.

"Let's get out of here before a bear eats us or something," Joan says, looking around in the darkness. We make our way back through the forest to Cooper. I pull around and park him in front of the post.

Joan pulls the chainsaw out of the back of the car and primes it. I hop in Cooper and wait for Joan's signal.

"Okay, do it!" Joan says as she taps the back of Cooper.

I start the engine and rev it three times.

Joan is quick with a chainsaw. It was down in a matter of seconds. She sliced it up and set everything in the back of Cooper.

"Let's get out of here," she says, sitting next to me in Cooper smelling like gasoline and charred wood.

"Okay, let's go get stuff for s'mores and have a bonfire on the beach," I say, looking at Joan. I want to make this better for her.

We find a spot on the beach. I grab the gasoline and matches from Cooper's trunk. Joan puts what remains of the post in a trash bag. We walk half a mile up the beach before we find the perfect spot. I dig a hole and Joan places the wood inside. I pour the tiniest bit of gas on the post and throw a match to light it. I put my extra shirt over Joan's shoulders. The fire is slowly dancing and weaving in the wind. There's nothing to say. The wood is going up in flames like Joan's marriage, and all we can do is sit here and be mesmerized by it.

Rebounds Aren't Just for Basketball

The next morning comes with a loud banging sound.

"What the heck is that?" I ask, holding my hands over my ears and looking for Joan.

"The hotel is under construction, remember?" Joan shouts. "And I recall someone saying, 'Oh, that's okay,' last night," Joan says, imitating my voice.

"It's not like we had a lot of choices so late at night," I say, plugging my ears harder. "What kind of construction workers work at 6 a.m.?"

"It's 8 a.m. Stupid," Joan says, looking at the clock.

I blink, refocusing my eyes. "Okay, what kind of construction workers work at 8 a.m.? I guess there's no sleeping now," I shout, hopping out of bed.

When I get out of the shower, Joan has a map spread out on the bed. She has little black dots traveling across it. Nevada, Colorado, Texas, Louisiana, Georgia, and New York

"What ya got there, another stone tablet?" I ask, bouncing on the foot of the bed to see if I can bounce hard enough to snap back to my feet.

"Well, I thought that we should pick out some places we want to go. I marked Nevada because I want to know if 'The Loneliest Road' is, indeed, the loneliest road. Colorado because there is a huge swing *you* can ride on the side of a cliff, and, of course, if we are that close, we should swing by and see mom and dad," Joan says, following the line with her finger.

I give myself one more, hard bounce and make it to my feet.

"I'm okay with that as long as I have some sort of input, too. And I noticed how you exaggerated 'you' in that whole swing on the side of a cliff thing. If I go, you go!" I say, jumping my jeans on.

Back in the car, Joan pulls out her map. She has it rolled like a treasure map, instead of folded like a normal person

"Why is your map rolled like that? Why don't you fold it like it should be?" I ask, trying to snatch it out of her hand

"Because it's easier to open like this," she nods, agreeing with herself.

"You look like Dora the Explorer like that. If a monkey jumps out of your purse, I'm gonna freak out."

"Whatever," Joan says, pointing. "Get on highway 50. You know, it's considered the Loneliest Road; I think because it's in the middle of nowhere. There's no cell service."

The Loneliest Road is the Nevada section of US 50 and is literally in the middle of nowhere.

"What was that?" Joan asks.

"What was what?" I say, looking around.

"What was that we just passed? It looked like a dog." Joan turns around in her seat.

I make a U-turn and drive slowly back. "What in the world would a dog be doing all the way out here?" I ask.

As Joan and I hop out of the car, the dog runs farther off the road.

"For heaven's sake, it is a dog!" Joan says squatting to the ground.

"Here sweetheart, here love..." I say, making a kissing sound with my lips.

Hesitantly, the dog begins crawling toward us with its head down.

"Awe, sweetheart...How did you get all the way out here?" Joan scratches him behind his ear.

There hasn't been anything around for at least a hundred miles.

"We just can't leave him here." I frown at Joan.

"Why are you frowning at me? I'm not arguing," Joan says, looking just as sad as I am.

We walk back to the car and the dog follows us. I guess he isn't arguing, either. I pull my seat forward and he hops into the backseat of Cooper. He quickly makes himself right at home, snuggling into one of Joan's shirts.

"Hey, I think we should name him right away. You know, to give him some sense of identity. What do you think?" I say, giving him a once over.

"Well, he looks like a pug, what about Junior? Or Oscar? He has the cutest most irresistible face," Joan says, reaching back and giving him a rub on his head.

"Or how about Hurley from *Lost* since he was lost...or Sawyer?" I jump in my seat, excited "How about Lone-Lee? Since we found him on the Loneliest Road, and he is some sort of Pug mix...we could call him Mr. Lee for short."

We shake hands and nod in agreement. Mr. Lee it is. Lone-Lee is our fellow traveler, our spirit animal. Just like that, what once were two travelers, are now three. I wonder how long it's been since Lone-Lee has eaten. I mean a Pug isn't exactly an agile dog. They probably aren't great hunters either; his body is evidence of that. He's quite skinny.

"I think we need to get Mr. Lee something to eat," I glance back at him. He's snorting around in the backseat licking the remaining crumbs left from the ill-fated cupcakes.

Joan looks over the map, "It looks like Delta, Utah is only a couple of hours away. Lone-Lee needs food and should be checked over by a vet."

Joan begins calling a vet she has found on her phone, the cell service isn't the best, though. Every time she gets through to someone she gets cut off.

"Ugh! Dang it!" she shouts into the phone.

I mock her and yell in an overexaggerated way, "Darn you Loneliest road!" I shake my fist in the air to let her know how silly she sounds. "You know the way you use the phone to look up a vet? You can do the same for the map." I give her a slight smile. "Don't get so mad. We'll be there in a little over an hour. Let's just call when we get into town," I say, trying to calm Joan's increasing irate temper.

Lone-Lee has made his way onto Joan's lap. She begins to mindlessly pet him. Huh, who knew? Maybe we needed this little fellow.

"The Loneliest Road is not lonely, after all," Joan says, reevaluating her situation.

"You're right, we found vast amounts of land, an open road, beautiful mountains, music, and best of all: we found Lone-Lee," I say, reaching over and giving him a scrub on the head. I turn my head to him and talk in a baby voice, "Isn't that right Mr. Lee?"

Funny how babies and animals have you talking like a crazy person. We pull into Delta and decide to eat fast food in the car, which is about the only option. We get Mr. Lee his own burger, which he quickly scarfs down. After our meal, we drive through the one-block town to the vet.

"We found this little guy on Interstate 50 about two hours from here," Joan tries to explain our situation and why Lone-Lee looks so rough.

The vet's eyebrows furrow. "Unfortunately, Interstate 50 is a dumping ground for dogs. He might have had litter-mates at some point," the vet says as he checks Lone-Lee's teeth. "He's not very old. I would say about three months. I'll take him to the back and test him for heartworms and give him all his shots. Do you want to put him on preventatives?"

"Yes, do everything, give him everything," Joan says.

I chime in, "And is it possible to get him groomed while he's here?"

"We'd like to get him a leash, dog food, and some supplies. Is there a place nearby we could do that?" Joan asks, taking on a motherly roll all of a sudden.

It's just like when we played house with our animals as kids.

"Yes, there's a country store two doors down from here, ask for Ms. Sue."

I kiss Mr. Lee on the head and head to the store with Joan.

Mr. Lee needs a bowl, food, bed, blanket, collar and a leash. Plus, we should probably pick up a couple of gallons of water, just in case. He might need some sort of shirt since it's still a bit cool. I pick two; one says, 'The Ruff Life' and the other 'I Kissed a Human and I Liked It.' We also buy him a sweatshirt just in case it gets colder.

"Joan, do you think Mr. Lee needs a pair of boots?" I hold up what looks like a tiny pair of rain boots.

"You never know, grab them just in case," Joan says, piling supplies into our basket.

An older lady walks up behind us, "Can I help you ladies?"

I swivel on my heels, "We found a pup on the side of the road and took him to the vet to get checked out. We just need some things to make him more comfortable."

"I'm Ms. Sue," the older lady says extending a hand. "That's awfully nice of you girls, not many people would pick up a dog on the side of the road."

I shoot Joan a confused look. Who wouldn't pick up an animal on the side of the road if they knew it needed help? That's a ridiculous notion to me.

"What brings you girls out this way? I've never seen you around," Ms. Sue asks, inspecting our cart.

I try to keep it light, "Oh, you know, just two sisters looking for the meaning of life."

"I'm divorcing my husband because he is a cheater," Joan says not lifting her head.

Sue raises her eyebrows, "Oh, I see."

Joan pretends to read the back of a bag of dog food in an effort to excuse herself from the conversation. I don't blame her, there are only so many times you can relive that memory without it killing you.

"We haven't had much luck with men, we thought a road trip would help clear our heads," I say.

"Your husband cheated on you, too?" Sue asks, shocked.

"No, just hers," I point at Joan. "But what happens to her might as well happen to me."

"I think I got everything we need; we should go pick up Lone-Lee," Joan says.

In other words, 'let's get out of here.'

"Your total is $148.17," Sue says with a look of accomplishment on her face.

That will be her biggest sale all week. Joan and I make the quick walk back to the vet's office. Lone-Lee is sitting next to the receptionist. As, soon as he sees us, he pops up and runs over to our feet.

Joan picks him up in one swoop. "Who is the luckiest fella in the world?"

I reach over and scrub him on the back of the ears, "You are!" I tug on his Ruff Life t-shirt over his little, frail body.

Who in their right mind would dump this little fella on the side of the road? Their loss is our gain. We rescued him, and he rescued us. I make him his very own place in the backseat with his new bed. He has the whole backseat to himself. Mr. Lee hops right in the car and into his bed. He makes himself comfortable, like he's never been anywhere else. He knows he has found a home.

Joan pulls out the map again. "Okay, the next stop is Grand Junction, which is almost five hours away. I think we should stop sooner; it will get dark way before that."

"Okay, let's just head that way and pull over if we get tired." I pull into a gas station to top off the tank, just in case.

Joan runs around the back of the car into the station. I watch her as I rest against Cooper, waiting. She's on the phone grinning from ear to ear. It can't possibly be Frank, or anything about Frank. She puts her phone back in her pocket when she makes it back to the car.

"Don't pretend you weren't just on the phone. Who was that?" I ask.

"Umm..." Joan blushes, "it was Will. He wanted to know how I was, and where we were," Joan tries to say flatly but fails.

I have no idea why she even bothers trying to hide her feelings from me. I know her too well. Plus, even if I didn't know her, if she was a complete stranger, her cheeks would call her bluff.

"Oh, Will... It's only been about two days. Someone has a crush!" I look at Joan like I'm examining her through a magnifying glass. "Do you like that he called?"

"Yes and no...it is completely the wrong time. I can't even possibly think of having something with someone else. I still thought I had a happy marriage, you know?"

"You know what they say, the best way to get over someone is to get under someone," I try to lighten her mood.

I don't want Joan to start thinking about Frank again. Not that she has stopped thinking about him. I just wish there was a magic spell I could put on her so she wouldn't have to go through the pain. Or that clicker from *Men in Black* that erases people's memories of aliens. Frank is an alien.

"I just don't want him to be a rebound," Joan says quietly. "I don't want to drag him down with the ship."

"But you do want him?" I exaggerate my point. "Plus, I think he's a big boy. He can make his own decisions."

"Of course, I want him, he's hot; I'm not dead. It took everything in me not to kiss him back at the hotel." Joan adjusts her shirt. "I just don't want it to be because I'm trying to get over someone."

"Just because you sleep with him doesn't mean he'll be a

rebound. It just means you really, really like him." I pause. "I hope you at least kept that door open because he is hot! It's been more than obvious that he's liked you from day one, and, not to mention, you like him. You can just see where it goes; no harm no foul," I shrug my shoulders.

"I guess you're right," Joan says, reluctantly agreeing with me. "He said he was going to call again later. I told him we would most likely be in Colorado by then. I also told him about Lone-Lee. He said he wasn't at all surprised and asked if you had found a goat."

"Ha! Well, good! What's next on the playlist?" I say, determined to get some miles behind us. I wiggle down to get comfortable in my seat.

"How about a little John Mayer?" Joan asks, knowing my answer.

"Sounds good to me, you know I'm always up for a little John Mayer."

This song always makes me feel like wandering aimlessly. Kind of like we are today…me, staring off into the distance; Joan with her feet on the dash and wind in her hair; and a snoring dog in the backseat. I put my hand out the window and move it up and down through the wind. I pretend it's a bird gliding through the air. Nothing feels as right as right now. I put my chin up in the air and feel the wind and sun on my face.

It's just past seven when we cross the state line of Colorado, 'The Colorful Colorado.' I hear Joan's phone go off.

"Is someone texting you? Is it dad?" I ask.

"It's Will, he wants to make sure we made it to the hotel." Joan turns the brightness up on her phone. "I told him we were headed to the Marriott in Grand Junction." Joan looks up the address and punches it into her phone.

I'm not really sure I like him tracking us; I instinctively look up in the sky for a drone. On the other hand, I do want Joan to stop thinking about Frank. It's six one way and almost half a dozen the other. We pull up to the front of the hotel. I put Cooper in park and walk into the lobby.

"Hi," I lean against the counter. "We'd like a room. We also have a small dog." I gesture towards our car as Joan and I both flip through pamphlets of local attractions.

Mr. Lee is standing against the back window pressing his face against the glass and slowly giving it a good lick. He's all ankles and feet. He has no height to him. His eyes are larger than normal, and is cute as cute can be. His nose is smashed in which makes him snort if he gets too excited.

"Would either of you be Joan?" the hotel clerk asks.

Joan looks up, laying her pamphlet down, "Me. Why?"

The clerk lifts a huge bouquet of flowers from behind the desk and a box of chocolate-covered strawberries.

Joan's eyes widen, "What in the world?" She cocks her head sideways.

"Read the card! They're from Will, right?" I ask impatiently.

"How did he manage to get this here so fast? I literally told him thirty minutes ago," Joan says with a hint of excitement in her voice that she's failing to suppress.

I shrug my shoulders, "If you want something, you find a way."

We drag ourselves up to our room with Mr. Lee in tow. I brush my teeth and land face down on the bed. I'm exhausted.

"Don't wake me up until next year," I say, my voice muffled by the pillow.

It feels like I just blinked when I hear Lone-Lee whimpering. I look around to see Joan put on her shoes and attach the leash to his collar. I slept the whole night without moving.

"I'm going to take him out, so he doesn't make a mess up here. I'll be right back," Joan says, halfway out the door.

I lay in bed for a minute. "Must get up...and shower." I try to find the strength. There's no need to get up. Honestly, I could lay here and watch the morning news. I wrap myself in my sheet and roll around, getting a good stretch. I search for the remote and flip on the T.V.

I hear the card in the door.

"Morning Love!"

"Back so quick? Why are you so chipper?" I look at Joan with a suspicious eye.

"What? I can't be happy in the morning?" Joan says, bouncing around the room.

"You can be happy in the morning, it's just that you are extra happy today," I roll myself out of bed. "Spill it."

"Will called last night and we stayed on the phone until I fell asleep," Joan says, falling onto her bed like she's falling onto a cloud.

"What? I didn't even hear you on the phone!" I say, looking confused. I must have been dead to the world. "Well, what did you talk about? What did he say?"

"He wants to take me to dinner when I get back to Yountville," Joan smiles.

"And...?" I prod Joan for more information.

"And...I said yes!"

"That's super exciting!" I say with more enthusiasm in my voice than needed, but I want Joan to know this is a good thing. I know he asked before, but this sounds like she will actually do it; before it sounded like a 'no'.

We order room service. I'm staring into space. It's my go-to when I haven't fully woken up in the morning. I'm mindlessly eating bacon when I feel two eyes staring at me. "Oh, Mr. Lee, do you want some bacon?"

He hops on the bed next to me and looks up at me with his large, googly eyes and tilts his head.

I nonchalantly pass over some bacon. I'm such a sucker. Then, I tear off a piece of toast and give it to him.

"Don't give him that! He's going to have a massive stomachache," Joan says, scowling at me.

"All dogs eat bacon. It's their God given right!" I say with a smirk on my face. "It's abuse if you don't give him some and he's forced to watch you enjoy it."

"Okay, you're handling it if he has problems later," Joan says, tasking me.

I laugh at her and stick out my tongue, and whisper into Lone-Lee's ear, "She's a mean old lady, don't listen to her."

"Well, where to next 'O' Keeper of the Bacon?" I ask sarcastically.

Joan pops up on her elbow, "I was thinking we could drive to Manitou Springs and hike around The Garden of the Gods."

"Sounds good to me. Maybe we should pick up some hiking shoes and a backpack?" Mr. Lee is faithfully sitting on my bed waiting for more food.

"We better go, Google says we are about four hours away. That would put us there about lunchtime," I say, carefully folding my clothes into my duffel bag.

Joan smirks, "Come on *Rain Man*, we don't have all day for you to fold your things." I start to reach into my pocket for my bird, but she cuts me off, "I know what you're doing, keep that finger in your pocket!"

We check out of the hotel and make our way to Cooper. Joan pops open the trunk.

I place the bags in carefully. I need to take this in. I stare at Joan. I don't know what I would ever do without her. Lone-Lee hops into the car, makes three circles before laying down in his spot in the backseat.

June, June Like the Month

"Is I-70 left, right, straight or what?" I ask, looking into my rearview mirror, fixing my lip-gloss. You would think I couldn't miss my lips since they are practically my whole face.

Joan shakes her head, "Don't you think it's about time that you get your directions straight?"

"Jeez, just tell me! Is it up, down or sideways from here?" I bark back, exhausted with this age-old argument.

"What? Yes, it's up from here, that doesn't even make sense," Joan says, giving me a confused look.

"Yes, it does. It's like 'did y'all go up to Houston?' No one ever says, 'Did you go north to Houston'!" I say trying to prove my point.

"Still doesn't make sense, Stupid...Plus, that's only a Texas thing. Most everyone else needs an actual direction."

I shake my head at her, "Maybe...but it makes more sense my way."

"No, it doesn't!" Joan is getting more frustrated now that I still can't see her point. "You need directions for everything! Map reading, road signs...Let's just agree to disagree!" Joan says giving up.

Her voice raises two octaves higher as she says, "Hey, I have an idea."

I look over as Joan is scrolling through her phone. "Quick, take a left here."

"Where are we going?" I ask, craning my head around to safely cross the road.

"Here! Pull in here!" Joan shouts and gestures with her hand.

I read the sign out loud, "Shady Willow Senior Living." I pull Cooper into the parking lot and turn off his engine.

"We can't exactly take all these flowers with us," Joan grabs them out of the backseat.

"Oh, great idea!" I call. "This is why I love you!" I hop out of the car, looking around. I spot a donut shop across the street. "I'll be back!" I yell as I high-knee it across the road.

I walk in and the young man behind the counter greets me with a, "Hello, welcome to Little Miracle Donuts."

I look at his nametag, 'Robbie.'

"Uh, hi Robbie! How many donuts do you have on hand?" I ask, perusing the display case.

"About twelve dozen," he answers.

"I'll take them all! Is there anyone that can help me carry these across the street?" I ask, looking for someone else behind the counter. "I'll also need two jugs of milk."

"Of course, I can help you. Are they going to the senior living community?" the sweet young man asks.

"Absolutely and thank you!" I say.

I run across the street holding up six-dozen donuts, with Robbie lockstep behind me carrying the rest.

"And *this* is why I love you!" Joan says smiling back at me. "How many donuts did you get?"

"I got twelve dozen, and two jugs of milk. Might as well stay for breakfast while we're here," I shrug my shoulders and walk towards the building.

Joan turns back to the car and dumps my clothes out of my duffel bag. She shoves Mr. Lee into it, "We can't leave him in the car for that long."

I nod my head in understanding and hold the building's door open with my foot.

Joan strolls up to the counter, "We were just passing through and hoped we could drop off these flowers, have breakfast, and visit for a while."

"Oh, sure," the nurse says, taking the flowers from Joan. "Here I'll show you where the dining hall is."

Joan looks back at me, giving me a wink as Mr. Lee pops his head out of the bag.

"That's a service dog in your bag, right?" She knows darn well it isn't. "Next time bring his badge."

I pipe up with a hardy, "Sure thing!"

We walk into the dining hall. The silence is deafening.

I clear my voice, "Hi, everyone! My name is Marguerite, and this is my sister, Joan. We'd like to have breakfast with all of you, if that's okay."

An old lady in the corner catches my attention. I walk over and she grabs both of my hands. I squat down beside her as she asks in an English accent, "Do you sing, Sweetheart?"

"Yes?" I answer.

It comes out sounding more like a question because, in all honesty, I don't sing—at least not to anyone but my shower and the occasional messing around with Joan; never, actually for people.

"Could you sing us some songs?" she asks, holding onto my hands tightly.

I'm pretty sure she's not going to let go unless I say 'yes.'

Joan shakes her head, "Yes, yes! We can do that! What's your name, Love?"

The little lady raises her head up towards us, "My name is June, June like the month."

I could kill Joan right now.

She said 'we,' but what I think she really means is me. "Okay, June, June like the month, I can sing, but I can't promise I'm any good." A nervous smile stretches across my face. I look to the nurse for the okay. She shakes her head as if to say, 'Go for it.'

Joan turns and walks off with the nurse by her side. Oh, great!

She's ditching me! She's the one who said we would sing in the first place! Sheer panic begins to set in. I'm just standing in the middle of the room. I guess I'll have to pull out my pretend microphone and just go for it. Just as I'm about to stumble my way through a haphazard production of "It's a Hard Knock Life" from *Annie*, I spot Joan rolling in a piano. Where in the world did she get that? I shouldn't be at all surprised. I feel a bit braver now that I have a piano to hide behind.

"Any special requests?" I ask, leaning in towards June.

"How about, 'Will You Still Love Me Tomorrow?' by The Shirelles. Do you know that song?" June asks with the biggest smile on her face.

"I *do* know that song," I say nodding my head in approval.

I pull up the piano stool and look at Joan. June couldn't have picked a better song; I remember singing this song over and over in my bedroom. I remember each and every word because my dad had it on vinyl. Sometimes his records were all we had access to as kids.

I start off, my voice coming out a bit shaky and quiet.

All my nerves subside when I see an old man stand and slowly shuffle across the floor. As he reaches June's chair, he holds his hand for her. June's eyes light up as she stands and wraps her arms around his neck.

I force myself to sing louder.

Slowly, one by one, people start to couple off. Joan begins dancing with a cute old man in the middle of the makeshift dance floor.

The song comes to an end, and from the corner of the dance floor I hear, "Keep it going, Honey!" from June, June like the month.

She's a real firecracker.

Joan mouths, "Do it."

"Okay, this one goes out to all the lovebirds out there, 'My Funny Valentine.'" I feel a bit like a DJ from the 1960s. A wave of electricity goes through my body. The hair on my arms stands up. I'm embarrassed, but something pushes me on. I barely got out the first song. I can't let June down, not to mention Joan.

I clear my voice.

My stomach churns as I glance up at Joan. She's standing completely still in the middle of the floor and staring wide-eyed back at me. I quickly look down so that I don't bust out laughing. For the rest of the song I stare down at my feet. I hit the last note and Joan rushes to my side, sliding onto the bench with me. Thank goodness!

She keeps the momentum going as she begins to sing, "Son of a Preacher Man".

I join the beat at the chorus. I look around at everyone's faces. Could they possibly be enjoying our off-tune concert? I give a cheeky grin to Joan and she gives one back. My heart feels ten times bigger as I stand there singing at the top of my lungs. Joan is happy.

"When did you learn to sing like that?" Joan looks at me, stunned.

"Like what? 'My Funny Valentine' is like one key," I say.

"Like you know what. Why haven't you sung like that before in front of me?" Joan asks, searching my eyes for an answer.

"I guess because we are always just joking around. Plus, I've never had to be a guest singer at a senior sock hop," I wink as I brush off her compliment.

Someone taps me on my shoulder.

I spin around to see June standing in front of me, "I've been waiting for Arthur to dance with me for two years."

"Aw, is Arthur your boyfriend?" I ask, smiling.

"Heavens no, dear; he's my husband. We've been married for sixty-two years. We got married right out of high school. The song I requested is our song."

I swallow hard, trying to keep the lump deep down in my throat. I can feel the tears starting to well up in my eyes.

June continues as she holds my hand, "He doesn't remember much these days. I spend my days watching him from afar. He hasn't remembered me in two years. Thank you for bringing him back to me, even if it was only for a moment."

"I can only wish to have a love like that someday," I squeeze her hand gently.

"You will, dear. Just take your time. The right one will come along when you least expect it." She squeezes my hand back to make a point, then changes the subject, "Do you girls live here in Grand Junction?"

At this point, I would if it made things better for her and Arthur.

Joan interrupts, knowing I'm trying hard not to cry, "We live in California. We are just passing through, traveling."

"Where are you traveling to?" June inquires, giving us a concerned look.

"Oh, a little here and there until we reach New York. Then we'll drive back to California again. Today we are headed to Manitou Springs to hike up the incline with our dog."

Joan begins casually looking around like she just realized something.

"Well then, you should go visit my grandson. He owns a bed and breakfast in Elizabeth. Elizabeth, like the Queen of England...No, that's not right." June closes her eyes and thinks for a second, "The town is called Estes Park."

June has this way of describing things; it's like her own version of the phonetic alphabet. Just in case you didn't understand what she said when she said Elizabeth, or her name June, June like the month.

"June, I noticed your accent, is that Scottish?" Joan asks, trying to buy me time to pull myself together.

"No, it's English," she says matter of fact, then continues, "Like I was saying, Love, you should stop in and meet my grandson. Stay at his place for a couple of days. It's a fantastic bed and breakfast you know? It's the least I can offer for what you've done for me today."

I shrug, "Maybe."

"There will be no maybe about it! I'll call him and tell him you girls are coming." June writes his number on a piece of paper she's found on the table next to us.

"Thank you," I say, shoving the piece of paper in my pocket with no intention of calling.

From the corner of my eye I see Joan frantically looking around. "What?" I yell.

She holds my empty duffel bag up in the air. Mr. Lee is gone! We must have completely lost track of him during all the singing. I turn and scan the room. I notice a few little ladies gathered in the far side of the dining hall. I slowly walk up behind them and there's Mr. Lee on his back wrapped in a pink blanket, living the dream.

I motion Joan over, "I found him! Hello, ladies," I say as gently as possible.

The little lady sitting in the wheelchair holding Mr. Lee looks up, "Oh, we've been busted." She hands Lone-Lee up to Joan.

"Thank you for taking such good care of Mr. Lee. You've been a sweetheart," Joan says, cradling Lone-Lee in her arms.

We walk around saying our good-byes and giving big hugs. Some of these people haven't had loved ones visit in months. I make sure to acknowledge each and every one. I give them a heart to heart hug for as long as they want, waiting for them to release first.

As we walk back to the car, I feel ten feet tall. Joan puts her arm around my shoulder, "You did good, sister."

I fire back, "We did good, sister. This was a great idea."

With our hearts full and Mr. Lee safely back in my duffel bag, we set back on the road towards Manitou Springs. Our visit only cost us a couple of hours, but the feeling is going to last all week. Mr. Lee crawls up onto Joan's lap. She gently begins rubbing his fur and round little belly. All the commotion must have taken it out of him. Just a few days ago he was homeless, now he is the center of attention. In the beginning, I thought that Joan and I would have to split custody, but he is really Joan's dog. He has chosen. I've heard that an animal knows where they are needed, and she needs him now.

Joan interrupts my thoughts, "I have an idea. Just hear me out before you say anything...I think you should try singing."

I look at her like she's crazy, "I can't sing, Joan. It was just the moment. Everyone was so excited."

"Someone really smart once told me, 'If you want something bad enough you will do it, if you don't, you'll make an excuse'." Joan smirks.

I roll my eyes. I know I just told her the same thing yesterday about Will. "You act like I don't have a job."

Joan puts her hands up in front of her chest waving them, "I'm just saying, I think you are really good. This could be something you could explore."

I nod my head, "Maybe."

"Why do all your 'maybes' sound like 'no's?'" Joan says, slightly laughing.

I shrug my shoulders and grin at her.

"You're ridiculous, I'm going to get a nap in, if that's okay? Stay on I-70 until you get close to Denver," Joan says, sliding down in her seat and snuggling in with Lone-Lee.

"Shouldn't have stayed up all night having phone sex with Will," I joke with her.

"We did not!" Joan says, sounding embarrassed and way too defensive.

"Aw, but you were thinking about it..." I trail off, hoping she will fill in a detail.

She wraps her hoodie over her face and pretends she's fast asleep. "Maybe," Joan muffles from under her hoodie.

I laugh, "Your 'maybes' sounds like 'yes's'."

She giggles under her hoodie and blindly tries to punch me in the arm. She accidentally bumps her fist against the steering wheel instead.

"Don't make me wreck, Stupid!" I say in a joking voice, "You've already tried to kill me once."

"I'm rolling my eyes under here just in case you were wondering. That was low!" Joan says with a fake sadness to her voice.

I push play on our road trip playlist and settle in for the four-hour drive. I turn up the volume. I love this song! It's exactly how I feel driving across the country with Joan. Sometimes songs just speak to you. This is one of them. It's called "I, Love and You" by The Avett Brothers.

The Avett Brothers are a folksy band Joan and I saw in concert at Stubbs in Austin. Their voices always comfort us, like a warm bath and being rocked to sleep. I look over at Joan; she's curled up in the seat. She looks so small lying there. My thoughts wander back to when we were kids. I thought she was invincible, and now, she seems so broken. It feels like I'm getting my first look behind the curtain in the Wizard of Oz. I wander off in thought.

"What happened to the music?" Joan asks, straightening up and pulling her seat back to an upright position.

"Umm...I didn't notice it turned off. We are about sixty miles to Denver. Want to stop and grab a bite to eat?" I shake the thoughts from my head.

"No, let's just press on since we've lost time already. Do you want to call June's grandson to see if he has a room tonight? Or do you want to continue on to Manitou Springs?" Joan says, starting the playlist again. "I'm just going to look up the bed and breakfast online, just in case."

I nod my head giving her the go ahead to at least investigate.

"Oh, Mar it's adorable. The bed and breakfast is in this refurbished red barn. The grass is so green. Oh! And it's a farm with miniature horses. Please let's go here! It has us written all over it. It has an 'About' page..." Joan clicks the tab and opens the page.

"Mar, this guy is hot!" She turns her phone to show me his picture.

Tiny Animals Living Together

"Holy Hell! He's hot! Not to mention all the tiny animals. This is our kind of place, but I just feel weird. Why would we drive all the way to Estes Park just to stay there?" I say, squinting my eyes at Joan.

"Why wouldn't we? Did I mention that they have miniature animals...?" Joan says scrolling through the photos page.

"Jeez, okay, call him!" I drag out my words.

Joan lets out a squeal, "This is going to be awesome! We're gonna stay in a barn. We're gonna pet tiny animals. We are going to stare at a hot guy. We are going to promise not to look creepy doing it," Joan is turning her words into a song.

I begin singing back to her, "You're weird. Call him already! We aren't petting tiny animals, sleeping in a barn, or staring at a hot guy if he doesn't have room for us tonight."

Joan types in the number. She turns and whispers to me, "It's ringing." She holds up three fingers indicating it has rung three times.

A formal English voice comes on the line, "The English Countryside...Hello?" Joan spits out her water onto the dash, choking in the process.

She hits her chest hard with her fist trying to get the water up. She covers her coughing and laughter with her hand, trying to muffle any sound. She begins to fumble with her phone trying to turn it on speaker.

"Hello? Hello? May I help you?" A distant voice can be heard coming from her phone.

Joan straightens up in her seat, trying hard to pull herself together, "Hi, umm...My name is Joan. I was wondering if you maybe had a room for tonight?"

"Joan and Mar, the women that sang to my grandparents today?" I can hear the smile in his voice.

Apparently, June, June like the month, already called.

"Umm...yes, guilty as charged," Joan says clearing her throat. Joan looks to me, and mouths, "OH MY GOSH," and starts fanning herself.

"I am called Winston. Of course, we have a room for you! Would you be here in time for dinner? It would be my pleasure if you could join us as a 'thank you' for your kindness towards my grandparents?" His voice is rich and smooth. He speaks with the perfect English accent; he could even make reading mathematical equations sound seductive. 'The Pythagorean Theorem states...'

I imagine bras flying off, being lit on fire and swung into the air.

"Will you be needing one room or two?" Winston asks with a voice as smooth as butter on hot toast.

"Just one would be fantastic," I chime in.

"Is that your sister?" Winston asks with curiosity in his voice.

"Yes, my baby sister." Joan emphasizes the word 'baby' and pokes me on my side.

"Well then, I will see you tonight."

"Thank you, Winston. We will see you shortly." Joan pushes the button on her phone.

"Maybe we should do the hike tomorrow? I don't want to cut our hike short because it's so late in the day. Plus, I've driven all day. I'm kind of beat," I say throwing my arm over my head for a good stretch. "I could use a slow down."

"I agree, let's leave Manitou Springs for another time." Joan reaches over and squeezes my shoulder.

As we drive up a long, dirt road, I can see the top of a barn. It looks like a fancier version of an old, red barn. It's rustic and industrial. The grass is as green as I have ever seen; I thought maybe the picture was photoshopped, but here it is before my eyes exactly as it was on the website. A quintessential white, picket fence surrounds a large pasture with a small, tan and white horse standing at the entrance. It's absolutely perfect.

The gravel crunches under the car as we creep up the driveway. A tall, blond man strolls out of the barn. He walks straight to my side of the car opening my door, then steps around and opens Joan's.

"Welcome ladies, we spoke earlier on the phone. I'm called Winston," he says jetting out his hand to Joan.

Joan doesn't miss a beat, vigorously shaking his hand and replying, "I shall call you Winston." Joan sometimes adopts this formal way of talking when she is around anyone from England.

I burst out laughing and swiftly turn, burying my face in Mr. Lee's fur, avoiding eye-contact with Joan.

"I'll show you to your room, so you can get settled. Then, you are welcome to explore the grounds as you wish. The dining room opens at 6 p.m." Winston grabs our makeshift bags from the trunk and leads us up the stairs.

"I know you said one room would be suitable, but we have a nice suite I thought you would enjoy, instead." Winston sets our bags inside the door and leans against the doorframe. "My grandmother said that you were on some kind of trip?"

"Yes, we are. We kind of are just going where the wind blows us. The plan is to go all the way to New York then back to California," Joan says, looking around the room.

"That sounds like quite the trip. I'm glad the wind chose to blow you here." The corner of Winston's mouth creases into a smirk.

"It was more like Hurricane June, June like the month," I say, not being able to keep a smile from spreading across my face. "She's quite the firecracker. We should have kidnapped her and brought her with us."

The room is absolutely beautiful. There is a huge, stone fireplace in the living room with a cognac-colored leather couch in front of it. The kitchen is small with a stocked wine rack.

"I hope you like the room. I will leave you to it. See you at dinner." He nods his head as he turns and shuts the door behind him.

Joan puts Mr. Lee down and he makes himself at home by jumping on the couch and stretching out. I can't possibly see how he could continue to sleep; he slept the whole way here. I grab my bag and walk to one of the bedrooms. The bed is like a huge cloud. It is covered in a big, fluffy, white comforter. The whole room is in gray tones, except for the furniture. The furniture is made of heavy, dark wood and leather. The bathroom has a reclaimed wood floor and a white sink top. We have the choice between a tub or shower: the shower is made of river rock with a rain showerhead; the tub is a fabulous deep, old, claw-foot tub.

I walk out of my bedroom the same time as Joan. "Is your room as amazing as mine?" I ask, walking past her into hers. "It is! Wow, June sure did us right."

"Wanna get a look around?" Joan asks, now inspecting each bottle of wine in the rack.

"Yea," I slip on my running shoes.

"Did you see the wine selection in this wine rack?" Joan asks, looking for a glass and setting it out on the bar.

"Set out a glass for me, too!" I say, opening the door.

I take a deep breath as we step outside. There's just something about Colorado air. It smells cleaner, crisper. Not to mention the sky seems bluer here than in California. We begin walking towards the white, picket fence when I feel a tug at my knee and look down. A tiny goat is nibbling a thread from my ripped jeans.

I squeal, "Oh my gosh! Look at him!" I kneel down and look him straight in the eyes. "Who's the cutest thing in the whole wide world? You are!"

I scratch his tiny beard, then lift him up and stuff him under my arm, continuing to pet his head. Joan and I walk across the field to the fence. I put the tiny goat down as I rest both elbows on the rail and lean against the top. There's a large, green pasture with a number of tiny goats and horses trotting around. The grass smells sweet here; like a field of clover.

"Goats and tiny horses living together, it's chaos," Joan says with a smile.

"Look, there's a donkey over there!" I point in excitement. "This is so our kind of place. Thanks for convincing me that it wasn't weird. I don't know what I was thinking. We are on an adventure after all, aren't we?" I say with more gusto. "We should do more things outside of the box."

Wincing and raising her eyebrows, Joan shoots me a look, "I'm not sure I like the sound of that. Last time I heard that come out of your mouth, we were in Hawaii. I think I remember something about extreme parasailing. I have serious trust issues with you. Not to mention that one time you mixed Skittles and M&Ms together."

I snort, "*You* have trust issues?" I narrow my eyes at her. "*I* have trust issues! Let's head back. I need to change, and I'm going to need all the time I can get."

"You got that right," Joan laughs, jumping on my back, trying to tackle me to the ground.

"Get off of me, you cow!" I shout, losing my balance and landing face first in the grass as she crashes on top of me. I feel broken. I think I got a concussion.

"Pardon me," comes a man's voice in a questioning tone.

Joan rolls off of me, startled.

I roll over onto my back and put my hand to my face to shield my eyes from the sun. I can only see a silhouette of a man. He's tall, or maybe he just seems tall because I'm still on my back.

"Pardon me, are you okay?" comes the man's voice for the second time.

Why do people keep asking us that? This guy sounds a lot like

Winston, but better. I didn't think that was possible. I get to my feet as his back blocks the sun, creating a halo effect around him. I swallow hard. My heart feels like it's about to burst, and my face gives me away. He is drop dead gorgeous. He has bright blue eyes, the color of the bluest of Colorado skies, not to mention he has the longest lashes. It is so unfair; women would kill for lashes like that. He has a strong jawline and a dusting of freckles across his face. His hair is blond and cut short. Even though he is trying hard to keep it under control, I can tell he has springs of curls on the top of his head. His arms are strong and have huge veins running down them. He is wearing a simple watch with a black band. A runner's watch, I note. My eyes are running over him.

My mouth drops open, "Ugh…" I manage.

I must look like a deer in headlights. I instinctively bat my eyelashes at him. I feel like I've blacked out. How long can I reasonably stand here undressing him with my eyes? That's a valid question. I want to take every second that's reasonably possible.

I finally find my words. "Oh, Ummm…we were just joking around." I extend my hand, "I'm Mar…Marguerite." I gesture to Joan, "and this is my *older* sister, Joan." I emphasize older and wink at Joan.

When our hands touch, I feel an electric vibration go through my hand directly to my heart. The hair on my arm stands straight up. It's true, I never believed it, but it's true, there is such a thing as a spark between people. I never thought that was a real thing. I thought it was more like chemistry, not an actual shock to the heart. I wonder if he felt it, too.

Joan makes a circle with her index finger pointing at my face. Confused, I wipe my mouth. She shakes her head and widens her eyes at me.

Noticing Joan pointing at me, the man turns to her and smiles. "Excuse me, where are my manners? I'm called Thomas, I'm Winnie's cousin."

"Winnie?" Joan screams in laughter. I can't imagine Winston

ever being called Winnie. That definitely knocks him down a couple of notches. We thought Winston was hot, but he is nothing compared to Thomas. If another hot guy pops out from somewhere like Russian dolls of hotness, it's going to be more than I can handle.

Thomas is choosing his words very carefully. "If I had to guess, I'm guessing you are the ladies from California? My Nan talked you up this afternoon on the phone. She said that you two were the most delightful girls and that you sang songs to her." He points to me, "She said you were really good."

"Ummm, I'm not a good singer, but that doesn't stop me from singing," my cheeks flush.

"That's not what I heard." He taps his finger on his chin, pretending to think. "She told me that you could sing, that your voice was like a time machine, and that my grandfather actually danced with her!"

"Your grandpa did dance with her, it was adorable. They are the sweetest," I say, blushing at the way he is looking at me. I look down, breaking his gaze.

"We were just headed back to our room to get cleaned up for dinner," Joan says, trying to make it less awkward that she's been standing here and the two of us have barely noticed.

Thomas is standing in complete silence, but I can hear him saying a million things to me. It is taking everything in me not to reach up and kiss him full on the lips. That would be completely awkward, since I just met him, and probably a shock to us both. Thomas is now looking down at my lips. I can tell he is thinking the same thing. It's almost like we are in slow motion. I part my lips slightly and then bite my bottom lip. I feel like I'm going to spontaneously combust.

"I'll accompany you back, if that's okay," Thomas says, clearing his throat.

It is more than okay. I just hope my heart can take it.

"Yes, that would be... yes." Holy hell, I'm blowing it. I'm

making a complete fool of myself.

Joan is nonchalantly standing behind Thomas, making funny faces at me. She begins rubbing her two index fingers together like she's sharping a knife. I know exactly what she means. It's a hand gesture from when we were kids; it means shame, shame. I pick up my tiny companion and stuff him back under my arm, surfboard style, and walk back towards the barn.

"I see you found a friend," Thomas says, pointing to the tiny goat I'm clutching under my arm.

"Yes, he was trying to chew my jeans," I say, lifting my knee to show him the strings.

"Oh, he's a cheeky goat. I don't blame him, though. Did he rip your jeans like that?" Thomas asks in surprise.

"No silly! He was just chewing the thread. The jeans came like this," I say, smiling like a schoolgirl.

Winston is walking out of the barn as we approach.

"Hi, Winnie!" Thomas says, clapping his hand on Winston's shoulder.

"Stop calling me that! I haven't been called that in thirty years!" Winston says, sounding mildly frustrated.

Thomas reaches up and pinches Winston's cheek. "Until then, ladies." He gives us a quick bow.

Winston turns his head as he looks at Thomas, "Sometimes he's impossible."

I set the tiny goat down. He wobbles off back towards the barn. I turn on my heels and grab Joan by the arm and rush inside as if I've stolen something. "My, gosh! I thought Winston was hot. But he's nothing compared to Thomas," I turn and pull Joan into our room.

Joan interrupts me in a dry tone; "You have a giant grass mark on your forehead Stupid!"

I turn and look in the mirror. "Crap! Why didn't you tell me?"

"I was trying to tell you, but you just weren't getting what I was saying then Thomas caught me...plus, you were all, 'oh, singing was nothing, your grandparents are so adorable...blah, blah, blah...'.'"

Jeez, I'm never going to live this down. I throw myself back onto the bed like a bratty teenager. I'm so embarrassed. "I'm going to hide in my room. Just bring me something back from dinner," I say, feeling mortified; all the wind and momentum deflating out of my sails. Maybe he wasn't into me like I thought. Maybe he just felt bad for me because I'm a colossal idiot.

"Pull yourself together. You're going! It's not the end of the world. Get over yourself. He likes you!" Joan says, trying to sound convincing.

"He does not! I looked like a fool!" I say, waving her off and burying my face in my pillow.

"He did! You would have noticed that if you could have snapped out of it. It was like I wasn't even standing there. At one point I thought he was going to kiss you! You need to do something cool tonight," Joan says, thinking and staring off into space like the idea was written somewhere on the ceiling.

I sigh, rubbing the back of my hand around my face, resting it under my chin. "Who, me? I am the epitome of cool. I can't turn this off." I rub my eyes with both my hands. "But, seriously, did you see me out there? I can't show my face tonight. Tell them I'm under the weather, tell them aliens abducted me, tell them anything, I don't care!"

Joan twirls her hand in the air like she's casting a spell over me, "Look at yourself! I've never seen you act like this. Just go out there and be yourself. I'm just saying, do something cool to erase the vision of you with a grass mark on your head!"

"Do something cool like my baton twirling from the sixth-grade talent show? Or the clog dancing I learned last summer?" I say, smiling.

"Never mind, you're not allowed to come up with something on your own," Joan acts like she's exhausted from my foolishness. "Sing? Sing something for him! Something that lets him know you think he's cuter than a bug's ear in July."

"Like…? I know! How about, 'I Touch Myself, by The Divinyls'?" I clutch my arms to my chest.

Joan whacks me hard in the face with a pillow.

I giggle and begin singing the lyrics.

Joan tries to talk over me. This only encourages me to sing louder.

"Get serious!" Joan snaps.

"This is me being serious!" I say, laughing as I walk to the wine rack.

"Remind me not to ask you to do my eulogy," Joan says.

I look at Joan perplexed, "That's a bit morbid! Stop that! Really, what if I make a complete fool of myself?" I gulp down a glass of wine. "You didn't poison this, did you?" I give Joan a suspicious look.

Joan laughs, "You will make a fool of yourself if you keep drinking like that. Plus, if you do happen to make a fool of yourself, we can leave tomorrow and you'll never have to see him again. I'll sneak you out, I'll say you had to leave early."

"Okay, I'll go, but promise me if I do anything crazy you will rush me out of there," I say, holding my breath and raising my eyebrows, waiting for Joan to agree.

Joan starts, "You haven't said what your plan is for tonight."

"Why do I have to have a plan? Why can't I go and just hang out?" I ask, working on my second glass of wine.

Joan squints her eyes at me, "Do you remember the grass skid mark on your forehead?"

I shake my head, "Right…" like anything I do at this point will make that memory any better.

"So…what you are going to do? I'm reconsidering your baton act from the sixth grade but, unfortunately, we left your baton back in Cali."

"I don't know, Joan. I guess it will come to me," I shrug my shoulders and slink off to my room.

I turn around and wrap my leg around the doorframe and slide down it as I begin to sing The Divinyls again. I run my finger over my lips and throw my head back like I'm in a 1980s hairband video.

Joan laughs, "Get in there, Stupid! We don't have all day to get dressed!"

Animal Attraction

I clean up with a pair of black chinos and a silk spaghetti strap camisole.

"Well, well, look who's looking hot, but there's one thing missing..." Joan begins to walk around me, inspecting my face. "Yes...something is missing... I got it. You're missing the giant grass mark on your forehead! That would really pull this whole look together!" Joan reaches up and tugs on my hair.

I furrow my brow, "You're not making this any easier. I just forgot about that. Thanks for the confidence booster."

"Oh, I thought it was my job to make it harder," Joan says, fluttering her lashes and smiling at me. "Hey," Joan says, grabbing my glass. "You need to slow down; this is your second glass of wine. You know how you get when you drink a little too much."

"Oh, really? How's that?" I ask with a smirk on my face.

Joan gives me that, 'I know about you look.' "You become a social butterfly, sing karaoke super loud, and become a certain male Avenger!"

I raise my eyebrows and stick out my tongue.

"See?" Joan points at me. "I told you! Stop drinking now and save yourself."

"Where is your sense of adventure? Weren't you the one just telling me that we were on an adventure?" I nod my head, agreeing with myself. "Good thing this isn't a karaoke bar, and only dinner." I look at Joan, thinking I have the whole thing figured out.

"You're right. I did just say that. Go for it! Knock yourself out, but don't come crying to me when you embarrass yourself." Joan shakes her finger at me.

Joan and I walk into the dining room when I notice Winston walking towards us.

"Good evening, ladies. I'm so glad you could join us," Winston ushers us to our seats.

I take in the atmosphere. The dining room is two, huge, white canvas tents joined together to make one large tent. There are a few iron tables on the grass with string lights hanging from one side to the other. A piano sits on a raised platform at the far end of the tent. The walls are sporadically lined with olive trees and Italian cypress in large pots.

Winston pulls out Joan's seat, then hands us a wine list. "Here's the wine list. All our food is organic and grown right here on the grounds."

"Thanks, Winston," I say, scanning the room for Thomas.

"He's not here yet," Winston says in a whisper.

"Who?" I say, my face burning.

"Tom, he should be here shortly. Trust me, the feeling is mutual. I heard about the cute grass mark on your forehead and the way you carried the goat under your arm, and about a million other things." Winston shakes his head. "You have him rattled."

He told Winston about me? I look to the ground and run my hands nervously over my knees. He thought the grass mark was cute? I swallow. I feel like my heart is going to burst right through my chest.

Winston taps his finger on the table, "I'll be back in a couple of minutes to check on you. We usually have a band here on the weekends, but tonight I thought we'd do something different." He straightens up, "Well, Tom convinced me to do something different."

I clasp my hands together in excitement, "I can't wait."

Winston walks off as I turn to look at Joan. I put my hand over my heart. "What the hell is wrong with me?"

"It's called chemistry. Animalistic attraction…" Joan exaggerates the word animal as she makes a clawing motion with her hand.

"Well, I don't like it," I say, sounding like a two-year-old throwing a temper tantrum. I don't like the feeling of not being able to control my emotions. Who does he think he is, anyways?

I look at Joan and finally say out loud, "Who does he think he is anyways?"

"Why are you mad at him? He didn't do anything to you. At least not yet," she gives me a wink.

"I don't like that I feel out of control. I'm mad because he's just so damn hot," I say, throwing my hands in the air. "I don't know. I don't know!"

"You're letting your head get in the way. Just relax," Joan says, putting a hand on my knee and giving it a squeeze.

I feel like I'm going to laugh, cry, cheer, and die all at the same time. I feel like each body part is doing its own thing and everyone can tell.

I lean over and whisper into Joan's ear, "Is love at first sight possible?"

As I say 'possible,' I feel a hand on my shoulder and let out a yelp and practically slide down my chair and onto the floor.

"I'm sorry, excuse me. I didn't mean to startle you." I turn to see Thomas standing there.

Please tell me he didn't hear me ask Joan about love at first sight.

I clear my throat. "Hi."

"Do you mind if I sit down?" Thomas says, eyeing the chair.

"Please," Joan gestures to the chair beside me. "We were just looking over the menu. What do you recommend?"

Thomas' white shirt is tailored to his lean body. I let my eyes run over his chest where each button is doing their part to hold themselves together. I know exactly how they feel.

"How is your forehead?" Thomas asks with a wide grin on his face.

I reach up and touch my head with my hand. "Oh, I just looked ridiculous. I wasn't hurt." I say, dying a little inside.

"It wasn't ridiculous, it was adorable," Thomas says, reaching over and grazing my hand with his.

I'm watching his mouth move but I'm so mesmerized with his lips that I don't register what he is saying. My eyes follow his jawline and up to his cheekbones. His face is manly, but he also has this wide eyed innocence.

Thomas points his index finger into the air. "Would you trust me enough to have the chef pick for you?"

Joan steps on my toes under the table. I refocus on the sound that's coming out of Thomas' mouth instead of just watching it. Has he been talking this whole time?

His words hit me like a ton of bricks. "The chef, Anna is Winnie's fiancé. She went to The Culinary Institute of America in Calistoga."

"Oh, we know a guy who went there," Joan interrupts. "It's such a small world."

"Oh, I wonder if Anna knows him. I'll have her come by the table," Thomas says to Joan, not taking his eyes off of me.

"His name is Will," Joan says with a glint in her eyes.

"I see, very well," Thomas says, dragging out his words and slowly rising from the table. "I'm going to talk to Anna. I'll be back with a bottle of wine."

I'm not sure he even registered anything Joan just said. As he stands from the table his thighs are straining against his dark blue, suit pants.

Joan turns to face me, "Did you see the way he was looking at you?" she asks, pushing my shoulder with her hand.

My face turns bright red. I am so glad people can't see my thoughts right now because I'm pretty sure they would be considered X-rated. My third-grade teacher once told me that she knew what I was thinking. I spent the rest of my elementary career thinking that my thoughts popped up above my head like in one of those thought bubbles. I still worry about that from time to time, but only when I'm thinking things I don't really want people to know. For instance, from time to time I think: that guy has a nice ass, or I picture Mrs. Carson, my fifth grade math teacher with green gas coming out of his mouth because she smells like garbage.

A petite brunette in a chef apron heads to our table. "Hi, I'm Anna. I'm Winston's fiancé." She holds out her tiny hand.

I can't imagine her being able to do much with how waiflike she is; waiflike in a beautiful way. "Tonight, I have something specifically prepared for you since you are our special guests. I'm going to start off with a creamy mushroom soup, followed by short rib with root vegetables, and a salted caramel chocolate tart for dessert."

My mouth begins to water.

"That sounds fantastic," Joan says, smiling and looking Anna right in the eye. She isn't hiding the fact that she could care less about what we eat tonight. Or maybe I am the only one who notices because I know her so well. I know exactly what she really wants to know. She wants to cut to the chase and get the low down on Will.

Almost as if she could read Joan's thoughts, a smile stretches across Anna's face. "Oh, Tom said that you know Will! I know him very well. He was like my best friend while I was going through school. He's such a nice guy." Anna shakes her head. "It is a small world isn't it?"

"You can't just say he was a nice guy and leave it at that," I prod Anna for Joan's sake.

"Ummm, I know his dad. He held a party at his castle when Will graduated. He never really had a serious girlfriend that I know of. He was always very focused on opening a restaurant and getting that going." Anna is spitting out facts like bullet points in an email.

"Yes, he opened a restaurant. Matter of fact, we ate—or tried to eat there—the other night," Joan fills Anna in.

Anna looks at us with a puzzled look on her face.

I wave my hand at her, "Long story."

"Well, I'll have to catch up with him sometime. Do you have his number?" Anna says as she turns her sights on me. "Mar, I hear you caught Tom's eye. He will not shut up about you. He's probably watching us through the tent flap. Don't let him fool you. He is completely malfunctioning right now. He keeps second-guessing everything he has said to you. It is sure giving Winston something to pick on him about."

"The feeling is mutual, but don't tell him that," I say, blushing.

"I won't, but he'd have to be completely blind to not see it," Anna says as I stand, she gives me a hug. Anna turns to Joan and hugs her. "Will is a super nice guy. If he is interested in you, then that's a big change for him. He was, at one point, all about his work. If you like him, go for it. He's not a fly by night kind of guy."

Joan scribbles Will's number down and hands it to Anna. "Thank you, Anna," Joan says. "We look forward to dinner tonight. I'm sure it's going to be spectacular."

I sit back down, watching Anna disappear back through the curtains.

Thomas walks over to our table burnishing a bottle of Stag's Leap Cabernet 2014. "Anna is making you the short rib; this wine will be perfect with it." He places his hips against the table and leans over and pours me a glass.

He looks up at me, "Enjoy."

I watch his mouth, even the word 'enjoy' sounds ripe with innuendo. I swallow hard and try to crack a smile.

Thomas mirrors my smile. "Let me know if you need anything."

The word 'anything' hangs in the air.

"Do you work here?" I ask, trying to keep him at our table.

"No, I'm just visiting. I help Winnie out while I'm here," Thomas says, shrugging his shoulders. "Please don't hesitate to call on me, really, if you need anything."

There's that word again being flown by on a little imaginary airplane banner…anything. I unknowingly start to fan myself with the wine list.

Without turning, Joan reaches over and grabs it from me and hands it to Thomas, "Thank you."

He turns on his heels and I watch his perfect ass as he disappears through the crowded tables.

"Does he look familiar to you?" Joan asks. "It seems like I've seen him somewhere before."

"No, but I'd like to get familiar with him," I say to Joan as I put my hand on my chest to feel my heart race.

We are just finishing up our entrée when I hear a single note on the piano. I look up to see the spotlight shining on it. Thomas grabs his pants that are stretched tight over his thighs and pulls them up to sit down. The piano starts slow and quiet. I'm trying hard to recognize the song. It sounds like "Something" by the Beatle's, but he is playing it slower. He starts to sing, and I know it immediately. His voice is clear and warm. Like I've heard it for a million years. I feel safe. Like I've heard his voice every day of my life. Thomas looks straight at me. I feel like I'm going to melt into a hot puddle. People start to move in their seats to turn and look at me. I lift my hand and give a short awkward wave.

Joan whispers to me without moving her head, "He's looking at you, and he's not being shy about it."

"Holy crap! He's really good," I say, looking at Joan.

"I know! And he's singing to you," Joan says, with a smirk on her face. We look like two deer frozen in headlights with only our lips moving. I'm hanging on every word; awestruck. It's like he wrote this song just for me.

As Thomas finishes, the dinner crowd begins to clap. He stands and takes a slight bow. I look straight at him and put my hand over my heart and bow my head.

A lady behind me shouts, "One more!" Then she whispers to someone beside her, "I can't believe he's here!"

I wonder who she thinks he is? He is beautiful enough to be a model.

"As you wish," he looks straight at me and sits back down.

The piano plays as I rest my chin on my hand and begin to drift off in a daydream. He is absolutely magnificent. The way his pants bunch up where his thigh bends and meet his pelvis is enough to think about for a lifetime. His fingers play the keys softly and I imagine him running them over my body, up my thigh and over my hipbone. His wrists are perfect with his white shirt rolled up just enough to see his forearms.

I imagine tracing his tiny freckles with my finger. I think about rolling in soft white sheets. I walk to the stage and begin slowly dancing around him. I drag my hand over his collarbone. I run my hand over his strong shoulders, then straddle him, leaning my head on his chest while he continues to play. I slowly unbutton his white shirt, nibbling his ear letting my hair land on his chest.

I'm lost in thought when the lady behind me starts to clap and like a bolt of lightning my mind snaps back to reality. The room grows silent as I notice that most of the people are watching me. I hope I wasn't acting out anything from my daydream.

Thomas stands and walks off the platform.

I didn't even clap. I was too lost in my thoughts. I hope he doesn't think I didn't like it. Buzzing dinner chatter surrounds me again as people go back to their conversations.

"Hey," I clear my throat, "I'm going to find a bathroom and freshen up," I whisper to Joan as I push my seat back.

"Don't get lost. But if you do, make sure it's somewhere amazing, if you know what I mean," Joan says, shooing me away with her hand.

I roll my eyes, "Please."

I walk towards the opening in the tent, not sure where the

bathroom is. I'll probably have to head back to the room. I really hope I didn't hurt Thomas' feelings by not clapping. If he only knew what I was actually thinking about, he'd forgive me. An arm reaches out and pulls me through an opening in the curtain. Before I can react, a hand covers my mouth. My eyebrows shoot up. It's Thomas! Good thing he's so hot, or he would be in serious trouble right now. "Hi," he draws in a deep breath and slowly blows it out against my neck. He presses his hips firmly against mine, pinning me to the wall. "I'm going to move my hand from your mouth but, don't scream. I mean, unless you really want to, of course."

Even now he's polite. Scream? I can hardly breathe…much less scream.

He leans down to me rubbing his nose against mine. His eyes look down at me, questioning. I take a deep breath in, inhaling the bergamot on his skin. His lips part mine as he pushes his tongue into my mouth, slightly sucking on my bottom lip. Everything in me turns on like I've just been plugged into a generator that could power Vegas. I can feel my cheeks flush red-hot. I reach up and grab his face, desperately pulling him into me. I can feel him against me, as he reaches down and lifts me slightly off my feet. My hands untuck his shirt and explore his chest. His body is burning hot. Everything inside me is about to explode when he slowly sits my feet back on the ground.

In a breathy growl he whispers in my ear, "I wanted to do that all day."

I mentally picture a person with a fire extinguisher spraying me down. My lipstick is all over his mouth; I stand in front of him in stunned silence, panting, trying hard to control my breath.

I tiptoe up and kiss him, "Me too." I purr. I bite my bottom lip, "That was amazing."

I run my hands through my hair, trying to pull myself together. I have forgotten completely about finding the bathroom. I start to slowly walk towards my room and glance back at him. He is standing there with one hand pressed against the wall. I want him to follow me, but he just stands there watching as I walk away. Why isn't he following me? I pass a man in the hall and he gives me a strange look. I promptly put the key card in the door and walk in. I shut the door with my back and slide down to the floor. I put my head in my hands and beat my feet against the carpet. That was the best kiss I've ever had. I jump up and run to the bathroom to quickly brush my teeth, hoping Thomas will come to his senses. I glance at myself in the mirror. No wonder the man in the hall was looking at me strange. My hair is a mess and my cherry red lipstick is smeared all over my mouth. I look like a deranged clown. I grab a washcloth and scrub my face. I'm running a brush through my hair when I hear a knock on the door. I straighten my shirt and walk to the door, hoping Thomas has come to whisk me away, but when I open the door there's no one there except for a note at my feet. I look back and forth down the hall but it's empty. Can he do magic too? Of course, he can.

Meet me in front of the barn. I'll bring dessert and you bring yourself. —Thomas

My heart skips a beat. I replay his breathy growl in my head. Just the thought of his voice makes me hot and sweaty all over again. I can't wait to get back to Joan and tell her what just happened. When I make it back into the tent, Thomas is already there, talking to Winston in the corner of the room. I catch his eye and his gaze follows me back to my table.

"Where in the world have you been, or do I want to know?" Joan asks.

"Shush," I say, putting my finger to my mouth and sliding down into my seat. I lean into Joan, "Thomas kissed me! It was the hottest kiss ever. Think, *50 Shades of Grey* and *The Notebook*, hot."

Joan raises her eyebrows at me, "Really? And…?"

"He asked me to meet him later for dessert. And by 'dessert' I hope he means sex," I say, fanning myself.

"Good thing he invited you for dessert because you missed

dessert here and it was fantastic," Joan says with a snort. "I packed yours up for *me* to eat later."

"Keep the dessert. It will never be as fantastic as the kiss I just had," I trail off, reliving his hot body pressed against mine.

Joan leans in closer, "Well just be careful. Use protection."

I jerk back in my seat, "Did you just turn into mom? Eww! Please, stop that! For your information I have the five-year plan and the proof is right here in my arm. So, stop it!"

"I'm just saying," Joan says.

"You're just turning into mom that's all." I elbow her in the ribs. "Stop it."

"I'm going to stay here awhile and finish this glass, then I'll head back to the room to call Will. I won't wait up," Joan says, shooing me off. "Have fun."

"I'm going to go do a quick shave. If you know what I mean? Nothing major, I'm not a Neanderthal!" I raise my eyebrows at her.

"Too much information! Why aren't you waxing, anyways?" Joan asks like shaving is so old school.

"Well, if you haven't noticed we've been a bit busy." I look around for Thomas. I plant a light kiss on her head. "Toot-ta-Lou." I say as I wave at her over my shoulder.

"That's not how you say that," Joan yells at me but I'm already halfway through the dining area. I start to rush back to my room to prep for my dessert date but, by the time I make it outside, Thomas is already waiting for me at the front of the barn. He has a blanket and a small basket in his hands.

"Hi," he says as he leans down to kiss my cheek.

"Hi yourself," I say with a smile.

"So, I was thinking that we could take the dessert and wine out to the pond." Thomas holds out his arm for me to grab, waiting for my reply.

Two women pass by and give Thomas a long, hard stare. I mean, I have to admit, I would be staring, too. He's got to be the most handsome guy I've ever seen. But come on, ladies.

"Do you know them? I ask, taking his arm.

"I've never met them in my life," Thomas says, lifting one hand in the air.

"Well, they want to know you." I give his arm a soft squeeze.

Thomas turns, "I want to get to know you."

As we turn to walk out through the pasture, the ladies watch us go. I feel like asking them if they need something, but I figure that would just come off as jealous. We make it to the edge of the pond. Thomas stretches the blanket out. We both sit down as he pulls out two pieces of chocolate cake covered in strawberries and another bottle of wine.

"So, tell me Marguerite, what do you like to do for fun?" Thomas reaches up and traces my ear with is finger. He's making it almost impossible to concentrate. "Hum...I guess that's a hard question to answer. I don't have a specific thing I like to *do* for fun. I mean...I'm having fun all the time. To say the one thing I do for fun isn't fair. I will say this: I like trying all kinds of adventurous things. How about you, Thomas? What do you like to do for fun?" I'm interested in unraveling his inner workings.

He casually leans back on one elbow, "I like to travel. I run and I absolutely love to spend time with my family."

"Ah, a family man," I say with twinkling eyes.

Thomas rests his temple on his hand, "So, what brings you and your sister to Colorado? I mean I know why you are in Estes Park, but why did you choose Colorado in the first place?"

"That's a long story, but the short of it is that we are road tripping from California to New York. Kind of just letting the road take us where it takes us. Joan is getting a divorce and we needed to do some soul searching. But like I said, long story." I rush my words so that I can get to my question. I see how this is going to go. It's a back and forth interview. "How about you, why are you in Colorado?"

"I come and visit Winnie. He's like a brother to me. His parents moved to Colorado when he was a teenager. I used to spend summers with him, but now I visit when I need family time."

He's lying on his side, as he inches closer his shoulder rubs against my arm. His long legs are stretched out on the blanket and my eyes are soaking him in. Kicking off his shoes, his feet find mine. He leans over and kisses my shoulder. "Is Joan your only sibling?"

It is getting harder and harder to concentrate. I turn my head towards him. He's talking, I'm watching his mouth move. I lean in to give him a sweet kiss on his lips.

His hand grabs the back of my head, his fingers intertwine in my hair as he pulls me in closer. He casually breaks off and spoons a piece of chocolate cake into my mouth. I wish he would never stop kissing me.

I try to keep my cool, I rapidly ask another question, "Where do your parents live?"

"My parents live in London. I do, too, most of the time." He spoons another piece of cake into my mouth.

My heart drops. London...he doesn't even live in the States. I try to put that in the back of my mind.

"I'm back and forth to California a lot." He plants another kiss on my neck.

I lay back onto the blanket. He follows me, never moving his lips from my neck. His hand wraps around my bare waist as he pulls me into him. I try to keep the conversation going. I mean, I don't want to look easy.

In a growl, he leans into my ear, "I want you, Marguerite."

I love the way he says my name; my whole name. It rolls off his tongue nice and slow every time. I reach up and grab both his strong shoulders and pull him closer to me. Is this happening? Am I okay with this? Hell yes! I'm okay with this. He reaches down and unsnaps the button to my pants. Thank goodness I decided earlier to wear sexy, white cheekies with a tiny white bow on the front.

Thomas leans down and kisses my belly button then the tiny bow. He uses both his hands and slides my pants down. He kisses my inner thighs, then my knees and then my ankles as he goes. He sits back on his knees to unbutton his shirt.

I sit up and help. He has a chiseled chest. Not a body builder's chest, but a chest a girl could really curl up on. I run my hands over his chest and down his abs. When I reach his pants, I slowly unbutton them. I run my hands over his hip flexors and around his backside. I'm tracing every line and every muscle when I see a flash.

"Should we go inside? It looks like there might be weather," Thomas says, never taking his lips from my skin.

"Yes, let's go." I reach up and give him one more kiss before I reach down and shrug my pants back on.

Thomas squats down beside me, "Hop on. I'll give you a piggyback ride back if you carry the basket."

I hop on his back and lick his ear.

Thomas squeezes my calf. "You better stop, I won't be able to control myself."

Thomas' white shirt flops open in the breeze and everything in me decides that I've made the right decision.

He looks over his shoulder, "We'll go back to my room. I'm not sharing with anyone."

Thomas bounces me up to get a better grip.

I nod in agreement. Something is following behind us. It must be the goat from earlier.

"Hey, I think something is behind us," I whisper to Thomas.

"It's okay. There's no one else out here," Thomas reassures me as he rubs my knee with his thumb.

"No, I just heard it again. I'm pretty sure there's something behind us. I think someone is following us." I make it a point to get a better look. "Oh, my goodness! It's a goat!"

I hop off Thomas' back and reach down to pet it. Thomas lifts the tiny goat to his chest. I'm supposed to be there, not some stupid goat!

"We better take him back. He isn't supposed to be out overnight. Do you mind?" Thomas tucks him under his arm.

Of course, I mind, but I'm not going to say that. Plus, I would feel horrible if I found out he was eaten by a bobcat all because I didn't want to put him back in the barn.

Thomas leans over and kisses me, reminding me that he hasn't for one second forgotten about me.

With his free arm, he scoops me off my feet so that I reach his lips. "Let's drop him off at the barn. My room is really close." Thomas opens the barn door and drops the goat in the hay and locks the door behind him. "There, that should keep him. Now, where were we?" He says as he presses my body against the barn door.

"I think we were just past this part," I smile at him.

"Right, right. I think you're right," He says, smiling back at me. He grabs my hand and we walk to his room. His room is a stand-alone cottage. It's just as beautiful as our room. The door barely shuts behind us when Thomas reaches down and quickly unbuttons my pants. I am working just as fast on his. I fumble on his shirt buttons. He pulls my shirt over my head. We are hastily discarding clothes as he lifts me onto the bed and lies on top of me.

"You're amazing," he says as he runs his hand over one of my breasts.

"You're amazing," I pull him into me. I'm kissing him now like I need his kiss to breathe.

"Don't stop, Marguerite. Please don't stop," Thomas pants.

I don't want to stop. Nothing has felt so right.

Thomas' strong hands devour my curves. There's not a part of me he hasn't touched, and I love it. I roll over on top of him, giving him a full view of my bare chest.

"You are so beautiful," he moans as I rock back and forth. His fingers trace my breasts. It feels like we are the only two people in the whole world. I don't know where he ends and where I begin. It's like we are and have always been like this, forever. Thomas begins to match my rocking. I bite my lip in an effort to keep control, to hold off a few seconds longer. I watch as his ab muscles flex under me. I trace my finger from his lips down to the middle of his chest. My hands are exploring every inch of his torso. His eyes gently squeeze shut and his fingers grip my hips tightly. He pulls me to his chest enveloping me. It sends me right over the edge. My own climax is close behind. I throw my body back, exploding, arching over him. I collapse down back onto his chest, breathing in his smell. He smells like summer, like oranges and sunshine. I catch my breath and lay my head on his chest.

Thomas brushes my hair off my face. "Marguerite, this is the most amazing night." His hand intertwines with mine. "I would like to see you."

"You're seeing me right now," I say, pressing myself into his chest.

"No, I mean this is something different for me." He raises my chin so that my eyes meet his, "This feels like something different to me." He presses his lips to the top of my head and kisses me.

If feels like I just closed my eyes when the sun beams through the crack in the curtains, waking me. I rub my eyes and run my fingers through my hair. Oh, crap! I better try to get back to my room before I have to do the walk of shame in front of too many people. I slink out of bed and gather my clothes off the floor and swiftly put them on. I tiptoe across the room and quietly shut the door behind me. I feel like a cat burglar sneaking out after I've stolen the rare, diamond necklace. I'm feeling pretty happy with myself. It's been more than six months since I've been with anyone. I hope I was good. I mean, that's a legitimate concern, right?

I slide my key in the door and try my best to slip in without Joan hearing me.

"OH, MY GOSH, Mar! Did you see the news?" Joan shouts at

me, practically standing on the couch.

T . M . I = T . M . Z

"When would I have seen the news?" I point to my hair. I thought my sex hair was self-explanatory, but obviously not. It's really very impressive. I'm going to have to use a good amount of conditioner to get this out.

"It's 6 a.m.!" I rub the day-old mascara out of my eyes. "I don't immediately roll over and scroll the news like you, Joan. Plus, isn't it apparent that I've been quite busy?"

"Stop fooling around and come over here! Did you know who he is? You know, before...?" Joan asks scolding me like a child.

It's a vastly different tone than she had last night. What ever happened to go have fun, blah, blah, and blah?

"Did I know who he is?" I ask sounding confused. "What do you mean, do I know who he is? Yes, I know his name if that's what you're asking? What's wrong with you? First you tell me to go have a good time, and when I do, you're all upset about it!"

"I'm not upset you spent the night with him. I'm just mad. I'm mad at the situation. Did he tell you what he did for a living?" Joan repeats herself.

I'm getting more and more confused. As long as he's not a serial killer, I'm fine. It's not like we had the whole conversation about jobs, favorite color, or pets. I don't date people for their job status.

"What 'situation' are you talking about?" I ask, finally waking up and registering the alarm in her voice.

I plop myself next to Joan on the couch. She shoves her phone into my hands. I look at the screen and my jaw drops.

"Oh, my gosh! What is all this?" I yell as my stomach hits the floor.

"Keep looking! Read the article. There's more!" Joan sounds like a late-night infomercial.

"He is a big-time actor in England! He just filmed a movie in Montana." The realization sinks in. That's why those women were staring at him. I thought it was because they thought he was hot. Why didn't he tell me? My blood is beginning to boil. I flip through tabloid article after article. My half naked picture is on every tabloid I open. There I am in my full glory, white cheekies and all!

"Don't get too upset," Joan interjects. "Did you tell him what you did for a living? Maybe he didn't want to lead with 'Hey, I'm kind of a big deal in England'," Joan says, trying to smooth over my anxiety. "Let's be fair."

"No, but he could have said he was famous!" I say, getting more and more angry.

Joan's playing devil's advocate, "Mar, think of how that would have sounded to you. You wouldn't have liked him telling you."

"Joan, my picture is everywhere… everywhere!" I snap.

I begin to rock myself back and forth. "In my panties no less, in a very compromising position! Mom and Dad are going to freak!"

"Crap! I forgot about Mom and Dad! Maybe they won't read this since it's gossip news," Joan tries to sound convincing.

She knows very well that it will get back to Dad. I get up and start pacing the room with my face in my hands. "OH, MY GOSH! Everyone in the world has now seen me in my panties!"

"Well, at least they were sexy panties," Joan says, looking for the silver lining. "Plus, it's no worse than people seeing you in your bikini, isn't it?"

If she says 'the obstacle is the way' I'm going to freak. It's one of her mantras. She read a Ryan Holiday book last year and decided it was her new way of life. A new way of looking at things. It's a take-off of a Marcus Aurelius quote, 'what stands in the way becomes the way.' But I swear, if she says it right now, I'm going to choke her.

A knock at the door bolts me out of thinking about choking Joan. I shoot Joan a look. "Are you expecting anyone?"

Joan shakes her head, "I'm not expecting anyone."

I open the door, still in last night's clothes and looking like a raccoon.

"Good morning, Beautiful. I brought you some eggs and soldiers for breakfast," Thomas says in a chipper voice.

Any other time, I would love this, but instead I snatch him in by the front of his shirt. "Have you seen the news this morning?"

Thomas looks even more confused than I did, "Hum, no; I saw that you were gone so I went to bring you breakfast. Was there some kind of natural disaster?" Thomas asks with innocence in his voice.

"You could say that! We are all over the internet in our skivvies." I turn Joan's phone towards Thomas.

Thomas quickly sets the breakfast down on the counter and turns to look at me, grabbing for my hands. "Marguerite, I'm sorry. I can't believe this! I didn't think anyone would know I was here. I should have told you last night what I did for a living. I just didn't think it mattered."

"It doesn't matter. I just didn't expect to be on the internet in my panties!" I run my hand through the front of my hair and pull it.

"I'm sorry. I thought we were protected here. I would have never intentionally hurt you." Thomas sits down on the sofa next to Joan. "Can I please see your phone?"

Joan gladly hands it over.

Thomas begins to swipe through page after page. Then he throws his head back. "I can't say 'sorry' enough, Marguerite. I just never thought…"

"That's what the flash was last night. It wasn't a storm coming! It was someone in the bushes taking pictures!" I plop myself down beside Joan; sandwiching her in between us.

Thomas rubs his forehead with his hand, "There might be more digging. You might get more attention than you bargained for, and for that I'm sorry. But I'm not sorry for last night. It was magical for me."

Joan tries to make herself smaller.

"It really meant something to me. *You* mean something to me. I don't want it to end. I want to continue to see you."

I can tell Thomas is conflicted.

He looks from me back to the phone. "I'm just so sorry this happened."

Frustrated, I blurt, "Me too! But this is just too much for me right now! It's just too complicated. My parents…!"

Thomas holds his forehead. "Please don't tell me I lost my shot because of some crazy person in the bushes. I think we really connected last night."

Joan starts to slide farther and farther off the couch onto the floor. When her bottom hits the floor, she crawls on all fours away from the couch and towards the kitchen.

"I see you, Joan." I finally realize she is still only wearing a t-shirt and panties.

She throws her hand back and shoos me away. In the kitchen she starts to eat the breakfast Thomas brought. I'm guessing she still hasn't realized that she's missing the bottom half of her outfit.

Thomas turns back to me and puts his hand on my shoulder, "Marguerite, I really am sorry. Please accept my apology."

There's another knock at the door. Joan hesitates to answer it but walks over and slowly cracks open the door. Joan stands in the door for a sec, long enough that I begin to crane my head to see who's there. She opens the door a little wider and Will steps in. She quickly shuts the door behind him.

Will stands frozen in the middle of the entryway trying to piece everything together. Joan, still standing there in her panties, I'm dressed for dinner, and a man is sitting on the couch.

Joan grabs him by the hand and walks him into the doorway to her room. "What are you doing here, Will?"

"That's what you ask? What I'm doing here? What are you doing here? Why is Thomas Blaine on the couch? Where are your pants?" Will is firing off questions in rapid secession.

"Do you know him?" Joan asks, sounding surprised.

"Of course, I don't know him, but he was in that mini-series, *Analog*, last year. It was on Netflix." Will says. "So... what's he doing here?"

Joan tries to fill Will in, as Will's eyes dart back and forth from Joan's missing pants to Thomas. The atmosphere is thick, I could cut it with a knife.

I hear them whispering but can't make it out. My mind is spinning from having my most intimate moment photographed and put on the internet for all the world to see. I glance back at Joan and she is smiling at Will as if she has completely forgotten all about me and Thomas. He beams at her as if she's the only person in the room.

Joan beams back at Will, "Want to get out of here?"

"Yes, I think we should. Let's go down and have breakfast. Maybe these two lovebirds need some time to sort things out," Will says as he watches Joan walk pant-less into her room.

Joan throws on a pair of jeans and gives her teeth a quick brush.

"Hey, Mar, we are going to go down and have breakfast. See you in a bit," Joan says, giving me a wave as she walks out the door.

"Yeah, okay. See you in a bit. Hi, Will." I give him a slight wave.

I figured that Joan told him and I am mortified. I've had my first one-night-stand and it's plastered all over the internet for the world to see. I guess that's what I get.

"Marguerite, I don't want to leave, but I have to go back to my room and try to figure some stuff out. Plus, I need to tell Winston there is someone here selling our pictures. I'd do it here, but I left my phone back in my room. Do you want to come with me?" I can appreciate how Thomas is handling this, but I need some time to think.

I shake my head, "I better stay here and try to wrap my head around this. I think I better call my parents before they hear it from someone else. Oh, gosh! How am I going to tell my Dad? Thomas, please just go. I can't do this right now," I'm about to cry. My bottom eyelashes are like dams that are about to crack and overflow.

Thomas reaches his arms around me and hugs me tight. He releases his grip a little and leans back to look at me. His fingers trace my ear, brushing my hair behind it. He runs his thumb across my cheekbone. "Listen, please don't let this change what happened between us last night. It was meaningful to me."

I shake my head and swallow hard. We both stand up and walk to the door.

Thomas turns to look at me one last time. He starts to say something but stops himself. He manages to whisper, "Sorry."

I can tell he is torn. My heart sinks as I shut the door behind him. I rest my forehead on the back of the door, and whisper, "Me too."

My phone buzzes in my pocket. I pull it out and slide my finger over it. "Hello."

"You slept with Thomas Blaine?" Comes a yell from the other end of the line.

"Oh, hi, Marie." I walk back to my room, face-plant onto the bed, and roll the covers over me. "Yes, I did. I didn't know he was a famous actor before I did. God, could this get any worse?"

"You don't remember that cheesy movie we saw on Amazon Prime last year? The one about the prince meeting the tutor and falling in love...? Remember they get married and now she's the princess. Her dad was a janitor..." Marie trails off, waiting for my brain to click.

"Oh, you're right! I do remember that now. I just didn't make the connection." Another wave of panic rushes over me, "OH MY GOSH! How did I miss that? What a royal fuck up!"

"I mean would you have really changed anything, Mar, if you knew? You like him, right? You weren't sleeping with him because he is famous. Think about the price he has to pay. Being famous must be cool but having to protect yourself all the time must be exhausting."

Marie is right. I don't think I would have thought about any precautions. I might have…who am I kidding? I would have still slept with him. I mean, I like him, I don't care that he is famous.

"I really like him, Marie. It felt like there was a real connection, but I can't have something complicated, right now. I mean, I have to get Joan through this. I can't have baggage," I say, feeling a little sad.

I can hear Marie breathing on the other end of the line. I know she's trying to think of something to say. "Mar, I mean, think about it. He didn't do this to you. He had it done to him also. It's not like having your private moments being splashed all over the internet ever feels normal. I bet he feels very intruded on, also. Cut the guy a break. Plus, don't give me this bullshit that you have to get Joan through this, she's a big girl."

"You're right, but I just can't right now," I say.

There's silence on the line.

"You can't or you don't want to? Stop making excuses." Marie has a way of cutting through the bullshit and getting straight to the point. "So, what are you going to do?"

"I'm just going to leave. We are headed to Texas next. Maybe some time at home will help me sort things out. It always helps to be home for a bit."

I try to change the subject; it seems like months since I've actually talked to Marie. "How have you been? Sorry I haven't checked in about the shop. I know you are more than capable."

"Oh, all good here. Don't worry about anything," Marie says, reassuring me. That's one of the reasons I decided to go into business with her. I never have to worry about her going off the deep end. If there's a problem, Marie just figures it out.

"Thanks, Marie." I breathe a sigh of relief. "Thanks for everything," I say as I gently hang up the phone.

I lie under the blankets for a few minutes staring up at the stitching on the comforter. I just want to hide here for the rest of the day. I mean, I could. I could hide here for years. I could become a hermit. Turn into a Howard Hughes of sorts, minus the growing my fingernails out and peeing in jars. I have to pull myself together. Joan and I should be moving on. At least, that was the plan before Will showed up out of the blue.

I turn on the shower as I hear Joan slide the key into the door. Mr. Lee gives a quick bark but must have realized it's only Joan. I step in the shower and let the water run over my face as I get lost in a daydream. Last night was amazing. He is so different from anyone I've ever met. He's so caring. So, open. Except he didn't tell me about the whole famous thing. I wrestle with myself for a couple of minutes. Why would he tell me? Maybe it's hard to find someone that likes him for him. I can see that.

I step out of the shower with my temper cooled and a little more clarity. I quickly pull on a plain, gray t-shirt and jeans and walk out into the living room. Joan and Will are sitting on the couch, they both go completely silent as I sit down next to them.

"Hey, Mar…" Joan hesitates, "I called Mom and Dad. They know. I didn't go into too many details, but they are okay with it. They are just worried about you."

"Thanks, Joan. I was trying to figure out a way to tell Dad that I had a one-night-stand and it was all caught on film." I bury my face in my hands. "Gosh! This is so fucked up!" I yell, finally breaking.

"I saw Thomas slip through the restaurant while we were down there. He looked like he was sad," Joan says, filling me in.

I change the subject. "So, what do you want to do today? Want to get on down the road?" I glance at Will, waiting to see if he has anything to add, hoping he will fill me in on why he's here. He doesn't.

"What's going on, Will?" I ask, trying not to sound rude.

"Anna called me last night and I thought it was serendipitous that you guys were here and with someone I know," Will says, smiling at Joan.

I look at Joan, confused.

Joan notices so she adds, "Will flew in last night to surprise me. Remember he and Anna know each other from culinary school?"

I'm still confused, "Anna...?"

"Anna, remember...? Winston's girlfriend, the chef," Joan says, prodding me along.

"Oh, yes. Okay. Now it makes more sense." I look down at my feet.

"Hey, we were talking, and we can move hotels if you feel more comfortable. Or we can do anything you want," Joan says, rubbing my knee.

What does she mean, 'we?' What sort of 'we' is she talking about? Why would they be talking and making decisions? I just want to disappear, but I know very well that Joan needs me. Gosh, or maybe I need her? I'm here to help Joan, not worry about my little fiasco. I repeat in my head: I am here to help Joan.

"Let's go do that big swing off the side of the mountain," I say out loud. I'm feeling risky. I need something to get my mind off of Thomas. I need something to get my mind off the whole naked pictures. I pull my phone out one more time and sit it on my knees as I swipe through the pictures. Well, if I'm seriously trying to find the silver lining, he does look super hot lying on top of me.

I'm so humiliated that I can't even let myself go there. I lock my phone. "Let's go!" I say, shoving it in my pocket.

"Yea, cool! Let's go." Joan agrees easily. I know she's just agreeing because she wants to please me. Normally, I would get major push back. Joan is the least adventurous of the both of us. Matter of fact, Joan hates heights. Scratch that, Joan is petrified of heights. She was practically on the floorboard driving into Estes Park. I was trying to enjoy the mountains and the view. Anytime I would say anything to her or point anything out she would start screaming. After a while I would just do it to scare her. I mean, if she was going to make it miserable for me, I was going to make it miserable for her.

I'd say, "Oh, look at that cabin way over there on top of that mountain. Who would ever live up that high?"

Joan would grip the side of the seat and yell, "Keep your eyes on the road, Stupid! We are going to die!"

I'd just shake my head and laugh. Mind you, we were nowhere close to the edge of the cliff. I think she was just scared because there wasn't a guardrail. I told her cars just don't fall off cliffs, but she made me promise to drive ten miles an hour the whole time we were on the mountain. I had to pull over three times to let people pass. If she would have seen the pull off, she would have really flipped out. It was even closer to the edge. She looked hilarious siting in the passenger seat with her hoodie over her head, screaming: "We're gonna die."

I would have taken a picture if I weren't driving. Every once in a while, I'd let out a blood-curdling yell. Just to break up the boredom. I mean we were driving ten miles an hour for more than an hour. I had to do something to keep my mind occupied.

I smile at the memory, "Let's just stay one more night here. It's no big deal. Plus, I don't want to have to go check in somewhere else. Let's just go and have fun today. Is that okay?" I ask, looking at both Joan and Will.

Joan stands and grabs her bag, "I have to go call the gallery really quick before we go. Could you give me a minute?" Joan says, putting her phone up to her ear and walking into her bedroom.

Will and I awkwardly look at each other. "So, you really like Joan?" I ask. "I don't know that she's ready for anything. I mean, she just found out her husband was cheating on her two weeks ago." I examine Will.

"I know, I know. It might not be the right time, but I'm drawn to her. I want to be here for her. Even if it's just friends," Will says, reassuring me.

Joan walks out of the bedroom and gives Will a nod. I give Will a sharp sideways glance.

They have a secret. Joan has a secret she's not telling me. I know it, I can tell by her face. I don't like this; I don't like this, not one bit.

"We can go in my car. I rented a SUV. I don't think I'll fit in the back seat of the Mini," Will says, trying to gently make his point.

"Cooper," I snap, feeling a little overwhelmed. I instantly regret it. "Sorry, Will. This has all been a little overwhelming for me. Now you're here. And to be honest, it feels like you are intruding a little."

Joan stares at me. I've never been one to not say how I feel, but I've never been one to be a complete ass, either.

"I can leave. I didn't mean to intrude. I just thought it would be nice to see Joan again," Will says, sounding embarrassed.

Why do I keep digging? This is horrible. Now because I'm hurt, I've lashed out on a guy that has done nothing to me. I really just need to chill out.

"I'm sorry, Will. I didn't mean to snap." I look at him.

"It's okay, Mar. It's not every day that the whole world sees your private moments," Will says. He reaches around me and pulls me into his chest, like a big brother would, and I let him.

He's more understanding than I would have been right now. I got to give him credit for that. We sit like that for a moment. Joan places a couple of bowls of rations out for Mr. Lee. He is lazily resting on the couch. He lifts his head as I reach over and rub his ear. "You sleep, we'll be back later."

We walk towards Will's SUV. It's a nice black Jeep Cherokee with tinted windows. Will opens the passenger door for Joan, and she hops in. I don't really like someone opening the door for me. I know it's the polite thing to do, but it makes me feel awkward. I quickly hop in before he makes it to my door. I look up in shock. Thomas is sitting in the seat next to me.

He's Got Some Nerve

"Hi, Marguerite," Thomas says in a hushed voice.

"What are you doing here?" I'm immediately red hot at Joan. That's what she and Will were up to.

"I wanted to see you. I figured if this was going to be your last day here, I sure wasn't going to let some pictures get in the way of me spending it with you," Thomas says as he grabs my hand. "I mean, if it's okay with you."

I smile from ear to ear. It is about time I get over myself. It wasn't like he did this on purpose. I go through my pros and cons list. Pros: 1. I do really like him. 2. He's hot. 3. He can really get it on in the sack. 4. Chemistry. Cons: 1. People taking his picture all the time. 2. Lack of privacy. I mean, I can handle it, now that I know. The pros outweigh the cons. I curl my fingers tighter around his. He makes me feel calm, safe.

We ride in silence until Joan realizes that we are headed back on the same road that we rode in on. She starts to scoot down in her seat little by little.

Will notices. He turns and looks at her, "Are you okay, Joan?"

"Um-huh… I'm fine," Joan replies to Will.

I know she's completely freaked, and she's trying to keep her cool. That's the last thing you want to do. I mean, lose your cool at the guy you like. She continues to slide farther and farther down in the seat.

"Is the height bothering you, Joan? Would it help if you drove?" Will asks, trying to comfort her. Honestly, it's kinda like trying to pet a bear right now. Bless his heart; he doesn't know how close to death he is.

Joan nods her head, indicating that she would like to drive.

Not a good idea. I don't think being able to see the drop will do her any good. It would be better if she was wrapped in a tarp and shoved in the trunk.

On a straight stretch of the road, Will pulls off into a parking lot. It's a little cabin that sells jam, sandwiches and water. Who would have thought a store would be way up here? I saw it on the way in but didn't think it was a good idea to stop and prolong Joan's anxiety.

Joan crawls out of the passenger seat, pressing her back against the Jeep. As she makes it to the front of the Jeep, she turns to face it. She leans forward and presses her chest flat against the top of the hood as she slowly makes it around to the driver's side. She is completely freaked out even though we are nowhere close to a cliff.

Will gets out and watches her make her way to the driver's side. Once she is in, he takes her seat as the passenger. I lean into Thomas, "This ought to be good."

He gives my hand a squeeze.

Joan slides into the driver's seat and buckles her seat belt. She gives it a tug to make sure she is nice and buckled.

I bite my lip and squeeze my eyes shut to keep from laughing.

Will, looking a bit more nervous now, shoots me a glance. I just shake my head at him. This is the worst idea, ever.

Joan cranks the engine and puts the Jeep into gear. As the Jeep pops in gear, Joan lets out a yelp. The Jeep slowly rolls backwards as Joan is holding the steering wheel in a death grip.

Will clears his throat, "Joan, do you think it's a good idea to drive if you are that scared in the parking lot?"

Joan puts the Jeep into park and pulls the emergency brake, hard. At this rate we will never get to where we are going. But, I have to admit, I'm glad she put the Jeep in park.

"You're right," she slides out of the driver's seat. Her hand glides against the black slick metal of the Jeep as she makes it back around the front of it. She hugs it, pressing her head against the hood.

Thomas, Will, and I just stare in utter amazement. Will gets out and holds the door open for her.

She makes it to the side of the Jeep and around to the passenger's seat and gets back in.

I throw my jacket up to her, she quickly wraps it around her head.

"Okay, go, don't worry about me. I'll be fine. Just drive," she says in a muffled voice from under my hoodie. "I'm good, really."

I don't know if she's trying to convince herself or if she's trying to convince us. Will puts the Jeep back into drive and we continue to the giant swing. I Google where the swing is. I figure asking Will won't be a good idea. I don't want Joan to fixate on the distance. It's only five more miles from here. Thank goodness Joan didn't give Will the ten miles an hour limit.

We pull into the parking lot and Joan must have had some time to reflect. She hops out of the car and makes it around the front of the Jeep without holding on this time.

"I'll go get the tickets. Four?" Thomas asks.

I look at Joan, she holds four fingers up and says in a confidant voice, "Yes, four!"

I cringe at the thought of Joan up on the side of a mountain strapped into a swing.

Thomas gives me a kiss on the forehand and walks towards the ticket counter.

"Are you sure you're up for this?" I ask Joan. "I mean, you don't have to do this. Not for me."

"It will be good for me," Joan says, putting on a brave face.

I know that look. It's the same look she gave me as a kid when our dog died. She didn't want to cry, trying to hold strong for me.

I throw my arm around her and whisper in her ear, "We can say

I'm sick if you want to leave. I'll fake a bout of diarrhea."

"Nonsense, we are here now. Let's just do it," Joan rushes her words just to get them out.

Thomas comes back with four tickets and hands one to each of us. "Alright, who's first?"

Joan sits in the seat and her legs are visibly shaking.

One of the workers gives us the rundown on safety, then tugs hard on our safety belts. "All strapped in."

Will and Thomas are standing a few feet away looking a little rejected since Joan and I decided to go together. I reach my hand over to Joan; she grabs it tight.

I can hear the guy behind me, "On the count of three."

Joan turns to me, "I've been thinking..." I can tell she's trying to fill space and get her mind off of what's happening.

"One... two..." I hear the mechanism click and just like that my stomach floats up into my chest.

I don't know if Joan is scared or if she just feels free, but she yells from the top of her lungs, "I don't think I ever loved Frank!"

I turn to catch the look on Will's face as the swing swings us over a giant canyon. It's the most adrenaline-pumping ride I have ever been on. I know most people would say they felt like a bird flying, but that's some next level bullshit. It's only because they want to make it sound like a freeing experience. Not wanting to let on that they are scared witless.

I, on the other hand, would describe it more like being in the front seat of a car that's about to crash, just to realize that it's not crashing at all, and it's all just a dream. But then you also wet yourself... and just like that it's over.

We are getting cranked back in when I look over at Joan, "Did you really mean what you said about Frank?"

Joan looks at me, "I've been thinking about it for the last couple of days. I really don't think I actually loved him. I was just going along with, you know, what I thought was supposed to happen next?

I never really stopped to think if it was love or if I was in love."

"Oh, Joan…," I say with sadness in my voice. "Good thing you figured it out now, before children. Now you can get on with your life without Frank."

As we reach the top again Will and Thomas are just getting strapped in. Thomas looks over at me and gives me a thumbs up.

He cups his hands around his mouth and yells, "Was it amazing?"

I give him a wide grin and two big thumbs up. Not because of the ride, but for the breakthrough Joan just had. This changes everything.

"How do I know if I'm in love? How do I even know what love is?" Joan asks. It's more of a hypothetical question.

But I answer, "Gosh, Joan, I don't know what love is. I've never been in love. I guess when you know it you know it. Maybe we should ask Mom and Dad. They would probably have a better answer."

Just as Will and Thomas get unhooked, a guy with a camera walks up to me and snaps a picture ten inches from my face. Startled, I quickly jerk my head back.

"What's your relationship with Thomas Blaine? Is he your boyfriend? Has the notorious bachelor been taken off the market?" He hits me with a barrage of questions like he's firing a machine gun into the air.

I squint my eyes and hold my arm up to my face. My mouth drops open, I try to say something, anything. I'm standing a little in shock when Thomas puts an arm around me.

"This is my girlfriend. There's no crazy tabloid story here. We are just a normal couple on a normal vacation." His words come out more polite than I would have sounded. That is, if I could have said something in the first place.

I smile, not knowing what else to do. I tiptoe up and plant a kiss on his cheek for good measure. I have to confess; I do like the sound of 'girlfriend.' But we hardly know each other. How would his life and job in London mix with my life and job in San Francisco?

Thomas leans over and in a low tone whispers, "Sorry, Love. I didn't mean to presume...," he trails off. "I hope you don't mind. Sometimes if you make the story normal, it's more unappealing and it makes all this disappear." He waves his hand around at the photographer. "Instead of them splashing headlines like, 'One Night Stand in Colorado,' or 'Off the Market for One Night.' It's better if we give them a more normal story."

I deflate a little. He didn't mean the girlfriend thing at all.

"That's okay," I say.

To be honest, I kind of want to see where this thing goes. If he doesn't mind telling the whole world that I'm his girlfriend, then that means he isn't attached to anyone else, right?

He signs a couple of autographs and then he politely turns away.

I'm not sure I will ever get used to that. Even now, when I barely know him, I don't want to share him. I guess all this attention would be hard on a relationship; having women throw themselves at him all the time. I mean, if your boyfriend is hot, it could happen no matter what they do for a living.

"How was the swing?" I ask Thomas, sliding one arm around his waist.

"It was exhilarating, but not as exhilarating as last night," he growls in my ear.

It's like someone set me on fire. My cheeks turn red hot, as he pulls me in closer and kisses me. A few flashes go off, and he turns me away from them and pulls me in for a deeper kiss. I've never been one for excessive PDA. I pull away and plant my face into his chest, mainly to hide my blushing face. My whole body tingles. I swear the hair on my legs just grew half an inch. He smells fantastic. Like blood oranges and summertime.

"Want to go?" Joan looks at me, searching my face for my real answer instead of what comes out of my mouth.

She knows me all too well. I hesitate; I'm not really comfortable with people walking around snapping pictures of us, but I guess I could make the best of it. If this is the price I have to pay to be with Thomas, then I guess it's something I can deal with. At least for now while I'm figuring out if I like him or not... if this is something or not.

"No, let's do what we are going to do," I say. Besides, I'm still not ready to get back in the car with Joan and her craziness.

I catch Will still smiling at Joan from ear to ear. It's kind of creeping me out. Poor guy heard what Joan yelled and now is in some sort of euphoric state. I can tell he is ramping himself up to ask Joan something. I look away because it feels like I'm in the middle of a private moment Joan has no idea is happening.

"There's a gondola that you can take across the canyon. On the other side is a cliff side restaurant." Will finally gets his question out, "Can your heart handle a gondola ride?"

The better question is, can we all handle Joan on a gondola ride? A few seconds pass before Joan gets the courage to answer. I'm guessing it's taking everything in her to say 'yes.' The swing probably took everything she had today.

Thomas intertwines his fingers with mine. His hands are smooth, strong, and make my hands feel tiny.

"If I can swing across the canyon strapped onto a chair, I think I can ride in a gondola. Plus, there's food on the other end...there is food at the other end, right?" Joan says, sounding more like she's trying to convince herself; or maybe she just sounds like that to me because I know her so well.

Will must have missed Joan's uncertainty because he runs off to buy the lift tickets without a moment's hesitation. We are all in for it now.

As we wait in line, I press my back against Thomas. This is everything I needed and didn't know. I'm not sure where this is going, but it feels good right now. The gondola comes to a swaying stop in front of us.

We silently decide to let Will and Joan have a car to themselves. It's mostly because I want to have a private second with Thomas without all the watching eyes, and, to be honest, I can't handle another meltdown by Joan. I hop in the gondola and Thomas sits next to me. The doors shut and we are finally alone. He turns to me and puts his hand on the back of my neck and pulls me into him. He kisses me long and deep, and I never want to be anywhere else except right here, right now, in this gondola with Thomas.

"I really like you, Marguerite." Thomas says looking straight into my eyes. I melt every time he does this, like I'm the only girl in the whole world. Like I'm the only person in the world.

"You don't really know me," I say, trying to sound level. I attempt to change the subject and withdraw myself from the gravitational pull he has over me. "So, have you always wanted to be an actor?" I ask, hoping that it doesn't sound like I'm drilling him.

Thomas gives me a quizzical look. Most of the time this would be called getting to know someone, but since he's famous it could easily get confused as an interview.

"Are you interviewing me?" Thomas asks with a cheeky grin on his face.

"You could say that." I smile. "I have to figure out if you deserve my time. I'm interviewing you for that boyfriend position you mentioned earlier." I nudge him with my shoulder, "So, have you always wanted to be an actor?"

Thomas looks down at my hand pressing into his, "As a kid, I wanted to be a cowboy. I still do; if this acting thing doesn't work out, you can find me in Texas being a cowboy."

I scoot back and sit a little straighter. He's got my attention. I study him for a second. "Why Texas?"

"All the best cowboys live in Texas," Thomas manages. He has this little boy look in his eyes.

I laugh, until I realize he's serious. I cut in, "Thomas did you know I was from Texas? I lived there my whole life until I moved to

California." Thomas looks at me like I just gave his six-year-old self a lollypop.

I guess it's the same for people that haven't lived in London. They make up this grand idea of it. Not all people in Texas are cowboys. Not all cowboys are Texans.

"Is your dad a cowboy?" Thomas asks.

"No, my dad owns a gas station," I say.

A smile stretches across my face thinking of my Dad sitting at the gas station with Tex.

"I'd like to meet him some day," Thomas says like it's totally normal to want to meet someone's dad this early in a relationship—if that's what we are calling this.

"Hold your horses, cowboy. Not so fast." I tap him on his knee, "Let's not get ahead of ourselves. Don't put your cart before your horse!"

What the hell is wrong with me? I'm using every horse reference I know. I just can't control myself. The gondola comes to a stop and I can see Joan smiling at me from the sidewalk. She's holding on to the rail for dear life. I can tell the gondola almost sent her over the edge but she's keeping it together. As I step off the gondola, Thomas grabs for my hand like he's been doing it his whole life.

"I made reservations for lunch," Thomas says, ushering us towards the restaurant.

I turn and shoot him a wide-eyed look, "When did you have time to make a reservation?" I have to admit, I like a man that thinks ahead and just takes care of things.

Thomas shrugs his shoulders and I see a look of embarrassment flash across his face. "I messaged my assistant and he called."

He has an assistant? What the hell is that about? The restaurant is called The Songbird. The entire front of it is made of glass from floor to ceiling. The hostess' eyes light up when she sees Thomas.

"Hi, reservations under Thomas," He points at her clipboard.

I black out every word but 'under Thomas.' My mind immediately steals a car and drives it straight into the ditch.

"Yes, right this way." The hostess walks us to a table in front of the large, glass windows. "Enjoy your meal," she says, straightening her back, popping her butt out as she walks away.

I want to karate kick her in the back. Gosh, this has to get old.

Thomas pulls a chair out for me. I sit down and begin to peer out the window. I wonder how high up we are. It must be over 10,000 feet. There's something so beautiful and peaceful being up this high.

"The gondola has stopped running!" Joan looks at me with alarm and stands up from her seat. "The gondola stopped running Mar!"

I crane my neck to see, "I'm sure it's nothing," I say, trying to reassure her.

Will reaches over and rubs her shoulder. How did our *Thelma and Louise* party of two end up becoming a party of four? I can't help but feel a little intruded on. I might as well enjoy it while it lasts, we are headed to Texas tomorrow. I'm pretty sure Dad needs rescuing by now. Mom has probably given him an earful about letting us just 'run off.' Not that he had a choice.

"Oh, look the gondola is running again, see?" I point out the window.

"It's only going down, no one is coming up," Joan says, sounding satisfied that somehow she's proved me wrong.

"Well, lucky for us, down is all we need. But, if gondolas are going down, they have to be coming up." I shoot Joan a look like I've just taken back control of the argument.

I look around. She's right, something is going on. The restaurant is almost completely empty. That's weird, it's lunchtime. Where is everyone?

Concerned, I tap Thomas on the thigh. God, his thighs... "Looks like something is going on with the gondola. Do you think we should head down?"

Thomas looks up from his menu. "I don't want people bothering you and taking your picture while you are eating. It seemed like you were uncomfortable earlier."

"You broke the gondola so that we could have alone time?" I ask, impressed.

"No, silly. I reserved the restaurant," Thomas says, rubbing my face with his thumb.

Who does that? Joan shoots me a look and raises an eyebrow.

Will gives Joan a look like he's in our private conversation, even though he's in the same boat as Thomas. I'm not sure if I like this. I mean, who rents out a restaurant for lunch unless it's someone's birthday, even then you don't get the restaurant. You only get a room and it's usually in the back. Not in the front…and most definitely not the whole place!

Laying It All Out

"Thomas..." I say slowly trying to think of the right words to say. "Thomas, you don't have to change anything for me. I get it, I get that people are going to follow you around. We don't even know what we are, what this is. We're just having fun, right?"

Thomas is staring at my mouth, watching the words come out. His eyes glint with hurt, "I don't know, Marguerite. I think this is something."

I stumble on my words, "I mean, how can it be? We don't even know each other?"

Oh, this is bad. I can feel this conversation going south. Joan and Will are sitting in silence. I wish I had never said anything. Why can't I just keep my big mouth shut? 'When someone does something nice for you, just smile and say "thank you." Now look what you've done.' I mentally argue with myself. I imagine an angel popping up on my right shoulder and a devil popping up on the other, like that *Tom and Jerry* cartoon I used to watch as a kid.

"I have to disagree," he says as he stares into my eyes.

"You're right, I'm sorry. I don't like to be told what to do," I say reaching over and grabbing his hand.

"Marguerite, I'm not telling you what to do. I'm just telling you that last night meant something to me and I wanted this time today, right now, to be special because I don't know when I'll get to see you again. I just didn't want it to be interrupted with people walking up to the table. That's all." Thomas puts his hands in the air sounding more exhausted and hurt.

I turn to Thomas, smile, and simply say, "Thank you." "You're impossible," he whispers under his breath.

"Yeah, I've been told," I force a laugh. I feel like a lump sitting here. Why did I say anything?

Thomas leans over and brushes my hair behind my ear, "I forgive you. Don't worry about it. It isn't like any of this is normal."

I'm not entirely all that hungry but I will make myself order something. I mean, he did rent out the whole place. The last thing I want to do is offend him more by not eating.

I try to lighten the mood; I lean in towards Joan. "Thomas wants to be a Texas cowboy. I mean, if the acting thing doesn't work out."

"Really? Have you ever been to Texas?" Joan asks, trying to sound even. "You should visit Texas sometime. It is everything outsiders say it is. You should ditch the acting gig and buy a horse and be a cowboy." Joan is ribbing him pretty hard.

"Does everyone drive a big truck covered in mud?" He's genuinely asking.

Joan nods her head, "Oh, yes, everyone!"

"Does everyone sit on their front porch with ice in their tea?" Thomas asks, sincerely curious.

I look up at Thomas and smile, "It's called 'iced tea,' and 'front porch sitting'." I try not to giggle. He's so cute. I can just picture him on the front porch sipping hot tea in 100-degree weather.

"Well then, I will just have to visit; I mean, if Marguerite ever invites me," Thomas says, looking straight at me for emphasis.

I just smile. This is much better than opening my mouth and sticking my foot in it. I really like him. I'm just not used to having a man be so forward. I know exactly what he's thinking. There's no guessing, no game playing.

"You know, I would be just as happy on the roof with a cup of soup, watching the planes fly over," I say, looking at Thomas. "It doesn't have to be this big hullabaloo all the time. We can just be normal."

"I like that, *The Jungle Book* is one of my favorites!" Thomas says with such enthusiasm in his voice, I almost forget that I have no idea what he's talking about.

I give him a strange look. It's like he changed the subject altogether.

"What does *The Jungle Book* have to do with anything?" I ask, looking confused.

"I thought you said, 'Baloo'." Thomas starts to sing "The Bare Necessities" from *The Jungle Book*.

I slap my forehead with my hand and laugh. He has the biggest grin on his face. He's just too adorable. Thomas' smile is infectious, I can't help but smile right back at him.

I look at Joan and shrug my shoulders; if you can't beat him, then join him. I love breaking into song. I have a song for every occasion in life. It's like my life is some kind of a running musical. If I could sing to communicate, I would. I'm really getting into the song when Joan stands up and excuses herself.

"Need to go to the bathroom...Mar?" Joan asks as she scoots out her chair. I don't, but I know this is code for 'you better get your butt up and go to the bathroom with me.'

I stand and give Thomas a flirty look, "I shall return!"

I'm punch drunk with musical happiness. I spin around, still feeling like I'm on cloud nine. I'm almost skipping to the bathroom when Joan shoots me an 'act cool' look. As we round the corner, she practically pulls me into the bathroom.

I'm still giggling, "What's wrong, Joan?"

Joan looks around me and shuts the door. "Nothing is wrong. I just thought we needed a meeting, a pause...What do you think about Thomas?"

Isn't it obvious what I think about Thomas?

Joan is holding me by my shoulders, "I think he's really sweet, but correct me if I'm wrong, you did just meet him last night. Right?"

I step back and lean against the sink. "It's a bit fast, but I'm just having fun. Who knows what's going to happen? We're leaving for Texas tomorrow. He's going back to London and he'll forget all about me. It's not like I'm falling for him. You know?"

I feel a strange tickle in the pit of my stomach. I can't quite place it.

"Yeah, but you also just slept with him, too. It seems like you guys have some major chemistry," Joan says, trying to make her point.

"I'm an adult. I've slept with guys before and haven't gotten all stage five clingy. You're the last person I expected a lecture from. Let's just get out there and live in the moment. You've spent your life doing the right thing and look where it got you." I can tell that stung, but there's one thing about Joan and me: we don't hold back.

"Are you suggesting we do the wrong thing?" Joan raises her eyebrows at me, giving me a devilish look. "You're right, I don't have to always do the right thing. I just have to do what's right for me," Joan says to me but then repeats it.

I know, she's telling herself more that she's telling me. "I don't always have to do the right thing; I just have to do what's right for me."

I extend my hand to her as we shake in agreement, then I pull her to me for a hug.

"Right, we don't always have to do the right thing. I mean, look at us. How lucky are we? We are traveling the country, we are free, and we are having fun. No rules!" I pull my head back and look at her.

"No, rules!" Joan shouts.

We both walk out of the bathroom like John Wayne who just won a gunfight. Thomas is turned, staring out the window with his long legs stretched out in front of him. He looks magnificent. Thomas has his hand pressed against his chest as he's leaning back and laughing about something Will is telling him. Will catches a glimpse of us and turns to look at Joan as we walk back, towards the table. I catch Thomas' eye as they both stand at the same time.

Honestly, I could get used to this.

Joan smiles at Will and sits down.

Thomas leans in and kisses my forehead. How can he be so passionate and also so sweet? He's a perfect combination of devil in bed and angel in public. His devil is only lightly veiled. At any moment he could show up and give my angel the boot.

The corner of his lips curls up and I know he knows exactly what I'm thinking, or at least knows that's exactly what I'm thinking. I sit down next to him; he holds my hand firmly.

Thomas is smiling from ear to ear. "Will was just telling me the funniest story about meeting you guys in Cannes." He isn't even trying to control his laughter. "Did you guys end up having to pay for the trike?"

"Not exactly," I chime in. "Our dad got the bill for that one." I shake my head, thinking about Joan's face with all the dirt between her teeth.

"Have you made your decision about lunch?" He squeezes my hand then gently runs his thumb over my fingers.

I feel a flutter in my stomach. "Umm...I think I'll have the Avocado salad."

I look deeper into my menu trying to hide the fact that I'm blushing. I've never felt this way about someone just simply holding my hand. I almost feel like I should at least hide our hands under the table. I'm trying hard to only have clean thoughts in the bubble above my head. I imagine a construction worker planting down a sign in the imaginary grass of my mind. 'CLEAN THOUGHTS ONLY, MAR!'

I'm concentrating hard; green grass, *Tom and Jerry* cartoons, Tom in the green grass...his strong arms wrapped around me, and springy blond hair. His mouth and the dusting of freckles across his arms... his hands pressing into mine. Well, that went in the gutter fast.

"Earth to Mar...hello? Is that all you're going to order?" Joan is kicking me under the table.

I snap my head up and notice the waiter standing at the table holding out his notepad. I didn't even notice he walked up.

I slap my menu shut, "Oh, yes! Sorry," I say as I hand the menu back to the waiter. My face flushes bright red. I can tell because I can feel my ears burning.

Thomas reaches his hand over and brushes the hair back around my ear, "Are you okay?"

I can physically feel my heart pounding in my chest. "Yep, good!" I manage to squeak.

He knows darn well how I'm feeling and exactly what I'm thinking. I think everyone at the table now knows what I'm thinking. My red-hot ear is exposed. My body starts to shake and I wonder if anyone can see it, or if it's more of a quiver that feels bigger than it is.

I scoot out my chair, "I'll be right back."

I excuse myself to the bathroom. I have to pull myself together. What the hell is happening? Maybe I'm sick. I must have caught something. I lean over the sink, grabbing the edge, when the bathroom door creaks open. I look up. Thomas is standing just inside the bathroom doorway.

"Are you okay, Love?" he asks as he leans down, looking at my face.

My stomach gives a lurch. What is this feeling? It's him. I'm not sick. He's making me feel like this. It feels like flying with cement shoes. My whole body is stingy.

"Yes, I thought maybe I was sick but I'm not," I say, shrugging my shoulders a little.

Thomas begins rubbing them, pulling my hair back.

"Good, I was hoping you were alright," he says in a rushed voice.

He wraps his hand around the back of my neck and presses his mouth against mine. Without moving his lips from mine he whispers; "I apologize, I couldn't wait one minute longer. I need you."

An image of us on the bathroom floor flashes through my head. That will never work. Plus, that's extremely disgusting. I want him too, just not here. I grab him by the shoulder and push him back gently.

"I want you too, but here isn't the place," I whisper.

His mouth is hot on mine again. I'm struggling to slow my breath. I give in a little and kiss him deeper this time. I want this. I reach down and unbutton his jeans, releasing the pressure pressing straining against them.

He reaches his hands into my jeans and pulls them down as I shake them off my feet. He lifts me up and presses me against the wall. Who knew? The floor doesn't have to be an option.

Every cell inside me is exploding. The pit in my stomach is burning now. My whole body is shaking as I throw my head forward and muffle any noise into the side of his neck.

Thomas holds me pressed against the wall for the next couple of minutes as we erupt in laughter.

"You're amazing," he whispers as his lips brush past my ear.

My body feels like molten lava, "No, you're amazing. We better get back out to the table," I say, pulling on my jeans.

Thomas glances at his watch, "We've only been gone for seven minutes."

"Seven minutes in heaven," I smirk as I pull my hair back into a nice ponytail and reapply my lipstick.

Thomas is watching me in the mirror. He has this wide-eye innocence about him. I don't know how it's possible that he could pull off hot-sex and cute-puppy-adorable, but he does, and he does it well. Thomas runs his hands through his hair, and it stands straight up. His hair is naturally curly, but he must use some major product to try and keep it in place.

I look up at his hair and giggle, "Your hair is standing straight up!"

Looking a little frustrated, he runs his hand in it a few times more, "Is this better?"

The more he does, the wilder it gets. I put my hand over my mouth and try not to laugh, "It's getting worse!"

Thomas glances in the mirror and raises an eyebrow, "Bloody hell, sit down!" he's forcefully trying to make it lay down.

That makes me giggle even more.

Finally, he just gives up, "Well...I guess there's no explaining that."

I make a mental note not to pull his hair if we are in public. I grab him by the hand and lead him back to our table. His hair is beginning to look back to normal except for one tiny, springy curl popping out the side of his head. I laugh as I reach up to smooth it down.

I slide back onto my chair. Joan and I lock eyes. She knits her eyebrows together then smiles at me.

"Feeling better?" she asks.

"Yes, Thomas was so much help." I give Joan a cheeky grin.

Thomas chokes on the water he is sipping. He tries hard to clear his throat. For heaven's sakes, I slap him on his back with my hand. He's turning bright red and I'm not sure if it's from choking or if it's from embarrassment.

"Maybe you need to go back to the bathroom?" Joan adds to make matters worse.

"Shush it!" I giggle as I continue to pat Thomas on the back.

There's no use hiding it. Thomas sits in silence for a couple of minutes; coughing every few seconds, still trying to clear his throat. I don't think it occurred to him that we would be found out. I'm not sure what he expected.

I try to redirect the focus and put the spotlight on someone else other than poor Thomas. "So, Will, what's happening in your world? I mean, it's been a whole two days since we've seen you. If I were a betting woman, I would bet that you like someone at this table." I lean my face forward to look right at him.

I raise my hand, pretending to hold up a magnifying glass over one eye. I examine Joan, "Very suspicious."

"You found me out," Will says, "I like Thomas."

I scratch my head, over exaggerating my words, "Sorry Will, Thomas is currently off the market," I say, giving a light laugh.

Thomas squeezes my hand and I feel warm and tingly all over.

Just as we finish our dessert the gondola starts running again. This time we decide to all ride down together. It's about a ten-minute ride from end to end. As we inch closer and closer to the bottom, I notice a small crowd gathering.

"What's happening down there?" I ask as I stretch my neck to see.

Thomas wraps his arm around my shoulder and pulls me closer, "Just brace yourself."

The gondola doors slide open and the flashes start to go off. Thomas reaches his hand out and helps me step off. I feel like a deer in headlights. Are they all here for him? Of course, they are all here for him. They wouldn't be here for us. Stupid question. I guess word travels fast. Thomas doesn't let go of my hand; instead he wraps his fingers around mine even tighter. He lifts his other hand into the air and gives a wave and a shy smile. I stand there as he signs a few autographs and helps a few people snap selfies. Maybe I don't like this, I want him all to myself. Is that selfish of me?

I feel someone pull my shirt from behind. It's Joan. Thank goodness! "Come here!" She says hastily.

I look around and see Will making big circles with his hands, gesturing me over to him. I have to admit, I'm a little bit stunned. I mindlessly walk towards Will. He's standing in front of an ice cream stand. "How about some ice cream, Mar?"

I stare at the many choices when a voice from behind me whispers in my ear, "It's a hard choice. Isn't it?"

I whirl around, "Thomas!" My face immediately flushes.

He plants a kiss right on the mouth. A few flashes go off. He gently puts his hand on my face and rubs my cheek with his thumb. "Thanks for being so understanding," he says as he slides his hand into mine.

I shrug my shoulders. Whatever hesitation I had earlier is gone. He's totally made up for it.

Joan chimes in, "We weren't really thinking about getting a second dessert." She winks at me.

I wasn't thinking about anything. Frankly, I was just standing there and if someone would have asked me what I wanted I would have been on autopilot and answered, 'Rocky Road, please.' I think we have exhausted this place. Maybe we should head back, but to be honest I don't know if my nerves can handle Joan's psychotic fear of driving down the mountain again.

"Hey, I have an idea," Will says, looking at Joan. "Do you mind?" He whispers in her ear.

I'm straining to hear. I'm watching Joan's facial expression closely. I can hear her say "four," as I squint my eyes, focusing to hear. Which is ridiculous. It's like turning down the radio in the car when you're lost. Will is messing with his phone, he begins tapping in numbers as he walks away. He presses a finger against one ear and holds the phone up to his other. He's nodding his head up and down. Whoever he is talking to, he must be agreeing. Will turns and points to Thomas, gesturing him over.

I turn to Joan, "What's going on?"

"Will thinks we should rent a house for a couple of days and not go back to Winston's because people know where Thomas is staying."

I shake my head and ponder this for a second. We don't have clothes, or a toothbrush. Honestly, I'm just going to start carrying a backpack with me. How many times are we going to be somewhere without anything? "Joan, we don't have anything with us. The only thing I have are those little toothbrush sticks I carry around in my purse," I say, feeling a little nervous.

I'm not ready for Thomas to see me in the rough. I'm sure we could easily fix this, but I'm feeling a bit bombarded. Maybe it's because it wasn't our idea. Maybe it's because Joan and I had a plan and now Will is here trying to change it. We were supposed to be leaving for Texas in the morning. Who is he to assume he could change our plans? It's not like I don't want to spend more time with Thomas. I tell myself that Will is trying to make the best of the situation. After all, he might not be changing our plans. We could still easily leave tomorrow. Will starts to walk back towards us; I make an effort to smile and keep myself even.

"I found a place we can rent for the night or for however long we want. If that's something you would like to do." He looks back and forth at us.

Thomas is standing next to him. "My schedule is clear, I'm in if you are," he says, looking at me with that boyish look in his eyes.

One look from him could easily convince me of anything. His hair is still springing about and he gives me a wide, cheeky grin. Damn it, I'm sold.

I nod my head, "Yes!" I jump a little and throw my arms around Thomas' neck.

Flashes go off like crazy around us. Jeez! That sounded a little more enthusiastic than I expected. They must think we are getting engaged.

A reporter looks back at the others, "She said yes!"

Someone shoves a microphone into Thomas' face. "What happened? What's the good news?"

Thomas gently pushes the microphone away, "We all woke up today to have another day, now please."

Paparazzi

Thomas puts his arm around my shoulders as we walk to the car. "Can we finish this conversation in the car?" he asks as the paparazzi casually follow behind us.

How are all these so-called paparazzi here? They're like ants. You never see ants, then you leave a crumb out and all of a sudden out of nowhere there are hundreds. Where did they come from? How did they know food was there? How long did they have to travel?

Will slides into the driver's seat not giving Joan the option to drive. Which I think is a marvelous idea. I throw my jacket at Joan, preparing her. She shoots me a mean look and sticks out her tongue.

"Okay, if we are going to stay out, we need to stop at a store. We're girls. We need things," I say, matter of fact. "Right Joan?"

Thomas raises his eyebrows and bites his bottom lip, "What sort of things?"

Joan shoots back dryly, "A toothbrush and toothpaste for one, and panties."

Thomas leans over to me and whispers, "You don't need panties."

"How far are we from the house?" I ask, tapping Will on the shoulder.

"About two hours. It's deep in the mountains. The distance isn't far, but we probably should drive slowly. We could stop at the store here. It's remote," he replies, thumbing through his phone.

"I found a few stores about six-miles from here. Let's head there, if that's good with you," Will says, putting in the address.

Will cranks the engine as Joan wraps the jacket around her head. At least she knows her limits.

I giggle as we slowly make our way down the road. Luckily, the road to the store is completely flat and not on the side of a mountain at all. Not even remotely close to what we drove in on. We must be in the town part. I give out a little yelp anyways; just to freak Joan out.

"Jeez, that's a long way down!" I say with extra urgency in my voice. Thomas squeezes my knee as Joan holds the jacket tighter around her head. For added pleasure I add, "I can't believe they'd make a road up here, especially without guardrails!"

Joan starts to nervously tap her foot on the floorboard. "Shut up, Stupid! I don't need the play by play!"

Will ruins the fun. He reaches over and lightly touches Joan's hand, "We aren't on the side of a cliff. Joan, look. I promise!"

Joan slowly unwraps the jacket from her head. She immediately throws her head back and laughs. "Have we been on this road the whole time?"

I slug Will on the arm. Even though I'm playing like I'm upset, I know where his intentions lie. He has been protective of Joan since day one. I love that about him. He's almost the exact opposite of Frank. Frank was nice but there was never any meat to him. With Will you can tell that he has so many layers to him. Frank was pretty one-dimensional, always keeping things on the surface. He would never dig deeper. You know, like if you're having a bad day and someone asks if you are okay and you say 'yes' but you really aren't? He would just take the 'okay' and move on. Even if he knew Joan wasn't okay.

Will finds a spot right in front of a store on the main street. I hop out as Thomas makes his way around the back of the Jeep.

"Should we split up, or should I go with you?" Thomas asks, slipping his hand in mine. His hand feels warm in mine and I want him to hold it forever.

"Come with us, it'll be fun!" I lean into him playfully. It

doesn't take much convincing. We walk into the first store. It's mostly touristy stuff, but I manage to grab a pair of shorts and a plain t-shirt. Thomas is talking to the girl at the counter. I stand still for a second admiring his form. I think to myself: 'I've seen him naked.' Oh, what a wonderful sight. Not only does he look amazing, he does things to me that I can't even begin to describe. Everything about him does it for me. I'm not sure how I feel about that. I think about how swept away Joan was by Frank in the beginning of it all and look how that turned out. I'm shutting this down right here right now. I can't be doing this. Whatever *this* is. I promise myself not to get too wrapped up too fast like Joan did.

Thomas turns and notices I'm staring at him; I duck down behind the clothes rack. I'm squatting down, pretending to tie my shoe, when I hear footsteps come my way. I can see his shadow on the floor. Crap! What did I expect? He definitely saw me; I don't know what I was thinking. I must look ridiculous.

"Marguerite, is everything okay? Are you spying on me?" Thomas squats down next to me.

I still love how he says my whole name.

He leans in and presses his forehead to mine, "I like you. You have nothing to worry about, Marguerite."

"I wasn't worried, I was just looking at your fabulous ass." I pretend to crane my neck to get a better look.

"Then why are you on the floor behind the rack?" Thomas playfully looks at my chest.

"Tying my shoe of course," I giggle.

He eyes me suspiciously. Thomas knits his brows together, "Your shoes don't have laces."

"What are we doing?" Joan asks as she squats down next to me.

"We're robbing the place!" I say, putting a finger in front of my mouth pretending to shush her.

Will walks up beside us, "Should I even ask what's happening right now?"

I look up, "Shush! We are robbing the place!"

Will's eyebrows shoot up.

"I'm kidding. Jeez, calm down," I laugh at him.

Will shakes his head and walks off. If he's going to pursue Joan, then he is going to need to loosen up. We are rarely serious. Well, I'm rarely serious. Joan is more serious than I am, but still rarely.

"Marguerite, I was asking the girl at the counter if there were any boutiques close by. She said there's one about three stores down. Would you rather go there?" Thomas asks, looking pretty proud of himself.

I love that he thought about that. At some point he's going to have something wrong with him, right?

We leave the store we're in without buying anything and find the shop the cashier told Thomas about. I walk into the boutique shop and everything is cute and lacy.

I turn to Joan, "How long are we staying? I need to know how much clothes I need to buy."

I'm thumbing through a small rack of lingerie.

Thomas is slowly moving clothes back and forth, mindlessly, on the rack in front of him. His chin is pointing down but his eyes are lifted, watching me look through each lacy piece. I show Joan a pair of pink panties, pretending not to notice Thomas looking at me.

Joan nods her head, "Those are good."

She winks. I notice Will walking our way, but he only gets about two feet from us when he quickly makes a U-turn and goes back the other way. He must have just realized what we were looking at. Joan puts a hand over her mouth to muffle her giggle. Poor Will, we really aren't trying to put him through it.

I look back at Joan, "You haven't answered me. How long are we staying?"

"How long do you want to stay?" she drags out her words.

"A day?" It comes out more like a question. I don't want to get hurt. I don't want to get too attached.

"Okay, a day it is. Just grab three days' worth of stuff, just in case," Joan says, sounding disappointed.

"Just in case of what?" I ask. I want her to say what she really means.

"Just in case you spill something on the first outfit, or just in case we stay longer, or just in case..." Joan says, a little irritated. "Jeez!"

"Don't get mad at me. If you want to stay longer just say it, Joan," I encourage her to confess.

Embarrassed, she finally confesses, "I'm sorry for being snappy. I just want to see where this Will thing goes."

"Joan don't hitch your wagon to the first horse that comes along," I say. I'm saying it to Joan but truthfully, I'm scolding myself.

Joan looks at me flummoxed. "You're the one who told me to have fun. That the best way to 'get over someone is to get under someone.' How can I have 'fun' alone?"

I wink at her, "If you don't know how to have 'fun' alone, I can explain it later."

"Jeez! You know what I mean! Besides, don't you want to spend as much time as you can with Thomas?" Joan asks, sounding curious.

Thomas walks up behind me, startling me, before I can finish my thought. God, I'm glad I didn't answer that with him behind me.

"Are you ready, ladies?" Thomas doesn't seem one bit embarrassed that we are still standing at a lingerie rack.

Will on the other hand, is circling like a shark about three racks away.

"Yep." I randomly grab a few more things off the rack in my size and walk to the counter.

Joan follows me, biting her lip. I can tell she wants my answer, but Thomas is standing too close for me to give it to her. The answer will have to wait. I slap my credit card down on the counter as Joan throws her clothes on top of mine.

"My husband cheated on me," Joan whispers in my ear.

I smile at Joan and whisper back, "I was poisoned by my big sister."

"My husband had his penis in another woman...," Joan says, knowing she's won the argument.

I nod my head at the girl at the counter to ring Joan's stuff up with mine and she gives us the biggest smile. She must work on commission. Since it isn't tourist season, this must be quite the payday.

"$463.27," she says as she picks up my card.

I turn to look at Thomas and survey the clothes in his hands. He has a handful of things in his arms. It only looks like a couple of blue shirts and a pair of jeans. Does he not want to stay more than one day? I don't know why I feel so hurt; I just said the same thing to Joan. Thomas puts his clothes down on the counter, rubbing his thigh against my bottom as he scoots past me. I'm sure he didn't mean it on purpose, but I have to admit, I love the way he always has to be touching me one way or the other.

"Will that be all, sir?" the salesgirl asks Thomas. She hesitates and holds her gaze a little too long. "Don't I know you?" she asks, staggering her words.

"I don't believe so," Thomas replies. This is just painful to watch.

"No, I do know you! Do you work at the ski lodge, the one by Glacier Park?" I can see her wheels turning.

"I'm not from here," Thomas looks up and smiles.

"No...Oh!" and like a bolt of lightning I can tell she's figured it out. "You were in that show on Netflix, *Dialog*", she stops ringing up his items for a second. "No, it's called *Analog*."

Will walks up behind Thomas and claps a hand on his back, "Chris, what's taking so long? We have a schedule. I'll take care of this; Mom needs you in the car."

Thomas turns and nods his head at Will. He tosses his credit card on the counter and walks away, leaving Will to handle it.

I like the way he never confirms nor denies who he is.

"You're such a Boy Scout," I whisper as he passes. He snatches my hand, pulling me along to follow him.

"What do you mean, 'Boy Scout'? He asks as he opens the car door for me and we both slide in.

"Boy Scout... like you always do the right thing. You're sweet and innocent," I flirt a little. "Are you always so good?"

"I'm a good boy when I need to be and a bad boy on other occasions," He says with a slight curl to his lip.

"What occasions would those be?" I breathe in his ear.

"I'll show you later," he says, pressing his lips to mine.

Joan and Will slide into the car. "That girl was convinced she knew you, but Will did a pretty good job trying to convince her you were his brother," Joan says, turning in her seat.

"Thanks mate, I don't mind people recognizing me. I just sometimes think that it's better to go unrecognized. So, thank you," Thomas says returning Will's clap on the back.

"Should we stop at the grocery store for food, or do we plan on coming back into town for dinner tonight?" Will shoots Joan a look.

I could tell it wasn't something she thought of.

"Let's just stop by the grocery store since we are here," Joan says, looking on her phone. "There's one about three miles from here."

Once they got to the grocery store, Joan and Will make quick work of the groceries while Thomas and I scroll through the Airbnb website. We are thirty-five miles from the house. It's a sweet little cabin tucked into the mountains. Just the type of place I imagine for a romantic getaway.

Joan is standing on the basket as Will pushes her back to the car. They have a whole cart full of stuff. I haven't seen her this happy in a long time.

"Having fun?" I ask as Joan hops back in the car.

I like *this* Joan. It doesn't seem like she's thinking about Frank at all. If she had any worries, you couldn't tell it by the look on her face. She smiles at me and nods as Will loads the groceries in the back of the Jeep.

We start heading toward the cabin. Joan is actually sitting in the front seat without my jacket wrapped around her head. I'm waiting. Any second now Joan is going to freak out. The flat part of town is short lived and we're on a cliff again. It doesn't have a guardrail, but I guess the tall trees are giving the illusion of it not being a cliff. It must be that. Why else would she not be in full meltdown mode?

As we drive deeper into the mountains, the trees begin to make a tunnel over the road. The leaves are so dense that I can only see little glints of sunlight. I roll down the window. It must be about to rain; I can smell the dirt and pine trees. Funny how a smell brings you back to a memory. It brings you straight back to a certain place and time. I will now always think of this drive when I smell rain. Like how the smell of tortillas will always remind me of my grandma and sitting on her red, front porch with my bare feet in the sun.

I tap Joan on the shoulder, "Hey, want to make a playlist for this drive?"

"Yea," Joan's eyes widen as she begins to shuffle through songs on her phone. Getting a music subscription has been one of the greatest things that could have happened to us. Besides, of course, developing boobs.

"I have an idea!" Joan points her finger in the air. "Let's each come up with a song. We could call it 'Cabin Tripping'." Joan is smiling like she just came up with the best idea ever.

I do have to admit, she did. Plus, this is a sneaky way for me to see what Thomas is like. You can tell a lot about someone from their choice of music. Music is a big part of my life. It always has been. I mean, if he loves techno it's not a deal breaker, but he better make up for it somewhere else.

"Okay, I have one!" I clap my hands, "Since it's about to rain I'm going old school. My song is, "I Love a Rainy Night" … the original Eddie Rabbit version."

Joan types in the song and adds it to our list.

The music starts and with every word, Thomas' smile widens on his face. "I've never heard this song; I quite like it. It's catchy."

Joan is scrolling through all the playlists on her phone. "I've got one, it's kind of like how I'm feeling right now. Let's stick with a theme, here."

The air is thick, and I can almost hear Will thinking. There's a moment of silence as the song starts. The first couple of notes play.

I yell from the backseat, "Oh, I know this! It's "I Can See Clearly Now" by Nash." I feel pretty proud of myself. Joan and I always try to stump each other with random songs. It's been a game of ours since we were teenagers. It's almost like whomever gets stumped the most doesn't know music as well as the other. This just put me ahead of her, at least in my mind. I reach up and tug her hair and write an imaginary check mark on my imaginary board, "That's one point for me!" I say, sounding smug.

"We aren't playing a game, Stupid," Joan says, sounding agitated.

"Oh, we are always playing a game." I give her hair an extra hard tug.

She knows we are always playing a game. She's just mad because I guessed the song so fast. I love this song. Who am I kidding? I love most songs. Well, until I don't. There is that one song by that group Goat or something. There's a reason she cut you off, buddy, and acted like you were nothing.

Thomas squeezes my hand and looks around the car. "I've got one, but you'll have to pull over, Mate."

Will looks confused but pulls to the side of the road.

"Okay, my choice is, 'Can't Take My Eyes Off of You'. I'm not sure who sings it." Thomas leans against my shoulder.

"I don't think I have that, but I can find it," Joan says, quickly opening her Amazon Music App. "…Found it!"

Thomas grabs my hand and pulls me out of the car. His warm arms wrap around me. I never noticed how much taller he is than me; he's at least a foot taller. If I am being honest, I guess it's hard to gauge when you are horizontal.

As we sway back and forth, my mind drifts off to the pond and the green grass, his hands, when Thomas begins to playfully sing.

I immediately feel my insides turn to putty. I forgot how well he can sing! Is there anything he can't do? I make a mental note: turns me to putty. He can start fires all over my body and put them out all at the same time. Not to mention he's absolutely adorable. He's hot and adorable all at the same time. How is that?

He spins me around; I throw my head back and laugh. We are dancing on the side of the road like a couple of crazy people. My heart gives a little start. I can't place this feeling. Maybe I have residual effects from the pills? I ignore it since I'm having so much fun. He isn't afraid to make a fool of himself—not that he is. I think he's wildly romantic. He wears his heart on his sleeve. I can't complain; I love that about him.

Will jumps out of the car and pulls Joan with him. She doesn't seem to notice how high we are. Will twirls her around and around. She seems so carefree. Take that Frank! As the song comes to an end, it begins to rain. The earth smells fresh and new, like dirt and freshly cut Christmas trees.

Joan looks at me and throws both shoulders up, "Guess we did a rain dance!"

I giggle as we run back to the safety of the Jeep.

Will reaches over and flips on the seat warmer for Joan. I like the way he just instinctively takes care of her; its second nature to him.

"Okay, who's next?" Joan turns to look at Will.

"I have one, 'Going Up the Country', I think it's by Canned

Heat," Will says.

Joan shakes her head, "I actually have it."

Will taps the steering wheel as he drives.

I snuggle into Thomas' shoulder. His skin smells like oranges and fresh linen. The feeling in the car is electric. There's a lot of talking without talking. Music can do that for you. Joan and I have this invisible frequency, it's hard to explain unless you have a tight bond with a sibling. Even though we aren't saying a word, we are speaking volumes.

Everyone's feelings are just hanging in the air, just ready to be picked; like if you slightly bump the tree all the apples would fall to the ground. I can tell Joan is beginning to feel a bit edgy. I clear my throat and she instantly knows what I'm thinking because she's feeling it too. Lord knows Joan obviously doesn't need any more complications right now. I mean, really, we took this road trip to get away from stupid men. Or should I say, one stupid man? I can sense her thinking… Sending me a S.O.S. I picture her brain shooting tiny flares up into the air. I can't imagine what she's going to pick. She seems a little distracted.

I push the back of her seat with my knee, "Pick something already."

Joan looks at Will and cracks a smile. I roll my eyes. Jeez, it better not be something cheesy like the Go-Go's. I mean I'll sing the hell out of some Go-Go's, just not feeling it right now.

"It doesn't have to be so complicated. Just pick something and go on," I say.

I have a feeling that isn't what Thomas did. To be quite honest, that's not what we normally do ourselves. Every playlist we have has a theme. After all, isn't that the whole function of a playlist? It's to get you to run, to relax, to get in the mood, or sing on a road trip? Or in this case, break the mood in the car.

"What is it already?" I say, sounding exhausted from the wait.

"Okay, okay…. 'Rapper's Delight'," she says quickly, cutting me off and denying me the ability to grab another imaginary point.

"Ah, I know this song," I clear my voice and put one hand over my mouth like I'm about to beat box. I snap my fingers on my other hand. Come on Joan, you know you want to join in."

She shakes her head at me. She's the one who picked the song after all. Will looks over at Joan and shrugs his shoulders, then joins in.

Joan's mouth drops open.

I look at Will, "Alright, Will!" I start to clap with more enthusiasm. I guess he isn't as conservative as I thought. Whoever knows every word of 'Rapper's Delight' can't be all that stiff. Never in a million years would I have thought he would know this song. He knows every single word, no less. We have our own little concert back and forth.

Will points to Thomas, "And next on the mic is my man named Tom. Come on Tom, sing that song."

Thomas seamlessly joins in.

I throw myself back against the seat and clap my hands over my eyes. This is too much. I don't know if I'm more impressed that Thomas knows this song, or that it is completely adorable that he's rapping with a British accent. All the resentment I had about Will intruding on our trip is disappearing every time I see Joan laugh. Now that I think about it, maybe I was being a bit selfish.

"OKAY, last song, the house is coming up soon," Joan says, holding up her phone, looking at the map. I'm proud of her; she might have no choice, she can't use that prehistoric map of hers if she doesn't have it, but I'm proud of her.

"'Never Be the Same', by Camila…" I start before anyone else has a chance to add a song.

Joan interrupts me, "Cabello! Got it!"

Just as the song comes to an end, Will begins to slow down. "There's supposed to be a driveway around here."

The Cabin

There's a small, gravel road with the cabin address only marked with a wooden post stuck in the ground. The sides of the driveway are overrun with wild berry bushes and wildflowers. If ever there was a perfect cabin, this would be it. We come to a stop at the end of the driveway. The cabin is adorable, it looks like a tiny gingerbread cabin. It's tan with a red door and roof. There are patches of wildflowers lining the cabin.

I slide out of my side of the Jeep, reach up and get a good stretch. Joan joins me.

I elbow her in the ribs, "Super cute, right?"

Thomas stands beside me and grabs my hand again. My stomach starts to do the wave, and my cheeks begin to tingle. The tingle goes all through my body down to the tips of my fingers. If I throw-up right now, I will never forgive myself. The feeling is kind of like... I stop and give it a thought. Remember when you were a kid and you got tricked into sticking your tongue to the end of a battery? Thanks, Joan. It feels kind of like that; a tiny shock all over my body. I wonder if he can feel it through my hands. I'm sure everything I'm feeling is invisible to everyone else. That is until I make it apparent by squirming around.

Thomas notices and squeezes my hand lightly three times.

That stops me in my tracks. I immediately bend down and pretend to get something out of my shoe to stop me from barfing all over the place. He's like a magnet: I feel strangely pulled to him. It's strange because I've only known him for forty-eight hours. I don't believe in that whole love at first sight BS. Maybe lust at first sight, that's obvious. I mean, I wasn't exactly putting up a fight last night.

I try to pull myself together and not hyperventilate. Or ridiculously stand up and shout, 'I love you, too.' I bite my lip and stand. "So, shall we take a look around?"

Joan wraps her arm around mine and walks me towards the house. "Pull yourself together, Smalls," She whispers.

I pretend to giggle in her ear, "Is it that obvious?"

Will hops in front of us and unlocks the door. "I found the key, they left it in the mailbox." He opens the door, "Welcome, ladies."

I survey the layout, two rooms and four of us. How is this going to work? I'd be completely happy to share a room with Thomas, but Joan and Will aren't exactly a thing.

"We'll take this room," I pull Joan towards a bedroom.

Will interjects, "Wait! You guys don't need to share. Thomas can stay in Mar's room, Joan can have her own, I'll just sleep here on the couch."

Thomas' head shoots up. "I think that's a grand idea, but I can take the couch since I'm the intruder here. I did stow away in your Jeep, Will."

Will nods his head, "No, Thomas. It's decided."

I raise my eyebrows at Joan. I give Thomas a small smile and quickly put my head down; trying to avoid being called out by my blushing cheeks. I walk into my room and close the door behind me. My heart is thumping hard in my chest. I plop my butt at the end of the bed and start to bounce up and down. I throw myself backwards on the bed when Joan cracks the door open and slides in. She catches me mid jump and startles me. I roll myself up in the comforter.

"What are you doing in there?" Joan asks, lying next to me on the bed.

I curl deeper into the blankets.

"Mar, what's going on with you? Are you feeling well?"

I give myself one more good twist in the blanket.

"That's it, come out of there before I pull you out." Joan pretends to act mad. She reaches under me and gives the blanket a good tug.

I know it's coming so I snatch the blanket around myself tighter.

"You can't stay in there all day! Just say it! What is happening with you?" Joan starts to shake the bed.

It squeaks as it shifts across the floor. It's one of those old brass beds that someone has painted white over the years. It has tiny, metal wheels on it. Who thought putting wheels on a bed in the first place was a good idea? And if it was such a good idea, then why don't beds still come with wheels? I can imagine getting it on and ending up on the completely other side of the room.

"I don't feel sick…well not in the contagious type of way," I say quietly under the blankets.

"Then what the hell is it?" Joan gives the blanket one more tug.

"My stomach feels like I'm on a roller coaster, my whole body is tingly, and my cheeks won't stop blushing. And all I want to do is kiss Thomas again. There I said it!" I feel a little embarrassed to admit it out loud.

"Is that all? You like Thomas and you can't keep your cool about it?" Joan says with a slight giggle in her voice. She gives a harder tug and unrolls me halfway.

I frantically kick my legs in the air, trying to get her to stop.

"You're acting like a big baby. Do you love him or something?" Joan keeps a steady hold on the blanket.

With that I stop moving completely. Do I love him? Impossible. I've only known him for forty-eight hours and some of those were spent sleeping. Joan struck a nerve, "Love him? I don't even know him!" I shriek.

Why I am so mad at the thought? Joan tugs my blanket harder. The blanket unravels and rolls me onto the floor. My body makes a loud thump on the hardwood.

"Hello!" I can hear Thomas' voice through the door.

The door handle squeaks as he turns it. I'm lying flat with my face pressed against the floor when I see two, new sets of feet walk into my room.

"Umm...Mar was stretching when she fell on the floor," Joan says as she shifts herself off the bed.

Last time I was on the floor like this it was Joan's fault. This makes two times I'm lying on the floor because of Joan. I'm writing this down so future grandchildren can know what a horrible sister she really is.

"Is she alright? Marguerite, are you alright?" Thomas asks as he makes it around the bed.

I see every step as he comes closer and closer. Like he is walking in slow motion. If I could have a superpower right now, I would wish for the power of invisibility. 'Please make me invisible,' I whisper to no one in particular.

"Are you doing okay, Dear?" Thomas says with concern in his voice.

I pop up to my feet, "Of course. I just rolled off the bed and wasn't expecting it. Those yoga stretches are tricky. I'm just going to change; I'll be out in a sec," I say, ushering Thomas out of my room.

Will follows suit, shooting Joan a look. He shakes his head. I give him a half wave and shut the door behind him.

"You are so stupid, acting like a baby!" Joan says, pressing her lips together.

"Joan, do you believe in love at first sight?" I manage to whisper.

"I'm the wrong person to ask. Before, I would have said it was possible, but I'm so messed up right now; I don't know what I believe. I would say lust at first sight. You can't truly love someone without knowing every layer of them."

I nod my head. She's right. This is stupid. I'm just really

attracted to him. That's it. I start to dig through my plastic bags and pull out the stringiest pair of panties. If it's just string, is it really considered panties? What makes panties, panties? I guess if its material wrapped around your bottom then these could be considered panties. They are a lovely shade of purple. I bought the matching bra, too.

"What do you think about these?" I swing the panties around my finger in the air.

"I think they wouldn't be hard to take off," Joan snickers as she turns to leave the room. She stops at the door and turns to look at me.

"What?" I stop twirling the panties in the air.

Joan reaches out for my hand, "Don't let my bad experience stop you from opening your heart. I think you love him, and I'm so glad I'm here to see my little sister fall in love." She turns and quietly steps out of my room.

I slowly sit back down at the edge of my bed. Do I love a guy I barely know? I pull on the purple panties and bra. Then I tug a white t-shirt on and some denim shorts. I walk out of the room. Thomas is sitting on the couch texting on his phone. I sit diagonal from him on an overstuffed chair.

"Hi, Love. Come sit here with me." Thomas says, patting the cushion next to him. "I was just texting Winnie to make arrangements to have Mr. Lee taken care of while we are gone."

Oh! Crap, I didn't even think of Lone-Lee. Some pet owner I am. "Thank you so much. I had totally forgotten about him!" I say in alarm.

"Don't worry, I talked to Joan a few minutes ago and we have it all set up. Winnie is going to keep him at his place while we are out," Thomas reassures me.

"Where is Joan by the way?" I listen for any sound coming from her room.

"She and Will went for a walk. I stayed back to wait for you."

Thomas stands up and reaches for my hand.

I happily grab for it. I study his hand in mine. My eyes travel up his arm. He has a sprinkle of freckles on his arm and his hair looks like strands of gold in the light. For a split second, I allow my mind to wonder. What if he was mine forever? What if I could be like this with him forever?

The grass is still moist with fresh rain; Thomas and I walk hand and hand down a small dirt path that opens to a clearing and a small pond. Thomas sits in the grass and pulls me down next to him. We both sit in silence. He is making tiny circles on my knee with his finger, it shoots electricity straight up my leg.

Joan and Will are sitting across the pond from us. I catch Joan's eye and she gives me a big wave. I respond, giving her a two-finger salute.

"So, you're from Texas? What really brings you to Colorado?" Thomas asks, stretching his legs around me.

I nervously cross my arms over my chest. "Well, it's kind of a long story... but kind of not. The short version of it is, Joan's husband cheated on her, so we are driving across the country. Soul searching."

"And the long version?" Thomas positions himself to face me.

"It's basically the same. Joan was planning to poison Frank, her husband, when she found out he was cheating on her. Instead, she accidentally poisoned me. Now we are driving across the country," I suppress the urge to say, 'running from the law'. "To soul search and give Frank time to move out of the house," I say, stumbling over my words.

Thomas sits in stone silence for a good minute. Crap! Have I said too much? He probably thinks I'm crazy. Crap, crap, crap.

"What? Say something!" I ask Thomas.

"Alright then," Thomas says, giving one solid nod.

'Alright then?' What does that mean? I can't tell if he thinks it's okay or if he is about to look for his exit. "Well.... Do you think I'm crazy?" I hesitantly ask, looking at Thomas.

"I don't think you're crazy, but your sister is a different story." He gives me a mischievous grin. He looks like the cat that just ate the canary. "He deserved it. I'm not sure what I would do if I found out someone was cheating on me. I mean, I wouldn't poison her, but I don't blame your sister. Betrayal makes you do crazy things. Does anyone know what she did?" Thomas asks, looking genuinely concerned.

"Only me and Will...and now you. No, my dad, also. We told him at the hospital, and if dad knows, that also means my mom knows. Frank might have figured it out, too." I'm telling him too much information. Mar just shut up. Stop talking. Kiss him, do anything, just stop talking.

"Why were you guys at the hospital?" Thomas asks with apprehension in his voice.

"Like I said, she poisoned me by accident. I drank the wine that had the sleeping pills in it. To be fair, she wasn't trying to kill him. She was just trying to knock him out. I drank the wine and passed out while I was talking to my dad. My mom thought I had Ojo. She rubbed an egg all over me to cure me..." I laugh at the thought.

"An Egg!" Thomas is laughing hard now. "Like a scrambled egg?"

I see his confusion, "No an egg out of the refrigerator. It's supposed to help take away evil spirits. They ended up calling the ambulance. I didn't find out about the sleeping pills until I woke up a few hours later," I say, sounding a little more relaxed.

"Ah, come on... you can't stop there. What did you do when you woke up?" Thomas reaches for my hands.

"Well, I just gave Joan a fist bump." I look down at my arm. The bruise from the IV is barely visible. It does seem like a million years ago. Now that I think of it, we do kind of sound crazy.

"Well, I'm glad you got poisoned. Remind me to thank your crazy sister. If it weren't for that and my sweet, Grandma June, we would have never met."

"June, June like the month," I remind him.

"Just think of all the things that had to happen to have our paths cross." Thomas looks into the air like a list is hanging there. "Not to mention, the coincidence that Anna knows Will. I saw you fall in that field. Then Winnie invited you for dinner, and now here we are."

I nod my head, "Funny how things work sometimes..."

Thomas begins to hum, "My Funny Valentine". "You will always be my Grandmother's favorite person. You made her day. Thank you," Thomas says, raising my hand to kiss it.

I look down and begin to blush. "Your Grandma is the sweetest. Not to mention your Grandpa scooting across the floor to get to her... it broke my heart, in a good way. They made my day," I say, remembering the mile-high feeling I had walking back to the car. My heart is floating at just the thought of them.

The sun is starting to set. From the corner of my eye I see Will waving us over. "We were thinking that we would head back to the cabin and I could start dinner," he says glancing at his watch.

When did they become, 'we'? I'm overacting. There is no 'we'. There's only Joan and me. I envision that old, black and white *Frankenstein* movie. I can almost see two bolts starting to protrude out of the side of my neck as I repeat in my head, 'Will good, Will Friend.' I just don't want Joan to get hurt again. Call me overprotective, but I'm looking out for both our interests. Plus, I don't want to get poisoned again. So, really, I'm looking out for my best interest.

I manage a smile, "Perfect."

Will sounds excited, "Give me about forty-five minutes, then come up for dinner." Cooking is where Will shines.

"Are you going to make bread again," I ask, thinking back to the loaf he made for us back in California.

"You liked the bread, huh?" Will rubs his chin, "I'll make something you will like just as well. How about that?"

"Oh, that sounds amazing." I turn to look at Thomas, and I can see a tiny smirk on his face.

My whole body stands to attention. I'll be left out here all alone with him. I'm not sure that's a good idea. I could get myself into real trouble out here.

The Interview

For heaven's sake, what's wrong with me? He's not a werewolf or something. It's not like he's going to eat me. On second thought, I wouldn't protest. This could be very dangerous since I can't seem to manage five minutes without thinking of him naked.

"We'll see you up at the cabin in forty-five minutes," I say, swallowing hard.

Thomas growls low and soft in my ear. His voice comes out almost like a soft purr, "What ever shall we do with all that time?" His lips brush my ear. Every tiny hair stands up straight. My mind immediately steals another car, jumps the curb and lands straight into the ditch.

Thomas interrupts my train of thought. "So, I was thinking.... Maybe we could get to know each other. Let's play twenty questions."

That's not at all what I was thinking. But I guess this is good, too.

"Do you mean where I try to guess who you are thinking of?" I ask, sounding confused.

Thomas shakes his head, "That would be too easy. You would be able to guess who I was thinking about every time. My answer would always be you." Thomas leans forward and pecks me on the lips.

My lips tingle. He's a charmer for sure. I can feel myself putting up walls around my heart. I imagine a tiny construction worker franticly hammering boards together.

"Okay, I'll go first so you can get the hang of it," Thomas says, leaning back on his elbows. "How many siblings do you have?"

"Just Joan," I say, pointing my thumb back down the path.

"How many brothers and sisters do you have?" I shoot back.

"I have two sisters, no brothers," Thomas says. "They both torture me relentlessly. You know what I do for a living, what is it that you do?" Thomas shifts himself on the grass.

How does he expect an answer when he is so close to my face? All I can think about is kissing him. He does this thing with is tongue when he is listening. He sticks the very tip of it out, sucks in his bottom lip, then smiles wide. It drives me crazy. I'm trying to think of every horrible thing I can think of, so as not to kiss him. Death, tsunamis, starving animals, famine…

"Marguerite…" Thomas rubs his index finger across my cheek. "Everything okay?"

"Ummm…yes, right. What do I do? I own a bakery in San Francisco with my best friend, Marie. I moved there to be closer to Joan. As you already know, I'm originally from Texas."

"Texas, okay, your turn." Thomas pulls me closer. "What do you want to know about me? Ask me anything. I'm an open book."

There are a million things I want to know about him. Like, why doesn't he have a girlfriend? Or does he have a girlfriend? How many people has he slept with? What made him pick acting? Where did he go to school? I can imagine little thought bubbles pop above my head rapidly like fireworks. I pick one question. So, you live in London?

"I'll pick up where we left off earlier. My main home is in London, but I frequent Los Angeles for auditions." Thomas says, laying me flat on the grass. He traces the lines of my lips with his fingers. Then traces my nose and each eyebrow.

Thomas stares deep into my eyes and curls his fingers in my hair, "I love your hair." He runs his thumb over my lips. "I love your lips, I love you…" He jerks his head back. He's just as surprised as I am. It's too late. He's said it.

I just lie there, not moving. We are both frozen. After a moment I sit up and run my hand through my hair. I'm waiting for him to take it back. What happens now? I shift in discomfort.

Thomas matches my body language. Then firmly grabs my face with both of his hands. I can tell he is searching for the words. It seems like we are suspended in time.

He disrupts my thoughts and, in a whisper, he says, "I really think I do..."

My eyes widen. What do I say to that? I can't say it back, no matter how I'm feeling. Two days is too soon to love someone. It's not like we are fourteen and in eighth grade.

"Marguerite, please say something. I don't need you to say it back. I didn't even know I was going to say it, myself. My mom always told me to wear my heart on my sleeve. If you love someone let them know. Don't wait. Although this was unexpected, it doesn't make it any less true." Thomas pulls me closer.

I lean into his chest and inhale deeply. Ah, oranges and everything good. I'm falling hard. How could this be? I barely know him. Maybe I'm just infatuated with him. Maybe I've dated so many jerks that I'm confused. I press my face harder into his chest, and just breathe him in.

Thomas begins, "Marguerite, you are everything good. You are smart, funny, and your heart... you have the best heart. I love being around you. Even though I didn't mean to say it, I love you and I won't apologize for that. We don't have to talk any more about it. We can just be here, right here, right now."

I pull myself up to look at Thomas, then lean over and kiss him full on the mouth. He runs his fingers through my hair and around my neck and pulls me deeper. Sirens are going off in my head as my whole body begins to tingle and a line of fire goes straight to the lower part of my body. I have an epiphany: this is how people spontaneously combust.

Thomas lays me down onto the grass. His eyes are questioning as he slowly unbuttons my shirt. I run my hands underneath his shirt and up his back. I can feel him pressing against my leg.

"We better stop," I say without pausing for more than a second. "Last time we did this outside my butt ended up all over TMZ the next day."

Thomas sits up and adjusts himself. "You're right. But there's no story here, just a boy with his girlfriend."

I like how Thomas tries to downplay it, or maybe that's what he really thinks of himself. Truth is, it's not just a boy with a girl. Every little thing in the media could be twisted. Maybe the way you overcome it is that you just don't care what's written. You find someone who doesn't care either. He's lost all privacy since he has become well-known. I feel a bit sad for him. Having a real relationship must be hard.

I try to console him, "I wish that were true, but people care what you are up to. I know it's not fair, but I guess it's the price you pay."

Thomas shrugs his shoulders. "It's more like this in America. It's not like this as much in England. I can still ride the tube without being hounded."

I think about that for a second, "So, in London you are freer to live like a normal person."

"Yes, for whatever normal is. I still live in the flat that I've lived in since moving to London after uni. It's just me, so I don't feel the need for a bigger place. I like it. I walk to the coffee shop, I run in Regent Park, I go to the theatre."

I watch the words come out of Thomas' mouth and lean in and kiss him. I press my forehead against his.

Thomas places a hand on each side of my face, making a makeshift blinder from the outside world. "It's only us. There is only us. That is all that matters to me."

I'm taken aback. I've never had anyone talk to me like this before. I feel a bit overwhelmed. I turn and press my back into Thomas, he wraps his arms around me. Can this moment last forever? Can we just sit here and forget about everything else? I don't want to think about responsibilities, him going back to London, or what is going to happen to Joan. I just want to sit here with his arms wrapped around me.

Thomas leans over, "I wish we could sit here forever." He glances at his watch, "But we better go back to the cabin. It's been close to an hour."

I pop up! "How inconsiderate of me! We better get back before Joan sends out a search party. I'll race you back!" I take off running before Thomas can answer.

Thomas is on my heels in no time. My short legs are doing double-time. He's striding next to me effortlessly. I hate that. I stick out my leg and pretend to try and trip him.

"I see you!" Thomas says lifting me up in his arms while continuing to jog.

I try to wiggle free, "Put me down, you giant!" I don't really want him to put me down. I could get used to traveling like this. This is actually a nice way to travel.

Thomas lowers me down to my feet and kisses me on my forehead. "If you weren't so cute, I wouldn't feel the need to carry you around."

If he wasn't so cute, I'd be offended.

Thomas opens the door. I walk in, in front of him. Joan gives me the once over. We are both out of breath, but I manage, "Sorry we're late. We lost track of time and ran all the way back to the cabin."

Will has made an impressive spread. I've never seen such a well put-together meal. This guy is growing on me. Everything smells so delicious.

Will starts, "I've made steak with a creamy polenta, and Mar—I made some fresh bread, had to forgo the yeast to make it work but I think I whipped up something you'll like." He sits the fresh bread in front of me.

I close my eyes and inhale the smell of the buttery crust, "I'm beginning to really like you, Will."

I shoot Joan a devilish grin, "You really ought to keep this guy around, Joan."

Thomas starts to set the table; I give him a quizzical look.

He shrugs, "I have two sisters and a Mom, if someone cooks the other one sets the table. That's the rule."

I kiss him on the cheek, "Oh, is it now?"

I can see the blood rush to Thomas' cheeks.

Joan is looking at me like she doesn't even know who I am. "Mar, could you help me with something in my room?"

"But we are about to eat..." I say, trying to avoid Joan; at least for the moment. I know she has a million questions, but I don't have answers for myself much less answers for her.

Joan's smile tightens into a line. She pulls out a chair and sits; sulking.

Will sits next to Joan, "The steaks are medium."

I reach for the bread. I'm craving carbs like crazy.

"We also have four bottles of Cote de Rhone. It's the best I could do," Will says, examining the bottle's label.

Thomas cuts into his steak, "So, I hear you went to the culinary school with Anna. Do you still live in California?"

"Yes, I still live in California. I own a restaurant there." Will puts a piece of steak into his mouth.

Thomas leans back in his chair and looks at me, "I want to know more about these bikes you two wrecked. Did you both wreck at the same time? Or did you wreck into each other?"

I correct him, "We were on one adult tricycle."

Thomas straightens in his chair and rubs his hands together, "This is going to be good. Two girls on one bike?"

"One adult tricycle," I correct him. "But we did not wreck! I got nervous about a truck coming too close... I veered off the road. I was able to keep the trike upright even when the wheels popped off. The only casualty was Joan's butt."

Will smiles at the memory, "I didn't know where to look. The whole bottom half of her dress was missing!"

Thomas raises his eyebrows at me, "And what were you wearing?"

My cheeks blush as I reach over and pinch a piece of bread off the loaf. "I was wearing everything I started the ride with."

Great now I can't think of anything but Thomas naked.

"Will was kind enough to stop and help us back to the bike shop." Joan looks at Will and smiles. "I don't think I ever said 'thank you', I mean, officially. So, thank you so much for your help."

Will gives Joan a sweet nod. "My pleasure."

"So, you've only known each other for a few days?" Thomas asks, a bit flummoxed. "I thought you knew each other longer."

"Nope, we are magnets for friendship." I shrug my shoulders.

"There's hope for me, after all." Thomas smiles as he makes a circle over my knee with his hand.

I stop and think for a second, "You're right. We met Will, then found Lone-Lee, and now you... like a magnet. A good magnet. Not a bad one that picks up sharp metal, screws, nails..." Hell, this is going downhill fast. Just shut up Mar. I give Thomas an awkward grin.

"Got it, not a magnet for picking up screws...or sharp objects." Thomas laughs.

I see the irony in it. Very funny... I just better sit here and shut up. It can only get worse if I try to add anything.

"Well at least I'm not a magnet for picking up screws," Joan winks at me.

I put my face in my hands.

Joan laughs, "Don't get so embarrassed, we all know that you and Thomas are getting it on; hell, the whole world does!"

"Thanks Joan...thanks for the reminder," I say, feeling my whole face light up like a Christmas tree. "Could we change the subject, please?"

Will clears his throat, "So, Thomas, do you have anything lined up next? Anything exciting?"

Thomas leans forward like he's about to sell state secrets, "I just read for a new movie that's starting to shoot in a couple of months. I don't know if I got it or not, though. It's an action movie."

"So, where is it filming?" I'm genuinely curious.

"Mostly in Los Angeles. I'm going back to London until then. I have a voice over for a cartoon. Then I'm back if I get the part," Thomas lays out his plans. "Los Angeles is only a forty-five-minute flight to San Francisco."

Wow! I can't believe he has already looked into that.

Joan starts, "I own an art gallery in Yountville. I'm an artist. Mar owns a bakery...."

Thomas breaks in, "And Will owns a restaurant. I can't say I own anything."

All of a sudden, I want to yell, 'You own my heart!' Crap where in the hell did that come from? I hop up instead and start to clear the table. Joan follows behind me with a handful of dishes. She puts the dishes down next to me, "What's the deal?"

"It's too soon to be in love with someone. Love is not a feeling, it's a commitment," I repeat something I read somewhere.

"Wow, look at the big brain on you," Joan says, sounding impressed. "You didn't answer my question."

There's a slight scratching noise on the kitchen door. I hold my tongue and look over my shoulder. Thomas might be coming in with some dishes. But nothing... I continue, "I definitely have never felt this way about anyone. But..."

There's another scratching noise outside the door. Joan quietly tip toes over to the door and swings it towards us. Thomas and Will go stiff as they stand there with their heads still pressed up to where the door was. They quickly walk back to the table and start to clear it.

"Not so fast, were you guys eavesdropping on us? Now think

about your answer, because it's obvious we know the truth," Joan scolds, putting her hand on her hip.

Thomas clears his throat, "I apologize. I was just concerned about Marguerite. It was completely wrong of me."

Joan points a finger at Thomas and shakes it back and forth, "If you want to know about Mar, just ask her."

"Mar, would you like to take a walk?" Thomas asks, holding out his hand.

I look at Joan.

"Go, I'll get the rest." She shoos me off with her hand.

Thomas grabs a blanket from the back of the couch as we walk by. My stomach immediately starts to flip. He wraps it over my shoulders.

We walk down the path towards the pond, Thomas turns to me, "Tell me, Marguerite. Are you feeling what I'm feeling? I just have to know if I'm crazy."

I suddenly get a lump in my throat, "I...I don't know how I feel. I know that I'm extremely attracted to you. But... is it something more? I don't think I know that. I don't think I know you well enough to say that," I say, trying to sound levelheaded without hurting his feelings. I don't want to say 'no' when it's a 'yes'. Why don't I just say 'yes'?

Thomas nods his head, "The last thing I thought I was ever going to say was 'I love you.' But I did. And I do. It's not like I ever planned this. I guess my body knew before I did. I guess what I'm saying is... I love you. I do. I don't know how. I just know that I do." Thomas begins to look up at the stars. "Do you think it's possible?"

I shrug my shoulders, "That's what I'm trying to figure out, myself. I don't think it's possible to love someone in only forty-eight hours. I've never heard of anyone falling in love that fast. Except for in the movies." I run my hands through the tall grass on the side of the path.

We reach the pond's edge, Thomas sits down. I sit down next to him and turn to look him straight in the eyes, "Thomas, what I do know is that I have never felt like this before. You make all my insides spark like little tiny sparklers..."

Thomas grabs the back of my head and pulls me closer as his mouth presses against mine. His hands are every which way in my hair. My whole body stands at attention.

He pulls back, "You were saying? I apologize for cutting you off. Your lips are just so perfect. I couldn't wait one second longer to kiss them."

I laugh, "Apology accepted. Just don't let it happen again."

"And if I do?" Thomas says with a twinkle in his eye.

"If you do, you'll be sent to your room," I tease.

"I'd like that. Would you be coming with me to my room? In which case, I don't apologize." Thomas begins to rub his nose gently against mine.

What is this guy doing to me?

Thomas lays back in the grass.

I lay next to him resting my head on his chest, "Could we just be here, right here, right now. I don't want to think about what this is, who you are, if this will work. I just want to be."

The world is completely silent. All I can hear is Thomas breathing and his strong heartbeat. As I look up at the stars, it's amazing how crystal clear the night sky is out here without any city lights. The rich smell of earth and pine trees drift through the air. There's a bullfrog croaking in the distance. I wonder if there is anyone else in the world tonight as confused as I am. As happy as I am... I don't know if this is love, but it feels so right. Thomas begins to stroke my hair and I'm trying hard not to doze off. But I do.

"Marguerite, Mar...wake up." Thomas is saying as he's shaking his arm underneath me. "We fell asleep."

I sit up and straighten my hair with my hands. I dig my phone out of my pocket and check the time, "It's only 10 o'clock."

"Oh, it felt a lot later than that," Thomas says shaking out the blanket.

As we walk back into the cabin, the lights are out. We try sneaking around the coffee table when I notice two empty wine bottles sitting on it. As I get closer to Joan's door, I hear her laugh. Thomas and I freeze.

I mouth to Thomas, "Is Will in there?"

Thomas shrugs his shoulders and whispers, "How would I know."

I knit my eyebrows together. I gently open my bedroom door and flip on the light.

I shut the door behind me, I ask Thomas, "Really! Do you think Will is in there?"

Thomas bites his lip. "My guess is that he is. Unless Joan is laughing by herself." He has a valid point. Thomas turns back towards the door.

I yelp in alarm, "Where are you going?"

"I need my things. I have to go back out to the living room," Thomas says as he opens my bedroom door. He quietly creeps out.

I follow close behind him; grabbing the back of his shirt so that I don't bump into anything. As we walk past Joan's door she laughs again.

Thomas and I pause to listen when we hear her say, "I love you, too."

The light turns on behind us and I scream, "Ahh!"

Joan flings opens her bedroom door; she looks around confused. "What happened, Mar?"

I glance around the room quickly, Will is standing behind us with his hand still on the light switch.

"Jiminy Cricket, Will, you scared me!" I say with my hand over my heart.

Joan slides her phone into her pocket. Jeez, she was on the

phone. "I just talked to Mom. She's happy that we are coming to visit."

Thomas sits on the couch and begins to ruffle up the pillows.

Joan narrows her eyes at me, "Okay then, goodnight." She turns and shuts her bedroom door behind her.

Thomas grabs his bag and walks back to my room without looking up.

I give Will a quick wave, "Night."

Will looks like the saddest guy in the world. Thomas just puts it all out there and Will is more of the silent type. I nod my head towards Joan's door indicating to Will to go and talk to Joan. I shut the bedroom door. I watch the light flicker as Will's shadow passes in front of my door towards Joan's room.

I turn and press my back against the door admiring Thomas standing in front of the sink in his white boxers. Could his body be more perfect? He's not super muscular, but he's fit. He leans over, washing his face; as he is drying it, he catches me admiring him. He stands up and turns around.

His hair in the front is springing in all different directions, "What? Do you like what you see?"

I raise my eyebrows up and down, "Maybe."

He raises a finger up in the air and motions me over. "Come here then."

Thomas lifts me up in his arms and slides into bed effortlessly. "You can like what you see, Marguerite. Just because I love you doesn't mean you have to love me."

I lift my face up to his and kiss him like it was the last time I would ever kiss him. Maybe it would be the last night I would spend with him like this. Maybe it is the last time I would kiss him like this...

As I pause, Thomas whispers, "I love you... How could I not with you kissing me like that?"

I reach up and put a finger over his mouth and shake my head. I roll him over and land on top of him. I slowly pull my shirt over my head and unhook my lacy purple bra, revealing my bare chest. Thomas takes a deep breath in. I slowly pull at the elastic on his boxers. He lifts his bottom up as I pull them down, past his knees. I lean forward and kiss him along his chest down to the inside of his thighs. Thomas' body jerks and I reach up and put one hand in his. He presses his head back into the pillows. As I slide my body over his, I can feel that he is ready. I reach up and take his earlobe in my mouth.

"Thomas…" I whisper in his ear.

Thomas turns his head slightly towards me. I lean in ever so softly and kiss his lips. Then press my head against his.

He wraps his hand around the back of my neck, "Only us, only here, only now."

"Angel of the Morning"

The morning light is shining through the curtains on Thomas face. The sun catches the gold in his hair. My eyes drift over his body. His eyelashes are long. His cheekbones are perfect. I reach over and trace the lines of his lips with my finger. The crisp, white sheets are wrinkled and pulled up to his chest. I scoot down and rest my head against his chest to listen to his heartbeat.

Thomas pulls me in closer to him and kisses the top of my head. "Are you awake?"

"Yes, I've been awake for a few minutes." I rub my face deeper into his chest. It still smells like oranges. "I was thinking of going for a run but didn't want to wake you."

"Go, I'll make breakfast," Thomas says as he stretches.

God, how could he possibly look so good? I can't imagine what I look like. I run my hand through my hair. My fingers get stuck in the back of my hair and I just leave them there and pretend like I'm resting on my arm.

"Your hand is stuck, isn't it?" Thomas asks, looking behind my head. "Lean forward, let me see."

I laugh and roll over. "It's not stuck, stuck. It's just a big rat's nest back there. And it's all your fault!"

Thomas slaps me on the bottom. "I think you had a lot to do with it too, Missy."

I get up, run a brush through my hair, and brush my teeth. I give a double tap on Joan's door as I walk by, but I don't dare do more than that just in case Will did make his way into Joan's room last night.

As I shut the cabin door behind me, Joan grabs it. "Hey," she whispers.

"Hey, yourself," I give her a once over.

"Where are you headed?" she eyes the shoes in my hand.

"I'm going running, why?" I ask, pulling on my shoes as I sit on the front, cement steps.

"Do you mind if I come?" Joan asks, glancing over her shoulder.

I can tell she needs to get something off her chest. "Yep, I'll wait here."

I shoo her back in the cabin to grab her things. I know Joan isn't a jogger so I rest in the knowledge that this will be a walk not a jog. It's just as well, we need to talk. I clap my hands together and blow on them. It's a little colder than I expected. Not that I could have done anything about it, I only bought a few things at the store. This trip is teaching me how to be outside of my comfort zone. We've been traveling around with the bare essentials and just when I thought I had what I needed, we decide to run off once again with nothing.

Joan slaps me on the top of the head as she steps off the steps beside me. "Okay, I'm ready!"

I begin to slow jog. To my surprise, Joan is keeping up right beside me. Without a word, I jog up along the path towards the pond. Joan follows, our minds are buzzing.

"This isn't what I planned at all," I start.

"That's because you weren't looking. It happens when you are happy with yourself," Joan says, huffing now and pausing to place her hands on her knees.

"For a skinny girl, you sure are out of shape," I say, rubbing her back. I don't dare mention the altitude. I look around and there is no sign of anyone but us.

"So, is there anything you want to tell me about last night?" I raise my eyebrows at Joan.

Joan leans up against a rock, "I slept with Will last night. I mean we slept. I didn't 'sleep' with him."

"Well, why the hell not?" I ask before I can catch myself.

"It was more of his choice than mine. I mean, I would have, but he ended up reading some ridiculous book about a man telling bear stories and I just fell asleep."

"You fell asleep because he bored you to death with nonsense," I giggle. "Cut ties now!"

"No, I actually fell asleep because I felt so comfortable." Joan looks into the distance deep in thought.

"I'm kidding, that's nice. Will seems like a really nice guy," I comfort Joan.

This whole trip was for her to get her mind off of Frank. I think it worked. She hasn't mentioned Frank in a couple of days. The last thing she said was she never loved him. Which is vastly different from where I thought her head was.

I lean against the rock next to her, "I think I'm having major feelings for Thomas. I don't think it's love, but I feel like I don't want him to go. Does that make any sense?" I kick the dirt in front of me.

"Mar, I know you better than anyone. I think you might love him, but you don't think it's possible. You think time only proves love and that's just not the case. Feelings prove love, not time," Joan says, beginning to kick dirt in line next to mine. "He's not asking you to do anything about it. So, there's no rush. Just wait it out until you know one way or the other. I don't understand the dilemma."

I look up, "There's not one, I guess. I'm just confused how he thinks he could love me when we don't know each other all that well. It's only been what, three days?"

"A lot has happened in those few days. It's like war: nothing brings you together like having your intimate moments splashed all over TMZ."

I throw my face in my hands. Jeez, those are always going to be out there. There's no hiding that we were together. Not that I want to hide it, but can you imagine thirty years from now if my kids come across those pictures? No use trying to tell my daughters about respectable sex. I hear a crunching sound and I look up to see Thomas running up the path. My heart gives a leap right out of my chest. I swallow hard.

"Hey, I was wondering where you ran off to. Breakfast is ready."

I turn my wrist and look at the time. "Jeez, it's been an hour, sorry!"

"No problem. I was just worried." Thomas tucks my hand under his arm. "I didn't know what you might want. I made bangers and mash. Will made eggs and some bread."

I shoot Joan a look. She reads my mind and smiles. She knows I'm laughing at the whole 'bangers' part. I don't dare ask what bangers and mash are. I guess I'll find out when I get there.

"Bangers and mash sound great!" I say, evenly. I'm picturing all kinds of sexual positions. I clear my throat thinking it would clear my mind of my thoughts.

Joan opens the door and the smell of fresh bread wafts out the door past me. Will is going to kill me with all the bread he makes. I love him but I hate him.

He looks up at Joan and pulls out a chair for her, "For the lady." He points to the chair where a spread of potatoes and sausage sit out in front of her. So, this is what bangers and mash is. I can't say I've had potatoes quite like this for breakfast, but it does look good. It's something a beer might go well with. Will slices the bread on a wooden cutting board and sits it in front of Joan. It smells divine.

I sit cross-legged next to Joan and Will sits on the other side of her. "What's on the agenda today?"

Joan looks at me and I stare back at her, willing her to answer so that I don't have to.

"Humm… we haven't thought that far, but I think we will leave in the morning. We are headed to see our parents in Texas," Joan says, waiting for me to show a sign one way or the other.

"Yes, I think that is a great idea. It would be good to see them before we move on."

Thomas' hand slides over mine, "Where is the next stop after that?"

"We are going to Louisiana then up the coast towards New York, then back across the states again to California." I point with my finger in the air like I'm tracing our route on the map.

Thomas begins cutting the sausage with a knife. I watch him closely. I love the way he picks up his fork. He holds it upside down with his index finger on the back of it. I try copying him but end up looking more like a caveman, so I return to using my fork like normal.

"The food is delicious. Thanks for breakfast," Joan interrupts everyone's silent thoughts. "I have to admit, I wasn't sure what bangers and mash were."

"I thought it was a sexual position, in which case I was all in," I laugh. If rolling eyes could be a language, Joan was fluent. I sink a little in my chair.

Will stands and starts stacking the dishes. "I think the sun has burned off the cold, do you want to go exploring the property or maybe go into town?"

Thomas shakes his head, "I think if we go into town it might get a bit crowded, but it's up to you. I'm game for anything."

He might be regretting he said that.

"Maybe the owners have some games around here?" I stand, open the closet door in the living room and rummage around. "Monopoly...chess...checkers. Hey, there are Nerf guns in here, a whole arsenal!" I begin pulling them out and lining them up on the floor. I nod my head at Joan. She instantly knows what I'm asking for.

She slyly walks over and pulls two plastic trash bags out from under the sink. Then nonchalantly walks over and hands me one.

We both casually start loading the guns in our bags.

Thomas stands to attention, "Bloody hell! Will! Get over here!" He picks up a gun, but Joan grabs it out of his hands just as fast as he is snatching them up, one by one. It's almost like he's just picking them up for her. He looks more and more confused every time Joan snatches one out of his hands.

Once my bag is full, I yell, "It's us against you." I throw my bag over my shoulder. "We'll meet you in the woods. We'll be building our bunker!"

Will and Thomas scramble for the remains of what we couldn't take. Which only happens to be one, large Nerf gun and two Nerf pistols. I see both their faces looking flustered as I shut the door behind us.

"Game on, boys," Joan yells.

I throw my head in the air to howl my battle cry. I catch a glimpse of Thomas standing on the porch in awe. Well, I don't know if he's actually in awe because he thinks I'm great or if he's in awe because he thinks I'm completely bat shit crazy. Either way; it's better for him to know now.

Joan and I run up the path to the clearing by the pond. I look for an area to set up our fort. I scan the trees when I notice a tree with a large, high branch=perfect for perching. I point up to the tree. This is one of my age-old tricks. When I was a kid we used to play 'war' in the woods next to our house. I would hide until everyone was out except one person. That made the battle fair. I tie my bag on my belt loop and climb up the tree. When I get my spot, I tie the bag around a small branch, securing my weapons. Joan runs into the woods and hides behind a large, pine tree that has fallen on its side.

I watch as Will and Thomas come sneaking along the border of the clearing. I hold still, quiet as a church mouse. They are about ten feet from Joan. Joan pops up from behind the log and shoots Thomas in the chest.

Will immediately shoots Joan on the shoulder. They are both

out. Will crouches down and scans the forest for me.

I hold my gun on him and follow him with it. As he gets about five feet from my tree, I shoot directly down, hitting him on the ear with a spongy bullet.

"Where is she?" he starts to wheel around.

I steady myself as I stand, holding on to the tree trunk. "There can be only one!" I drop my weapons down to the ground and climb down.

As I make it to the ground Joan reaches her hand out and gives me a fist bump. "Sacrifice for the bigger win. It's about the long game."

Thomas pulls out his phone and snaps a picture of us holding our weapons, basking in our win. "How in the world did you get up there?"

"I climbed, silly." I reach out and bop him on the nose.

Thomas shouts, "best two out of three!" and grabs a couple of our guns we left unattended. I didn't expect him to be so competitive, but in a cute way. We play two more rounds, and this time they knew my trick so I couldn't use it again. Will won once but Joan managed to break the tie and give us the final victory. The sun was well overhead at this point and we were all exhausted, lounging by the pond.

"So, what now?" Joan asks looking around the pond. What is there to do? It's not like it's very romantic with your sister sitting right next to you. Will seems to catch the drift when he chimes in, "Since it's your last night here, how about I make something special for dinner?"

I smile, "That sounds like a great idea." I hope in the back of my head that Will will end up making something amazing…like bread again.

"We'd have to head into town for some things but should be back in plenty of time to make supper," Will says, checking his watch.

"Why don't you give us a list? We can drive into town and pick up what you need since you will be doing all the work," Thomas offers, looking at me for approval.

I nod my head, "Yep, make a list. We'll go." Will agrees and we all head back to the cabin. We indulge in a small lunch because we want to save room for whatever amazing dinner Will is planning on whipping up.

As we get ready to leave, Will hands me the list and the keys to the Jeep. A thought occurs to me. Thomas and I will be completely alone for the first time since he told me that he loves me. I still don't know how I feel about it. I know what Joan said and what I'm feeling but it can't be love. Love doesn't work like that. Does it? I push those thoughts aside and focus on getting to the store. Bread is in my future and I don't want to keep it waiting.

I type in the address and place my phone in the cup holder. We pull out of the driveway and ride in silence for a few miles. Thomas reaches over and puts his hand on my knee. It feels like a line of fire goes up my leg, making everything in my body stand at attention. I wiggle in my seat to bring my focus back to the road. Even though we were together last night, I want him. His hand creeps up half an inch. I try hard to continue to focus. I keep my eyes straight ahead. I wonder if he knows his hand is inching up my thigh. Of course, he does. It feels like tiny fire ants are all over my body. My mind begins to wander off when I make a drastic move to break the invisible strings that are pulling me towards him. Everything in me wants everything he has to offer.

I clear my throat and smile at Thomas. "So, are you leaving Colorado when we leave tomorrow?" I tried avoiding that question, but it was either ask or pull over on the side of the road and rough him up—in a good way.

"I haven't thought about it. I need to get back to London but was keeping the next couple of days open so I could have options." A small curl breaks loose from the top of his head and my eyes drift up.

What kind of options? Was he talking about me? I don't dare ask. Instead I reach over and pat his curl down.

"It's standing up, isn't it?" Thomas runs his fingers through his hair, trying to flatten it down.

That's not the only thing standing, I avert my eyes as my cheeks flush.

"I wanted to talk to you about something. I don't want you to answer now, I just want you to think about it."

I pull over to the side of the road to give him my complete attention.

I turn in my seat as Thomas grabs both my hands. "I know this might sound completely crazy, but I would like you to come back to London with me."

My mind starts to spin. I'm glad I pulled over. Come back to London with him? What does that mean? How would that work? Confused stubbornness creeps into my brain. Who does he think he is? That I would just pick up and run off to London. Does he not remember? I own a bakery! I have a life, a family, here... I try to keep my face even. I'm not just going to uproot my life and shack up in London, despite how I'm feeling.

I can hear my mother's words in my ear, "Why would he buy the cow if he could get the milk for free?" I was taught that you don't just live with a man that you aren't married to. Not that I want to get married. Do I? Of course, I don't!

Finally, I manage, "How would that work, exactly?" I drag out my words. I'm not sure I want to know the answer. Depending on what comes out of his mouth could change everything. I'm mentally willing him to not say something stupid while my emotions are already running rampant.

"I would love for you to live with me. I mean, if you wanted to. We could do whatever you want though. We could move..." Thomas begins to scramble.

I can tell he is getting nervous. I didn't think he could ever get nervous. I mean, look at him. He could have anybody he wanted. And here he is fumbling over his words... for me.

I begin slowly, choosing my words carefully so that I don't hurt his feelings. "I have a life here. I just can't pick up and move halfway across the world. I mean, we barely know each other..."

I can see the hurt flash in his eyes.

I quickly follow it, "I really, really like you. That isn't it. I just don't know how all this would work. I have a business here. I've already off-loaded much of it onto Marie the last couple of weeks. What if I get there and we find that this was only a fling?"

Thomas interrupts me, "It's not a fling to me. I've said that. It may have started off casual, but I love you. When I said it, I meant it."

If there was ever a time to lay it all out there, this is it. I wince, "Thing is, I don't think love works like that. I think lust does. But love is a thick and thin kind of thing. Something you can't have unless you really know someone."

It's not like I'm not feeling it. I'm just worried that it's not real. I'm afraid to make a colossal mistake. Why can't we just try a long-distance relationship? Why do I have to move clear across the country?

"Are you saying you want to be exclusive? With all the other beautiful women swarming around?" I turn and press my back to the window to see Thomas more clearly.

Thomas leans over and kisses the very tip of my nose. "That's exactly what I'm saying. Dating a lot of women when I found the one just isn't my thing."

I rub Thomas' knee with my hand. "Could I think about this? I need time."

"No, no. Please take all the time you need," Thomas says, trying to calm my nerves but I can hear his words catch.

The hurt is easy to see, but I can't just run off and leave everything I know. No matter how I'm feeling. I turn back in my seat and crank the engine. I drive the next few miles on autopilot, lost in thought.

As we pull into the parking lot, I grab the list out of my pocket. "Are you ready to tackle this list? Will needs a lot of stuff I've never heard of."

Thomas grabs the list out of my hand and looks over it, "Can we just give it to someone and have them find it all for us?"

"You've got to be kidding me! What fun would that be?" I get out of the car and start walking towards the store. Thomas glides beside me, putting his hand in mine. It's like we've done this a thousand times.

Thomas grabs a basket as we walk into the store. "Want a ride?" he raises his eyebrows at me.

I smirk. "Do you mean in the basket?" I shake my head and laugh. Of course, I want a ride, but decide not to. I go down one aisle, then the next, making an effort to get everything on Will's list. I've lost Thomas somewhere in the store. I sent him for cocoa powder, but he's been gone for a good ten minutes.

I round the corner and distinctly hear Thomas' very distinct English accent. "What aisle is Cocoa powder on?"

I stop and listen. He sounds so cute when he's lost. Thomas comes around the corner and my whole face lights up. I feel like I have just been caught spying on him. He has his own basket now and a box of cocoa powder.

He smiles at me, looking so proud. "I found the cocoa powder!"

His basket is full of flowers. "I see that, and you found the flower section, too... Why do you have so many flowers?"

He must have at least four dozen roses and ten bundles of assorted flowers. "If this is the last night I'm ever going to see you, I want you to remember me. I want it to be special."

I reach up and grab his chin in my hand, "What? You think this is the last time I'm going to see you? Why would you think that?"

Thomas is looking like a lost puppy standing in the middle of the aisle with a cart full of flowers.

"Even if it were the last night, I was ever going to see you, I would never ever forget you. Stop thinking like that. I never said anything like that." I wrap my arm around his. "I think I found everything. Let's get out of here."

As we pull into the driveway, Joan is standing in front of the cabin. Will is taking pictures of her. Joan waves me over, "Let's take some pictures so we can remember this."

I look over at Thomas and he smiles. My heart breaks thinking about what he said in the grocery store. I stand next to Joan as Will continues to snap a couple of pictures. I motion Thomas over to me and wrap my arms around him then whisper in his ear, "So, you can remember me."

Drunk Thor

Joan opens the trunk to unload the car. "Is anyone going to say anything about the massive number of flowers in the back of the Jeep?"

I look at Joan and just shrug my shoulders.

Thomas grabs all the bundles and carries them inside.

"What in the hell did I miss?" Joan looks at me for an explanation.

It's like someone took a knife to a bag of beans; everything comes spilling out. "Thomas asked me to go to London with him! He wants me to live there!" I'm rushing my words, trying to tell Joan everything before Thomas gets back.

"Crap! What did you say?" Joan puts the bag of groceries back down.

"I said I needed time... that maybe we could try a long-distance relationship...that I thought this wasn't love." I rest my head against the side of the Jeep. I'm a colossal idiot! I have this perfect man standing in front of me spilling his heart out and I'm running away because I'm overthinking it. Not because I don't like him, but I like him too much and I think that it won't work.

"I wish I could make the decision for you, but this is something you have to figure out on your own. The only thing I can say is don't worry about being hurt. Hearts can heal from hurt but they can never heal from regret. The 'what could have been.' Hurt isn't a final thing. It's something that happens. Once the hurt happens you have the time to heal. Regret will last until the day you die. Nothing will change that."

I nudge Joan in the ribs, "Look at you being all Yoda-like. It's like you know what you're talking about." I give Joan a warm smile.

Joan shakes her head, "It only took a failed marriage, being heartbroken, poisoning you, and meeting Will to gather this wisdom. Take it from me little sis, I know."

Will pokes his head around the side of the Jeep and startles me, "Crap!" How long has he been standing there? Without saying a word, he grabs the last two bags and walks back into the cabin.

Joan slams the trunk shut and puts her arm around my shoulder. "Having someone in love with you is a good problem to have. Just roll with it."

In the cabin, Thomas is nowhere in sight. Joan shoots Will a look, he nods his head towards my bedroom door.

I swing open the bedroom door. Thomas is busy cutting the stems off the flowers and arranging them all over my room. It smells like a flower shop in here.

"Do you like it?" Thomas waves his arms around.

I shut the door behind me, "I'll show you how much I like it." I still can't get his hand inching up my thigh out of my mind. I plop myself down on the bed as I watch him pull rose petals from their stems and dust them over me.

He pulls my shirt over my head and rests me back on the bed. Leaning over, he kisses me right in the middle of my chest. He whispers, "Heart."

Thomas makes his way down to my belly button and unsnaps my jeans. He's going very slow and deliberate. I fight the urge to pull my jeans down and kick them off. My breath is quickening. I run my hands through his springy hair and pull him back up to me so I can see his face. his eyes are the bluest blue today. I don't think I've ever seen such a beautiful color. I could get lost for days. The way he looks at me, it's like the cat who ate the canary. I love that about him. It's a pure, innocent look.

Thomas leans over on his side next to me. "A penny for your

thoughts, Love."

I press my head against his chest. "I just don't know what's real. I don't want to hurt you."

Thomas squeezes me closer to his chest. "Don't worry about me. Like I said, I will be here."

He just seems to know the right things to say. To my horror, I feel tears well up in my eyes. I'm just going to lie here and try to be really still. That's the last thing I want: for him to see me cry.

Thomas brushes my hair back behind my ear. I'm lying on the bed half naked. This isn't how I expected the next few minutes to go.

There's a quiet rapping at the door, "Mar, are you coming out to help with the table?"

Jeez, thank goodness, saved by Joan. "Ummm... yes! Just give me a second," I shout towards the door.

I kick my legs over and roll out of bed. "We've been summoned. This will have to wait." I button my jeans and pull on my shirt; then blink my eyes a few times. I give myself a quick look in the mirror. Thank goodness, no sign of crying. I walk out of my room like I've just been introduced on stage. It comes off more dramatic than I hoped.

I try to tone it down; I'm buzzing around the kitchen placing wine glasses on the table. "Joan, put on some music. 'Into the Mystic' by Van Morrison!"

Joan begins to shuffle through her phone, "...Found it." She pushes the button and sets her phone down.

I look over Will's shoulder as I pass him in the kitchen, "Hey, good looking."

It's funny to think all the ingredients we picked up earlier turned into this amazing meal. Will turns the heat up on the stovetop. "I'm making the reduction for the ribeyes, the mashed potatoes are in the oven, and I just finished the double chocolate mousse. If you want to spoon it in glasses that would be nice." Will is right at home in the kitchen.

Thomas unwraps a bundle of flowers and arranges them on the table. Joan is setting the silverware on the table when I catch her eye. She's happy. She's glowing. This… this is what I wanted for her. I stand back and look around. Just to think, we didn't know these guys two weeks ago and I can't imagine not having them in my life.

It seems like this is how it's always been, how it will always be. My heart is full.

Will places the plates on the table and it feels like we are being served at a high-end restaurant. Everything is uniformed and exactly the same. He stands next to Joan and pulls her seat out for her. As he scoots her in, he lets his hand drag across her back. My head shoots up and my eyes widen. They had SEX! I know it!

I look over at Joan and stare directly at her until she finally has no choice but to acknowledge me. She turns sharply and looks directly at me. We stare at each other motionless for a couple of seconds. I raise my eyebrows at her. She gives me a smile and shrugs her shoulders. I nod my head at her. That was it. She confirmed my suspicions. I'm a little hurt she didn't tell me. When would she have? She was too busy wrapped up in what was going on with me. Gosh, how could I be so selfish? This trip isn't for me. How could I have forgotten that?

I reach over and grab a glass of wine. As I put the wine glass up to my lips, I look back at Joan.

She shakes her head and laughs. "I didn't put poison in that one."

Frank, San Francisco… the hospital seems so long ago. I just smile.

Thomas begins to examine his glass a little bit closer.

"She's kidding… She put poison in Will's." I give Will a cheeky grin as he slides his glass back away from his plate.

Joan shoots him an 'oh really look' so he grabs it and takes a gulp. Like he's willing to take a good, hard one for the team. Yep, he's completely whipped.

I'm working on my third glass of wine when Thomas and Will begin to clear the table. As Thomas walks back into the kitchen, Joan points to my glass and mouths, "No more."

I can't help it, though. I have all these emotions floating around. I figure if I'm drinking, I can't be talking, or at least not talking as much, or talking about anything that has to do with anything.

I finish off my third glass and start to tap it on the table, "More please." I raise my glass like Olivier Twist raises his bowl of porridge.

Joan is holding the wine bottle in her hand, ignoring me.

I clear my throat, "More please!" I exaggerate a British accent. It's a lousy British accent, I laugh and spit a little wine out of my mouth by accident. I randomly start trying out my accent, mumbling to myself... "Cheerio, top of the morning to ya...bloody hell...blimey...this is all going to pot, isn't it?"

Joan turns in her seat; she is completely ignoring me. I feel a little fuzzy. Joan must not hear me. I must raise the stakes.

"This drink I like it!" With all my force, I throw my glass to the floor. "Another!"

To my surprise my glass bounces off the floor hard and straight into the air. Everyone turns in stunned silence.

Joan reaches over and grabs the leg of my chair and pulls me over to her. "Knock it off! You aren't Thor!"

I cock my head to the side and squint my eyes at her. "Aren't I, though?" I snatch my plastic wine glass off the couch where it landed and walk over to Thomas. I thrust out my glass to him, "Another!"

Thomas looks up at Joan for approval. "If you give her another, you'll regret it," Joan says, pointing her finger at Thomas.

I butt in, "If you don't give me another, you'll regret it."

Will pats the chair next to him at the table. "Why don't you come here and have some mousse?"

Why is he talking to me like I'm a baby? I slowly walk over to the table and slide down into the seat next to Will.

Thomas sits next to me looking a little more relieved.

I glance around the table. "You guys are no fun!" I hop up and run in a circle around the table, grabbing the wine bottle next to Joan as I run out the front door. "Last one to the pond is a rotten egg!" I run down the sidewalk and up the dirt path towards the pond, kicking off my shoes as I go.

Thomas strides up next to me. "Well, I guess I won't be the rotten egg."

I look behind Thomas to see how far back Joan is. "Where's Joan?"

"She told me to bring you back." Thomas wraps his arms around me.

I feel strangely trapped. I start to jump up and down in his arms to get free. It's no use, he's on to me. He lifts me off the ground. I begin running in mid-air.

"Stop it! Stop jumping, Marguerite!" Thomas pulls me to the ground and onto his lap. He brushes my hair out of my face. "Just sit here for a minute. Shhh…just be still."

I put the wine bottle up to my lips and take a gulp. I'm not very good at hiding my emotions. I lean my head against Thomas' chest, then take another swig. "Why do you have to be so perfect?" I put my finger on his lips and trace them. "I think you are so hot. It's impossible to think straight around you." My body feels heavy as I curl up to Thomas' chest. "I mean, you're just so adorable."

"Ummm…I'm sorry."

I lean back to look at him. He has a smirk on his face. He's not sorry at all. "You're not sorry." My eyes begin to shut, as I snuggle my face deeper into Thomas' chest. Oranges…

"Let's get you to bed, Love. I believe you've had too much to drink tonight." Thomas lifts me up into his arms.

I wake up to the beat of Thomas' heart. I try to lift my head; it feels like it is a hundred pounds. A toy drummer crashes from one side of my head to the other. I look around the room. The wine bottle from last night is sitting on the nightstand. Thomas is stretched out next to me on the bed.

"Crap!" I put my face into my hands. I really can screw things up... What did I do last night? I hope I didn't say something I regret. I lift up the covers to check and see if Thomas is wearing underwear. Check, his underwear is still there. I'm still wearing my t-shirt. I reach under the covers and feel the lace on my panties. Okay, my panties are still there. I swing my feet around and slide out of the bed. I tiptoe across the floor to my pile of clothes. I quietly grab a few things and slink into the bathroom. Thomas is still fast asleep.

I let the hot water run over my body like all the thoughts running through my mind. I did have a bit too much to drink. I should have known better. I can't imagine the things I did last night. I'm just going to stand here in the shower for as long as possible. One: I don't want to face Joan's wrath, and two: we are leaving today. I hear the bathroom door open. I quickly wash the soap from my eyes. I have this paranoid thought that I'm going to get murdered in the shower. It's not like being able to see my attacker will help at all. I wipe my eyes and look wildly around. Thomas' face appears from behind the curtain.

"Shit!" I put my hand over my heart, "Sweet baby Jesus!"

"Sorry, Love. I was just checking on you." Thomas pulls the curtain back. "Do you mind if I join you?"

I motion him in. Thomas reaches around me for the shampoo. "Why are you so jumpy in the shower?"

"My sister and I watched *Psycho* when we were kids and I have never been able to take a shower without being paranoid."

Thomas wraps his warm arms around me, "Don't worry, I'll keep you safe from vicious murderers."

I poke him in the chest. "That's not funny."

I lean back into his body and we just stand there letting the water run over us. No words, no movement, just standing. I want to ask if I had said anything last night, but how can I ask? 'Uh… Thomas, did I happen to tell you that I love you last night?' Instead I opt for, "Thomas I want to apologize if you had to chase me around last night. I tend to start running when I drink more than two glasses of wine."

Thomas giggles, "I noticed. Good thing I'm a runner. And you hop more than you run when you drink."

I push his shoulder, "I do not! I run fluidly, like a gazelle. Graceful and beautiful."

Thomas turns me to face the wall and begins scrubbing my back. "You are beautiful, but I wouldn't exactly call you graceful when you drink. I think you hit Joan with your plastic wine glass."

Oh jeez, I definitely have some apologies today.

Thomas turns me back around and rinses my body. He reaches down, turns the water off, grabs a towel from the rack and wraps me in it. "I'm sure your head is pounding. Let's get you some breakfast."

I step out of the tub. I throw on my clothes and walk out into the living room.

Will is making French toast and Joan is on the couch reading a magazine. She looks up, "Hey, Thor! Sleep well?"

I shrug my shoulders, "I don't remember going to sleep." I casually look around the room. "Hey, I'm sorry if I did anything crazy last night. Thomas said that I may have hit you with my wine glass…" I sit next to Joan and rub my forehead.

Will walks over with the spatula still in his hand. "You didn't hit anyone with your wine glass. You threw it to the ground, and it bounced straight into the air. I'm pretty sure you didn't know it was plastic."

I plant my face in my hands, "Oh…my…gosh! I'm so sorry.

Joan shakes her head in one quick nod, "You challenged

everyone to run to the pond. Thomas ran after you and brought you back to put you to bed."

I curl up in a tight ball beside Joan. "I'm such an ass."

Joan turns to look at me, "Well, at least he will know what he's up against." She squeezes my knee and whispers, "Don't be so afraid of this. If you like him, go for it."

Thomas walks out of the bedroom pulling his shirt over his head. He begins rubbing my shoulders. "What can I help with, Will? I'm horrible when it comes to cooking, but I'm Dench at setting the table."

Will's head cocks to the side, like a dog who's heard something in the distance. He starts, "I'm sorry, I have no idea what you just said to me."

Thomas laughs and claps Will on the shoulder, "I just said I'm horrible at cooking, but I can set the table."

"Oh, right then!" Will hands Thomas a stack of plates.

Thomas starts setting the table. "I hate to ask but what's the plan for today?"

I look at Joan, willing her to say something. I just can't bring myself to say it.

Joan begins to look at the map on her phone. "We will need to head back to pick up our car and Mr. Lee right after breakfast. It will take us the rest of the day to get out of Colorado, then a whole day or two to get across Texas. We have a good seventeen-hour drive once we hit the Texas border."

Sadness flickers across Thomas' face.

Will sets the French toast on the table. "Let's eat!"

It's easy for him to say. Joan and Will only live about twenty minutes from each other.

Thomas pulls out a chair for me and I sit down next to him. I look around the table. "I want to say sorry again if I acted crazy last night. I usually don't have more than one glass of wine because of it. So, sorry." I smile and straighten my shoulders.

Everyone at the table is dead silent. You could seriously hear a pin drop, then everyone irrupts in laughter.

Will interjects, "I have to say, that was one of the funniest things I have ever seen. You threw your glass down and it came flying right back past your head, then you ran out the front door with a bottle of wine."

"Yea, and you thought you were Thor again!" Joan says shaking her head.

Thomas shoots Joan a look, "Is thinking she's Thor, a thing?"

Joan's rolls her eyes, "Yes! Almost every time I tell her she can't have anymore. She will immediately yell 'Another'!"

Thomas looks back at me, "I had to chase you down. You started jumping around. It was adorable. You were running in mid-air," Thomas says, laughing.

"OKAY, OKAY... I get it! I'm sorry!" I put my head down on the table and rest my forehead on the wood.

Joan tugs a strand of my hair, "It's alright tiny Thor, you'll get your hammer back..."

I reach over and rest my hand on her knee where no one else can see and raise my middle finger.

Joan is just finishing up her French toast when she stands up and starts to clear the table, "Come on, Stupid, help me with the table."

I drag myself to the sink and load the dishwasher. This will be the last time I'll ever be standing here. The last time we will all be here, like this, together. I swallow the lump that is forming in my throat. Don't cry! Whatever you do...don't cry.

I finish loading the dishwasher, "Okay, I'm going to pack." My voice cracks a little. That came out a little more rushed then I expected, but I really don't want to cry. How would I explain that? I don't even know why I'm crying in the first place.

I kiss Will on the cheek as I pass him. "Thanks for an incredible breakfast."

I glance at Thomas. He's pointing to his cheek waiting for his. I tiptoe up to kiss him on the cheek. He quickly turns his head and plants a kiss on my lips.

I blush, "You got me!" Heaven only knows he's got me.

I fold the few things I have and place them in a plastic bag and carry it out to the Jeep.

Thomas has the same matching make-shift plastic bag suitcase that I do. He loads it in the Jeep next to mine.

As I walk back into the cabin, I dust my hands together and try sounding sure of my decision "Well, that's that. I'm all packed."

Thomas walks up beside me, "Will and Joan are still packing." Thomas points towards Joan's bedroom. "Want to take a walk while we wait?"

I nod my head. He slides his hand in mine as we walk towards the pond. Our pond. I love this place. My thoughts are whirling around in my head. He's perfect. There's got to be a catch somewhere… not that I'm cynical. I'm just cautiously optimistic. Thomas turns his head slightly towards me. A wide smile spreads across his face. His smile could light the whole world, as far as I'm concerned. We reach the pond and walk down to the end of the small, wooden dock.

I slip off my shoes and dangle my feet in the water. Thomas sits beside me and wraps one arm around me. This will forever be our place. It feels like home. He feels like home to me, regardless of how much I am fighting it. My toe is making tiny ripples in the water, and my mind is on Thomas. It feels like I've always known him. How will we ever make the long-distance work? I turn into his chest and try to pull my focus on the here and the now. All we have is right now. It's foolish of me to think this will work, no matter if he thinks it will. If this isn't going to last, I want to hold on to every second.

I reach up and press my lips to Thomas' and whisper, "Right here, right now."

Thomas holds a hand to each side of my face and presses his forehead to mine, blocking out everything else around us. "Here and now. We are right here, right now."

Joan kills our moment as she yells from halfway up the path, "Hey, we're ready! Let's get on the road."

She turns and starts walking back up the path before I can say anything to her. Besides, what would I say? I want to stay here forever. I don't want to go back to reality. I want to live in this bubble with Thomas.

Thomas stands and holds out his hand to pull me to my feet. "I guess that's our cue."

Wake Me Up

Will and Joan are already in the Jeep when we make it back to the cabin. Will rolls down the window, "Hop in!" He points to the backseat.

Thomas opens the door and I hop in and slide over to make room for him.

Joan turns in her seat, "So, want to add to the playlist?"

My heart feels broken. I wonder if anyone can tell from the outside? I can't imagine the songs I would pick right now, but it's our thing. It's always been our thing. I can't say 'no.' Enthusiastically, I say, "Yes! You first. I need a second to think of one."

Joan picks her song but my mind drifts back to Thomas and leaving him today.

"Hey! Hey... your turn..." Joan's voice hits me like a ton of bricks. "It's your turn to pick your song?"

I didn't even know her song had played. My mind immediately goes into panic mode. I just spit out a song, "'Summer Nights'... *Grease*."

The first guitar cord plays and right on cue, Thomas starts singing. I absolutely love this about him. He loves music just as much as I do. *Grease* is my all-time favorite.

I pretend to pull my make-believe mic from the inside of my bra. *Grease* always pulls me out of whatever funk I'm in. By the time I realize it, I'm laughing and smiling like crazy. It's almost impossible to be sad listening to *Grease*. I can't get over how good Thomas is at this. He hits the high note at the end with no effort. It's absolutely amazing.

"Is there anything you are bad at?" Will looks at Thomas in the rearview mirror.

Thomas smiles at Will. "A lot of things, mate."

Will shakes his head. "I can't just sit here, I'm horrible at singing but I want to pick a song. Keeping with the theme... I've got to go big..." He looks at Joan and pretends to comb his hair back like John Travolta. "Play 'You're the One that I Want'." Will clears his throat, "Will you sing it with me?"

Joan puts her index finger to her chest, "Me?"

"Yes, you!" Will laughs. "Unless Thomas wants to sing again."

Thomas claps Will on the back, "Sorry mate, I'm taken."

Will begins to sing. He doesn't sound that bad. It's actually kind of cute.

Joan nods along with the music. She pushes Will back with her finger.

If any song was right on the button, it's this one.

Thomas and I sing backup from the backseat.

The atmosphere in the car is electric and it's keeping my mind off of leaving today. It seems to be calming Joan, too. Will is driving on the side of the mountain and Joan hasn't freaked out, not even a little. We are all so happy that Joan lets the whole album play. "Grease Lightning" comes on.

Thomas grabs each side of his collar and flips it up. I clap a hand over my mouth. He runs his hand through his hair. He even knows the dance. He improvises in his seat.

I look at him wide-eyed, "How do you know all that? That was absolutely awesome!"

"I played Danny Zuko when I was in boarding school."

My mouth drops open, "I played Rizzo in *Grease* when I was in high school! Joan played Sandra Dee! The music from *Grease* is my all-time favorite!" I slide my hand into Thomas' and close my eyes.

Thomas squeezes my hand, "We're here."

We are where? My whole body goes off in alarm. I missed the whole drive! I can't believe I slept the last two hours I had to spend with him. I stretch my arms above my head and yawn. Thomas opens my door and I slide out. I stand on my tiptoes and throw my arms around his neck. "I'm going to miss you."

"I'll miss you more. Keep in touch and we can make a plan for me to come back to visit. I'm headed back to London for work, but know that I will miss you every second," Thomas says, pressing his head down into the top of my head.

The front door of the barn opens, and Mr. Lee comes running full speed into Joan's arms.

Winnie and Anna are right behind him. "You made it back…"

Thomas hugs Winnie. I walk up behind Thomas and extend my hand to Winnie.

He grabs it and pulls me into him. "Come on now, stop that. Give me a proper hug."

I blush thinking about how much Winnie knows. "Thank you for taking care of Mr. Lee on no notice," I say as I hug Anna.

"No problem. He's such a dear." She hands me a box of things.

I rifle through it. "What is this?"

"I baked him some treats for the road and picked up a blanket and a couple of shirts for him," Anna says, opening the Tupperware to show me.

The smell of the most delicious peanut butter cookies hit my nose. To be honest, I could probably eat one of these and be totally happy.

"Thank you. That is very sweet of you." I put down the convertible top and set the box inside. Joan puts Lone-Lee in the backseat.

"So, what's the plan?" Winnie looks at me.

"We are headed to Texas to visit my folks then we are driving up the coast, maybe New York, then back to California. I have to get back to the bakery before Marie thinks I've abandoned her."

Anna hands me another box, "And these are for you and Joan for your trip."

I hold the box tight to my chest. "I can't even begin to thank you guys for all your hospitality."

Will comes over and hugs me. "See you back in California?" He walks around the car and opens the door for Joan; he leans over and kisses her.

I turn and open my car door then I sink down into the seat.

Thomas' warm smile spreads from ear to ear. "Take care, Love. I hope to see you very soon." He leans over and presses his forehead to mine and kisses me hard. It's not likely I will forget that kiss anytime soon. Matter of fact, I'm going to be thinking of that kiss for the rest of the day. Who am I kidding? I'll be thinking of that kiss for the rest of my life. I crank the engine and slowly turn the car around in the driveway. I blow a kiss behind me as I pull onto the road. I adjust my mirror to look at Thomas.

In the Mirror

"Song?" Joan looks at me, opening her Amazon music app.

"Okay, song…" I say, letting my mind drift. I'd do anything not to think of Thomas in my rearview mirror. I cup my hand around my mouth and yell at the top of my lungs; "Brass Monkey!"

I can only remember every other word. Strangely enough, though, I can remember every single word of the chorus and give it all I've got. Joan is singing along with me. She pretends to scratch a record on her knee. She knows some of the words that I don't and sings them. It sounds like we are actually rapping.

Joan pulls her map out from under the seat. She follows the highway with her finger. "Looks like you take Highway 36 for the next 100 miles." She taps her lap and Lone-Lee carefully crawls from the backseat onto her.

Joan gives him a good scratch behind his ears. He is putting on more weight, must be all of Anna's cookies. The music is playing in the background and I let my mind drift to Thomas and his face. His perfectly chiseled chest…his springy hair, his blue eyes…his smooth skin. The tiny, gold hairs on his arms. He even has gold flecks in the stubble on his face, it reminds me of Edward in that vampire movie.

For my sanity, I need to keep my mind off Thomas, at least for now. "Want to talk about Will? I mean, now that we are alone."

Joan is silent for a second, so I glance to look at her. "Spill it!"

"Well… it was just the one time," Joan says as her cheeks flush.

"Well, was it good?" I can tell it was, by how red her cheeks are getting.

"Of course, it was good! In fact, it was more than good. It was everything I didn't know I was missing." Joan stares off into the distance like she is reliving the memory.

I raise my eyebrows at her and growl, "Does he do things to you that you only dreamt about?"

Joan smiles at me, "It's more than that. I don't know how to explain it. When I was with him, he was warm, caring, gentle…"

The way Joan talks about Will makes me miss Thomas again. The hundred miles just fly by. I'm lost in thoughts of Thomas, lost in Joan's words, lost in songs. I pull off at the next exit. The thing about Cooper is that he seems to need gas more than the average small car. Even so, I refuse to get a new one. I swipe my card at the pump and lean against his door while Joan takes Lone-Lee for a quick walk around the gas station. My cellphone dings as I hang the gas nozzle back on the pump. It's Thomas!

Love, I miss you already. Will and I are driving to the airport. Just checking on how you are doing. We are probably not too far behind you. We are stopping for gas.

I watch Joan walk around inside the store as I type back.

We just stopped for gas. I'm waiting for Joan to get back to the car. I miss you too! I wish I could kiss you one more time.

Just then a tapping on my window startles me. I jump and toss my cellphone into the air. I must be dreaming because Thomas is leaning over with his face pressed close to Cooper's window. I hop out of the car and into his arms. I kiss him hard, I missed him. It's only been a couple of hours, but I missed him.

He presses his lips against my ear, "Your wish is my command."

"I like the sound of that." I lean back to look at his face without letting him go.

Joan walks out of the gas station looking flummoxed. "What are you guys doing here?" she asks, giving Will a quick kiss on the lips.

"Marguerite wished for another kiss," Thomas says, leaning over and giving me a sweet kiss on the cheek. "We stopped for gas, now we are both headed for the airport."

A sinking feeling churns in my stomach. I don't want to have to say 'goodbye' again. I let that rumble around in my head for a second. I can feel a lump forming in my throat. I swallow hard, "Well, we better go. Texas is a very large state to cross." I give Thomas a hug as he lifts me off my feet. I dangle there for a few seconds. Talk about sweeping a girl off her feet.

"You don't think this is a sign that you should come with me?" Thomas whispers, holding his breath for my answer.

"I think that I will see you soon when you come to visit. It gives me something to look forward to. Good things come to those who wait." I lie to him and myself. I feel like throwing caution to the wind and running off into the sunset with him. But that's not how this can work. I have a life here. I have to remind myself of that.

I give Thomas a quick kiss on the cheek and hop in Cooper before I say something I'm not ready to say. Or before I make a rash decision.

Joan pulls out the map again and blows a kiss to Will. "See you in Cannes!"

Just like that, I watch Thomas in my rearview mirror for the second time today. Joan and I ride in silence for the next fifty miles. I am concentrating on counting down the miles and the lines on the road. It helps to keep me from thinking about Thomas and the horrible feeling that I've made a big mistake. It's funny, after driving for a while your driving kind of goes on autopilot.

Joan breaks the silence. "Seems like it's getting harder and harder to say 'bye' to Thomas."

I press my foot down on the gas a little. Like the farther I get from the gas station and Thomas, the farther I get away from my feelings. Truth is, my feelings are sitting right here in the car, pressing on my chest against my heart.

I manage a, "Yep."

Joan waits for me to go on. I take a second. I'm trying to gather my thoughts. I take a breath and I begin, "I'm just really confused about how I feel because it really hasn't been that long. I'm afraid that I'm just infatuated. Or, even more, that he is just infatuated. That I am going to just pick up my life for something that isn't real. I mean it's fun, but is it real?"

Joan realizes that I'm not really asking her a question, so she sits there letting my words hang in the air.

We are somewhere in the middle of New Mexico, Oklahoma, and the Texas border when Joan finally interrupts my thoughts again. "Have you ever tried peyote?"

"What do you mean 'have I ever tried peyote?' Where did that come from? Of course, I haven't. Have you?!" My mouth goes loose as I look at Joan with a skeptical eye.

"Well, no...but I saw it advertised on a sign a couple of miles back, I thought we might want to get back to our roots."

"Just because we are part Native American doesn't mean we have to smoke peyote." I knit my eyebrows together. "You're crazy. The last thing we need to be doing is smoking peyote. I shouldn't be the one telling you this, as your much younger sister, you know?" I give her a wink.

"My much shorter sister. Let's just go check it out. Remember, we are on an adventure after all. What's the harm of looking?" Joan says, craning her head around to read every road sign. "See," she points. "See, it's the next exit."

"I don't think it's a good idea to stop at a peyote shop advertised on a billboard. That doesn't seem legit. I mean, is peyote even legal?" I mark that down as things I never thought I'd hear myself say.

"Stop being a Fuddy Duddy. That's my role. You can't all of a sudden be me, as much as you would like to be." Joan knocks me on the shoulder.

"Okay, okay...I'll go. But we are only looking. And I'm texting Thomas my location." I put my blinker on and exit the highway.

This is the worst idea I've ever heard of. We follow the makeshift signs off the highway to a large teepee in the middle of a cornfield. I put Cooper in park and pull out my phone to share my location with Thomas. I quickly type:

Pulled off the highway. Stopped at a peyote shop with Joan. It's a teepee in the middle of a field. Sending you my location just in case we get murdered. What time is your flight?

A texting bubble pops up immediately.

What do you mean you are stopping at a peyote shop? Please get back on the highway. Doesn't sound like a great idea. My flight leaves in 4 hours. Will and I are just having a drink at the airport bar. He is texting Joan. He also thinks that you need to get back on the highway. Don't stop. I love you!

Joan snaps the leash on Mr. Lee as we walk towards the teepee. The hot sun has burned the grass, turning it into straw. Next to the teepee is a small shack. Like the ones that pop-up to sell fireworks during the Fourth of July. A woman is standing in the opening of the shack and there's an old lady sitting on a chair behind her. The old lady's skin is cracked and weathered but her eyes sparkle dark brown. As we approach, the old lady starts waving her hand for us to come closer. She says something to the younger lady.

The younger lady waves her off. "Hi, my name is Doli. This is my grandmother, Chooli. How can we help you?"

"Oh, we don't need any help. We were just curious, so we stopped," I say, looking around for some pamphlet or something to read.

Joan walks up behind me and pokes her head around me.

The old woman says something again, that I can't understand, to the younger woman. The younger lady shoos her away with her hand, then asks, "Are you Native American?"

"Yes, our grandpa is 100% Apache," I say, feeling like we have a foothold here.

The elderly woman tugs on the younger lady's elbow, seeming to be a little irate.

Joan stops the younger lady mid-sentence and points to the older woman, "What's she saying?"

"She says that there is soul searching here and great grief. Big hurt, soulmates. But she's a foolish old woman."

Joan looks at me and widens her eyes. How would she know any of this?

"What else does she say?" Joan asks, playing devil's advocate.

"She says you were a broken bird, but your wings are fixed." She then points to me, "And this one is a jail cell. Lots of walls." The younger woman shakes her head. "She says you must stay and find yourself and purge yourself of what blocks you."

I have to admit, she sounds quite convincing. But there is no way I want to smoke peyote for the first time, or ever, in a teepee in the middle of nowhere. It can't be safe. I'm not afraid of the people. I'm afraid of the surrounding cornfields in the middle of nowhere. I have an irrational fear of werewolves. The old woman stands and walks to the opening of the shack. She locks arms with Joan and begins to mumble something as she pulls Joan in the direction of the teepee. I quickly follow Joan as she looks back and shoots a 'what did we get ourselves into' look at me.

The old lady gestures for Joan and me to sit down. There is a pile of wood in a semi-circle in the middle of the teepee. The top of the teepee is covered in black tar like soot. My lungs are never going to forgive me for this. The sun is setting. This is the last place I want to be after dark. What in the world has Joan got us into? All I can think of is *Texas Chainsaw Massacre* and having to drag Joan to the car. I'm a runner when I get scared. Joan, on the other hand, just falls to her knees.

The younger lady appears in the doorway of the teepee and takes Mr. Lee by his leash. A couple of energetic millennials come bouncing in and sit on the other side of Joan. Several men and a few women walk into the tent and sit on the other side of me, filling in the circle. The old lady ties the teepee doors shut behind her, shutting out the last of the light from the sun.

One of the elderly men stands up. "We are here to find our true selves. To rid our bodies of illness and earthly barriers."

He lights the small pile of wood in the middle of us and picks up a bowl, handing it to the woman sitting on the ground next to him. She takes a sip and passes it to the man beside her. It goes from one person to the next until it reaches Joan. Joan takes a small sip and passes it to me. I hold the bowl with one hand and reach over for Joan's with my other hand. I guess we are doing this. I swear... I take a small sip, never moving my eyes from Joan's. Humm... I feel absolutely nothing. This can't be entirely bad. The two ladies begin to drum beside me.

The bowl makes it around to me again and I look at Joan silently asking if she's still okay. I take another sip. I still don't feel anything. I close my eyes as the drumming syncs with my heartbeat, or my heartbeat syncs with the drumming... I'm not sure which. One of the elderly men stands and rakes the lit wood into a semi-circle. The smoke weaves through the air like tiny, white ribbons. The drumming is getting louder. The women shake bamboo sticks that sound like rattle snakes. They begin to chant.

My body relaxes more. I float up to the top of the teepee. I can see myself from up here. It's peaceful. I feel like everything becomes clearer.

Joan nudges me, my body floats back down and I open my eyes to focus on her. She places a tiny bowl of small, dried up cactus in my lap. She motions to put one in my mouth, the way you show a child to eat. I place one in my mouth and start to chew. My body feels like it's turning into vibrations. Like I'm dissipating with every drumbeat. I lean back on my elbows when the woman next to me shakes her head and straightens my body back up to a stiff, upright position.

Time feels irrelevant. I'm floating. I can't hear the music anymore. I only feel it. I look over at Joan and angel wings have sprouted out of her back. She's glowing. I smile at her, or at least I think I'm smiling. I look around the teepee. I see a beautiful, giant wolf sitting in the corner. He seems friendly enough. On the other side of the tent sits an eagle. I can't tell if the animals are real or my imagination. Everyone else is gone. Where did everyone go? When did everyone else leave? The teepee flap is open. I walk out and look up to the night sky. It is completely black except for the stars which are like pin pricks of light all around us.

I walk to a clearing and lay my head in the dirt, facing the night sky. It's quiet here. I slowly turn my head; Thomas is lying in the dirt next to me. He doesn't say a word. His electric, blue eyes are staring back at me. His eyes turn into ponds. I reach out to place my hand on his face and he disappears. Don't go Thomas. I feel calm. Like I'm water slowly flowing back and forth, kissing the sandy shore. I like it here. I wonder where Joan is. I turn my head to find her.

She is running in a dead sprint past me.

I bolt up in a fog. "Where are you going, Joan?"

I place my hand over my eyebrows to shield the sun in the complete darkness. I get to my feet in a wobble and scuffle after her. She is running straight for the open cornfield. I struggle with the idea of whether or not to follow her. I mean, I've seen *Children of the Corn.* I know how that goes. I'm not crazy. I try to run faster, but my legs don't feel like they are moving even though I'm gaining ground on her. "Joan! Joan! Holy crap! Stop running!"

Joan is slapping at her hair like a bee is chasing her. "The snakes! The snakes!" I turn to look behind me.

I don't see any rabbits. "Joan, there aren't any rabbits! Please stop running!" I notice a few older people watching us in the distance.

This can't be something new. They've had to have seen it all. Joan drops to the ground and starts rubbing her legs from hip to ankle.

I grab both her hands and hold them tight. "Joan, stop! What are you doing?"

"I'm scaling my legs! I'm a mermaid..." Joan tries to pull her hands free.

I hold her hands tighter and shake them. "One: you are not a mermaid. And two: if you were, why would you scale yourself?"

Joan gets to her feet and starts running again. I'm worried that she will hurt herself. I hop up and chase behind her. "Joan, damn it! You ate peyote. You are okay. None of this is real!"

Joan speeds up. I run up behind her and tackle her to the ground. She turns and looks me right in the eyes, but she is looking through me.

"I swear, I'm never going to let you talk me into something this stupid again. I was having the best time relaxing and you have to go and ruin it. For heaven's sake, this was your idea!" I scowl at her.

Joan reaches up and feels my face with her hands. "You look weird…"

As if she couldn't get any more annoying. She lays flat on the ground and I lay on top of her, staring up at the sky. She can't run off now, not without me knowing. We must look like quite the sight. I lay in silence and take in the blackness of the night sky.

"Mar, hey, Mar… did you see the stars? The sky is so crystal clear," Joan whispers in my ear.

She sounds calmer now, I roll off her and lie beside her. I hold her hand tight and swing my legs over hers. "The stars are breathtaking. I'm excited to do most things with you, but I have to say, I will never do this again. Sometimes you are really stupid. Sometimes, we are really stupid." I turn on my side to face Joan, "Stupid…"

Joan is fast asleep. Maybe that's for the best. I dig the phone out of my pocket then snap a quick picture of Joan passed out next to me. I text Thomas. I figure he is still on the plane to London. I shoot him a quick text, anyways. I scroll to Will's number.

I'm not sure if Joan texted you. We stopped and an old lady talked us into drinking peyote tea. Joan ate some, also. We are okay, but Joan was running through a field. She's sleeping now. Just wanted to tell you we were okay if you try calling later. Picture to come…

Next, I text Marie.

Please remind me never to drink Peyote tea with Joan in the middle of nowhere. I swear… I'll explain later. Pics to come…

I lay next to Joan counting the minutes. Mr. Lee comes sneaking across the field, putting his head under my hand. I sit up and place my face in my hands.

I reach over and shake Joan's shoulder. "Wake up, we need to make it back to the car. I can't drive right now, but we can't sleep in the field. It's not safe."

Joan makes it to her feet, and we amble to Cooper. We quickly fall into a deep sleep.

The sun comes creeping through the windshield in beams. I raise my head. "Sweet Baby Jesus!" the old lady from yesterday is standing next to the car window, smiling. I stare at her for a second when she knocks on the window. I hesitantly roll it down. "Umm…Hi…"

She thrusts a cup into my hands.

"Oh, no… no thank you." I try handing it back.

Her granddaughter from yesterday walks up behind her. "It's okay. It is only coffee. Folgers…"

I put the cup up to my nose and take a tiny sip.

The grandma mumbles something to her granddaughter.

"She is asking if she can tell you something?" Doli, the granddaughter, timidly asks.

I glance over at Joan; she is sleeping in the seat next to me with Lone-Lee on her chest. Chooli, the grandmother, begins to become very animated with her hands.

"She says, 'your sister is shedding here old life. She will start a new life soon. You…. you have met your soulmate. He can travel and his spirit was with you last night. You have a connection that is beyond this world'."

I twirl the thoughts in my head for a second. I did see Thomas last night when I was resting in the grass, right before I had to tackle Joan. All the memories come flooding back. She was scaling her legs! She thought she was a mermaid!

Chooli becomes more animated. Doli is trying to explain as fast as Chooli is talking.

Joan raises her seat upright, "What's happening?" She looks around the car and pats the dashboard with both hands, as if she is making sure it's real.

"Chooli," I point to the old woman, "was just telling me that you were shedding your old life last night." I lean over to Joan. "It makes sense to me, since you were trying to scale your legs…"

"Holy crap, really?" Joan reaches down and rubs her calves. "This was such a bad idea."

Joan opens the car door and stands Mr. Lee on his feet. Mr. Lee stretches his body and happily walks off, wagging his curly, pig-like tail. "So, I'm shedding my old life…"

Chooli nods her head up and down.

Joan turns and looks at Doli. "What is she? A psychic?"

Doli's smile stretches across her face. "No, ever since she was a little girl, she could see things in people. That's why she wanted you to stay yesterday. She thinks you needed to realize something you already knew but didn't want to admit."

I step out of Cooper and squint my eyes at Chooli. "I can't say I understand what you do or how you do it, but thank you for the best and worst experience of my life." I grab her thin hand in mine. I pull her closer to me and give her a warm hug. "Now, stop poisoning people. That's Joan's job."

Mr. Lee leans up against my leg. I lift him up and put him in the backseat.

Joan hugs Chooli, and hands the empty coffee cup back.

I put Cooper in reverse and turn back onto the main road. Joan pulls the map out from under her seat. There is complete silence in the car. I clear my throat, trying not to laugh. Joan copies me, clearing her throat. Then, at the same time, we both bust out laughing.

"You are so stupid sometimes!" I say, looking at her. "You thought snakes were chasing you!"

Joan claps a hand over her mouth. "I was so scared. I was running towards the field to lose the snakes…then I turned into a mermaid…and couldn't run anymore!"

"I know, dumbass! You told me. I caught you, remember? I should have pretended to catch you in a net, but I was too afraid that you would start running again."

"You're an ass sometimes." Joan punches my knee.

"You had me drink peyote! I don't want to hear anything from you." I laugh, searching for the road to get back onto the highway. I point to the sign, "Oh, how fitting, Dumas, Texas…look, they named a town after you."

Deep in the Heart of Texas

Joan glances up from her map, "Ha! Ha…very funny. We have a ten-hour drive from here to Portland. Do you think we could make it all today?"

I glance at my phone. It's only eight a.m. "Yeah, I think we can make it if we don't stop and explore too much. You better shoot Will a text. Last I texted him, I told him you had passed out because you had too much peyote." I make a gun out of my thumb and index finger and point it at her.

"Oh my gosh, you told him what?!" Joan stomps her feet on her seat.

"I sent him a picture, too! You know, I had to send proof of life." I give her a cheeky smile.

"I guess I deserved that," Joan whispers under her breath.

I toss Joan my phone. "Could you text Thomas for me?"

Joan pulls up Thomas' name, "Okay, go…what do you want to say?"

I start, "Good morning from Texas."

"He's texting…" Joan says holding the phone so that I can see it.

"What does it say?" My stomach does somersaults.

"Hang on, he is still typing, it says…" Joan squints her eyes.

I got in late last night. I was surprised to hear about your Peyote adventure. Thought you might still be sleeping. I miss you. My eyes miss you; my mouth misses you; my soul misses you. I miss you.

Joan raises her eyebrows at me, "His soul? This boy has it bad."

I can't think of anything witty to say. I sit there lost in thought, letting Thomas' words float around in my head. I quietly watch Joan fiddle with her phone, looking for just the right song to add to our playlist. She touches her screen and looks at me satisfied. I roll my eyes at her. The first few notes play. I know this song, it's called, "Deep in the Heart of Texas". I used to play it on loop. Instead of Gene Autry, it was the Mickey Mouse version.

Joan begins to sing. She leans towards me, urging me to join her.

I jump in at the clapping part. I give four good claps and join Joan in singing.

This song always makes me happy. It's a throwback to old country. When country songs told a whole story. It doesn't take long until Joan and I are smiling from ear to ear. Joan lets her phone play song after song as we drive south towards home.

I love the roads here in Texas. They are so wide. I guess it's because most drive huge trucks here. It makes driving Cooper a breeze. I could literally drive side to side and still not cross the line into oncoming traffic. I'm on autopilot as we make it into Austin city limits. "Want to drive by the old house, since we are here?"

Joan turns her head, "No, let's just try to make it home tonight."

I immediately regret asking. I forgot all about Frank. It seems like he never happened, but certain places can trigger memories of a person...even when you don't want them to linger. I know it's not that easy for Joan to forget.

"Okay, let's drive on. I can't wait to see Mom and Dad," I say, trying hard to get Joan to think about anything other than what I had just said. "Hey, play another song."

Joan looks lost in thought so I grab her phone from her. I open her Amazon app and search for my song choice. I scrub Lone-Lee behind the ears. "Are you ready for the next song?" I ask him in a high-pitched voice.

He sits up, excited. He has no idea what I'm saying but he wags his tail and lets his tongue roll out of his mouth.

Joan laughs, "You get me. Say we will always be like this. Tell me when we are in our forties and have kids that we will always be like this, that we will take vacations. That we will still go on adventures. Tell me that nothing will ever change."

I look deep into her eyes, "Nothing will ever change. We will always be like this. We will always go on adventures. No matter how close or far, we will always be like this." I reach over and squeeze Joan's hand three times. "Even if I follow a boy to London."

"You're thinking of going to London?" Joan turns in her seat and looks at me.

"Yes, I'm thinking of going to London. But, just thinking. I just don't know how it would work. I mean, with the cupcake shop and all. Which reminds me, I need to call Marie and check in." I put my blinker on and pull into a gas station.

Joan hops out and begins to pump gas as I walk off with Mr. Lee. The phone rings.

Marie's voice comes on the line. "Feeling Whisky. How may I help you?"

I smile, "Hey, it's me! How have you been?"

In her always upbeat voice, "Oh, hey stranger! How's the trip been going?" I can hear customers talking in the background. "Hang on, I'm going to walk to the back. Kevin is here. He has been helping out, part-time."

"Oh, that's good! Our trip has been crazy. I'll have to tell you all about it. I just wanted to stop and give you a call. Is there anything you need? I mean, is everything okay?" I feel bad for leaving Marie short staffed. "Have you been able to handle it? If you need to hire someone else full-time, then go ahead."

"Things have been good. We had a sudden rush of people last week. I think because you were on TMZ, we had some Looky Lou's here. Mr. Horowitz loves it, though. He's had more visitors in the last week than he's had, well… ever! Kevin has been taking his trash to the curb and he's been at the house a few times for dinner. Hey, I want to hear about Joan and the peyote!"

I interrupt Marie, "Oh my gosh! Joan and the peyote. I think we need to write a song about that. She thought she was a mermaid. Next time you see her, you need to ask her about it. But, listen, on a serious note, we need to talk. I was thinking of going to London, but I want to talk to you first. I haven't made my decision yet. I just want to run it past you."

There's a hesitation on the line, then Marie starts, "Are you thinking about actually moving there, or just going for a visit?"

I can feel a lump starting to form in my throat. "I don't know about moving, but I might be gone for a while. I could hire someone in my place. You can rent out my room if you want."

Marie is silent on the line. I can tell she's thinking. "Go! I've got it handled here. I'm doing what I love. We can hire Kevin full-time since he already knows the ins and outs of the shop. If, by chance, you decide to stay longer, Kevin could move into your room and it would help him out to not pay rent for a while."

"Thanks, Marie! You're the best! You've been so understanding through all of this." I feel guilty for leaving Marie high and dry. "I just feel like I'm abandoning you."

In one breath, Marie shouts, "What? Mar, you moved across the country with me. You opened a bakery with me; it was my dream, not yours. Your dad bought you this building. It brought the bakery to life. Without you, I would have never been able to do this on my own. You haven't abandoned me. If anything, you helped me."

I take a deep breath and slowly let it out. "I'll of course let you know what I decide. But I'm glad to know you feel like you can handle it."

Marie hesitates, then adds, "Kevin has been sleeping on the couch for the last week. He was having a tough time making rent since his roommate moved out. So, he had to let his apartment go."

I laugh, "Have you played Dirty Scrabble?"

"No, I haven't taught him the ways of Dirty Scrabble, but I will. Our game is still on the table. It's your turn." Marie lets out a laugh. "Your last word was 'balls'."

"Ha! Can you blame me? I didn't have a lot to choose from. I better go. Joan is circling the car. She must be done pumping the gas. By the way, we have a dog. We named him Lone-Lee since we found him on The Loneliest Highway. I'll send you a picture." I feel like I'm saying 'goodbye forever,' even though I know I'm not. I whisper, "Bye, love you. I'll talk to you soon." I hang up, my heart aching, and walk back to the car.

"Did you get ahold of Marie?" Joan asks, sliding into the seat next to me.

"Yep, all is good. Things are going well." I stare off into the distance. "She told me to go to London. She could totally handle the shop; she will take Kevin on full-time."

"Is that what you want?" Joan asks, staring straight ahead.

"I don't know yet." I shrug my shoulders as I turn back onto the highway.

Joan stuffs the map under her seat without rolling it up. We could make this drive with our eyes closed. We are about an hour from home. I'm getting a little nervous for some reason. Maybe it's because I have to explain the whole naked picture thing. Maybe I have to tell my parents about Thomas. Maybe I'll have to confront my feelings head on.

"Hey," I look at Joan. "You know what song to play."

Joan types in John Denver. I love that about her. We are so much alike she knows exactly what song I'm talking about.

"I'm adding it to our playlist," Joan says as the song begins to play.

Tears roll down my cheeks. I reach up and wipe them off my face with the back of my hand. I don't know what it is about this song that always makes me cry, but it does. No matter how much I protest. I've tried to figure this out so many times. Maybe it's because I miss my parents, maybe it's because I miss my youth and being at home where there wasn't a care in the world, maybe I miss riding in my go-cart, or ground-in dirt in the knees of my jeans. I mean, I have a pretty great life. I guess I just miss the time when we were all there at home and we ran around until the sun went down. When time was something meant for other people. When time didn't exist; not for us.

Joan notices the tears streaming down my face. "Ah, you cry every time... why do you put yourself through that?"

I clasp my hand with Joan's. "It's a good cry. It's like bad dreams. People want to go to sleep and have good dreams, but I would rather have bad dreams because when I wake up, I wake to an amazing life and the bad dream is just a dream."

"Okay, well, let's listen to something happier." Joan looks through her song list.

She digs under Mr. Lee and pulls out her make-believe microphone. I throw my head back and laugh. She really knows how to make me laugh. The song begins to play. I rock my shoulders to the music.

I wish we could always stay just like this. This young, this crazy, this wonderful. Just as the song is ending, we turn off Highway 77. The road has one lane each way. There's a small causeway that is surrounded by shallow water. If it rains, even a little, you would need a truck to go this way. A truck and a whole lot of faith, since the road is underwater. We are only a couple of towns from being home. The towns are so small we could blink and miss them. We take the back-way home. At least, it used to be the back way. The town has grown out past what used to be corn and cotton fields. We used to only have Whataburger and a Pizza Hut, now there are more restaurants than you can count. The old high school is now the junior high, a brand new, shiny high school was erected across the street from the old one. The football stadium could rival any college stadium around. The stadium itself cost more than a million dollars, but that's Texas football for you. The stadium went from The Wildcat Stadium to Roy Akin's Stadium, and rightfully so, he was an amazing football coach. Mom and Dad still go to every home game during the football season.

Everything past the high school looks the same. The wicked curve cutting between the farmer's field is still there. I remember Joan running off the road into the field on the way to school one morning. Thank goodness she wasn't going fast and we kind of just drove into the field. I've been leery of her driving ever since. That's why I usually drive, but I never tell her that. I just simply drive. As we pull into the driveway, I can see the glow of the living room lights through the window.

Dad is sitting in his burnt orange recliner. It's from the '70's but he refuses to get rid of it. All the furniture in the house has changed over the years, except for Dad's burnt orange chair. My mom hates it. One of the happiest days in my mom's life was when Dad almost burned it to the ground with a cigar. That was the last time he was allowed to step in the house with a lit cigar. The cigars were out, but the recliner stayed; even with the huge hole in the side.

Joan and I sit in silence in the driveway for a minute watching Dad in his recliner. Mom walks into the living room and runs her hand across the back of Dad's shoulders. She sits on the couch next to his chair. They look perfect. Like they have always been together, and that's just the way they will always be.

It looks like Dad is having something built on the property next to the house. I hop out of the car and quietly meet Joan on her side of Cooper. She knows exactly what we are about to do, we do it every time we come home. She holds Mr. Lee in her arms as I slowly push open the gate. We are walking so quietly and sneaky that Mr. Lee begins to growl in confusion. Joan rubs her fingers on his head and he snuggles into her arms. We both step in front of the large living room window and wait.

Mom glances up and sees us standing in the window like the twins from *The Shining*. She yells, "You crazy girls! Te voy a pegar! When will you ever grow up? Henry, your daughters are here."

I love how anytime we do anything that Mom doesn't like we are automatically not hers. Dad turns in his chair and stands up, a huge smile spreads across his face.

I open the front door and Joan and I struggle to both get through it at the same time. Joan puts Lone-Lee on the carpet.

"I see you got a dog. How did that happen?" Dad asks, looking at Lone-Lee like he's the most pathetic animal on the planet.

I have to agree, he has a face only a mother could love. It's a good face.

Mom calls Lone-Lee over, "What's his name?"

Joan laughs, "His name is Lone-Lee, or Mr. Lee. We named him that because we found him on the side of Highway 50 in Nevada."

"Are you girls hungry?" Mom asks as she starts pulling things out of the fridge without waiting for our answer.

I slump into a chair at the table, "Mom, you don't have to make anything. We can go out to eat."

Mom's brows knit together, "That's nonsense. I'll make you something. No use going out and spending money when I can make you something better here."

Mom apparently never got the memo that she and Dad are rich. Mom is Mom. Mom and Dad were dirt poor most of their lives. She comes from a very large family; she has nine brothers and sisters. Being frugal is ingrained in her.

She rolls out tortillas as she talks. It's like second nature to her.

Dad pours himself a glass of sweet tea and sits in his spot at the end of the kitchen counter. "So, girls tell me about your adventure," Dad says, taking a swig of tea. He gives Mom a nod to let her know the tea is just right.

I blurt out, "Joan drank peyote and was running through a field. She thought she was a mermaid! I had to tackle her!"

Joan's eyes widen. She shoots me a look. "Mar! Well, let me tell you about Mar. She met a boy; her naked pictures were all over the news!"

Joan and I are always competing. Even now, we are trying to spill the most embarrassing things about each other. I'm having a hard time coming up with dirt on Joan, though. Besides the peyote, I mean.

"Joan met a man. He really likes her." Jeez, that was lame.

Joan looks at me sideway, "You're so stupid."

Mom is mildly annoyed, "Girls, girls, knock it off."

Dad is sitting in silence enjoying the show. "Well, it sounds like you girls are having a good time. As long as no one is hurt."

"Speaking of getting hurt," I shrug my shoulders, "Oh, by the way, sorry about the six-hundred-dollar bill. Joan's big butt broke the tricycle we were renting."

Joan's mouth drops open, "I really hate you sometimes. Tell them about Thomas. Go ahead, tell them." Joan shoots me a smug look. She thinks she just won the competition. She may have won the battle, but she will never win the war.

Mom sets a plate of freshly made tortillas and refried beans in front of me, "Tell me, Mijita, about this boy."

"Well, I met him in Colorado. We ended up going to this bed and breakfast place we had heard about from a woman we met traveling. We spent a few days together."

Joan clears her throat, "Spent? … And he thinks he loves Mar and wants her to move to London."

Dad nods his head up and down, "I see. Well, how could he not be in love with Mar? He must be a smart man."

Mom pulls out a chair next to Dad. "Do you love him?"

I can feel my face flush. "That's the thing. I feel like I do, but I think there's no way I can. I barely know him."

Mom looks at Dad and then looks back at me. I can tell she wants Dad to tell me something.

Dad's face cracks into a smile. "I met your mother when she was cooking at a place called George's Kitchen. When I walked in, she immediately caught my eye. She was working as a line cook and waitress. She looked up at me and that was it."

"What do you mean, 'that was it'?" I ask, waving my hand in the air. "Did you guys just run to each other like in a fairytale? I need more information here!"

Mom reaches over and pops me on the hand, "Deja de ser un smartass."

I laugh. The only thing I caught was 'smartass.'

Dad tries to clarify. "What I mean is, it was love at first sight. We met after her shift; I think we dated a week."

Dad looks over at Mom for confirmation. "At the end of the week I drove over to her house and picked her up."

Mom interjects, "We married two weeks later at the courthouse."

"We bought a piece of land, set a trailer on it. Then worked to build the house." Dad waves his hand around gesturing at the house. "It doesn't take time. Love is a feeling. It has nothing to do with time. What comes after the feeling is the commitment. That's all you need. It doesn't matter if it's one day or one week. Love can hit you in one glance." Dad leans over and grabs Mom's hand. "I've loved your mother since the day I saw her. I told her so."

Mom squeezes Dad's hand, "I thought he was crazy! Gringo Loco." She trails off, muttering something in Spanish I don't quite catch. I can understand Spanish more than I can speak it, but I can never understand it when Mom starts rattling things off at top speed, which she mostly does when she's mad. Sometimes, it's best not to know what she is saying, anyways.

She slows down and looks at me with a serious look on her face, "Marguerite, I'm talking to you. Do you love him... this boy?"

I pause for a second, "Yes, maybe...I don't know...how can I feel this way about him? I barely know him."

"You don't need to know him; at least not fully. I'm still learning things about your Dad every day. A heart knows love long before your brain will concede." Mom's face begins to glow;

something we rarely see. She likes to keep this tough exterior, but everyone knows it's just a front. She was the disciplinarian growing up. Dad, on the other hand, would let us get away with murder.

As I'm finishing up the last of the tortillas and beans, I look up to see Tex standing in the back door.

Joan stands and wraps her arms around his neck. My eyes meet my Dad's. He's said everything he needed to in just one, long look. I break our look and stand to throw an arm around Tex as he slides down into a chair at the table. Mom fills a plate and sets it in front of him.

Tex clears his throat. "I was in love once...Her name was Alice." Everyone turns to focus on him. I think I've only actually heard Tex talk at length a couple of dozen times. He isn't much for words. "I walked into a diner; she was the most beautiful girl I had ever seen. I met her before the draft. She was standing behind the counter. Her hair was twisted up into pin curls and she wasn't wearing shoes. I thought it was the most adorable and unusual thing I had ever seen. We were together every second of the day. I was studying art at the university; she was still in high school. When the draft called, I had to leave. We wrote..." Tex begins to stare into the distance, then sucks in a deep breath. "We wrote almost every day. We lost contact for a while. When I came back, she was gone. I never knew where she went. I looked for her for years. Back then, there wasn't a good way to find people. I never married. I chose to come back here in case she ever came back this way, she could find me."

A lump immediately forms in my throat. Dad stands and puts his hand on Tex's shoulder.

"You never married?" I ask, curious.

"I never married. She was it for me. When you know you know. Times were simpler back then. There wasn't all this craziness with internet, mass information, etc."

I put my hand to my lips, thinking... sitting in silence for a minute.

Tex interrupts my thoughts, "It's better to act on things, even if you are wrong, because it is more harmful to live in regret. I've spent the last 50 years regretting not marrying her before I left. The hardest thing in my life wasn't the war; it was losing her."

I have never seen Tex so hurt. Tears prick my eyes. I blink, hoping no one notices. He must have thought this was important enough to tell me. I won't let his words fall on deaf ears. Tex is like a dad to me, a silent partner kind of dad. I kiss Tex on the cheek and press my face against his cheek. "Thanks for telling me about Alice."

I walk to my room. As I turn to shut the door, I see Dad dealing out the poker cards between him and Tex. It's his way of trying to make things better. I sit at the edge of the bed and let all the words from my family soak in. Can you imagine loving someone your whole life and waiting for them? I've always wondered about Tex not having a wife or family. He has been with us for every holiday, graduation, and special event for as long as I can remember. I guess, I never really thought of it too much. He and Dad have this unspoken bond. Now that I think about it, he has always been just with us.

I dial Thomas' number and lay back on the bed. I stare at the ceiling as the phone rings. My ceiling is still purple with iridescent glitter. I mentally count the time difference in my head. He's six hours ahead. It's 2 am there! I begin to hang up the phone when I hear Thomas' sleepy voice come on the line.

"Hello?"

"Umm...hi..." I say in a whisper.

"Marguerite, Hi! Is everything okay?" Thomas says in alarm.

Will must have really filled him in on our antics. After last night, I get why he would be worried.

"Uh, yes.... I just... I just..." Why can't I just say it? I will myself to lay it out there. "I just miss you."

I can almost hear him smile over the phone. "I miss you, too. Did you make it to your parent's house?"

"We did, I just wanted to call and tell you that I missed you today." There are so many things I want to say, but I'm holding off until I actually know how to say them. I would hate to say something that I don't follow through with. I just need time to think.

"Okay, beautiful. It was good to hear your voice. I'll talk to you soon?" Thomas' voice is slow and smooth.

"Yep, tomorrow, at a better time." I bite the inside of my cheek so that I don't say what's on my mind.

"Until then. Goodnight, goodnight! Parting is such sweet sorrow, that I shall say goodnight 'til it be morrow." Thomas speaks like a seasoned Shakespearean actor.

Everything in me turns to mush. I click the phone off and curl up under the covers. I have it bad.

Home

The next morning, I drag myself to the kitchen table. Dad is up, making biscuits and gravy. The smell of Folger's brings me right back to my childhood. I slump in a chair as Mom slides over a cup of coffee, black.

"Joan up yet?" I ask, looking around.

"She's out on the front porch talking to someone on the phone." Dad points to the front door.

I take my hairband out of my hair and scratch my head, loosening the tight shape it has taken against my scalp. "So, what are you guys building next door?"

Dad puts the biscuits into the oven. "Tex and I are building him a cottage."

I stand to get a better look out the window.

"It will only be a two bedroom. It's just enough space for him," Dad says as he sips his coffee next to me.

"Oh, that's really nice, Dad," I say, looking to see my mom's reaction.

"Tex doesn't have family. His forever home needs to be here," Mom says, not looking up from the griddle. "He belongs here with us; we are his family."

I crisscross my legs and pull them close to me on the chair. I slowly sip my coffee and think about life. What amazing parents I have. I guess I have never really thought about it before. I just assumed all parents are like mine, taking them for granted. I realize now that that's just not the case.

"Good Morning," a gravelly voice says behind me. I swivel in my chair to see Tex walking through the back door. Tex pulls off his cap and sets it on his knee. Mom gently sets a plate in front of him.

Joan comes walking back into the kitchen. She's practically floating.

"Let me guess…that was 'Hi, I'm Will' on the phone." I poke her in the ribs as she walks by.

Joan seems to be having no problem moving on from Frank. I'm happy about that. It could have been worse; I mean, she could have taken him back. In which case I would have had to resort to something drastic.

Joan plops down into the seat next to Tex, "So, what's on the agenda today?" She sips her coffee and looks back and forth between Mom and Dad.

"We should go shopping," Mom says, looking happy now that she finally has someone to go shopping with.

I'm itching to get some alone time for a few minutes to think. I hop up from the table, "Whatever y'all decide, I'm in. Just let me know. I'm going to walk around outside for a bit."

I pop open the garage and take a look around. My old go-cart is sitting in the corner. I wonder if it still runs. Who am I kidding, it never ran to begin with. I haven't cranked the engine in forever. I put one hand on the steering wheel and one on the back of the seat and push it out. I give the rope one good pull. Nothing. I open the gas tank. It has gas. I turn the idle up and give the rope another good pull. It starts! I hop on the brown, velvet seat and take off. I retrace the route I made as a kid, even though the grass has reclaimed the path, I know it by heart. The oleander bush used to be the gas station. The mesquite tree in the far corner of the yard was the grocery store.

As I make the second loop past the house again, Joan walks to the side of the driveway, waving her hands, "Hey! Pick me up!"

She used to do the same thing when we were kids. Even though the go-cart was mine, when Joan was outside, we would have to take turns driving it.

I make the loop and pull up next to Joan. "Get on…if you must."

Joan happily runs around the back of the go-cart and plops her butt down next to me. We were a bit smaller the last time we rode this thing together. Joan shifts onto one side of her hip and holds on for dear life. I slam my foot down on the gas and we begin to go full speed around the loop. Sometimes, you just have to drive. This brings me straight back to when we were kids. The smell of the dirt, the grass, and rain—even though there is no rain in sight. When I needed time to think, I would mindlessly drive the loop.

We do about three laps going full speed when Dad walks outside and watches us zoom by and make another loop.

I pull the go-cart to a stop in front of him and hop off, "So, did you guys decide what we were doing today?"

"Your mother would like to go shopping. Then we could have a nice dinner tonight." Dad puts an arm around me. "When do you girls have to leave?"

Joan rounds the go-cart to stand next to us. "We were thinking about leaving in the morning and heading to New Orleans, then up north to New York, then back straight across to California." Joan draws a straight line in the air with her finger.

I exhale, realizing I have been holding my breath. Thomas is on my mind this morning. I wonder what he is doing. My mind drifts back to laying in his arms. I try hard to shake the thought out of my mind.

"Yep, shopping sounds fun. I'll go get ready." I put my head down and walk towards the house.

As I walk off, I hear Dad ask Joan, "So, do you think she's going?"

I see Joan shrug her shoulders. I turn to walk inside and head for my room. What am I going to do? I love him. The only harm I could do is to not go and possibly regret it for the rest of my life. If it doesn't work out, then I just come back. No harm, No foul. Tears are streaming down my face when Mom walks in with a basket full of my laundry. She must have dug all my clothes out of the trunk of Cooper.

"What's wrong, Mijita?" Mom gently sits me on the bed. She starts to scratch my back. "Why are you crying?"

I look at her as a tear rolls off my cheek, landing on my knee making a tiny, blue sun on the fabric of my pajamas.

"You are really conflicted about this boy?" Mom asks, narrowing her eyes on me.

I adjust myself, uncomfortable, "I am. I just don't think it's the real thing. I mean it's only been a week..."

Mom sits in silence for a minute. "If you didn't love him, then why would you be crying right now? You wouldn't give him a second thought."

I let her words sink in.

"When I met your father, I was scared, too. I didn't know if it would work, but I knew that I had enough feelings that I didn't want to not take the chance. I didn't know anything about life, money, or relationships. That's the thing, love is inherent."

I bury my head in her shoulder. Mom always make things better. If running to London to be with Thomas is the wrong thing, I will always have the support from my family. It makes taking the chance easier.

"Go, Mijita. If you love him, go to him. Everything else will work itself out." Mom pulls my hair to the side, tucking it behind my ear.

I rub my face onto Mom's shirt. "You're right, Mom. I'm just scared that it couldn't be love. It happened so fast. I don't really know all that much about him."

Mom pulls me off her shoulder to look at me. "Well, no one said there was a time limit on things. You have time to figure it out. There isn't this magic clock that when it runs out it will drop you into lava."

I shake my head. She's right. What am I worried about? Maybe I'm not worried about *if* I love him, but *if* he loves me. Maybe I don't want to be so far from my family. My phone rings in my pocket. I stand and dig it out. It's Thomas! I turn the phone towards Mom. Thomas' face pops up.

She raises her eyebrows at me.

"Hello!" I can barely contain my excitement.

Mom gives me a wave as she walks out the door.

I give her a thumbs up and turn back to my conversation with Thomas.

His smooth voice comes over the line and melts me like butter being sliced with a warm knife. "Hello, Baby. What have you been up to today?"

"Oh, not too much yet. I've been hanging out with my parents. I cranked up my old go-cart...drove it around. We are about to go shopping. Then tonight we are all having dinner together."

Thomas' voice comes out in a low purr. "So, you did what? You have a pushcart?"

"What? No, it's a go-cart. It's like a small car without a shell. I had it when I was a kid." I pause. What the hell is a pushcart, anyways?

Thomas begins to laugh. "You rode in this? I would have paid top dollar to see that."

A smile stretches across my face. Everything I was worried about disappears. "Well, just you wait, maybe someday you will."

"Oh, will I? I'm such a lucky man." He adds a little growl to the end of his sentence.

I wonder if he knows that he is driving me absolutely crazy. "You don't even know the half of it." I intentionally slow my voice. This is my attempt at being sexy, but it's quickly all going to crap.

"Is that so?" Thomas says. I can hear him let out his breath.

I drop my voice a couple of octaves, "Next time, the very next time I see you I will... eek!" I catch Joan out of the corner of my eye. "Dang it, Joan! You scared the crap out of me!"

Joan is bent over in the doorway, laughing. "Mom wants to know if you are ready." She winks. "I mean, if you are done at your miserable attempt at phone sex?"

I can feel the blood rush to my cheeks. I really hate her sometimes. Not really, that's a lie. I grab a pillow off the bed and throw it at her.

She dodges it and straightens. "Did you just throw a pillow at me?"

I lift my hand and try to shoo her out the door. I mouth, "Please get out of here!"

She cocks her head to the side. "You aren't going to get away with it that easy. Do you think you can physically assault me and pretend it didn't happen?" Her voice is getting louder with each word.

I widen my eyes at her and turn my back to block her out. Joan jumps on my back before I know what's happening and tackles me onto the bed. I fall into the pillows face first.

I let out a yell, "Get off me, cow!" My voice comes out muffled as Joan forces my face back into the pillow. I shift my head to the side to yell for Mom. "Mom! Joan is trying to kill me, again!"

My mom comes running in from the kitchen with her chancla in her hand. She starts spanking Joan on the butt with it. The shoe isn't working, Mom throws her shoe to the ground and jumps on Joan's back, trying to pull us apart. This must be quite the sight.

"You girls…stop it!" Mom manages to pull her other flip-flop off. She begins swatting at Joan, hitting her a few times on the back.

I fling my head back, trying to hit Joan.

Mom finally succeeds on getting Joan off of me. I'm still gripping my phone tight as Joan stands up and adjust her clothes. Mom puts the shoes back on her feet and walks out of the room, shaking her head.

Joan turns back to me with a mischievous look in her eyes. She reaches down, grabbing me by my ankles and pulls me off the bed.

My bottom hits the floor, hard. I throw my leg up to kick her but miss. Thank goodness she doesn't see me, or I would be in for it.

I clear my voice, "Thomas... sorry about that. My sister is a jerk."

Thomas laughs, a little flummoxed, "Were you guys fighting? I was worried about you for a second. So, you were saying?"

I know what he means, but I have completely lost my nerve. "Can I call you later? I have a day full of shopping. My mom is getting antsy to go have some girl time." I don't want to get off the phone. I just want to crawl under the covers and pretend I'm curling up around him.

"Okay, Love. Take care and goodnight if I don't hear from you again today." I can tell Thomas feels the same way I do. I can hear him breathing, and there is a slight hesitation on the line. "I love you."

"Bye." I sit on the floor in silence with the phone in my hand. I feel horrible, but I just want it to be the right time. It feels like a bowling ball hits me hard in the chest. I imagine this is what a heart attack feels like. When I walk out of the house Mom and Joan are already in the car.

Dad is standing in the yard watering the grass. He gives us a quick wave as we pull out of the driveway.

After six hours of shopping, my feet are throbbing. We finally make it back to the house for dinner. Dad is sitting at the end of the table drinking a glass of sweet tea. Two, huge bouquets of flowers sit in front of him. "These came for you today... you and your Mother."

He sent Mom flowers? Wow, what a gentleman. The front of the tiny white envelope has 'Marguerite's mom' written on it. I pull out the card and hand it to Mom. She looks at the card and smiles.

"Well, come on! What does it say?!" I ask excitedly.

Mom begins, "It says:

Thank you for making the most perfect, most beautiful girl in the world. I look forward to meeting you in the future.

Tom."

My heart flutters. Mom hands the card over to Dad.

He gives it a look and shakes his head in approval. "That boy of yours is quite the gentleman, isn't he?"

My words just spill out, "He is! He's more than I've ever expected. I love him."

What's for Dinner?

I clap my hand over my mouth. My words take me off guard. It's the first time I actually said that out loud. Do I love him? Is it 'I love you' or 'I love ya?' There's a difference.

Mom gives me a hug, trying to calm me. "It looks like you have found a good one."

Dad stands, "I will want to meet him sooner than later, and I'll be the judge of that."

After Frank cheated on Joan Dad has been beating himself up over letting Frank into Joan's life.

I throw an arm around Dad's neck. "Actually, I know he would love that. He wants to be a cowboy."

Dad jerks his head back and furrows his brow in confusion.

"He thinks everyone in Texas is a cowboy," I wait for Dad's reaction.

Dad shakes his head, "Well, we will introduce him to Tex. That's as close to a cowboy as he's going to get."

Mom is laying out our newly purchased clothes on the table. We've hit the mother lode. I haven't bought this many outfits since I lived at home.

"I told Thomas about 'front porch sitting'. I can only imagine him out there with a small cup of hot tea," I say to Dad, elbowing him in the ribs.

He claps his hands on the table in front of him and laughs. "Well, we will just have to teach him."

Dad eyes the clothes that Mom has spread out on the table, "Did you girls get what you needed?"

That's Dad's way of asking it we got what we wanted.

Joan is happily pulling off price tags and folding her clothes into a neat stack. "Dad, I think we got more than we needed. Mar had to buy two, new luggage cases just to carry her stuff. I didn't buy another since Mom said I could have one of hers." Joan gives Dad a smug look. She knows Mom would be proud of her for saving money.

Mom comes out of the bedroom carrying a suitcase just as Joan finishes her sentence. It must be from the '80's. It is covered in a dark green pattern with needlework, and pink roses all over it. It's the ugliest thing I have ever seen. I catch Joan's eye; she turns to see why I have a smirk on my face.

"Mom! What the heck is that?" Joan's mouth drops open. The horror on Joan's face is worth all the pennies in the jar!

Mom furrows her brows together. She holds the luggage up in the air. "What? It's the suitcase you wanted to borrow."

Joan grabs it from Mom and twirls it in the air. She says exactly what I'm thinking. "Mom! This is the ugliest thing I have ever seen. Besides, where are the wheels?"

I stomp my feet on the floor and hold my stomach laughing. I'm so glad I sprung for new luggage. I would have ended up with the matching, smaller version of this monstrosity.

Dad stands and pulls his pants up by the belt loops, trying to change the subject. "So, are you girls ready for some dinner?"

He can tell Mom is about to go into her rant about using what you have, especially if it still works. If I was the one that had to borrow it, I would argue that it doesn't work because you have to actually carry it. For now, I'll just laugh at Joan.

Dad is wearing his usual dark blue Levi's with a light blue, snap up shirt. Either he's a genius that doesn't like wasting time picking something out, or he just likes what he likes. His go-to shoes are Red Wing boots, size eight triple E. He has the squarest feet I have ever seen; a close second is Fred Flintstone. Dad begins walking to the truck before we answer.

Mom follows him without question.

I shrug my shoulders at Joan, "I guess we're going. I was going to call Thomas, I guess I can't call now."

As we walk towards the truck, Dad is placing a step stool on the grass so mom can get in without a running start. I know what you're thinking: why doesn't he just get running boards? He does have running boards. The step stool is to reach the running boards. I joke that he should put RV stairs on mom's side so that a set of tiny stairs pops out for her.

I open the back door behind Dad and slide in. I begin looking through my phone at pictures of Thomas.

Joan opens the door on the other side of the truck and hops in. She notices. "You miss him?"

I just nod my head up and down but don't say anything. My door opens and Tex shoos me over without a word.

Dad looks up in the rearview mirror. "Okay, we are all here. Let's get this show on the road. Joan, you're in charge of the music."

"Dad, before I do that. Mar needs to make a quick call to Thomas before it gets too late there." Joan gives me a cheeky smile.

"Mar?" Dad adjusts his mirror to point directly at me. "Do you want to call Thomas right now?"

I really don't want to do that with everyone in the truck listening to my every breath. As my thoughts drift off about my breath and Thomas, my phone rings. Thomas' face pops up on my screen. It must be the Universe talking. My eyes widen, the ringing is coming over the truck speakers. My phone must still be connected to the truck from the last time I was home.

"Go ahead and answer it, we will be quiet," Mom says, turning in her seat and giving me a smile.

I slide my finger across the screen, answering it. "Hi." My voice is an octave higher than normal and a little shaky.

"Hi!" everyone in the truck chimes in, in unison.

What happened to 'we will be quiet' ? I should have known better. My eyes narrow as I look around, making eye contact with everyone in the truck. I throw my arms in the air, turning into a silent mime. I shake my fist and point to each person in silent warning.

"So... I'm in the truck, and you are on speaker phone," I say, emphasizing speaker phone.

"Hello, who do I have the pleasure of speaking to?" Thomas doesn't skip a beat. He actually sounds excited to be on speakerphone.

"Well... my dad, mom, Joan, and Tex." As I say each name, a hello follows right on cue. This has to be the most awkward phone call. Even if it is, Thomas doesn't seem to mind, he's good like that.

Dad puts the truck into park as we sit in the driveway.

Thomas clears his voice, "Good evening, Mr. and Mrs. Becker. It's nice to speak with you. Marguerite has told me so much about you. I hope to meet you soon."

Dad chimes in, "Sooner than later, son."

There is a slight silence on the line, "Yes Sir, indeed. I would love to come for a visit."

That seems to please Dad.

To my surprise, Mom goes right in for the kill, "Mar says that you love her..."

This is just getting more and more embarrassing by the second. I quickly interrupt, "Thomas you don't have to answer that!"

Thomas laughs on the other end of the line. "I don't mind. You are right. I love her. She's amazing!"

My heart gives a hard thump. He just told my whole family that he loves me. No hesitation, no stutter... he just put it all out there.

Mom is completely silent. Well, I guess that's one way to shut her up. There's no way to argue with honesty.

I interrupt the silence and muster up all my courage, "It is good to hear your voice." Even saying this little bit in front of my parents seems too risky.

Joan grabs my knee, "Aw, Mar is in…"

I slap my hand over her mouth, silently threatening her. It feels like I'm in a dream, falling through the sky and everyone is watching to see what happens.

Thomas' voice comes over the truck speakers, surrounding me in his deep, rich voice, "I miss you, Baby. I hope to see you soon. I love you."

I'm melting into the backseat, "…Kay." I slowly slide my finger across the screen of my phone, hanging it up.

Without a word, Dad puts the truck in reverse.

I quickly start texting Thomas on my phone.

I'm sorry that was so awkward. I miss you too. K… wasn't how I wanted to end that.

The little texting bubble pops up. I stare at my phone. Then the bubble disappears. I feel like crying but then the bubble pops up again.

How did you really want to end it?

I type as fast as I can:

I wanted to say I missed you. I can't wait to hold you.

I shove the phone in my purse, trying to change the atmosphere in the truck. Maybe it's just me that feels awkward. "Joan, I think Dad requested some music."

Joan types a name into her phone. As the first few notes start to play, I began to laugh. My dad loves this song.

He starts to sing along.

Ray Stevens is just what I needed. Dad makes funny faces at us in the rear-view mirror. As we pull into the parking lot of the restaurant, Dad shuffles in his seat. Even though he has been playing with us, I can tell he has been thinking about something.

He turns in his seat to face me, "You're young. It's the right time to take chances. Even if you aren't sure, you should go. There is nothing that says you have to stay if it isn't what you thought it was."

I let Dad's words soak in. He's right. What am I so afraid of? I just hope I haven't screwed up things with Thomas tonight. I wish I had the courage to blurt it all out.

As soon as I open the door of the truck, I get a whiff of BBQ. We drive to the town over to get BBQ. It's been open since the 60's. When you say we are going for BBQ no one in town asks where, they already know. Like if you say, 'let's go have BBQ' you don't have to say where, you just say a time. It's that kind of place. It's been forever since I've had Texas BBQ. Not the BBQ you get in Kansas that claims to be Texas BBQ. I mean, *real* Texas BBQ. From Texas *in* Texas. Nothing beats it. Many states claim to have Texas BBQ, but none really ever do. It just ends up being very frustrating. I better eat my fill, who knows when I will have good BBQ again; especially if I go to London. I happily eat my fill and let the dinner go by in a blur. Once all of us are full and happy, we head back home and get ready for bed.

I pull the covers to my chin and stare up at the ceiling. I lay in bed looking from one shelf to the next at all the trophies and trinkets from my childhood. I can't sleep. I decide to see if Joan is awake. Our two bedrooms share a wall in between our closets that, as a kid, I poked holes into to spy on Joan.

I walk to the closet and press my face to the wall, "…you awake?" The closet is almost like a confessional. I can speak freely here.

I can hear Joan get out of bed and slide against the wall in the closet. "I'm awake."

"Hi," I say quietly.

"Hi," Joan replies.

"I need you to be serious. How do you know if you are in love?" My voice is barely audible.

"Gosh Mar, I thought I knew, but look at me now. The best thing I can say is, life is always evolving. Do what feels right. If that ever changes, change with it."

I can feel Joan press her hand against the thin paneling and I match hers with mine. We sit in silence for a while. That is until I hear Joan snoring on the other side of the closet.

I whisper, "Goodnight Joan." I slowly crawl across the floor to my bed and pull the covers around me. The blankets smell like home. I make a little tent and scroll through my phone.

The next morning, I wake up and reach over, searching in the covers for my phone. Last thing I remember I was writing in my notepad and looking at pictures of Thomas. I pick the phone up and try to focus on the time. 10:44... Could that be right? Ouch! I reach under my back and find my pen. I throw the covers off of me and crack open my bedroom door. The house is quiet. I walk to the fridge and grab the milk and unscrew the top, chugging it without getting a glass.

"Sucia! Stop that! You aren't the only one that drinks milk!" Mom says as she pulls off her garden gloves, setting them on the table.

I wipe my mouth and screw the top back on the jug. "Where is everyone?"

"Oh, everyone is over looking at Tex's cottage." Mom points out the window. "Get dressed and go over."

I quickly brush my teeth and run my fingers through my hair. I bust out the door like I did when I was a kid, like I always had some place to be and I was five minutes late.

"Hi, Dad." I give him a big hug and rest my hands on my hips. "Looks like it's going to be super cute."

Tex walks up behind me, "Good morning, Sugar Bear." Something he has called me since I was a kid. I still don't know why. I guess I never thought to ask. Like you never think to ask why your name is your name.

"Good Morning!" I wrap my arms around him and pull him in for a tight hug. "Looks like you are going to have an awesome place here."

"I'm going to plant a small garden behind it and raise my own vegetables." Tex begins pointing things out. "On the front I'm going to have a large porch."

"That sounds really nice, Tex. I can't wait to see it finished." I cuddle under Dad's arm.

Joan joins me under his other arm. She looks at me, then at Dad, "We are leaving today. We're headed to Louisiana. Might check out what Bourbon Street is all about."

"We will be back soon, though. We need to see this cottage finished," I reassure dad.

Tex gives us a big smile. I can tell he is proud of his cottage. I think he likes being closer to Mom and Dad. I mean, who wouldn't? Mom feeds him every chance she gets.

"How about a quick lunch before you girls take off?" Dad asks.

It's never easy to leave, even if we all make it a point to see each other fairly often. I throw my luggage in the back of Cooper. I watch as Joan struggles with the monstrosity Mom gave her earlier.

She gives me a dirty look as she throws it on top of mine. "I don't want to hear anything from you."

"Don't scratch my luggage with your hideous... whatever that is," I say.

I slam the trunk shut as Mom comes out to the patio holding several plates.

Dad is sitting at the head of the glass, patio table, feeding Mr. Lee bologna slice after bologna slice. That can't be good for him, but I'm not going to be the one to tell Dad that.

Mom sets a plate down in each spot. It's like ten degrees cooler than the underworld, making it a nice day in Texas. I grab a seat next to Dad and stretch my legs out in front of me.

Tex steps through the bushes and pulls a chair out next to me.

Mom is serving my favorite: a combo of bologna, mayo, and Dorito sandwiches.

Mom scoots in next to Dad and reaches her hand out for the lunchtime prayer. "God please keep Joan and Mar safe during their travels. Wherever it might take them."

I can't be for certain, but I think I can feel Mom give my hand an extra, small squeeze. We end lunch with small talk and laughter. Just like we always do. Mr. Lee has made it onto Dad's lap during the course of lunch and doesn't look like he has any intention of leaving. He's gotten his fill of belly scratches and bologna and is sleeping on his back.

Joan and I stand to give our quick goodbyes as Mom drops a groggy Mr. Lee into the backseat. She knows if she doesn't drop Mr. Lee into the back seat, she will be the proud new owner of a bologna-eating dog. I manage to hop in Cooper without bursting into tears. I give everyone a quick wave without looking back at them in the mirror. Leaving is always the hardest. I resist the urge to yell, "Hasta la vista, bitches." I seriously don't know what's wrong with me.

Okay, Joan. Next song..."

Louisiana

Joan pulls the map up on her phone.

"Want to head on to Louisiana? We can finally check out Bourbon Street," She says as she traces her finger along the highway.

I shrug my shoulders. "Yes, Bourbon Street. That sounds like the perfect plan for us."

Marie and I went our junior year in college; Joan seems to have blocked that out. She didn't go with us. She and Frank were pretty serious by then and he never wanted her to be involved with 'things like that,' whatever 'things like that' meant. We should have known then what a colossal asshole he was going to turn out to be. He was allowed to go out with the boys, but when it came to Joan it was a different story. If she did something he didn't like, he would give her the silent treatment; she thought it was just better not to rock the boat. I don't know how she lived like that.

"Hey...don't you remember, Marie and I went to Bourbon Street for Spring break that one time?" I wait for her to remember. She doesn't so I push it along. "You helped pay for a hotel bed... Marie and I had this not-so-bright idea... we tried to carry our mattress to the top of the roof via the balcony. Like I said, not the best idea. It fell to the street below and was swallowed up by the crowd. Luckily, the hotel was only two stories high and the mattress didn't hurt anybody."

"Oh! That's right! By the way, you owe me $1,200 bucks!" Joan holds out her hand for payment.

"Consider us even, since you poisoned me. And I had to catch you while you were tripping on peyote." I hold her hand tighter for her to shake on the deal.

She shakes it and throws my hand away from her. "I hate you! Well, only most of the time." She hammers her fist against my knee.

"Well, I hate you when you poison me and run through a field like a complete jackass. So, I guess we're even! And if we are keeping score, that's a whole 2% more hate for you." I hold up two fingers in front of her face.

Joan reaches up and grabs my fingers. "Shut up stupid!"

Joan and I play the license plate game until we both forget we are actually playing the license plate game. The eight-hour drive seems to fly by. We cross the Louisiana state line without even realizing it.

Joan is in her seat texting away, typing like a court reporter.

"Who are you texting over there?" I ask, not taking my eyes off the road.

"Mom, Will…. Thomas." Joan says Thomas' name so quietly that I almost don't catch it.

I turn and look at her. She has my full attention. "Thomas! Why are you texting Thomas?"

"Actually, he texted me. He was wondering where we were staying tonight. I told him that I wasn't sure. I kind of got the feeling he was going to show up somehow." Joan shakes her head and shrugs her shoulders.

My heart flutters at the thought. He can't be headed here, can he? I mentally count the hours from the last time I talked to him to now. Well, he has had enough time to fly here, he surely wouldn't do that… Would he?

That has me thinking, "Where are we staying?" I point my finger up and down indicating that Joan should start looking for a hotel.

Joan immediately starts scrolling through the hotels. "Want to stay close to downtown, or does it matter?"

I think about it for a second, "With Uber these days I don't think it matters too much, but the closer the better."

Joan's phone dings. She presses the button and smiles.

"Who is it? ...Will?" I look curiously at her phone.

Joan shakes her head. A smile stretches across her face. "It's Thomas...He got us a hotel... hang on, he's typing. He sent us the confirmation." Joan turns her phone to show me the screenshot of the confirmation.

I glance, "The Windsor? Holy crap! That's a super fancy hotel. I guess that takes care of finding a hotel. Type in the address!" I kind of like the fact that he found us a hotel. It's actually pretty sweet. I love knowing that I'm on his mind. I pull over and send a quick text:

> *So sweet of you to get us a room. The only thing better is if you were in it. I miss you. You're the best!*

A text bubble immediately pops up. My heart drops to my toes, I wiggle them around.

> *No, you're the best. I know firsthand. Have a great time! I love you.*

I pull Cooper to the front of The Windsor; two bellmen rush out and open our doors. I pop the trunk and yank my luggage out, but the bellman quickly takes it from me, loading it onto a trolley. He grabs Joan's hand-me-down luggage out and tries hard to not make a face. I notice though, and point at Joan. That's what she gets for borrowing anything from Mom.

As we walk into the lobby, a man walks around the counter. "Ms. Becker?" he extends his hand out to me.

I shake his hand. "Yes, I'm Ms. Becker."

He hands me a small envelope. "This is your room key. If there is anything you or your sister may need, please do not hesitate to ask. You are on the twenty-second floor, the penthouse."

I raise my eyebrows to Joan. We get into the elevator and press the button for the twenty-second floor. Lone-Lee is trying to wiggle free from Joan's arms. The elevator door opens right into our room. This is the most amazing hotel room I have ever stayed in. It's like a small apartment.

I glance around, "Joan, it has a full kitchen!"

Joan drops Lone-Lee from her arms so that he can explore. She walks from door to door, opening each one. "Look there's a library here, and a piano!" She pulls out the seat and starts playing "Fields of Gold" by Eva Cassidy.

I half hum and half sing along to the music.

I come to a door with my name neatly written in scroll. I open the door, cautiously peering around it. There's a note on my bed. I sit down and rip open the envelope.

> *I hope you like the room. I wish I was there making fort tents out of sheets. Please enjoy the room. I lined up a couple of things for you, but feel free to cancel anything that you want. Love, Tom*

I lean back on the bed and bask in the warmth of his words. I wrap the top comforter around me and hide in my cocoon of warm, glowing feelings.

"Hey… hey Stupid! What are you doing? Are you sleeping?" Joan's words jolt me upright. Lone-Lee jumps up onto the bed and licks my face.

I hand her the card and smile. I scoot to the end of the bed and finally get a good look around the room. Thomas has filled my room with flowers.

"Look at all the flowers." I wave my arms around in a circle, pointing out all the flowers. My room smells like the best English garden. I imagine myself sitting in the grass of a garden with my arms wrapped around his, leaning my head against his chest. The only thing that smells better is his bare chest. I let my mind go there and I float there for a minute.

A bell rings from the living room. "Do we have a doorbell?" Joan asks, looking back at me as she heads to the living room.

"Who is it?" I hop behind her. I'm half hoping its Thomas.

There is a man standing just inside the door. I forgot the elevator came straight into our room.

"It's our luggage." Joan ushers the bellman in. He wheels the trolley in and hands me a packet.

I quickly open it and spread its contents out on the table.

As the bellman leaves, Joan sits next to me at the table. "What do we have here?"

I spread out different pamphlets in front of her. "He said we could cancel anything we wanted. He made dinner reservations for us at an authentic creole restaurant, hired a driver for us, and he signed us up for a ghost tour. A ghost tour, Joan!"

Joan hands me a note, "Looks like this note is for you."

I open the letter and read it out loud.

Dear,
The driver is yours all night as long as you need him. He will take you anywhere you want to explore tonight. I just want you to have an amazing time without worrying about driving. A box will be coming up for you shortly. Have a great night!
Tom

I sit in awe. I have never had anyone think to do this for me. I really want to call Thomas right now.

I stand from the table, "I'm going to call Thomas, then grab a shower... should we shoot for being ready by 8:30?" I turn my wrist over to look at my watch.

"Yep, sounds good." Joan drags herself to her bedroom with Mr. Lee in tow.

I reach in my pocket and pull out my phone to dial Thomas' number. He picks up on the second ring, "Hello, Love."

His voice comes over the line like smooth, warm honey pouring over the back of a shiny, silver spoon. It makes me melt.

"Hi," I say in a whisper. I try to make it come out like a sexy breathless whisper, but it comes out more like I ran up the stairs and can't breathe whisper. "I wanted to thank you for the gifts and the room. It is an amazing surprise. I love that you planned something for Joan and I. Especially the ghost tour. We've always wanted to do something like that."

I can tell Thomas is happy. "I'm glad you like it. I've been thinking a lot about you today, I miss you."

"I miss you, too." I say, feeling an ache in my chest. There's a slight silence. I want to tell him. I want to tell him I love him. I want to run to him and jump into his arms and stay there forever, but I opt for, "How have you been?" I steel myself for his answer. I don't want to hear the sadness in his voice.

"I got a dog today. I rescued him from *Tyson's Rescue,* it's a rescue here in London. I found that my flat is too quiet these days."

I smile at the thought of Thomas with a puppy. "What's its name?"

"His name is Charlie. He lost his mother. I use a bottle twice a day to supplement his soft puppy food."

I hear the happiness in Thomas' voice. This little fellow doesn't know just how lucky he is. I imagine Thomas feeding Charlie with a bottle. It softens my heart and I feel warm and gooey inside. Just like warm, freshly baked chocolate chip cookies.

Thomas giggles on the other end of the line.

It makes me smile, "What are you laughing at?"

"He's chewing on my chin while I'm talking to you." I can hear Thomas playing with Charlie.

"Okay, I'll talk to you soon. I better get dressed so that we don't miss our dinner reservation."

"You..." Thomas' voice comes out in a smooth growl.

"You...what?" I say a little flummoxed.

Thomas clears his voice. "I was thinking of you." His words are slow and drawn out. I let his words sink in and settle in the bottom of my belly. It sends tiny firework messengers in all directions. I feel like I'm vibrating. "Goodnight, Goodnight! Parting is such sweet sorrow, my sweet Marguerite." When he quotes Shakespeare it's exactly how I imagine it is supposed to sound. I have nothing near that fancy to say.

"Goodnight, Thomas. Sweet dreams." I slide my finger across my phone and hang up.

I'm waiting on the couch when Joan opens the door to her room. I look up, "Hey! Did you get to talk to Will?"

Joan nods her head. "Yes, he was out at the vineyard site all day. He is now headed over to the restaurant with Howard for dinner."

The elevator chimes, Joan walks over to it.

It's the same bellman from before. He's holding a fruit basket and a small box. He sets the basket on the kitchen counter. Joan takes the small box from him and reads the attached card.

To: Mr. Lee
From: Charlie, Enjoy!

That has to be the cutest thing I've ever seen. I scrub Mr. Lee behind the ears. "Looks like you have a present."

Joan opens the box, it's freshly baked, peanut butter, dog biscuits. I walk over and pick one out of the box and lean down to give it to Mr. Lee. He takes it and jumps onto the couch. He makes three circles and plops himself down to enjoy his biscuit.

I sit on the couch beside him to pull on my boots. "Well, ya ready?" I slap my hands on my rear, dusting them off.

Joan grabs her purse, "Bye, Lone-Lee. Don't get into too much trouble."

As we take the elevator down to the lobby, I mentally make a checklist. Phone, key, gum, lipstick. Yep, I have everything.

"Are you Marguerite?" A medium-built, slender man in a black chauffer hat is standing in front of me.

"I am and this is my sister Joan." I grab Joan and pull her in front of me.

Joan jets out her hand and shakes his, "I'm Joan, nice to meet you."

"I'm Pranab. I will be your driver tonight." He pulls out a small notebook from his pocket. "Looks like Marie Laveau's first." He snaps his notebook shut and leads us to the car. He opens the car door.

I scroll down to Marie's name and type:

Male, about 5'9", black hair, our driver for the night. Silver Lincoln Town Car. Sending our location.

I push send as I slide in and lay my phone down on the backseat to buckle my belt. A text bubble immediately pops up.

Call me when you guys get back to the hotel. Don't make me hop a plane, looking all crazy.

Pranab drops us at the front of the restaurant. The hostess leads us to a table next to a giant, wooden case behind a thick glass with quite the wine collection. There must be over a thousand bottles. A waiter appears out of nowhere and sets down a plate of oysters.

I smile up at him. "We didn't order oysters." My smile isn't what it's supposed to be right now. It's more of a disgusted grimace. I've never tried oysters for a reason.

"Tom sent them. Enjoy." He gives a quick bow and saunters off before I can express my opinion on oysters.

"Thank you," I call after him. I look over at Joan.

She has a smile stretching across her face. "As I see it, we can do one of two things. One: we can gift them to another table, or two: we can try them."

I knit my brows together at her and blow out a breath. "You first…"

"No, no, no… you first." She begins to gag as she puts her hand over mouth.

"Together, then?" I wait for Joan to back out. I'm trying to give myself the easy way out, but she calls my bluff.

"Okay, together, then. How are we supposed to eat these, anyways?" Joan picks up a shell and examines it.

I begin to giggle. It's the only thing I can do to keep myself from throwing up. I wonder who the very first person was to eat an oyster. I mean, think about it. How did anyone ever think to crack open a rock and eat what is inside? Especially when it looks like a giant, gray booger. If I was the taste tester that day, modern times may have never discovered oysters.

Joan begins stabbing one with a miniature fork. It keeps slipping around in the shell until she finally gets frustrated and stabs it hard, then hands the fork to me. She gets one on another fork then looks at me, "Okay, you ready?"

"Ready as I'll ever be." I put it up to my nose to smell it. I involuntarily gag, then press my hand over my heart. It's going to take everything in me to do this. Honestly, I may lose it right here at the table.

Joan is cracking up and stomping her feet on the floor.

My eyes begin to water.

She mumbles, "Slimy, gross…"

"Shut up, Joan!" I laugh between gags. "Pick up your fork! On the count of three."

Joan nods her head in agreement. "One…two…three…"

At the same time, we both drop the oysters into our mouths. I begin to chew.

Joan turns to the wall, *slowly* chewing. She puts one hand on her forehead, as her face turns red. Little sweat beads form at her temples.

I'm having a hard time keeping mine in my mouth, but the sight of Joan makes me laugh, almost making me spit mine out by accident. I finally swallow mine as I rest my head on the table in complete elation that it's over. I curl my toes as tears stream down my face. I forcefully gag. I don't dare look up at Joan. I know she is equally having the worst time.

"Is everything okay?" I look up to see the waiter standing at our table. I clear my throat and shake my head, "Yes, we tried the oysters and they aren't our thing."

Joan is still facing the wall, not making eye contact with anyone.

I nudge her arm, handing her a napkin. "Just spit it out, admit defeat."

Joan swallows hard and swivels in her chair. Her eyes are wide and she's smiling like the Cheshire Cat.

I jerk my head back in surprise of how psychotic she looks. If this is her attempt to look happy and normal, she is failing. She's trying her best to hold herself together.

The waiter's eyes are darting from the crazy look on Joan's face to mine. "My name is Jay. Can I start you off with a nice glass of wine? May I suggest an Opus One from the Napa Valley?" He holds out the wine bottle, showing us the label.

"We'll take the bottle," Joan says, inspecting the label.

He nods in understanding. He opens the bottle and sits it on the table.

I glance over the menu. I don't know what most of these things are. I try to keep any trace of horror off my face as I scan over fried alligator and rabbit dumplings. I just take a stab at it and order the first thing my eyes land on. I mean, it can only get better from here. Right?

"I will have the smoked pork rib with the mac and cheese casserole." Thank goodness I didn't land on the rabbit dumplings. I would have cried. I close my menu and look at Joan.

"I'll have the Étouffée with a small house salad," She says in a rush.

The waiter turns on his heels and walks off. He knows we are out of our element here.

I lean over to Joan, pressing my head against her shoulder. "That was the worst thing I have ever eaten!"

I still can't get the taste out of my mouth and I feel like I have dirt in my teeth. I pour myself a glass of wine and take a large swig and swish it around.

I scoot back in my chair, taking on a more relaxed position. "Did you wear your comfy shoes?" I look under the table at Joan's feet.

She's wearing almost the exact same boots as mine. They have a very low heel. "You never know when you will have to run. I'm glad you wore flats."

She looks at me, flummoxed. "Why in the world would we have to run?"

My mouth drops open, "You didn't read any of the stuff I handed you earlier, did you? Remember, Thomas signed us up for a ghost tour!"

Joan shrugs her shoulders at me, "Not really. I like to be surprised."

"Well, you're in store for a treat. We are walking around the French Quarter and then we are visiting The Saint Louis Cemetery. I think we are taking a bus." I dig the paper out of my purse and slide it over to her.

She picks it up and pretends to shiver. "This is going to be a blast. What made Thomas pick a ghost tour for us?"

"I'm not sure, maybe I told him that we liked that kind of stuff? Or maybe he was just picking the best things to do in New Orleans," I think about it for a second. "However, he thought to sign us up, it's pretty nice of him."

My phone pings. I grab it out of my purse and look at it.

How is the restaurant? How are the oysters? I'm imagining you having a great time, lighting up the room.

I type back as fast as my thumbs can go:

Hello! Have you ever had oysters? It was so thoughtful of you to order them for us, but I don't think they are our thing. Joan almost barfed and I literally had tears running down my face. I still think you are the sweetest.

A bubble pops up.

Why in heavens did you not spit it out?

I text back:

I'm not a quitter and neither is Joan.

I can visualize Thomas shaking his head and it makes me laugh. I shoot another text, ending our brief conversation:

I'll try and text you again when we get back to the hotel tonight. It may be a late night. I'm thinking of you.

We are almost through the bottle of wine by the time we polish off dinner. We walked out of the restaurant on cloud nine, elbow and elbow, holding each other for support.

Pranab is leaning against the town car waiting for our return. "I take it you had a pleasant dinner?"

Joan squeezes my arm tighter, steadying herself as she gets into the backseat. "The wine was great, and dinner was interesting."

Pranab pulls out the small notebook from his pocket. "It looks like you have a ghost tour, *New Orleans Haunts,* starting in about forty-five minutes. Shall we head there now? Maybe do some people watching while you wait?" He flips shut his notebook. "At some point you will board a bus that will take you to the cemetery. In the event you want to leave, I will follow in the car." Pranab parks at the end of the block.

Joan and I walk to the meet-up spot for the tour. While waiting for everyone else to show up, we browse around.

"Hey, want to go into a shop while we wait?" I gesture to the shop in front of us. It is some kind of voodoo shop. These types of places are common in New Orleans. It's still open even though it's past 9:30. I open the door and let Joan walk in first. The place is crowded and dark. The smell of heavy incense floats through the air. Candles are lit everywhere. If one tips over this whole place is going up in flames in a matter of seconds.

There's an old lady walking past the candles towards us. Her back is bent from time. "Can I help you find something?" Her hard gaze holds me in her sights for a second. She nods her head up and down like I've asked her a question.

I politely smile back at her. "We're just looking around. Your store is very…uh…interesting."

She grabs a pouch out of her the pocket of her long, black sweater. She opens it up and sprinkles what looks like dried oregano on the top of my shoe. I notice Joan inching closer, becoming increasingly more curious about why the lady is putting something on my shoe. A music box begins to play on the shelf next to Joan, startling her.

Joan grabs my elbow. "Our tour is about to start." It's her polite way of saying, 'let's get the hell out of here fast'.

As I walk past the old woman again, she grabs my hand and presses what feels like a rock into my palm. I close my hand around it. I can tell from her eyes that she means me no harm. In fact, I feel like she is protecting me.

I step out onto the sidewalk and open my hand to see a small, shiny, black rock. I turn back to look at the shop and I see her black, shiny eyes looking back at me. I nod my head and squeeze my hand tight around the rock, then drop it in my pocket.

A smile spreads across her face. Her face loses all the wrinkles that time has etched across it. She turns into a very beautiful woman in her twenties but when I shake my head and blink, she turns back into the same old, bent woman standing in the window. Confused, I blink my eyes a few more times; must be the wine. Joan pulls me to a group gathering in front of the Irish pub next door.

"What did she give you? I saw her grab your hand. You got to admit, that store was creepy," Joan says, waiting for me to show her.

I pull the small, black rock out of my pocket.

Her eyes skeptically narrow. "You better ask someone what that means. She could have put a curse on you! Plus, what was that tea stuff she dropped all over your shoes." She lifts the rock out of my hand and examines it. "You better toss it."

"I will not! You don't just throw a gift away. Besides, I think she meant well." I shove it back into my pocket.

Joan gives me a frustrated look and pulls me through the crowd to the front. She pushes me towards what looks like the tour guide. "Show him, go ahead…show him!"

I pull the black rock out of my pocket. "Please tell my sister that I'm not cursed."

The tour guide gently takes the rock and holds it up to the streetlight. "Who gave this to you?"

I point to the shop next door. "The old lady in the shop."

The guide hands it back to me. "She's given you a gift. You are very lucky. This is a black tourmaline rock. It is considered to have the greatest protection to the person who possesses it. She intends to protect you."

I give Joan a smug look, "See, I felt that from her. I felt like she was protecting me." I shove the rock back into my pocket. As I walk away, I glance back at the window. The old lady is still standing there. I give her a small wave. She waves back.

After a few blocks, Joan and I grow complacent. The guide is droning on and on about each house. Frankly, it's boring. This is more like a history tour than a ghost tour. I wanted to be jumping out of my seat, scared out of my mind by now. I notice Joan's lack of enthusiasm.

I lean over and offer her a stick of gum. "Maybe the cemetery will be spookier?" I mean cemeteries are inherently spooky anyways; especially in the dark.

Joan checks her watch, "I wonder when the cemetery tour is." As we look up, a black tour bus pulls up to the curb with the named Ghost Tours of New Orleans plastered on the side. Joan grabs me by the elbow and pulls me to the bus. "Come on, Stupid, let's get a good seat."

The bus comes to a stop in front of what seems to be more than a block of mausoleums. Now that we are here, I'm kind of wishing we were back in town looking at old houses instead.

I notice Pranab is following close behind the bus as we step off. So, I guess if we really want to go, we can. I give him a wave of acknowledgement. I turn in a complete circle, getting a good look at the whole cemetery. I have never seen anything like this. There are rows and rows of mausoleums housing thousands and thousands of people.

Joan and I are at the back of the pack walking at our own pace. We are reading each and every name. Long forgotten people.... people that were once loved, people who once lived, once lived in this city with normal lives. I begin to feel sorry for them. Life is so short. I read each name out loud, hoping I can give someone the recognition that they have been craving for years.

The tour guide stops at a tomb. It's undeniably the most visited site in this whole cemetery. It's covered in beads and handwritten X's. Joan and I just stand, listening as the tour guide tells us about Marie Laveau and how she was the voodoo queen of New Orleans. I don't feel scared. I just feel sad. I squat down next to the plaster building and plop myself down onto the gravel. Joan follows suit. She reaches into her purse and hands me the flask we filled at the restaurant. I secretly take a gulp of wine and hand it back to her.

I'm studying the cracks in the plaster when I notice a pile of the same tiny, black rocks as I have in my pocket. I wonder what that's all about. I nudge Joan and point to the tiny rocks.

"See, I told you *not* to take random things from strangers." Joan smacks my knee.

I hear the guide say something that interests me. I stand up, smirking at Joan. If you write an X on the grave, spin around three times, and yell your wish into the air, Marie Laveau might grant your wish. If the wish comes true, then you are to return to the site and circle the X.

I raise my eyebrows at Joan. I know exactly what I'm going to wish for. Joan furrows her brows at me. I dig a pen out of my purse and draw a tiny X on the corner of the plaster. I hop back up to my feet and spin in a circle three times. I shout my wish into the air. "I wish that Joan finds complete happiness."

I lean down and add my tiny, black stone to the pile.

Joan grabs the pen from my hand and marks a tiny X next to mine. She spins in a circle, shouting, "I wish Mar love."

My mind quickly drifts to Thomas, his chest, his Armani

cologne, oranges and sunshine.

I give Joan a big hug and whisper in her ear. "I was going to wish that Frank got run over by a car but was afraid, just in case all this is real."

Joan slaps a hand over my mouth and we both giggle. As the tour heads back to the bus, Joan and I opt to ride with Pranab back into the city. We still have drinks on our 'things to do' list.

He opens the door to the car, and I slide in next to Joan. Pranab adjusts his mirror to look at us, "Okay, on to the next stop?"

"Of course! The next stop it is," I say, staring out the window as the rain begins to fall.

I don't know if it's the wine or the rain on the window, but I swear the same woman from the shop earlier is standing next to one of the mausoleums. I raise my hand and give her a small wave as she nods back. I watch her disappear as our car drives away back into the city.

Unicorn Pool Party

Pranab drops us off in front of our hotel. I hurry under the awning to keep dry from the rain. The rain is kicking up deep, earthy smells. I stand in the glow of the hotel light, inhaling the smell of trees, moss, and the laughter of partygoers from the balconies above. I'm happy. Joan and I make it back to our room to change into our swimsuits to head to the rooftop pool.

"I hope it stops raining or the pool bar is going to be a horrible idea," I say laying on the couch with Lone-Lee.

"Yeah, but there's an inside bar so not all will be lost," Joan says as she adjusts her top.

As the elevator door opens to the rooftop, the sound of partygoers hit me. This is a pretty happening place. Who would have known all this was going on up here? There's a giant inflatable unicorn floating in the middle of the pool. I immediately lock on to it.

"I call the giant unicorn!" I point to the middle of the pool.

For this being a rooftop pool bar there isn't anyone in the water. Lame. Do people just get dressed up and call it a pool party and not get in the pool? That isn't going to stop Joan and me from enjoying it. I mean, I already put my suit on. Joan looks at me sideways and starts to make a run for the pool. I grab her by the shoulder and pull her backwards as I pass her. I jump straight in, feet first, for the unicorn. Joan follows suit jumping in on top of me. By the time we make it to the unicorn we look like a couple of drowned rats. I pull myself onto the float and then help Joan drag herself up.

"Great, we are out here now and neither one of us has a drink." I look around for a way to get one. What does a girl have to do to get a pool boy around here? There's a swim up bar on the other side of the pool. Joan and I lay on our stomachs and use our arms to paddle our way over.

"I'll take two lava flows," Joan tosses her credit card onto the bar from her position on the unicorn.

"Where the hell did you have that?" I ask, looking her up and down. "You know we can charge everything to our room, but I like your style."

The bartender hands Joan both drinks and we kick off the side of the bar, propelling ourselves backwards. We lay stagnant in the middle of the pool. It reminds me of our childhood when we would spend all day swimming.

"Joan, I really love you. Well, most of the time." I elbow her in the ribs.

We stare up at the stars. Daydreaming. Three drinks later, Joan begins to doze off. I hop off the float and drag it to the edge of the pool. I nudge Joan, "Hey, let's call it a night. The last thing we need is to fall asleep out here."

I close out Joan's tab and wrap a towel around her shoulders.

Mr. Lee is sound asleep on Joan's bed. I pull the covers down for her while she's in the shower. I sleepily walk to my room and turn the nob for the shower. I stare into the mirror and brush my teeth on autopilot. I hang my swimsuit on the shower hook as I let the hot water pour over my back. I take a deep breath in and reflect on the last few weeks. My mind goes to laying in the hospital bed, singing along to songs with Joan in the car, and Thomas' smile. I step out of the shower and dry off. I slip under the covers without finding my pajamas. I cocoon myself in and dial Thomas.

"Hi, Baby..." his smooth voice comes on the line before I can chicken out and hang up.

I hesitate, "Hi."

"How was your night?" I can hear Charlie barking in the background.

"We had the best time! The restaurant, the ghost tour, and we ended the night on a giant unicorn drinking Lava Flows." I laugh at the thought of how ridiculous we must have looked.

"Why am I not surprised? I'm glad you had fun. I just came back from my run with Charlie and now I'm about to walk down to Ginger and White to have breakfast. Want to join me?" I know he is joking but I seriously want to join him.

"I wish," I say, feeling that familiar ache in my heart.

"You know you can. You could be here in a few hours." My heart skips at the thought of waking up next to Thomas again.

The next morning, I wake with a pain in my back. I reach to find my cell phone underneath me. Did I say goodnight to Thomas last night? Good Lord, I don't remember! I hope I didn't say anything stupid to him. A little red circle with a one appears over my message icon. I stare at it for a couple of minutes before opening it. It's Marie! Thank goodness!

Hey You! Just checking in. Haven't heard from you yet, whether you made it back to your hotel safely? I was getting worried. All is good here. Call when you can.

I dial Marie's number and wait. "Hey…"

"Hey, you got my message. Call a girl sometime, will ya?" Marie always has an upbeat lightness to her voice.

I laugh. "Sorry, I will. Joan and I floated on a giant unicorn last night and had some drinks. I even ate an oyster."

I hear Marie laugh on the other end of the line. "An oyster? OMG! I love oysters! How did that go?"

"Not so well as a matter of fact. I won't be doing that again." I think back to last night and begin to gag from the PTSD I now have. I can still smell it. I can still feel the grit in my teeth. "How are things going?"

"Things in the shop have been good. Our profit grew by 33% last week. If we could bump that up by another 17%, we will be doing extremely well. So, get yourself out there and show your butt again. We need the exposure. Your exposure is good exposure for us." Marie is never going to let this go. Rightly so; after all, isn't that what friends are for?

"Shut up Marie! Let's be serious for a minute. I think I want to see how this goes with Thomas. Are you still good with that?" I hold my breath waiting for her answer.

"I told you, Dummy. Go, I got it here." Marie sounds so sure that it puts my mind at ease.

"Okay, Crazy. I'll let you know what I decide. Joan and I are headed north. I'll call you soon." I hang up and hold the phone to my chest.

A light tapping sound comes from outside my door.

"Come in," I yell.

Joan drags herself around the side of my bed and plops down face first. "We must never drink that much again, ever..."

I just remembered that I didn't care to put on clothes last night. I tuck the sheets under me. Joan yanks my blanket. "Give me some blanket. I'm cold."

"Can't you go back to your room and sleep?" I ask, tucking the blanket under my butt a little more.

"Jeez, you're being rude this morning. Move over, Cow." Joan begins to tug at the blanket.

I free one leg and push her off the bed. "Go back to your room! You're invading my space." Joan hits the floor with a hard thud.

"It's not like you are naked under there..." Fully awake now, Joan cocks her head to the side. "Or are you?" Joan grabs the blanket and gives it a good yank.

I hold on for dear life. She manages to drag me off the bed, but I succeed on keeping the blanket tightly wrapped around me. I lie on the floor as Joan walks past me out of the room. "Okay, Stupid, have it your way. Get dressed!"

Cooper is parked in front of the hotel when we walk outside. I slide into the tan, leather driver's seat; it fits like a well-used baseball mitt.

I adjust the mirror. "Okay, Joan. Get the music and your

prehistoric map."

Somewhere in Between

Joan pulls the map out from under her seat and lays it on her lap while she searches on her phone for a song. She looks pleased with herself as she pretends to dig out her imaginary mic. The words of "Stuck in the Middle with You" start to play. I roll my eyes at her then lean over and pop open the glove box to pull out my imaginary mic and join in.

Joan and I harmonize the chorus. I'm going to miss her if I decide to go to London.

Joan is studying the map and tracing it with her finger. "Looks like if we take Highway 59 it will take us straight through Chattanooga and on to Bristol."

Joan rolls her map and stuffs it back under the seat. She pats her lap. Lone-Lee climbs over the seat and snuggles right in. We listen to the whole *Stealers Wheel* album, mindlessly tapping to the music.

"Hey, want to stop at a coffee shop?" Joan asks, looking at her watch.

"Indeed! Point me in the direction of the nearest coffee shop. And, for Heaven's sake, change the music," I say, messing with the radio station as Joan looks on her phone for another song to play.

Joan's face goes completely white.

"What?" I look over at Joan. "What is it?"

Joan points her phone towards me. Frank's face is on her screen.

"Answer it but turn on the speaker." I switch on my blinker, looking for a good place to pull over.

Joan presses the button, "What?"

Frank's voice comes over the line. How have I not noticed how annoying his voice is?

"Joan? It's Frank. I just wanted to let you know that I have moved out of the house. I'll be filing for support and ownership of half of the gallery."

My stomach turns. I look at Joan, my mouth hangs open. I can't believe the nerve of this guy. Joan's voice comes out in a boom. Gone is the broken Joan. "You've got to be fucking kidding me! You cheated on me, Frank! I'm not paying you a dime!"

I've never heard Joan talk like this. I have to admit, it takes me by surprise. I'm glad she is finally standing up for herself.

"You can't have half of the gallery. It's in my dad's name. Technically, it's his. I technically just work there. So, good luck with that. The house, by the way, isn't in my name either. As far as the bank account…well, this trip has been very expensive. You see, my husband has been cheating on me, so I had to take a break. But feel free to have what is left." Joan smirks at me.

Joan and I cleared out the bank account the day we left. I now have a little over two million in *my* bank account thanks to Marie and I for "selling" Joan part of Feeling Whisky.

Joan clears her throat. "Get a fucking life, Frank. Whatever you have to say to me, you can say to my lawyer." Joan slides her hand over the phone, hanging it up. It's less dramatic than the good old slamming the phone down, but it still gets the point across.

Joan presses her back into the seat and lets out a deep breath. "Wow, unbelievable."

"You okay?" I turn in my seat and grab Joan's hand.

She squeezes my hand, "I will be; especially after we get coffee." She punches me on my shoulder.

I turn my blinker on and pull back onto the highway. "Coffee it is."

The music is droning on in the back of my thoughts. I let the past few years brew around in my mind. I think back to all the times

Frank was late or had a business trip. Joan and I would spend the time on the phone, shooting the breeze. Has he been lying this whole time? Joan's phone buzzes. I glance down at it to see Will's face. I carefully wait to see Joan's reaction as she lifts the phone to her face. Any trace of being pissed off totally disappears. I don't know Will that well, but whatever he is doing, it's working. Maybe he isn't doing anything other than being himself. Maybe it's just because he is the right person?

"Hi," Joan lets out a breath and her whole body relaxes. I can visually see a wave of relief roll through her. I love Will for that.

I'm holding my breath in hopes that I could hear Will's side of the conversation. Joan lifts her finger indicating that I should take the next exit. I throw my shoulders up in the air. I hate not knowing exactly where I'm going.

"Take the next exit," Joan whispers.

I give her a thumbs up. She must have noticed my frustration. I pull into a tiny, mom and pop parking lot and give her a wave as I walk inside. I want to give her plenty of time to talk to Will.

At the counter, a tiny lady steps out from behind the espresso maker. "Hi, what can I get you today?"

I read her name tag, Rosa. I stare up at the menu, it's written on a large chalkboard. "I will just have two, medium, White Chocolate Mochas and two chocolate zucchini muffins, to go. Thank you so much."

I turn and lean against the counter to watch Joan while Rosa prepares my order. Her face is completely different when she talks to Will. She's relaxed, she's laughing. I helped Joan, even if it was inadvertently. Even if it was only by not dying when she poisoned me or driving our trike down the embankment. She somehow found Will. Even if he isn't long term, he is a nice distraction. Who knows, he may be *the one*, or maybe he's not *the one*? That's a good problem to have.

I hand Rosa my credit card. She rings it up smiling back at me. She hands me our coffee, and I take a sip. "Thank you! It's so good."

I carry our breakfast back to the car. I tap my elbow on the glass and Joan rolls the window down. I hand Joan her coffee. "What did Will have to say?" I ask, sliding in and putting my coffee in the cup holder.

"Not much. He just asked where in the world we were. He gave me an update on the winery. It's coming along nicely. He asked if I could do an artist showcase at Howard's next month. I told him I would love to." Joan sips her coffee and sets it back down. "Crap, that's hot! I burned my tongue!"

I put Cooper in reverse and pull back onto the highway. "So, how much more do you want to drive today?"

"Let's just drive until we get tired. It looks like we are about nine hours from New York. Maybe we should stop in about three or four hours." Joan puts her feet on Cooper's dash and sips her coffee, burning her tongue again.

Joan's knees are bent, smashing Lone-Lee's little, round body on her lap. He doesn't seem to mind, though. He is the most low-key dog I have ever met. Honestly, you wouldn't even know he was here if it wasn't for his putrid farts and obnoxious snoring.

"Okay, what's next on the playlist?" I ask, snapping Joan back to the here and now. "You're about to be fired from being the D.J." I laugh. "Play that new Lizzo song."

Joan types Lizzo into her phone. "Which one, 'Good as Hell?'"

I shake my head up and down. I can't keep the smile off my face. I know all the words by heart. I'm happy. Right here, right now. I roll down the window and let my free hand ride the wave of air up and down.

Joan slouches farther down in her seat and rubs Mr. Lee's ears. "Can you believe we found this guy on the side of the road? It seems like a million years ago."

It does seem like a million years ago. My phone dings, I glance down at it. "Can you check that? It's Marie. What does she say?"

Joan picks up my phone, "She says pick her up at the Chattanooga Airport at 5:05 tonight!" Joan looks at her watch. "That's seven hours from now."

"What? She's coming to meet us? Put it in Google Maps. Can we make it there in time?" I watch Joan as she types in Chattanooga Airport. She's finally getting the hang of using Google Maps. "I'm so proud of you. Isn't that nice they take out all of the guess work for you."

"Wow! You're right! It looks like we should make it there in six hours and 52 minutes. Right on time. She couldn't have timed that better," Joan says, looking impressed.

"Put on some Tom Petty, and Google things to do in Chattanooga. Looks like we are staying the night!" I settle in for the long drive ahead of me.

There's just something about Tom Petty. I reach over and turn the music up. I lose myself in the lyrics, nostalgia, and memories of Friday night football games.

"Hey, I found a hotel. It looks pretty cool. Do you want me to book it?" Joan asks, scratching Lone-Lee on the back of his neck. He truly has the life.

"Book it! Did you find something to do?"

Joan is jotting notes down on her bare knee. "Yes, we could do a riverboat tour, then we can tour the whiskey distillery. It's the oldest in the country. How does that sound?"

I shrug my shoulders. "Whatever, it all sounds fun!"

Chattanooga Choo Choo

We pull into the Chattanooga Airport parking lot. Joan straps my duffel bag over her shoulder as Mr. Lee jumps in.

"Hey, do you have any paper?" Joan asks with a smirk on her face.

"Yeah, I have a yellow legal pad in the trunk. Why?" I ask, opening the trunk.

"Just give it to me. You wouldn't happen to also have a marker?"

I begin digging out the legal pad. "As a matter of fact, I do." I hand Joan my extra-large sharpie that I bought to label totes in my closet.

Joan begins to write; I crane my neck to see what she's writing.

Marie,
Welcome back from rehab!
Porn addiction is real!

I squeeze my eyes shut and shriek. "That's perfect!" I high five Joan.

Joan and I position ourselves at the terminal exit. A bunch of people begin to shuffle through. I search the crowd for Marie. Joan holds the sign up higher and higher as each person passes. I catch a glimpse of Marie and frantically start waving my arms.

I cup my hands round my mouth and call out to her. "Marie! Marie!"

Marie smiles and waves back, running towards us.

Her face falls and her smile disappears as she sees Joan.

She throws her head back and laughs. "Joan! Oh, my gosh! Put that down!"

Marie passes us and begins to walk faster. Joan yells Marie's name, as she heads straight for the glass doors of the airport.

I catch up to her. "Hey, don't you need to get your luggage from baggage claim?" I point back towards the carousel.

"Nope," Marie holds up her backpack. "I've got everything right here."

Joan shuffles up beside us, tucks her sign into her pocket and gives Marie a hug. "You know we love you. Even if you do have a porn addiction."

Mr. Lee pokes his head out of the duffel bag and licks Marie on her elbow.

Startled, Marie looks down, "This must be the famous drifter dog, Mr. Lee."

"The one and only!" I say, scrubbing Lone-Lee behind the ears.

Marie throws her backpack in the trunk and climbs in the backseat with Mr. Lee.

"So, we thought we would check into the hotel then go on a riverboat tour. Joan read that the Tennessee River Gorge was the thing to do while here." I adjust the rearview mirror to see Marie. "Then we thought we'd do the whiskey tasting tour."

Marie nods her head in agreement. "Sounds fun. I'm up for anything."

"Anything? We know about you and your addiction." Joan drags out her words. She crumples up the sign and throws it back to Marie.

Marie bats it back, hitting Joan in the back of the head.

"Don't listen to this one, if it were up to her, we would all be drinking peyote tea and running through a field." I give Joan a cheeky grin.

Joan's mouth drops open. "You aren't supposed to tell everyone that!"

"I didn't tell everyone, I just told Marie." I give Joan a little knock on the knee.

I pull Cooper to the front of the hotel and unload my bag onto a luggage trolley. Joan pulls out her borrowed, needlepoint, green luggage from the trunk.

Marie jerks her head, "Is that your mom's luggage? I borrowed that for my fifth-grade overnight trip to the science museum. I stuck a note in the lining. Unzip it Joan, let's see if it's still there!"

Joan lays the luggage flat and unzips it. Marie reaches in and pulls out a tiny note from the lining.

"Well, what does it say?" I grab it from her hand and unfold it. I read it out loud.

I hate this museum. I wish Mar was here. In 15 years, I want to own a bakery in San Francisco.

"Looks like you got your wish." I laugh, handing the note back to Marie.

Joan rolls the trolley inside to check-in while I park Cooper. I meet Marie and Joan in the lobby and walk over to the window to look out at the river.

Joan joins me looking out over the river and hands me a key to our room. "We're on the third floor."

We get up to the room and I plop myself down on the first bed I see. I grab Lone-Lee to snuggle beside me. "I'm just going to take a ten-minute nap while you guys freshen up."

It feels like I just closed my eyes when Marie nudges me awake. "Hey, want to shower? I'm done."

I sit Lone-Lee on the floor and make my way to the bathroom. I take a quick shower and yank on a pair of skintight jeans and a black t-shirt. I walk out of the bathroom feeling on point. Joan and Marie join me in front of the mirror as we each do different Charlie's Angels poses.

I snap a couple of pictures and send them in a group text to Will and Thomas: *Here comes trouble.*

A text bubble pops up. Then disappears. Then reappears.

Thomas: *I was going to write something naughty but realized this was a group text. Looking sexy!*

Will: *ditto*

I roll my eyes and smile. Can he be any more adorable?

"Let's go!" I grab my purse from the chair and slip on my ankle boots.

Joan pulls out her phone and checks her Uber app. "Looks like the driver will be here in three minutes."

The driver pulls up and we scoot into the back seat. I look at Joan; Joan looks back at me and raises her eyebrows. Then we both look at Marie. Marie shrugs her shoulder. We just realized we have no one to send the description of the driver to. Everyone with our weird obsession is already in the car.

Joan pulls out her phone and starts clicking out a text to Will and Thomas.

Male, brown hair, early 20's. Honda civic. Uber driver. Headed to a riverboat tour. Chattanooga. Sending our location.

A bubble pops up.

Will: *I got it. Are you guys being abducted? I just saw your picture. How can you be in trouble already? Worried…*

Thomas: *My heart can't take this. Please preface it with, "we are all ok."*

Joan laughs, she quickly texts back.

Will, No silly! It's just in case we get abducted. Thomas, I will.

As our Uber pulls up to the dock, we see what looks like a steamboat from a Mark Twain book.

"Well, I guess that's our ride." Joan opens the car door and steps out. We make our way to the top deck and grab a spot leaning against the rail. As the boat begins to move away from the dock, we settle in for the hour-long boat ride.

"So…" Marie looks at me.

I turn back to her, "So…"

Joan's brow furrows, "So?"

"So, tell me about this London boy." Marie presses her back against the rail and sits on the floor of the boat.

I begin to feel a little nauseous. I don't know if it's the inquiry or the boat. I sit cross-legged next to Marie, Joan joins me. I shake my head in thought. "He's amazing…You know how some people say there's just something about him or whatever? It's just not *something* about him. It's not some obscure 'something' I can't put my finger on. It's *everything* about him."

The swaying of the boat rocks us into complacency. This is nice. Here I am with two of my favorite people. Life is pretty good.

As the boat floats to a stop at the dock, we make our way down to the main level. My legs feel like Jell-O. Marie grabs onto Joan's arm to steady herself. I grab onto Joan's belt loop as she passes me, making a human train off the boat. We stand on the sidewalk like drunk sailors.

"So…maybe riverboat cruises aren't our thing?" I say, pressing my head against Joan's back.

"I guess not," Marie says, squatting down, holding onto her knees.

Joan lands on all fours onto the grass. "Why is the world spinning? Oh, gosh! Please don't talk to me. Nobody talk to me."

Marie and I sit in the cool grass next to Joan. I put my head in my hands. "How did we not know we were all riverboat challenged?"

Marie rolls over and presses her face into the grass. "I just need to lay here for a while."

Fifteen minutes pass before my head begins to clear. My fingers crawl over to reach Joan. "Hey, Stupid. Are you okay?" I turn my head to see Marie still face down in the grass. "Marie, are you alive?"

Marie sits up and rubs her eyes. The grass has made little grass indentions all over her face. I guess a cruise is off the list for us in the future.

Joan pulls out her phone to order a new Uber. "What's the address again?"

I pull out the paper from my pocket. "It's on Lynchburg Highway. We are signed up to take the Flight of Whiskey Tour. Any objections?"

Marie gives me a thumbs up from her spot on the grass. I stand up and dust my butt off. I hold my hand out for Joan and pull her to her feet. I pick grass out of Marie's hair. I'm not sure drinking after motion sickness is a good idea, but I'm not a quitter.

Marie laughs, "That is the last time we take a riverboat cruise. I prefer my laying in the grass as a result of drinking too much, not from a Mark Twain riverboat."

The Uber driver pulls up and we pile in. "Going to the Whiskey Distillery? That's a good one."

"Yes, thanks." Joan texts his description in our group text.

Hello, we are all ok. 6'3" blond in his 40's, black Toyota Camry. Whiskey distillery.

A text bubble pops ups.

Thomas: *Please be safe and have fun.*

Will: *Should I even ask? Please don't get on a bicycle.*

Thomas: *What's wrong with getting on a bicycle? Never mind, I remember.*

Joan, Marie, and I saddle up to the bar. The host sets a long board in front of us. Each board has five shots on it.

I raise my eyebrows "Here goes nothing!" I lift the glass to my lips and throw my head back. I screw up my face. "Whoa! That's strong!" I nod my head to Marie. "Your turn."

Marie hesitates as she holds the tiny glass in front of her face and sniffs it. She clears her throat. "I don't think I can do it!"

I roll my eyes. "Just do it, Marie!"

Marie pinches her nose, puts the glass up to her lips and shoots it back. She reaches in her purse and holds up a tiny bottle of Apple Schnapps. "I've got to chase it down with something sweet."

"Where did you get that? I ask with a perplexed look on my face." I don't think whiskey is supposed to be chased with anything." Marie continues to take a shot of schnapps after ever swig of whiskey. I give her a nervous grin and turn to Joan.

Joan grabs the first one and throws it back. She doesn't need any prompting. She quickly follows it with the remaining four.

I raise my hands in the air, like I'm asking for permission to talk. "Hey! What the heck are you doing? We are supposed to listen to the guide before we go on. It's a tasting, not a frat party!"

Joan shrugs her shoulders, "Oops! I was just trying to get them over with."

"That's not the point, Stupid. The point was to actually taste them." I clap my hand on my forehead.

By the third sample I feel a little lightheaded. From where I'm standing, I guess Marie feels the same.

She's talking to a wooden post beside her. "So, where are you from?"

I grab Marie by the shoulder, "Having a good conversation?"

Marie leans back to focus on my face, "Did you meet my new friend, Post...Post Malone?" She's slurring her words.

I look at Joan, "Want to just head to the next place? Marie is talking to a post now."

Joan agrees. As we lock arms to get ready to leave, a guy walks hesitantly up to us. He asks, "Is that your friend over there with the post?"

I respond, "Yes! Why?"

He says, "Because, I think she's making out with it."

I turn around to see Marie in a loving embrace with Post Malone, sharing an intimate moment. I casually reply, "They're just kissing. Oh wait...there goes second base. Gotta go!"

I run quickly over to Marie and rescue Post Malone. We stumble our way outside to wait for our next Uber.

Marie begins to climb on top of a large wooden barrel in front of the building.

I take a couple of pictures of her before I walk over and grab her dangling foot. "Get down! You are going to get us arrested."

Marie looks down at me. "This reminds me of that Johnny Cash song. You know the one, right?"

Marie starts screeching out the first few words of, "A Boy Named Sue".

"Oh, shit! Get down!" I press my lips together and point to the ground with my finger. Joan dances circles around me and laughs. This doesn't at all remind me of the Johnny Cash song. Whatever narrative Marie has going on in her head is lost on me.

Marie's voice gets louder, "No! I'm going to finish my song. You didn't even get to hear the best part!"

I stomp my foot down on the sidewalk, "Jeez! Marie get your ass down from there!"

Marie shrugs her shoulders. As she slides down from the barrel, her shirt has rolled up to her shoulders. I pull it down. She and Joan lock arms and dosey doe around me.

"Pew! Pew!" Marie makes a makeshift gun out of her index finger and thumb. "Pew! Pew! I got you! You have to lay down! You have to lay down now! You've been shot!"

I crane my head around in hopes that the Uber driver is close. I see a car slowly approaching, "Joan, is that our car?"

Joan nods her head 'yes.' The Uber driver pulls up as Marie runs past. I open the door and shove her in.

"Oh, I'm being kidnapped!" Marie yells. "They are *stealing* me! I'm being stolen!"

"Shut up, Marie! You are going to get us arrested." I put her in between Joan and me; buckling her in.

Joan looks over at me, "Do you really think it's a good idea to go to the karaoke bar? Maybe we should stop while we're ahead."

I look at my watch. "It's only ten o'clock. Marie will rally." I glance over at Marie. She giggles and gives me an over enthusiastic wave.

We quickly find a seat at Lou's and begin looking through a large, black binder for a song.

Joan shuts the binder. "Maybe we should just sit here and listen for a while. You know, *sober* up a bit?"

Marie pulls the binder over and opens it back up. "Sober up? Karaoke isn't karaoke without being a little tipsy!"

Marie hops up and saunters over to the D.J. booth. I see our name pop up on the screen. We are the second one from the top. It's a name I haven't heard in years.

The D.J. walks to the center of the stage. "Let me introduce you to three girls, a long way from home. The Texas Hot-Totty's! Marie, Joan, and Mar!"

Marie takes center stage; Joan and I flank her sides.

The only thing that makes this so good is that Marie is a bit tipsy. She sounds exactly like a down and out housewife. She has the microphone in one hand, but she keeps singing into the top of the mic stand.

Joan joins in for emphasis.

As the song ends, Marie puts the microphone back in its stand. We make our way back to our table.

Joan throws her hand in the air as the waitress passes by. "Three Lava Flows, and three whiskey shots, please." She hands the waitress her credit card.

It's a big change from, 'we should probably sit this one out.' I plop down in my chair as Marie slides the binder in front of me. I scan over the names. There must be over a hundred pages of songs in here. I walk up to the D.J. booth and write my selection down. I turn and bow to Marie and Joan. Marie orders six more shots; two for each of us.

I shoot both of mine and grab Joan by the hand. "Come on! We have to pick out our costume."

Joan throws her two shots back and follows behind me. She gestures for Marie to follow her.

I begin digging through the trunk just off stage. I lean over and whisper in Joan's ear, my song choice. She laughs and gets on her knees to find her outfit. I pull up a white, Elvis inspired outfit with rainbow rhinestones in various patterns. I slip it on over my clothes.

Joan grabs a 1970's polyester shirt and pulls it over her head with a bright green, curly wig. Marie is still talking to the D.J. when the first notes of our song starts. Marie runs to the trunk as we walk past her. She is throwing costumes all over the place, frantically looking for something to wear.

The D.J.'s voice comes over the speakers, "Once again...The THT's with 'The Bohemian Rhapsody!'"

He shortened our name. I kinda like it.

Joan and I stand shoulder to shoulder with our heads down. We have rehearsed this dance over and over as teenagers.

We slowly raise our heads as the music begins.

Marie finally joins us on stage from behind. Joan and I step aside making a spot for Marie in between us. I turn and glance at her. Holy hell, she's wearing a Chewbacca costume. I try to keep my focus. She joins right in on her part. She also remembers from all the bedroom rehearsals. I try my best not to look at her. She's completely sauced! Looking at her at this point would make me laugh and, go down a rabbit hole I don't want to go down.

"Bock...boooock..." Marie starts to add the chickens from The Muppet version of 'The Bohemian Rhapsody' in the background. I guess the Chewbacca costume is the closest thing to a Muppet. She quickly switches to Animal's part.

I try to mutter out a couple of more lines before I completely lose it and bend over laughing. At least Joan is keeping it together. I give up trying to keep a straight face. I harmonize with Joan and laugh. Marie's antics make this whole song. The waitress walks over and hands us three more shots.

We hold them up and nod to the crowd. "Thank you out there! Whoever bought the shots!"

Marie shoots her shot then drags a stool to the middle of the stage. She positions herself on the stool and begins to sing.

Marie singing Cindy Lauper in a Chewbacca costume is hilarious; my stomach hurts from laughing. As Marie finishes her song, she hangs her head. I grab the mic and snarl my lip up like Elvis. Joan pulls her phone out and starts to record from the front of the stage. I don't care that she's recording. I lean into the microphone.

Marie is doing pirouettes around me, singing her own made up words in the background.

The song is building. I hold my hand out towards the crowd, then slide down the microphone stand to a squatting position.

Marie walks over to me and we sing the end together.

The D.J. walks to the side of the stage and holds out his hand to help us down. As we make it back to our seats, Joan has another round of shots waiting for us.

I sit back down in my seat. "Oh, I don't think I could have any more." I push my shot to the middle of the table.

"Oh, come on, Mar. I'm about to sing another song." Joan places the shot back in front of me, then scoots her chair from the table. "I'll be back."

As Joan stands behind the mic. The first few notes of Miranda Lambert's song 'Tin Man' plays. I see her face finally crack. Her heart is broken, that's something I will never forgive Frank for. That sobers me up a bit. I pull my phone out to record her.

I hand Marie my phone and join Joan on stage. I wrap my arms around her shoulders and sway back and forth with every word. Marie puts my phone in her pocket as she reaches around Joan. We both sway while Joan sings. We sandwich her between us, holding her hard. I hope if I squeeze her hard enough, I can push the pieces of her heart back together.

Marie

I don't know who is holding whom up as we stand at the curb waiting for our Uber. A white minivan pulls up and Marie tries pulling the door open. I stand behind her watching, waiting.

She starts to tug really hard on it. "It won't open! Tell the driver it's locked."

I tap on the passenger side window. "The door is locked."

Frustrated, the driver hops out of the van and walks around to where we are standing. He steps in front of Marie and slides the door open. Oh, who knew? You can't fault us for not knowing the dang door slides! We probably would have known had we not been so sauced. It just goes to prove we should call it a night.

The Uber drops us off at the front of the hotel. I step out of the van and make my way to a luggage trolley. I sit down on the trolley and spin to put one leg on each side. I ride it towards Joan and Marie. Joan sits behind me and copies my position. We both plant our feet down while Marie hops on behind Joan and straddles the cart. We are moving our legs in unison, like a well-practiced rowing team.

"Row! Row! Pull! Pull..." Marie yells from the back.

The girl at the counter just watches us as we make it into the elevator. Joan reaches up to push our floor. I turn and give the girl, who is now leaning over the counter watching us, a smug look as the elevator doors close.

I push open our room's door. We ride the trolley in and dismount in a roll.

The next morning, I'm the first to wake up. I drop off my bed and crawl to find Marie. I find Marie passed out on the couch in the corner of the room, still in her Chewbacca costume. I didn't even realize she was still wearing that when we got back to the hotel. What the heck is a luggage trolley doing in here?

A flashback hits me like a ton of bricks. I remember us riding it up from the lobby. I pull myself up to my feet and shake Marie. I walk over to see Joan. Lone-Lee is sleeping next to Joan's face with his paws in the air.

"Hey, Stupid! Wake up!" I wiggle Joan's foot. Lone-Lee quickly rolls over and gives a surprised bark. I reach over and rub him behind the ears.

"Hey, get up! Let's go for breakfast." I turn on my heels and walk over to where our suitcases are piled. "I'm going to get dressed."

I tap Marie again as I pass her on the couch. "I'm getting dressed. Breakfast in twenty?"

I glance in the mirror as I step in the shower. When I step out of the shower, I notice Marie is standing in front of my bathroom mirror with the Chewbacca costume at her feet.

"Please tell me we have pictures." She puts her face in her hands. "I will never drink that much again. No alcohol beyond this point."

Marie looks up. Her eyelids flicker. One of her eyelid's sticks, open. I jerk my head back, surprised. She doesn't even notice. "Seems to me like that's a reoccurring theme." I grab a towel and wrap it around myself. "Oh, and we have pictures alright. Joan has a video also, I think."

Marie bends over and presses her face on the cold marble of the counter.

"Get in the shower, you will feel a ton better," I say, pulling on my jeans. "I'll meet you in the room."

I'm sitting on the couch resting my eyes when Joan taps me on the shoulder. "Ready?"

We stand in front of the same mirror as last night, but a little worse for wear. Our faces are scrubbed clean and our hair is pulled into messy top knots. I quickly do a pose, Marie and Joan follow suit. We look more like The Three Stooges instead of Charlie's Angels.

Marie shakes her head, "We still have it!"

I'm not sure if she is trying to convince herself or us, but none of us believe it. We need major detoxing today. I haven't had that much alcohol since that one time in college. Fireball and I are no longer friends, and I can never go back to the Denny's on State Street. I'm sorry for that because I really like the cheese sticks there.

We stand silent in the elevator. Getting some food down will do us some good. Joan leans against the glass elevator wall, "Look at that scenery? It's beautiful." She takes a long deep breath in. The drive through Estes Park must have cured some of her fear of heights.

The hostess walks up behind us holding menus in her hand. "I have a table next to the window." She leads the way to a table closest to the wall of windows. Joan sits next to the window. I pull out the seat next to Joan, letting Marie have the other seat next to the window.

"So, check out is at eleven. I was thinking of what we could do to kill some time." I pass Joan a pamphlet of some local hiking trails. "What about hiking?" I point out the window. "I could use a good run today, but I'll settle for a nice hike."

Marie has her forehead resting on the table. She mumbles, "I could use it, too. So, it's settled then, drunk detox hike it is."

We load up Cooper and make the short drive out to the trailhead.

Joan pulls her map out from under her seat as Marie looks for a song. Apparently, old habits die hard; Joan can't quite embrace the 21st century.

"Does it matter what I pick?" Marie asks, shuffling through songs.

Mr. Lee is making cute, little snoring sounds beside her while curled up on her Chewbacca costume.

I reach down and turn the music up. Right on cue, Marie starts to sing.

I readjust my mirror so that I can see her. I roll my window down and let the wind blow through my fingers. I love 4 Non Blondes! It's hard not to sing along with them. It's impossible to do it at a normal volume.

Joan, Marie, and I sing at the top of our lungs. We startle Lone-Lee. He stands up and begins to look around.

I park Cooper near the trailhead. I look at Marie, "Are you up for this?"

Joan is loading Lone-Lee into what is now *his* duffel bag.

"Hey, let the poor dog walk. He isn't going to know how to use his feet if you keep carrying him everywhere." I lift the bag off of Joan's shoulder.

Joan pulls Mr. Lee out of the bag and sets him on the ground. "I'm just worried he is going to get a sticker! I mean, you never know."

The leaves crunch under our feet as we walk in silence, listening to the birds. The trail is an easy incline up to the top of the lookout. I sit at the edge, dangling my feet off.

Marie sits next to me and grabs my hand. "Isn't this amazing? Thanks for inviting me out here."

"I didn't invite you out here. You just said, 'Pick me up.' So, I didn't have a choice." I poke her in the ribs. "I'm kind of leaving you in the lurch; with the cupcake shop and all." I lean my head on Marie's shoulder and look back at Joan. "Hey, Stupid, come sit with us."

Joan army crawls up beside us and lays flat against the ground.

I reach my hand out to her. "What in the hell are you doing? I thought you were over your fear of heights?"

Joan closes her eyes tight and begins breathing hard,

"Apparently not. Just talk. I'm listening."

"Joan, Joan…open your eyes. It really is wonderful up here," Marie says waving her hand at the expanse of the overlook.

A bead of sweat forms on Joan's temple. I lean back, crossing my arms over my chest. "Okay, if you don't want to look over the valley, let's look up at the clouds."

Satisfied with that, Joan rolls over onto her back. "That's much better."

Marie leans back, "Hey, can I join this party?"

Lone-Lee wedges himself between Joan and me. He couldn't care less that he really doesn't fit.

I reach over and grab Joan and Marie's hands. "I wanted to thank you for always being my friend." I look over at Joan, "Even when it was hard, even when I was kicking boys in the nuts left and right."

Marie lets out a squeak of laughter. "I remember that. We would lay our blankets out on the grass. We'd sit and eat Doritos while watching the boys talk to Joan. You would puff up and tell me you'd be right back."

"God, I hated you for that…You should have kicked Frank in the nuts sooner." Joan laughs.

"I've thought about that a lot lately. We could go back and do it now. I'm just saying, for old time's sake." My smile goes into a straight line and I raise my eyebrows at her. "My offer stands."

Joan laughs, "No use now. Plus, I wouldn't touch his crotch with a ten-foot pole."

I turn to Marie, "Thanks for go-cart riding and Dirty Scrabble and lots and lots of fun bottles of wine. You're our other sister…Which brings me to something I wanted to talk to you guys about." I take a deep breath in. "I'm going to London."

Joan sits up and looks me straight in the eye. I guess she isn't worried about heights anymore. "Are you sure Mar? Is this what you really want?"

"Yeah, I've been thinking about it this whole week. Dad's right, I can just come back." I smile and turn to look at Marie for her approval.

Marie squints her eyes shut and begins to nod her head. Slow at first then faster. She jumps to her feet dragging Joan and I along. "Yes! Mar! Yes! A thousand times yes! Go get that boy!"

"It really does make me feel good to know that you guys have my back." I take in the hug Marie is giving me.

Joan squats back to the ground, realizing she is standing on the edge of a cliff. She slowly lays flat on her stomach and rolls away from us.

My eyes widen, "What in the heck are we going to do with you? Are you crazy? Get up!"

Joan gets onto all fours and stands up as she makes it back to the trail. We slowly hike the long walk back to Cooper; I begin fielding questions for Joan and Marie.

"What do you think his house looks like?" Marie asks, but it's more rhetorical. "I think he lives in a flat in the city. Probably a lot like our place."

I shrug my shoulders. "It doesn't really matter to me."

"You know that he will be the last person you will ever sleep with. You do realize that, right?" Marie starts pointing out facts.

"God, if I could be so lucky. He's amazing." I could go on for days about how he makes me feel. "He's handsome, but very humble all at the same time. I feel right with him."

Joan interrupts, "He sounds like the perfect guy."

I nod my head, "He is."

"So, when are you thinking of going?" Joan interrupts my thoughts of Thomas.

"I'm leaving when we get to the airport in New York. I'll buy my ticket when I know we will be there, no hurry." I lift Lone-Lee into the backseat. He turns in a circle and snuggles into Marie's Chewbacca costume.

We pull up to the front of the Tennessee airport. I hop out and give Marie a long hug, "See you soon. I'll call when I can; keep me posted on the shop."

"See you in Cali, soon." Joan hugs Marie then she gets back in the car. Joan exaggerates her words, "*Soon, right?*"

Marie shakes her head as she walks towards the doors of the airport, turning only to give us a quick wave 'bye.'

I yell, "See you later alligator."

Marie turns and I notice her cheeks are bright red. "After a while crocodile."

I slowly drive away, passing people giving hugs to loved ones. A hard lump forms in my throat. This is why Joan and I don't even make eye contact during our airport drop offs.

We have a long-standing protocol for dropping each other off at the airport. It's changed a bit since we now live so close to each other. We used to make the drop as quick as possible. We would let whoever was leaving grab their own luggage and the other would drive off without looking back. It was just easier for both of us that way. It gave us no time to fall apart. The very first time I came to visit Joan after she moved to Napa, she drove me to the airport. She barely slowed down long enough for me to hop out.

I start smiling as I reminisce about the details of that day. I could tell that Joan was on the verge of a complete breakdown. She drove off before I could get my luggage out of the trunk. I was still standing in the street when she broke the rule and glanced back. She pulled over thirty yards away, snatched my luggage out of the trunk and threw it onto the passenger seat, then drove off again. I watched her disappear into the distance. I was standing on the curb, dumbfounded, when I heard loud frantic honking.

Joan had made the short, airport circle. She threw my luggage out the window, it landed at my feet. Then she shot me the finger like I had just insulted her. I quickly returned the gesture. She later described leaving me there was one of the hardest things she ever had to do. She said I looked like a dirty little orphan standing in the street.

I should have used the protocol on Marie. I can only hope that Joan will be driving like an IndyCar racer when she has to drop me off at the airport tomorrow in New York.

New York Or Bust

"Welp, we better get a move on. How far is it to New York?" I swallow, trying to get rid of the lump in my throat and hide the tears in my eyes. "Pull out that trusty old map of yours."

Joan digs under her seat to look for the map. She starts to dig farther and farther under her seat. She bends down, trying even harder to find it. Maybe she's finally lost the damn thing…I lean forward to see. Joan smiles and exclaims, "I found it!" then precedes to pull her middle finger out from under the seat and sticks it right in my face.

I choke in surprise. "You're such an ass!"

She laughs, "But you're not crying anymore."

I pull over to get gas. Joan walks Lone-Lee around the small patch of grass next to the gas station. She's talking on the phone and walking in circles.

I lean against the car and begin to look up flights to London. It looks like I can catch a flight tomorrow at four. That gives me just enough time to get there. I pop the trunk and look in my luggage for my passport. That would put a real damper on things if I don't have my passport. It's something I always travel with, but it has been a crazy few weeks. It's not like I have needed it on this trip. I flip open my glovebox and dig around. Ah, it's there. I'm good.

Joan passes behind me, "What are you looking for?"

"Oh, just my passport. I found it." I say slamming the glovebox shut. "Who were you talking to on the phone?"

Joan leans against the car. "Just Will. I was telling him how the trip was going and that you were headed to London. He said he was happy for you; and, don't worry, I made him swear not to tell Thomas."

"Oh, thank you and that's nice of him. Hey, I was thinking about driving halfway there, or a little more tonight, and the rest in the morning. I got my ticket. My flight is at four tomorrow."

Joan's smile turns into a frown. "I'm going to miss you."

I put my finger in front of Joan's face, "Oh, no...no...no. Don't do this to me now. I'll leave you here."

"At the gas station?" Joan laughs and shakes her head.

"Absolutely, I will leave you at the gas station if you make me cry." I hop in Cooper and get back on the highway. "Play some music D.J. Anything. Just as long as it's not quiet in here."

Truthfully, Joan could pick anything and I would never hear it. I have too many things going on in my head. Joan and I ride in silence for a while. I don't think either one of us wants to say anything. I probably couldn't get a word out without crying, anyways. So, it's best to sit here like two bumps on a log.

Joan breaks the silence. "Hey, you know I'm going to miss you. Mom and Dad will probably be right behind you, be ready for that. And if they are going, I might as well come too. You know, to help them navigate the travel and all."

A wide smile stretches across my face. "Might as well."

Joan and I pull into the next hotel we see. Today has been a really long day. Maybe it actually hasn't been, but it feels like it since we drank so much last night. We must have had ten drinks in the span of five hours. I'm surprised we're alive. If truth be told, I never finished my flight of whiskey or my Lava Flow. I was too busy watching Marie have a great time. Don't get me wrong, I was lit, but not as lit as Marie in a Chewbacca costume.

I bring up all my things from Cooper. I have to repack everything. Joan and I are beat. I want to stay up and talk but decide to call it a night instead.

The next morning, I stumble out of bed. Joan is nowhere in

sight. Last I saw her she was next to me in bed. She's probably taking Mr. Lee for a walk. I casually brush my teeth and throw on my shoes to run downstairs and grab a quick cup of coffee. As I'm standing in line, I notice Joan a few people in front of me with Mr. Lee in his duffle bag. He looks ridiculous. He's got to be twenty pounds by now. It's like the time New York banned dogs on the subway unless they were in a carrier. People started carrying their large dogs around in bags. Some cut holes so their dogs could walk, others stuffed them in backpacks.

I tap Joan on the shoulder, "Got one of those for me?"

"No, this one is for Mr. Lee." She laughs and hands me a cup.

We stroll back to the room and gather our things. Joan checks out as I throw our luggage in the trunk and give Mr. Lee the last bite of my muffin.

"Let's go!" I yell.

Joan rushes to the car and hops in.

I look over at her. "Okay, Joan, you know the drill. Pick a song."

Leaving on a Jet Plane

I pull Cooper into the airport parking lot.

Joan turns in her seat, "You can change your mind, you know. Nothing says you have to go. He doesn't even know you're coming. You can back out. We can turn this car around and head back to San Francisco like none of this ever happened."

I let out my breath sounding like a long, drawn out sigh. I hadn't realized I was holding it. "Joan, I want to go. I love him. I can't believe it took me this long to allow myself to really admit it."

I move mom's ugly, patchwork luggage to the side and pull mine out. I stand, staring at my luggage. It's filled with all our adventures; all our treasures. Sand from the dessert, a postcard from the giant swing; the hospital gown we stole; the scrap of paper that June, June like the month wrote on; a Nerf gun bullet; the plastic wine glass...and a picture of Thomas holding me in front of the cabin.

Joan steps out of the car. "I'm going in with you. I can't just leave you in the parking lot."

"You're going to London with me?" I ask, confused.

Joan grabs my arm and pulls me for a hug. "No, Stupid, I'm going into the airport with you." I immediately begin to think about all the things that I hate, in an effort to not cry. I blink a few times to hold back tears, then return to thinking of the things that I hate: getting a toothbrush instead of candy on Halloween or biting into a chocolate chip cookie just to realize it's a raisin oatmeal cookie.

Joan interrupts my train of thought as a teardrop rolls over my bottom lash. This is all sinking in. Joan is leaving me at the airport. I don't know when I will see her again. My bottom lip begins to tremble. I bite the inside of my cheek.

Joan hugs me. "Don't cry. I'll see you soon. I've always wanted to visit London. I'll come with mom and dad. Let's go in, we can have coffee together." Joan smiles at me then drags out her words, "...one last time."

"Are you seriously trying to kill me right now?" I elbow her hard in the ribs, hoping the pain in her ribs replaces the emotions that are silently edging closer. It's a funny thing: no matter how good your life is where you are going, you are always sad to leave where you are. In my case, I'm going to tell the man I love that I was wrong, that I've loved him all along, that I was just too stubborn to see, too scared...It still doesn't make me miss Joan any less, or my parents for that matter. I'm taking the leap and not just a small leap. It's a monumental leap. It's not like if he decides this isn't what he wants, I can just hop in my car and drive home.

I gently roll my luggage up to the ticket counter. I look over to watch Joan ordering our coffee and scanning her phone app. This will be the last time in a long time that we will be together ordering coffee.

While the coffee is being made, she quickly runs to the gift shop. She grabs a travel pillow, blanket, and a couple of books. She turns and notices me watching her. She begins to frantically dig in her purse.

Oh no, she must have forgotten her wallet! I start to speed walk over to save her the embarrassment, when she pulls her hand out of her purse and shoots me the finger. I pivot on my heels and clap my hand over my mouth to muffle the loud obnoxious laughter that I know is coming. I throw up my finger too, not to be out done by her, then buckle over while snorting through the cracks of my hand. She really knows how to make me laugh. Just when I think I'm going to be a crying mess I'm laughing hard enough that the whole airport can hear me. I'm sure the ticketing agent is busily typing away, adding me to the NO FLY list. I turn to drop my luggage with the agent who furrows her brow at me. I give her a small smile and quickly make my way to Joan.

"You got me in trouble with Sue Sylvester over there." I laugh as I scoot into the booth next to her. "This has been the best trip of my life," I say, grabbing both of Joan's hands. "What are you going to do now?"

Joan shrugs her shoulders and gives me a wide smile, "I guess go back to California and pick up my life."

Mr. Lee's head is poking out of the duffel bag that has now become his official carrier. Joan is going to regret ever getting him in the habit of being carried around. He's going to be at least thirty pounds, fully grown.

She leans over and cups Mr. Lee's wrinkled face in her hands and pulls his chin up to look at him. "We are going to have many days in the California sunshine."

I bump my forehead with the palm of my hand. "Oh my gosh! In all the excitement I totally didn't even think about how you were getting back to California! Much less how Cooper was getting back!"

"Don't worry, Mar. I've already thought about that. That's what I was talking to Will about yesterday. He should be here in an hour. We are going to drive the car back to Texas and leave it with mom and dad. Then we are flying back to California from there."

My eyebrows shoot up, "Will is flying here? You're driving to Texas? He's meeting mom and dad...back to California...together?" With every question my voice goes up an octave. I couldn't be more excited for her.

"Of course, together...we both live there. Plus, it's only because I don't want to drive to Texas alone. I called him and he offered. So, I said 'yes.' I'm going to be saying 'yes' to a lot more things this year. See where it takes me." Joan gives one sharp nod of her head like she's set on her decision.

"Oh, only because you didn't want to drive alone...you could have called anyone. Hell, Marie was just here. You chose to call

Will!" I rub my two index fingers together, "Shame, shame. You like him, admit it."

"Yes, I like him! I just want to take it very slow," Joan says cautiously.

I give her a wink like I know exactly what she's talking about, "Take it slow…" I repeat, "I get it."

"Shut up Stupid! Enough about me, what are you going to do in London? I mean for work?" Joan asks, putting on her proverbial sister hat.

"You mean besides shagging Thomas?" I say, knocking Joan on the knee. "And spending your cool two million in my bank account?"

"Stop saying that, you sound like a hooker!" Joan clears her throat at me.

I think about that for a second, "Oh crap, you're right! I didn't mean it like that." I dig in my purse and pull out my yellow legal pad and slide it to Joan, "I'm going to write, I'm going to write our story."

Joan flips the legal pad over and begins to read. "Oh, Crap! 'This is not how I expected to die, lying here on my sister's living room floor.'"

I slowly breathe in and out, eagerly waiting for a flicker of anything to come across Joan's face. It seems like a lifetime when she finally looks up and meets my eyes. I can hear every breath she's taking. I can literally hear the clock ticking behind the counter at Starbucks. Never mind, that's just my heart pounding in my chest.

"Mar! This is going to be fantastic! I, of course, have the last say in what goes in it about me. You cannot put the peyote night in it." Joan says, scanning page after page. "When did you write all this?"

I shrug my shoulders, "Here and there, I only have about 100 pages give or take. Don't worry, I'll change your name. I'll call you Joann, but the rest stays in." I give her a cheeky smile.

The peyote story is too funny to leave out.

I check my phone and frown at Joan. "I have to go soon." I reach down and grab her hand as we sit in silence.

"I'm happy for you, Mar. You are fearless. You helped me get through one of the most terrible times in my life, and you turned it into something good. You brought me out of something that could have destroyed me. You're hopping on a plane, into the great unknown." A tear rolls down Joan's cheek.

I don't like seeing Joan like this. I nip her chin with my finger. "You are the fearless one." I try to lighten the mood. "You poisoned me. You drank peyote tea. For heaven's sake, your husband cheated on you and you opened your heart to love."

Joan shakes her head, "Yeah, we're both pretty badass."

I stand up next to the table as Joan scoots out of the booth. We have to improvise our airport goodbye. I give Joan a tight hug and rest my head on her shoulder.

"Go get the guy." Joan whispers in my ear.

I don't look up to meet her eyes. It's just too tough for me. "You go get the guy," I whisper back.

I turn and walk towards the security line. As I get to the line, I see Will coming down the escalator. I turn and watch him walk to Joan.

Joan still has her back turned avoiding me. He taps her on the shoulder. When Joan turns around her mascara has run down her cheeks. Her face turns from complete sadness into the widest smile I have seen in a while. She reaches up and throws her arms around Will's neck.

I smile and turn back to the security line. I know she will be just fine. My heart is happy. Mission accomplished.

Thomas

Eight hours later, the plane touches down at Heathrow airport. I didn't get a wink of sleep. I tossed and turned, reliving every word Thomas has ever said to me. Reading every 'How-to' Cosmo has to offer. I rented an Airbnb just north of Regent Park area. I have a car waiting to take me since driving on the opposite side of the street probably isn't going to be something that I'll get the hang of right away. Throw in the fact that the steering wheel is on the other side of the car…it's just a recipe for disaster.

I feel a little bit nervous. What if he did find someone else? What if he has come to his senses and decides that this was all just infatuation? What if he doesn't want to see me? Maybe I have made a big mess of things! I should have called before I hopped on a plane and flown eight hours. I've always been a fly-by-the-seat-of-my-pants type of girl. I guess that's how I ended up with a bakery in San Francisco, or on a road trip across the country with my sister. It's not all bad, look what it's gotten me. I have a very successful bakery, my sister is better, and I found love; love, just when I wasn't looking.

I stand holding my luggage, lost in thought, when a driver interrupts my daydream. "Madame, Madame…Are you Marguerite? Can I take your luggage? I'm George. I believe I am your driver. If you would, please…" George gestures towards the doors of the airport.

My phone rings, Joan's favorite Jimmy Buffet song comes on and I know it's her. She must have been tracking the plane.

"Hello…" I say clearing my throat.

"Have you landed?" Joan's voice says on the other end of the line.

"Of course, I've landed. How else would you be talking to me? The driver just picked me up." In a hurried whisper I begin to give Joan George's details. "His name is George. He's about 5'7" ...blondish gray hair, blue eyes, about 70 years old. The company is Penny Lane Services."

"Got it," Joan says. I know she's writing it down.

I can hear Will in the background, "I know, you don't have to tell me. I know she's not being abducted."

"Joan, what if I came all this way for nothing? What if he doesn't want me? What if he isn't even here?" I pause then add, "I better go because I'm about to get in the car. Black...*The Nanny* type of car."

I feel deflated, what if he isn't even in London? If I would've just picked up the phone, I would have known that. My stomach begins to churn. "I have to go Joan."

As I slide my phone to hang up, I hear Joan yell, "Call me when you see him!"

I shuffle into the backseat and throw my sunglasses on. George gets in and adjusts his mirror to look at me, "Where to Madame?"

"Ummm..." I pull out my phone to search for the email. "I know it's on Haverstock Hill, near Regents Park," I say quickly before my voice cracks. I scroll through my email, read out the address to George, then shove the phone back into my pocket. It's finally hitting me. I'm in London. "I'm in London!" I accidentally say out loud.

"Pardon me?" George looks up into the mirror that is still trained on me. "Are you not supposed to be in London?"

"There's no other place I'm to be other than London. I just can't believe I'm here," I say quietly.

"Oh, I see. If you don't mind me asking, is it for business or pleasure?" George smiles, making the skin around his eyes crinkle.

"It's a long story. I'm afraid if I tell you, you will think I'm a colossal idiot."

George looks at me a little bewildered, "I could never think that, Madame. Please, if I can help you, I'd like to."

I don't know how this seventy-year-old man could help me, but I'll take all the advice I can get at this point. Agreeing, I shake my head. "Okay…" I open my mouth, and everything starts spilling out. "I met this man. We spent a short time together. He told me he loved me, and I didn't say it back even though I am in love with him. I just thought it was too fast. I let him leave without saying it. I was just being incredibly stupid."

"And he lives here? Here in London?" George asks, trying to piece it together.

"Yes, he lives here, and I live in San Francisco, California."

"And you came here for him?" George says, adjusting his tie.

"Yes, I left everything back in the states to come here and tell him that I love him. He doesn't even know I'm coming. I haven't talked to him in a couple of days. Last thing I said was that I would call him soon since my sister and I were on a road trip. I've been talking to him on and off. I just haven't talked to him in the last couple of days."

George nods his head, "I see…"

What does he see? He's not giving me any advice! I suppose that he isn't at liberty to do so. I'm getting more and more nervous, "So…what do you think?"

"I think when it comes to the affairs of the heart, I ask my dear, Ruth." George looks up in the mirror and smiles.

He starts touching buttons on the console, "I can phone her if you would like."

"Sure, why not…" I throw myself back into the seat. I am thankful for the help.

"Hello, hello…" a very distinguished lady's voice comes on the other end of the line. "Hello, can I help you?"

"Hello? It's George. Do you have time to talk?" George smiles as he looks at me again in the mirror.

"Of course, dear, what is it? Let me sit down." I can hear a chair being scooted across the floor.

"I was wondering if you had some advice. I have a woman called Marguerite in my car. She has an affair of the heart and I thought you would be better suited for this," George says, looking at me for reassurance.

"I see, dear. Whatever is the problem?" Ruth's voice comes over the phone like a lullaby. For someone I've never met, there's something very soothing about her voice.

I lean forward in my seat and start explaining my situation. If I truly hope to get help, I need to lay it all out there. I hear a lot of, 'ohs…uh-huhs, oh dears…and I sees,' then one simple question. "Do you love him?"

Now I see where George gets it.

"Yes, I do. I love him even though I thought it was too fast. I love him. I love him with all my heart." I look down at my hands. "I love him. I don't know how it happened, but it did."

"And you've come here to tell him?" Ruth asks like she's formulating a plan.

With a little more confidence in my voice I say, "Yes, I came here to tell him, to start a life with him. That's if he still wants one with me."

There's a moment of silence on the phone and I look at George, wondering if the line went dead. Ruth's voice comes on the line again. Her voice loses the sing-song lullaby to it and sounds a little shrill. "Come, come and pick me up! Pick me up right now!"

George shrugs his shoulders and shoots me a questioning look.

"Yes, pick her up!" I want to get to Thomas, but I could really use some advice so I don't screw this up again.

After a ten-minute car ride, we pull up to the front of an old, brownstone covered in ivy. There's an old lady standing on the steps. She's clutching a hot pink, leather tote and wearing a pink, vintage Chanel skirt suit, complete with nylons and kitten heeled shoes. Even her hair is amazing. It looks like perfectly styled, white, candy floss. She has impeccable taste. When I grow old, I hope to be half as stylish. I thought that this might be George's wife, but she's about twenty years older than George.

George pops out of the car and opens the door for Ruth. She slides in beside me and extends her hand, "Hello Dear, I'm called Ruth. I'm George's mum."

She rolls down her window and gives a quick wave towards her brownstone. I look up to see a well-dressed, old man standing in the window blowing her a kiss. For heaven's sake, he's called his mother!

George chimes in, "Hello, mum. How have you been?" He readjusts his mirror.

"Mum and dad have been married for over seventy years. She's got some good advice, that one."

"Tell me, dear, are you headed straight to his house now? And he doesn't know?" Ruth asks excitedly.

I shake my head, "No, he has no idea that I'm even in London. I rented a place in his neighborhood."

Ruth rattles my knee, "Splendid! What's his name?"

"Thomas." Just saying his name sends tingling pinpricks all over my body.

"Thomas, a nice strong name. If you love this man, Thomas, you must go to him." She pauses as she puts her thin pale hands in mine.

"Ruth, you said that. Is there any more?" I ask, turning to face her.

"No, dear, it's just that simple. If you love him, go to him, tell him. I had George pick me up because I simply wanted to come along. I don't want to miss this. It's been ever so long since I've been on an adventure."

Deflated, I ride in silence for a block or two. I think about her words. It *is* that simple. I just need to see him and tell him. There aren't any magical words. There isn't a magic trick.

George looks back at me in the mirror, "We are almost there."

I precisely line my lips in my very best shade of berry lipstick, and I start to fix my hair in the reflection of the window when all of a sudden, I see him. My stomach does loopty-loops. I can't believe he's just here. Just here, walking up the sidewalk. "Pull over George! He's right there!"

George pulls the car over half a block up. I stare at Thomas out the tinted back window. He is wearing a black shirt and some black running shorts. His hair is springing up in all directions. The wind catches it and he runs a hand through it.

I pull out my cell phone and dial his number. A second passes, it seems like a lifetime. George, Ruth and I are sitting at the edge of our seats. I hear the phone ring as I turn my speaker on.

Thomas digs in his short's pocket. He pulls his phone out. I hold my breath, watching for his reaction. His eyes light up.

"Hello?" Thomas says in his smooth, British accent.

My heart gives a hard thump. So hard that I fear Ruth can feel it sitting in the seat next to me.

"Hi…it's me," I say sheepishly into the phone.

Thomas puts a finger up to his mouth then runs his hand through his hair. "I know. Your picture popped up on my screen. Plus, your ring tone is 'Can't Take My Eyes Off You.'"

"How have you been?" I anxiously interrupt him.

"To be honest, I've missed you. So…really not so well. I've been trying to keep busy though." There's so much melancholy in his voice I want to cry.

Ruth reaches over and grabs my arm, "Oh, dear."

"I would be better if I could see you. I could come visit you. I mean, if that's okay with you?" he adds.

I hesitate, "Thomas the thing is…"

I hear him let out his breath. I'm doing the absolute worst job of telling him I'm here. "The thing is I would love to see you, too. I just wish there was some kind of teleportation device so that I could see you right now," I quickly add.

Thomas stops in the middle of the sidewalk. People are walking all around him. It's almost like one of those high-speed photos where cars are racing around, and you have one single object in the middle completely still. All I can see is him. Him in his crinkled socks and springy hair…him with his perfect mouth and sharp cheekbones. Just him…I'm studying him carefully. He reaches up and rubs his eyes.

Then I hear him whisper, "I wish I could kiss your lips right now. I wish I could hold you in my arms."

This is killing me. I can visibly see his heart ache. I unsnap my seatbelt. Then open the car door and slip out. My feet touch the pavement. As I go to stand, my legs feel more like Jell-O than I expected. I begin to walk up the sidewalk. I can only imagine how I look.

I suck in a deep breath. There's no time to chicken out now.

Ruth slides out of the car. She's following a few steps behind me, hanging on my every word. I can hear her kitten heels clacking on the sidewalk. It's time for me to put it all out there.

Feeling a bit self-conscious I whisper into the phone, "I wish I could see you, too. I wish I could kiss your lips. I wish I could put my hands on your face."

As if I couldn't get any more nervous, George joins Ruth as they walk elbow and elbow pretending to hold their own private conversation behind me. My knees feel like they may buckle. If this all goes south, I could just have George take me back to the airport. I continue to walk straight for Thomas. I watch as he looks down at his feet.

I continue, "I wish I didn't wait…" I swallow the lump in my throat.

"Didn't wait for…" I hear him begin to say as I click off my phone and drop it into my pocket.

I'm standing right in front of him when he looks up to see why his phone went dead. I lock eyes with him.

"I wish, I wish that I didn't wait to tell you that I love you."

Dedication

To my loves, Rob and Robbie. You are my reason and my lifetime. Rob thanks for your undying support, your countless hours of proofreading, romantic comedy watching, and tucking me in at night...And also, for gently taking my glasses off my face when I've fallen asleep, waiting for me so I don't have to walk upstairs in the dark, and for doing all the things I don't want to do. You have been my biggest cheerleader and fan.

Robbie, you are a Rockstar! You are the wittiest kid I know, and your bravery and strength are beyond belief. Your style is awesome, and your laughter is contagious. I am thankful for you every single day. Even on the days I have to hide in the bushes to catch a glimpse of you at school.

To my dad for being that safe place to land and where we all get our sense of humor. To my mom for introducing me to the value of a shoe, not only are they nice to wear, but they can also double as a weapon.

To my family who has helped shape me into who I am today; we are one crazy bunch through thick and thin. To all my family and friends that have helped me along the way by proofreading, giving opinions or just being there. It was a labor of love. To Dustine who spent countless hours editing over text, reading, and laughing with me into the early morning hours. I will forever be grateful.

Last but not least, Joann. You are my best friend. I love all of the adventures we went on. All of the laughs and coffee we shared...our endless Scrabble games. You will forever live in my books, our adventures, and in my heart.

JB Teller is a fiction writer who grew up in a small town in south Texas. After moving to Europe for three years, she returned and was fortunate to have lived in many U.S. cities. She called the Bay Area home for ten years before moving to colorful Colorado with her handsome husband and charismatic and amazing son.

JB is an animal lover with four dogs and a rescue cat. Most days she writes, but on the off chance she isn't, you can find her trying new foods or going on adventures. She is a self-proclaimed music trivia champion, inventor of Dirty Scrabble, and a Mini Cooper enthusiast. Her favorite author is Sophie Kinsella. She's a huge Richard Curtis fan.

Her next book, "Open Bar," will be out in 2021.You can reach out to JB Teller on her various platforms.

JBTeller.com   jbrteller@gmail.com   Twitter @JBTeller1
Facebook J.B. Teller   Instagram jbrteller

References

Bare, Bobby. "Marie Laveau." Bobby Bare Sings Lullabies, Legends and Lies, RCA Nashville, 1974.

Beasty Boys. "Brass Monkey." License to Ill, Def Jam/Columbia Records, 1987.

Blanco, Benny, Halsey and Khalid. "Eastside." Friends Keep Secrets, Interscope, 2018

Canned Heat. "Going Up the Country." Living the Blues, Liberty, 1968.

Carter, Deana. "Strawberry Wine." Did I Shave My Legs for This?, Capitol Nashville, 1996

Cash, Johnny. "A Boy Named Sue." At San Quentin, Columbia, 1969.

Coldplay. "Fix You." X&Y, Parlophone, 2005

Denver, John. "Take Me Home, Country Roads." Poems, Prayers & Promises, RCA, 1971

Diamond, Neil. "Brother Love's Travelling Salvation Show." Studio Album, Uni, 1969.

Dixie Chicks. "Goodbye Earl." Fly, Monument, 2000.

Douglas, Carl. "Kung Fu Fighting." Kung Fu Fighting and Other Great Love Songs, Fox, 1974.

Fitzgerald, Ella. "My Funny Valentine." Pure Ella, 1994

Holiday, Ryan. "The Obstacle is the Way." Portfolio, 2014.

Lambert, Miranda. "Tin Man." The Weight of These Wings, RCA Nashville, 2017.

Lizzo. "Good as Hell." Coconut Oil, Atlantic, 2016.

Malone, Post and Swae Lee. "Sunflower." Spider-Man: Into the Spider-Verse, Republic, 2018.

Mickey Mouse. "Deep in the Heart of Texas." Pardners, Disneyland Records, 1980.

Nash, Johnny. "I Can See Clearly Now." Studio Album, Epic, 1972.

Notting Hill. Dir. Roger Michell. Perf. Hugh Grant. Universal Pictures, 1999.

Pretty Woman. Dir. Gary Marshall. Perf. Julia Roberts, Richard Gere. Touchstone Pictures, 1990.

Queen. "Bohemian Rhapsody." A Night at the Opera, Elektra, 1975.

Rabbitt, Eddie. "I Love a Rainy Night." Horizon, Elektra, 1980.

Simon, Carly. "You're So Vain." No Secrets, Electra, 1971

Sinatra, Frank. "Strangers in the Night". Studio Album, Reprise, 1966.

Stealers Wheel. "Stuck in the Middle." Stealers Wheel, A&M, 1973.

Stevens, Ray. "Mississippi Squirrel Revival." He Thinks He's Ray Stevens, MCA, 1984.

Sting. "Fields of Gold." Ten Summoner's Tales, A&M, 1993.

Taylor, James. "You've Got a Friend." Mud Slide Slim and the Blue Horizon, Warner Bros., 1971

The Avett Brothers. "I and Love and You." Studio Album, American, 2009.

The Beatles. "Something." Abbey Road, EMI and Olympic, 1969.

The Shirelles. "Will You Love Me Tomorrow." Tonight's the Night, Scepter, 1960.

The Sugarhill Gang. "Rapper's Delight." Sugarhill Gang, Sugar Hill, 1979.

Travolta, John and Olivia Newton-John. "Summer Nights." Grease: The Original Soundtrack from the Motion Picture, RSO Records, 1978.

Travolta, John and Olivia Newton-John. "You're the One That I Want." Grease: The Original Soundtrack from the Motion Picture, RSO Records, 1978.

Travolta, John. "Greased Lightnin'." Grease: The Original Soundtrack from the Motion Picture, RSO Records, 1978.

UB40. "Red Red Wine." Labour of Love, Virgin, 1983.

Urban, Keith. "Blue Ain't Your Color." Rip Cord, Capital National, 2016.

Valli, Frankie. "Can't Take My Eyes Off of You." Frankie Vallie: Solo, Philips, 1967.

Yoda. "Powerful you have become, the dark side I sense in you." Star Wars: Episode II- Attack of the Clones, 20th Century Fox, 2002.

Zevon, Warren. "Werewolves of London." Excitable Boy, Asylum Records, 1978

Made in the USA
Coppell, TX
07 October 2020